About the Authors

Maisey Yates is a *USA Today* bestselling author of more than thirty romance novels. She has a coffee habit she has no interest in kicking, and a slight Pinterest addiction. She lives with her husband and children in the Pacific Northwest. When Maisey isn't writing she can be found singing in the grocery store, shopping for shoes online, and probably not doing dishes. Check out her website, www.maiseyyates.com

Julia James lives in England and adores the peaceful, verdant countryside, and the wild shores of Cornwall. She also loves the Mediterranean, so rich in myth and history, its sun baked landscape and olive groves, ancient ruins and azure seas. "The perfect setting for romance! – rivalled only by the lush tropic heat of the Caribbean – palms swaying by a silver sand beach lapped by turquoise waters...what more could lovers want?!"

A bestselling two-time RITA® winner (with a further nine finalist titles), **Anne McAllister** has written nearly seventy books for Mills & Boon Modern Romance, American Romance, Desire, Special Edition and single titles—which means she basically follows her characters no matter where they take her. She loves to travel, but at home she and her husband divide their time between Montana and Iowa. Anne loves to hear from readers. Contact her at: www.an̶̶̶̶̶̶̶̶̶̶.̶̶̶̶̶̶̶̶m

The Greek Mavericks
COLLECTION

July 2019

August 2019

September 2019

October 2019

November 2019

December 2019

Greek Mavericks: Seduced into the Greek's World

MAISEY YATES

JULIA JAMES

ANNE McALLISTER

MILLS & BOON

First Published in Great Britain 2019
By Mills & Boon, an imprint of HarperCollins *Publishers*
1 London Bridge Street, London, SE1 9GF

GREEK MAVERICKS: SEDUCED INTO THE GREEK'S WORLD © 2019 Harlequin Books S.A.

Carides's Forgotten Wife © Maisey Yates 2016
Captivated by the Greek © Julia James 2015
The Return of Antonides © Anne McAllister 2015

ISBN: 978-0-263-27566-7

0919

MIX
Paper from
responsible sources
FSC™ C007454

This book is produced from independently certified FSC™ paper to ensure responsible forest management.

For more information visit: www.harpercollins.co.uk/green

Printed and bound in Spain
by CPI, Barcelona

CARIDES'S
FORGOTTEN WIFE

MAISEY YATES

To Megan Crane/Caitlin Crews. For all the times
we've sat around talking about how wonderful
it is to write these stories, and everything else.
You make my writing and my life more sparkly.

PROLOGUE

ANOTHER BORING PARTY in a long succession of boring parties. That was Leon's predominant thought as he pulled away from the ostentatious hotel and out onto the narrow Italian streets.

The highlight of his evening had been the most disappointing portion, as well. Being rebuffed by Rocco Amari's fiancée. She had been beautiful. Exotic. With her long dark hair and honey-colored skin. Yes, she would have made a wonderful companion for his bed tonight. Sadly, she seemed to be very committed to Rocco. And he to her.

To each his own, he supposed. Frankly, Leon did not see the appeal in monogamy.

Life was a glorious buffet of debauchery. Why on earth would he seek to limit that?

Though he had walked away empty-handed, he had thoroughly enjoyed enraging his business rival. He could not deny that.

The other man was possessive in a way that Leon could see no point in being. But then, he had never had feelings so intense for a woman.

He turned onto a road that began to lead out of the city, heading toward the villa he was staying in during his time in Italy. It was a nice place. Rustic, well-appointed. He preferred places like that to a penthouse in the middle of a busy business district. A fact that was, perhaps, at odds with other aspects of his personality. But then, being a contradiction had never bothered him.

He owned several estates worldwide, though none were as important to him as his estate in Connecticut.

The thought of that house, of that place, turned his thoughts to his wife.

He would rather not think of Rose just now.

For some reason when he thought of her after just attempting to bring another woman into his bed, he felt a tug of unaccustomed guilt. For the past two years, Rose had often made him feel guilty.

There was no real reason, of course. They were married, it was true, but in name only. He allowed her to do as she liked, and he carried on as he liked.

Still, it was easy to picture those wide, luminous blue eyes and feel…

His focus snapped back to the road, to a pair of headlights heading in his direction.

There was no time to correct. No time to react at all. There was nothing but the impact.

And a clear image of Rose's blue eyes.

CHAPTER ONE

"HE IS STABLE for the moment," Dr. Castellano said.

Rose looked down at her husband, lying in his hospital bed, broken, bandages wrapped around his upper arm, down over his shoulder and across his chest. His lip was swollen, a cut looking angry and painful at the center, a dark bruise bleeding color on his cheekbone.

He looked... Well, he looked not at all like Leon Carides. Leon Carides was larger-than-life, a man so full of power and charisma he was undeniable. A man who commanded respect with his every movement, his every breath. A man who stopped women in their tracks and demanded their full attention and admiration.

A man she had been on the verge of divorcing. But you could hardly hand a man divorce papers while he was lying in bed with severe injuries.

"It's a miracle he survived," the doctor continued.

"Yes," she said, her voice hollow. As hollow as the rest of her. "A miracle."

Some small part of her—one that she immediately set out to squash—thought it would have been much more convenient for him to have died there on the side of the road. Then she wouldn't have to face any of this. Wouldn't have to deal with the state of their union. Or rather, the lack of union.

But she banished it. Quickly. She couldn't stand being

married to him anymore, but that didn't mean she wanted him dead.

She swallowed hard. "Well, thank heaven for miracles. Large and small."

"Yes."

"Has he been awake at all?"

"No," the doctor said, his voice heavy. "He has not been conscious since we brought him in. The impact was intense, and his head injury is…serious. He shows brain activity, so we do have some hope. But you know, the longer someone stays unconscious…"

"Of course."

It had taken her about twenty hours to get to Italy from Connecticut, and Leon had been unconscious for all that time. But there were all kinds of stories of people waking up miraculously after years. Surely he still had hope after a mere few hours.

"If you have any other questions, don't hesitate to get in touch. A nurse will be by in the next fifteen minutes. But if you have need of anything, just text this number." The doctor handed her a card with a phone number on it. She imagined this was what it was like to get special treatment at the hospital. Of course Leon would get special treatment. He was a billionaire, one of the most successful businessmen in the world. Wealthy, and powerful. Which meant that these sorts of things—as difficult as they were—would always be easier for people like him.

She held the card close to her chest. "Thank you."

The doctor left, closing the door behind him. Leaving her standing there in the room with nothing but the sounds of machines surrounding her.

Panic started to rise in her chest as she continued to look at Leon's still form. He wasn't supposed to look like this. He wasn't supposed to be breakable.

Leon Carides had always been more of a god to her

than a man. The sort of man she had built up into fantasy as a young girl. He was ten years older than her. And he had been her father's most trusted and prized protégé from the time Rose was eight years old. She could hardly remember a period of time when Leon hadn't been involved in her life.

Carefree. Easy with a smile. Always so kind. He had seen her. Truly. And had made her feel like she mattered.

Of course, all that changed when they got married.

But she wasn't going to think about their wedding now.

She didn't want to think about anything. She wanted to close her eyes and be back in the rose garden at her family estate. Wanted to be surrounded by the soft, fragrant summer breeze, held in it as though it was a pair of arms, protecting her from all of this. But that was just a daydream. Everything here was too stark, too white, too antiseptic to be a dream.

It was crushingly real, an assault on her senses.

She wondered if there had been anyone else in the car with him. If there were, they hadn't said. She also wondered if he had been drinking. Again, no one had said.

Another perk of wealth. People wanted to protect you so they might benefit later. But the why didn't matter, as long as the protection happened.

Leon groaned and her focus was wrenched back to the hospital bed. He shifted, moving his hand, and the lines to the IV and the cord link to the pulse monitor on his finger tugged hard.

"Be careful," she said, keeping her voice soft. "You're plugged into…" She looked around at all the equipment, all the bags of saline and antibiotics and whatever else was being pumped into his veins. "Well, you're plugged into everything. Don't…*unplug* anything."

She didn't know if he heard her. Didn't know if he understood. But then, he shifted, groaning again.

"Are you in pain?"

"I *am* pain," he said, his voice rough, tortured.

Relief flooded her, washing over her in a wave that left her dizzy. She hadn't realized just how affected she was until this moment. Just how terrified she was.

Just how much she cared.

This feeling was so at odds with that small, cold moment where she had wished he could go away completely.

Or maybe it wasn't. Maybe the two were more tightly connected than it first appeared.

Because as long as he was here, she would *always* feel too much. And if he were gone, at least the loss of him wouldn't be a choice she had to make.

"You probably need more pain medication."

Though looking at him, at the purple bruises marring his typically handsome features, she doubted that there was pain medication strong enough to make it all go away.

"Then get me some," he said, his voice hard.

Issuing commands already, which was very much in his character. Leon was never at a loss. Even when her father had died and she'd been lost in a haze of grief, he had stepped forward and taken care of everything.

He hadn't comforted her the way a husband should comfort a wife. He had never been a husband to her at all, not in the truest sense. But he'd still made sure she was taken care of. Had ensured that the funeral, the legalities of the will and everything else were executed to perfection.

It was why, in spite of everything, it had seemed right to stay for the past two years. And it was also why, though it meant losing everything, she'd decided she had to leave him, no matter the cost.

But leaving him now…that didn't seem right. He hadn't

been a true husband, but he hadn't abandoned her when she'd needed him, either. How could she do any less?

"I will have to call a nurse." She picked her phone up and sent off a brief text to the doctor: He's awake.

Just typing the words sent a rush of relief through her that she didn't want to analyze.

His eyes opened, and he began to look around the room. "You aren't a nurse?"

"No," she said, her heart thundering hard. "I'm Rose."

He was probably still disoriented. After all, this was Italy, and she was supposed to be at home in Connecticut. She was probably the last person he expected to see.

"Rose?"

"Yes," she said, starting to feel a little bit more alarmed. "I flew to Italy because of your accident."

"We are in Italy?" He only sounded more confused.

"Yes," she said. "Where did you think you were?"

He frowned, his dark eyebrows locking together. "I don't know."

"You were in Italy. Seeing to some business." And probably pleasure, knowing him, but she wasn't going to add that. "You were leaving a party and a car drifted into your lane and hit you head-on."

"That is what I feel like," he said, his voice rough. "As though I were hit head-on. Though I feel more like I was hit directly by the car. With nothing to buffer it."

"With how fast you drive I imagine you might as well have been."

He frowned. "We know each other."

She frowned. "Of course we do. I'm your wife."

I'm your wife.

Those words echoed in his head, but he couldn't make any sense of them. He didn't remember having a wife.

But then, he didn't remember being in Italy. He wasn't entirely certain he remembered…anything. His name. Who he was. What he was. He couldn't remember any of it.

"You are my wife," he said, waiting for the feeling of blackness, the open space around this moment that seemed to take up his entire consciousness.

There was nothing. There was only her standing before him. This hospital room, this bright spot of the present, with nothing before or after it.

If he kept her talking, perhaps she could fill the rest in. Perhaps he could flood those dark places with light.

"Yes," she said. "We got married two years ago."

"Did we?" He tried to force the image of a wedding into his mind. He did know what a wedding looked like. Curious that he knew that and not his own name. But he did. And still, he could not imagine this woman in a wedding gown. She had light-colored hair—some might call it mousy—hanging limp around her shoulders. Her figure was slight, her eyes too blue, too wide for her face.

Blue eyes.

A flash of an image hit him hard. Too bright. Too clear. Her eyes. He had been thinking about *her* eyes just before… But that was all he could remember.

"Yes," he said, "you are my wife." He thought he would test out the words. He knew they were true. He couldn't remember, but he still knew they were true.

"Oh, good. You were starting to scare me," she said, her voice shaking.

"I'm lying here broken. And I'm only just now starting to scare you?" he asked.

"Well, the part where you weren't remembering me was a little bit extra scary."

"You are my wife," he repeated. "And I am…"

The silence filled every empty place in the room. Heavy and accusing.

"You don't remember," she said, horror dawning in her voice. "You don't remember me. You don't remember *you*."

He closed his eyes, pain bursting behind his legs as he shook his head. "I must. Because the alternative is crazy."

"Is it?"

"I think it is." He opened his eyes and looked at her again. "I remember you," he said. "I remember your eyes."

Something in her expression changed. Softened. Her pale pink lips parted, and a bit of color returned to her cheeks. Right now she almost looked pretty. He supposed his initial impression of her wasn't terribly fair. Since he was lying in a hospital bed and since she had probably been given the shock of her life when she had been told her husband had been in a very serious car accident.

She had said she'd flown to Italy. He didn't know from where. But she had traveled to see him. It was no wonder she looked pale, and drawn. And a bit plain.

"You remember my eyes?" she asked.

"It's the only thing," he said. "That makes sense, doesn't it?" Because she was his wife. Why couldn't he remember his wife?

"I had better get the doctor."

"I'm fine."

"You don't remember *anything*. How can you be fine?"

"I'm not going to die," he said.

"Ten minutes ago the doctor was in here telling me you might never wake up. So forgive me if I feel a little bit cautious."

"I'm awake. I can only assume the memories will follow."

She nodded slowly. "Yes," she said. "You would think."

A heavy knock on the door punctuated the silence.

Rose walked quickly out of her husband's hospital room, her head spinning.

He didn't remember anything. Leon didn't remember *anything*.

Dr. Castellano stood in the hallway looking at her, his expression grim. "How is he, Mrs. Carides?"

"Ms. Tanner," she corrected. More out of habit than anything else. "I never took my husband's name."

She'd never taken him to her bed—why would she take his last name?

"Ms. Tanner," he repeated. "Tell me what seems to be going on."

"He doesn't remember." She was starting to shake now, all of the shock, all of the terror catching up with her. "He doesn't remember me. He doesn't remember himself."

"Nothing?"

"Nothing. And I didn't know… I didn't know what to tell him. I didn't know if it was like waking a sleepwalker, or if I should tell him."

"Well, we will need to tell him who he is. But I'm going to need to consult a specialist. A psychologist. I don't often deal with cases of amnesia."

"This is not a soap opera. My husband doesn't have amnesia."

"He sustained very serious head trauma. It is not so far-fetched."

"Yes it is," she said, feeling desperate. "It is extremely far-fetched."

"I know you're worried, but take heart. He is stable. He is awake. Very likely his memories will return. And soon, I would think."

"Do you have statistical evidence to support that?"

"As I said… I do not often deal in cases of amnesia. Very often a person will lose a portion of their memories following a traumatic head injury. Usually just sections. It's uncommon to lose everything, but not impossible."

"He's lost everything," she said.

"He's likely to regain it."

"These other people. These people who have lost portions of their memory that you've treated. How often do they regain them?"

"Sometimes they don't," he said, a heavy admission that seemed pulled from him.

"He may never remember," she said, feeling dazed. Feeling her life, her future, slipping out of her hands. "Anything."

"I would not focus on that possibility." Dr. Castellano took a breath. "We will monitor him here for as long as we can. I would imagine that he will do much better recovering at home, monitored by local physicians."

She nodded. That was one thing she and Leon had in common. His business often kept him abroad, which for her nerves was for the best. But they both loved the Tanner House in Connecticut. It was her favorite thing she had left of her family. The old, almost palatial home, the sprawling green lawns and a private rose garden that her mother had planted in honor of her only child. It was her refuge.

She had always had the feeling it was the same for Leon.

Though they tended to keep to their own wings of the house. At the very least, he never brought women there. He had allowed her to keep it as her own. Had made it a kind of sanctuary for them both.

It was also a condition of their marriage. When her father had hastily commanded the union when his illness took a turn for the worse, the house and his company had been a pivotal point. If—before five years was up—he divorced her, he lost the company and the house. If she left him before the five-year term finished, she lost the house and everything in it that wasn't her personal possession.

Which meant losing her retreat. And the work she'd been doing archiving the Tanner family history, which stretched all the way back to the Mayflower.

So only everything, really.

And she'd been ready to do it, willing to do it because she had to stop waiting for Leon to decide he wanted to be her husband in every possible way.

Except now here they were.

"Yes," she said, feeling determined in this at least. "He will want to be moved to Connecticut as quickly as possible."

"Then as soon as it is safe to move him, we will do so. I imagine he has private physicians that can care for his needs."

She thought of the doctors and nurses that had cared for her father toward the end of his life. "I have a great many wonderful contacts. I only regret that I have yet more work to give them."

"Of course. But so long as he is stable we should be able to move him to Connecticut soon."

She looked back toward the room, her heart pounding. "Okay. We will do that as quickly as possible."

Going back to Connecticut with Leon was *not* asking Leon for a divorce. It was not moving toward having separate lives. It was not finally ridding herself of the man who had haunted and obsessed her for most of her life.

But he *needed* her.

Why does that matter so much?

The image came, as it always did, of herself sitting in the rose garden on the grounds of her family home. She was wearing a frothy, ridiculous gown, tears streaming down her face. Her prom date had stood her up. Probably because going with her in the first place was only a joke.

She looked up, and Leon was there. He was wearing a suit, very likely because he had been planning on going out that night after meeting with her father. She swallowed hard, looking up to his handsome face. Dying a little bit inside when she realized he was witnessing her lowest moment.

"What's wrong, agape?"

"Nothing. Just... My prom plans didn't exactly work out."

He reached down, taking her hand in his, and lifted her off the ground.

She couldn't remember Leon touching her before. His hand was so warm, his touch so intense it sent a shock of electricity through her.

"If someone has hurt you, give me his name, and I will ensure he is unrecognizable when I'm through with him."

She shook her head. "No, I don't need you or my father coming to my defense. I think that would only be worse."

He curled his fingers around her hand. "Would it?"

Her heart was pounding so hard now she could hardly hear anything over it. "Yes."

"Then if you will not let me do physical harm to the one who has hurt you, perhaps you will allow me to dance with you."

She was powerless to do anything but nod. He pulled her against his body, sweeping her into an easy dance step. She had never been very good at it. One of the many things she had never quite mastered. But he didn't seem to mind. And in his arms she didn't feel clumsy. In his arms, she felt like she could fly.

"It is not you, Rose."

"What isn't?" she asked, her words harsh, strangled.

"It's this age. It is difficult. But people like you, people who are too soft, too rare for this sort of assimilation required in order to fit in at high school, will go on to excel. You will go much further than they ever will. This is only temporary. You will spend the rest of your life living brighter. Living more beautifully than they could possibly imagine."

His words had meant so much to her. Words she had held close to her chest. Words she had clung to when she had walked down the aisle toward him, thinking that perhaps this was what he had meant. That this would be the bright, beautiful living he had promised two years earlier.

Their marriage had been anything but bright. Far from soaring, she'd spent the past two years feeling as though her wings had been clipped. She had a difficult time reconciling the man he'd been then with the man she had married.

Still, that memory was so large, so beautiful in her mind, even with everything that had passed between them since, that she could not deny he deserved her help.

And once he was better, once he was nursed fully back to health, then she would take steps to moving on with her life.

"Just tell me what I need to do," she said.

CHAPTER TWO

HE STILL COULDN'T remember his name when he was wheeled out of the hospital in a wheelchair and physically moved into a van designed to accommodate his limitations. But he did know that all of this ate at his pride. He did not like to need the assistance of others. He did not like to be at a disadvantage. And yet here he was, completely dependent, his pride in shreds.

Strange how he had no memories and yet he still knew these things. Bone-deep.

He *knew* his name. He knew his name because it had been spoken around him, over his head, as his wife and various medical professionals made decisions for him. But that was different than *knowing* his name. Than recognizing it. He was unable to remember who he was, but he wasn't stupid. Still, that seemed to constitute a compromise that he could not be trusted to make his own decisions.

The drive to the airport was long, and painful, every dip in the road aggravating some injury or another. He was lucky to have less broken than he did. But he was still far too sore to walk on his own. He had a couple of broken ribs, but other than that it was mainly deep contusions. So he had been told. He knew his extensive list of injuries. Had done his very best to memorize them, just so there was something in his brain he knew. Something he knew about himself.

But it was a rather depressing list of facts, he had to admit.

Still, they were the only facts he had.

According to his doctor, there were basics that he would be told. But there were some things that were best allowed to return organically.

He hated that, too. Hated that he wasn't just dependent on others for physical care. But that he was dependent on them for knowledge.

Every single person in the exam room earlier today knew more about him than he did. His wife knew whole volumes more than he did, undoubtedly.

He looked at her profile, her stoic expression as she looked out the window, watching the scenery go by.

"I know you very well," he said. He hoped that by saying it it would make it so.

He must. He must know what she looked like beneath her clothes. He had touched her. Kissed her. Countless times, he would imagine. Because they were young—reasonably so—and in love, he presumed.

"I'm not entirely certain of that," she said.

"Why wouldn't I?"

She blinked, looking startled. "Of course you do."

The startled expression, he realized, was her correcting herself. Realizing she had done something wrong.

"Now you are being dishonest with me," he said.

"I'm not. I'm just doing my best to follow the doctor's orders. I'm not sure what I'm allowed to say and what I'm not allowed to say."

"I don't know that it's detrimental either way."

"I don't want to put memories into your head that aren't there."

"Nothing is there at the moment. I'm a blank slate. I imagine I could very easily become victimized by you."

Color flooded her cheeks. Angry color, he guessed. "I'm not going to do anything to you." She turned away from him, her gaze fixed out the window again.

"So you say. But I am at your mercy."

"Oh, and I am so very terrifying."

"You could be. For all I know, this could be an elaborate ruse. I appear to be a very rich man."

"How would you know?"

"I had a very nice private room, and an awful lot of attention from doctors."

"Perhaps it is because you are a special case," she said, her voice so brittle it reminded him of crystal.

"Oh, I have no doubt of that. There are certain things that I seem to know. That I feel, down deep in my bones. Other things you have told me, such as my name, I simply have to believe. But my importance, the fact that I am a special case, that I know."

"Amazing," she said, her tone arch. "Apparently nothing can beat your ego out of you, Leon. That is an amazing feat, I will bow to that."

"So I am an egotist in addition to being special? I must be very charming to live with."

She blinked slowly. "You often travel for work. I typically remain in Connecticut. I suppose we find we get on best that way."

He lifted a shoulder. "Nothing unremarkable about that. I doubt very many people are suited to cohabitation."

"Another thing you're very confident about?"

"Yes. I am confident." He knew that. He felt that. He turned his focus to his wife. "This has been very trying for you," he said, trying his best to eliminate some of the waxen quality in her face. He did not like seeing her like this. Which was strange, considering he couldn't remember what she was like on a daily basis. Still, he knew he did not like her being in distress.

"Nobody wants to hear that their husband may never regain his memory."

"I can imagine. No man wants to hear he may never regain his memory."

She took a deep breath and let it out slowly. "I'm sorry. This has nothing to do with how difficult it is for me. You're the one who's injured."

"That isn't true at all. Of course it matters if this is difficult for you. We are one flesh, are we not, *agape*?" He leaned in slightly, her light floral scent teasing his nose and stimulating…nothing. At least nothing in terms of memory. He was a man, after all, so it did stir something in his gut, low and deep. She was enticing, if not traditionally beautiful. "And if we are one flesh," he continued, "then what affects me also affects you."

She shifted, delicate color blooming in her cheeks. "I suppose that is true."

They were silent the rest of the ride to the airport, silent until he was wheeled onto a plane. A private plane. He had no memory of this, either, so he imagined not remembering her scent wasn't any more remarkable.

Once they were settled in the opulent surroundings, he leaned back in his chair. "This is mine?"

Rose nodded. "At least I hope so. I would hate to abscond with the wrong private plane."

"Then we really would make headlines."

"And of course we don't want that," she said, her tone firm.

"Do we not? I would like a Scotch."

"Certainly not," she said, frowning. "You've had enough pain pills to knock out a large mammal."

"I *am* a large mammal. And I am not unconscious."

"A larger one. Adding alcohol to the mix is a bad idea." She sat down in the chair across from him. "We do not want it getting out in the press that you are having issues with your memory. I have called a couple of media outlets and let them know you are recovering nicely from what was a traumatic injury. But that you will be back to normal in no time."

"Efficient of you. Do you work in my company with me?"

She shook her head. "No. But I spent many years helping my father with various details. Particularly after my mother passed away. So I'm well familiar."

"Am I involved in the same business as your father was?"

Her expression became guarded. "I don't think we should talk about business. In fact, I know we shouldn't. That is something I discussed with your doctor."

"How very nice of you to leave me out of it."

"It's for your health and well-being," she said, her words stiff.

"As though I am a child and not a grown man."

"You may well know less than a child does, Leon."

"I know a great many things," he countered. "I do not need to be sheltered."

"You're also not in any condition to go to work. Which means you don't need to be troubled with the details of business."

"As I said earlier, I am at your mercy." His head was pounding, and he really could kill someone for a Scotch. He could not be entirely certain, but he felt as though he did not often go this long without having a drink. He found the experience unsettling. Or perhaps, he was simply unsettled because his entire mind was a vacant field, with nothing stretching as far as he could see.

"I don't intend to let you atrophy on me now, Leon. We have a bit too much of a history for that." Of course they did. They were married after all. "You should sleep. When you wake up we'll be in Connecticut. And it's entirely possible everything will seem a bit clearer."

When the town car pulled up to the Tanner house Leon expected...something. A rush of familiarity, a feeling that he might latch on to. Rose had said this place was very important to him. In fact, she had acted as though his being here would be key to his recovery, and he realized as they advanced on the large, palatial home that he had been expecting something of a miracle when it came into view.

There was no such miracle.

It was a beautiful home, comprised of brick, with ivy climbing up the sides, making it appear as though the earth was attempting to reclaim the space for its own. There were no other houses out here. There was nothing but a large building off to the side he assumed was quarters for the staff, or at least had been at one time. Otherwise, there were large sprawling lawns in a vibrant green, backed by thick dark woods that gave the impression this house was in another time and space entirely from the rest of the world.

It was a beautiful home. But none of the magic he had been hoping for was present.

"This is it," Rose said, her tone small, as though she had already sensed his disappointment.

How was it that she could know him so well, even as he now didn't know himself? It was as though she could see inside of him, see into things that he could not. She had done so on the flight, and then again once they had landed. Of course, none of it seemed to matter, as her sixth sense mostly involved realizing that he was craving alcohol, and then denying him the satisfaction.

"Yes," he said. "So it is."

"You don't remember it." She sounded crestfallen.

"No," he said, surveying the bricks and mortar yet again. Waiting for a feeling of homecoming to overtake him. Waiting for anything beyond this fuzzy, blank confusion.

"You have been coming here often for as long as I can remember," Rose said. "Ever since you first started working with my father. When you became his protégé."

"Is that how we met?"

She nodded wordlessly, the gesture slightly stilted. "You would always sit with him in his study, but I can't enlighten you as to the content of those meetings. I was not included. Which stands to reason since I was a child."

He wondered then how old she was. If she was much younger than him. She did seem young. But then, he had very little reference point for that since he wasn't entirely certain how old he was.

"How old are you?" he asked.

"I don't think that's relevant. Anyway, it isn't polite to ask a lady her age. Is that something you've forgotten?"

"No. Survival skills made sure that was instilled deep inside of me still. However, it seems relevant. If I was here having business meetings and you were a child then clearly there is an age gap between us."

"Something of one," she said, her tone airy, distant. "But it isn't important. Why don't we go inside and I can show you to your room."

Her words didn't strike him as odd until they were

wandering through the grand foyer of the home, surrounded by enough marble and fine art to make any museum curator jealous.

"To *my* room?" he asked.

"Yes," she returned.

"We do not share a room?"

She cleared her throat, fidgeting slightly. "Well, for the purposes of your recovery it would be extremely impractical," she said, neatly sidestepping the question. That was something he noticed she did with frequency.

"You did not make it sound like there would be any changes in our living arrangements when you talked about showing me to my room."

"You're making assumptions."

"I am. Enlighten me as to the situation, Rose. My head hurts and I find that I am in a foul temper."

She let out an exasperated sigh. "This is a very traditional house. With an obscene amount of rooms, as I'm sure you guessed. It's very much existing in its own time. And, I suppose you could say our living arrangement exists in the same time. We both like our space."

"Are you saying we live like some outmoded royal couple?"

"Yes. As I said, you are often away. For business. That means I often live on my own. So I elected to retain my own space, and that suited you just fine."

The answer seemed wrong to him. The arrangement seemed wrong to him. Which was strange, because he knew the man he was. The man who possessed all of the memories, all of the past experiences, had clearly found it the right way to conduct his marriage. Who was he to argue with that superior version of himself in full possession of all of the facts?

Still, he wanted to. Because his wife had come to his

side immediately when he had been injured. Because her blue eyes were the only thing he truly remembered.

"Will you be able to make it up the stairs?" she asked, looking at him with concern in her expression.

"None of my limbs are broken."

"Your ribs are."

He shifted, wincing. "Only a couple."

"Tell me if this is too taxing." She began to lead the way up the broad, curved staircase. The steps were carpeted in a rich dark red, the banisters made of oak, polished to a high-gloss sheen. Money, history and tradition oozed from the pores of this place. And he had a strange sense that he did not belong. That somehow all of this was not his birthright, in any sense of the word.

He looked at Rose, her delicate fingertips skimming along the banister, her long, elegant neck held straight, her nose tilted up slightly. She was a bit plain, it was true, but she was aristocratic. There was no denying it. She was fine-boned, and refined, each and every inch of her.

He had the feeling that her skin was like silk. Smooth, perfect and far too luxurious for any mere mortal man to aspire to.

Somehow, he had her. Somehow, he had this house.

And he could make none of it feel real. Everything seemed to exist on its own plane. As if it were a strange dream he'd had once long ago.

A dream he couldn't quite remember.

He paused, a sharp pain shooting up his side, somehow going straight up his neck and through his jaw, rendering him motionless. As if sensing his discomfort, Rose turned. "Are you okay?" she asked.

"I'm fine," he returned.

"You don't look fine."

"Pain is a very determined thing," he remarked, continuing to stand there frozen as he waited for the lingering effects to recede. "It doesn't like to stay at the site of the injury."

"I've never been seriously injured. So I don't really have any experience with that."

"I… I don't know if I ever have been before. But either way I don't remember it. So it feels remarkably like the first time."

That made him wonder what other things might feel like the first time, and judging by the suddenly healthy color in his wife's face, she was wondering the same thing.

Of course, with his ribs being what they were, that wouldn't be happening anytime soon.

It was a strange thought, the idea of going to bed with someone he didn't know. Except, he *did* know her. But he might be different with her now. He might not be able to be the lover she deserved, or the one she wanted.

"Can you keep going? Or do you need for me to figure out a way to fix you a room downstairs?"

"I'm fine," he said, welcoming the interruption of his thoughts.

Finally, they reach the top of the stairs and he continued to follow her down the long corridor that led to his bedroom. Though *bedroom* was a bit humble of a word for what was in actuality an entire suite of rooms.

There was a home office, an extremely large bathroom, a sitting area and a room that actually contained a bed. "Do you have something similar?"

She nodded in affirmation. "Yes."

"We really are quite a bit like a royal couple." It made no sense to him, and it also felt wrong. He felt…captivated by Rose. Drawn to her. He couldn't imagine agreeing to separate bedrooms.

But perhaps things were different when his head was full of other things. Right now, it was only filled with pain, and her.

She was preferable to the pain, no contest.

She tilted her head to the side. "I find it very strange. The things you know and the things you don't."

"So do I. In all honesty, I would rather forget my surface knowledge of world customs and reclaim what I know about myself. But no one has consulted me on this."

"I understand. I should leave you to rest."

He was exhausted. Which seemed ridiculous considering he had spent most of the flight sleeping. He felt like this was definitely out of the ordinary. Being this tired. Also, being this sober.

He definitely had some strong impressions about what felt normal and what didn't. But he still wasn't entirely certain he could believe them.

"It would probably be for the best," he said.

"I'm going to confirm arrangements with the doctor I have coming in to check on you. The nurse, as well."

"I'm not an invalid."

"You have a head injury. And while we're reasonably certain you aren't going to die in the night, this is definitely out of the ordinary."

He couldn't argue with that. "All right then," he conceded.

"I'll wake you up when it's time for dinner." And then she turned and walked out briskly. And it was only then that it struck him that she never made any moves toward touching him physically. No small gestures of comfort.

She hadn't even behaved as though she was tempted to lean in and kiss him before walking out.

But he supposed he would have to unravel the mysteries of his own mind before he set out to unravel the mysteries of his marriage.

CHAPTER THREE

ROSE FELT LIKE she was losing her mind. Which, really wouldn't do since Leon had so clearly lost his.

"That isn't fair. He hasn't lost his mind, he's lost his memory," she said, scolding herself as she paced the empty study.

The past two days had been the most trying of her entire life. And all things considered, that was saying something. She had endured an awful lot in her life. From her mother dying when she was a young girl to the loss of her father when she was only twenty-one. Continually feeling as though she didn't fit in with her peers, because she was too quiet, too mousy to be of interest to anyone. Because she would rather spend her time in dusty libraries than at wild parties. Because if she was going to shop for anything it would probably be stationery or books rather than the latest fashions.

She had spent the past two years married to a man who hadn't touched her outside of their wedding day.

Yes, it was safe to say that Rose Tanner had not had it easy.

Still, watching a man like Leon go through something like this, seeing him so reduced… It was… It was awful. She wished very much that she didn't care quite so intensely. Even when she was angry with him, even when she talked herself into believing that she hated him, it didn't change the fact that he was the most vibrant, powerful, incredible man she had ever met.

Seeing him injured. Seeing him unsure. Seeing him as mortal… It was as though the last remaining safety net in her life had been pulled away. She had already lost her other pillars. Her mother. Her father. And now, she was losing Leon, too.

Sure, he hadn't exactly been a fantastic emotional support in the past few years, but he had been steady. Predictable, at least.

He could have died a couple of days ago, and he might never again be the man that he had been. Acknowledging that was devastating in a way she could never have anticipated.

"Get it together."

Her stern admonishment echoed off the walls, and she bit back the rising hysteria that was threatening to burst out of her.

She should do something. Go out to the garden and tend to the roses. Finish cataloging her father's extensive library. Instead, she sat on a dark green settee in front of the fireplace and allowed a wave of misery to wash over her.

She wanted so very much to be done with this. To be done with all of this sitting still and waiting for something better to become of her life, for something better to become of her marriage.

She wanted Tanner house. Of course she did. But she knew Leon wanted it, too. Ultimately, she had been willing to walk away from both if need be.

But she couldn't walk away from him now. She needed to see him well. And then with a clear conscience she could go. She could get on with her life.

And if he doesn't remember anything ever?

For one brief moment the temptation to lie to him overtook her. To tell him that the two of them were madly in love. To tell him that he had married her because he couldn't keep his hands off of her, not because he wanted to inherit her father's business empire and the home that had become close to his heart.

Yes, for one moment she was tempted. She wouldn't be human if she wasn't. She had spent so many years fantasizing about what it would be like to have Leon want her. To have him look at her and see her as a woman.

She couldn't do it. It would be… Well, it would be disgusting, but more than that it would be the furthest thing from what she really wanted. She didn't want Leon to be her prisoner. That was basically what he was already.

Actually, you're his.

She couldn't really argue with that. She had agreed to marry him, and then she had basically been installed in this house and left to rattle around the vacant halls. Meanwhile, he had continued to live life as though he were a single man.

The entire world knew they were married. The entire world also knew that he was an incorrigible playboy. And nobody knew that she had been trapped in an agreement to stay married to him for five years in order to make his ownership of her father's company permanent, and for her to end up with the home in the event of a divorce.

That was the prenuptial agreement, dictated by her father before his death.

But she wasn't waiting anymore. He could have the company. He could have the house. She just wanted to be free.

She had come to the point where she'd known she had two choices. To sit down and talk to him on one of the rare occasions he came home, and let him know how badly she wanted to give their marriage a chance. To tell him how she felt. Or, to ask for a divorce.

She'd opted for a divorce. Because there was no good way for the other conversation to end. She would lay her heart out there for him to see, risk everything and get rejected.

She'd decided she'd rather skip a few steps.

"Is it nearly dinnertime?"

She turned toward the sound of the gruff, sleepy voice and her heart nearly evaporated, right along with her good intentions. He was wearing nothing more than a pair of black, low-slung pants. His chest was bare, and she ought to be concerned about his wounds. About the bandage over his shoulder, the dark purple bruises streaked along his torso. Instead, her eyes chose mostly to fixate on his muscles.

On his perfectly defined chest, on the muscles in his abs that were rippling with each indrawn breath.

"I think so," she said, well aware that she sounded a little bit like she was the one who had been hit over the head.

"I'm starving," he said, crossing his arms and leaning against the door frame. He was holding a gray T-shirt in his hand, but made no move to put it on. "This is the first time I've been hungry since the accident. It's quite nice. I don't suppose you'll allow me to have a drink yet?"

"Still medicated, Leon."

"I'm starting to think that I would sacrifice pain medication for a drink." He frowned. "Do I drink a lot?"

She tried to think of Leon's habits. She wasn't overly familiar with them, since they didn't spend all that much time together. But, come to think of it, he was rarely without a drink in his hand.

"A bit," she said, cautiously. "Though I'm not quite sure what you're getting at."

"I have been craving a drink ever since I woke up. I don't know if it's simply because I'm in a situation of extreme stress or if I potentially have a bit of a dependency."

"You go out a lot," she said. "And why don't you put your shirt on?"

She sounded a little more desperate than she would have liked, but if he found it out of the ordinary, he didn't show it.

She wasn't supposed to pile a lot of information on him. She really was supposed to wait until he questioned things. But she was finding it difficult. Part of her wanted to dump the truth on him and then leave him in the hands of a doctor or nurse.

But he had been there for her the night of prom. He had also been there for her when her father had died. And this was what her father would want for her to do. Because he'd cared about Leon. Leon had always been the son her father had never had. Oftentimes she had felt like she was competing for affection, though she knew her father had loved her, too.

Her father wouldn't want Leon abandoned right now.

And so she would stay.

And she would do her very best not to upset him.

"I can't," he said, standing there still, the shirt clutched tightly in his hand.

"What do you mean you can't?"

"I'm having trouble getting the shirt on. My ribs are too sore." He held his hand out slightly, the shirt still clutched in his fist. "Can you help me?"

All of the air rushed from her lungs, her heart beating a steady rhythm in her ears. "I—" She was supposed to be his wife. There should be nothing remarkable about the request. There was nothing remarkable about it either way. He was an injured man and he needed help. He didn't need her to be weird.

She cleared her throat and crossed the space between them, hesitating for a moment before she reached out and took hold of the shirt. Their fingers brushed as he relinquished it to her, and a shiver ran down her spine.

She needed to get a grip.

"When you say I go out a lot, you mean that I go to parties?"

She nodded, swallowing hard, her throat suddenly dry. "Yes." She held the shirt so it was facing the right direction and gathered the material up. "You need to…duck your head or bend as much as you can."

He bent slightly and she pushed the shirt over his head, dragging it down to his shoulders, his skin scorching hers as her knuckles brushed against his collarbone.

"And you?" he asked.

She looked up at him, her eyes clashing with his. He was so close. So close that it would be easy to stretch up on her toes and close the space between them. She'd only kissed him once. At their wedding in front of a church full of people.

What would happen if she did it again?

She blinked, trying to shake off the drugged feeling that was stealing over her. "Lift your arm as much as you can," she murmured.

He complied, his fingers grazing his bicep as he slipped into the shirt. "Do you go out with me?" he pressed.

She wasn't sure how to respond to that. She wasn't supposed to be dumping information on him, and beyond that, she didn't really want to. "I prefer to stay at home."

She pulled the shirt down the rest of the way over his torso, her knuckles brushing against the crisp hair and hard muscle as she did, a hollow sensation carving itself into the pit of her stomach.

It brought to mind all manner of things she'd scarcely allowed herself to fantasize about. Possibilities she'd only just now let go, as she'd accepted the fact her marriage had to end.

And now this. This unique and particular torture that brought her closer to her fantasy than ever before, and further away at the same time.

She took a step away from him, hoping to catch her breath.

He frowned, straightening. "I go out without you?"

He looked just as sexy with the shirt on. Tight and fitted over his muscular frame. She blinked and looked away.

"Sometimes." She looked up at the clock and saw that it was nearing six, which meant that dinner would be ready. She felt absolutely rescued by that. Maybe when they had a whole table between them she'd be able to breathe again. "I think it's time for us to go and eat," she said. "I'll show you the way to the dining room."

"You have a full staff here?" he asked, as they made their way through the house.

"Yes. I have kept everyone on since my father died. I didn't see the point in changing anything." She cleared her throat. "More than that, I guess I have desperately tried to keep everything the same."

"We both love this house," he said. "It's something we share. At least, you have told me I love this house."

"Yes, you do. And so do I. I was very happy here growing up. It is the only place I have memories of my mother. I remember hiding up at the top of the staircase and looking down, watching their massive holiday parties. My mother was always the most beautiful woman in

the room. She looked so happy with my father. I wanted…
I wanted more than anything to grow up and have that
be my life."

Her throat tightened and she found herself unexpect-
edly blinking back tears.

"Is that not our life?" he asked.

He sounded… He sounded hopeful. It was a very
strange thing. Typically, Leon spoke with an air of practiced cynicism. He was not the sort of man who held out
hope for much of anything. He was grounded. A realist.
It was why she cherished the very few soft moments she
had ever had with him. Because when he took the time
to be caring she knew that he meant it.

But when it came to things like this, flights of fancy,
romantic ideas about life and adulthood, she didn't expect him to care at all. Much less be able to envision
himself as part of it.

She found that she wanted to lie to him. Or, if not lie,
be a bit creative with the truth.

"This house is ours. To do with it as we wish. You have
been very busy since my father's death. Fully establish-
ing yourself as the head of the company, expanding. We
have not yet had time to throw any large holiday parties."

"But we intend to?"

"Yes," she said. That really wasn't strictly true. She
imagined that he never intended to. And she'd been planning on leaving him before next Christmas anyway.

Though she had wished… She had hoped, once upon
a time.

Recently, she had given up on it. She didn't even imagine her own future in this house, much less a shared future. But there was no benefit in telling him that now.

When they walked into the dining room the table was
already beautifully appointed. She had warned the staff

to keep a low profile. The doctor had told her that it was best to keep things as low-key as possible for Leon while he recovered. It was easy to focus only on the amnesia, which was of course the thing that both of them were most aware of, and forget that he also possessed quite a few physical injuries.

"They made your favorite," she said, sitting down in front of the steak and risotto that had been prepared for them. There was red wine at her seat. Water at Leon's.

"This seems a bit cruel and unusual," he said, eyeing her drink.

"I don't need to drink it."

"And that," he said, his tone hard, "seems remarkably wasteful. You can drink wine. I cannot. One of us should."

"Awfully giving of you."

"I feel that I am generous."

She couldn't help herself. She laughed. "Do you?" She lifted her wine to her lips and took a sip, suddenly grateful for the extra fortification that it would provide.

"Yes. Are you contradicting me?"

"Of course not," she said, looking down at her dinner. "You give to a great many charities."

"There you have it," he said, picking up his knife and fork. "Incontrovertible evidence that I am in fact generous."

"Perhaps," she said, slicing her steak slowly, "there is more than one type of generosity."

His dark eyebrows shot upward. "Is that so?"

She lifted one shoulder. "Perhaps."

"Do not speak in code. That is hardly less strenuous on my brain."

"I am not supposed to bombard you. Much less with my opinions. Opinions are not fact. You need facts."

"It is your *opinion* that I am not generous. At least not in every way."

She let out a long breath, feeling frustrated with herself. Feeling frustrated with him. With the world. She wanted to get up out of her chair, throw her cloth napkin on the floor and run out onto one of the grand lawns. Then perhaps she might rend her garment for dramatic effect and shout at the unfeeling sky.

Of course, she would do none of that. She never did.

Instead, she looked up at him and spoke in an even, moderated tone. "Of course you are."

"Now you are placating me."

She let out an exasperated sigh. "Are you trying to start a fight?"

"Don't be silly. We never fight."

"How could you possibly know that?" she asked, a strange sensation settling in the pit of her stomach.

Of course, he wasn't wrong. They had never fought. She had done nothing but idolize him for most of her life, and then she had married him. And in the two years since they had gotten married they'd had so little interaction they hadn't been able to fight. And, frankly, probably wouldn't have even if she had seen him every day.

He was indifferent to her, but he'd never been cruel. There had never been enough passion between them for there to be a fight.

"I just do," he said.

"You are so arrogant. Even now."

"Stingy and arrogant. That is your opinion of me. How is it that we never fight?"

"Perhaps because you are not often around," she said, taking her first bite of steak and making a bit of a show about chewing it so that he would perhaps cease his endless questions.

* * *

Leon looked across the table at his wife. He did not know quite how to read the exchange that had just taken place between them. She was irritated with him, that much he was certain of. He wondered how often that was the case. He wondered if this was unusual, if the stress of the situation was simply overtaking her, or if she didn't usually show him her irritation.

Or, more troubling, if he didn't typically notice it.

She had made several comments now about him frequently being away. She made him sound as though he was an absentee husband at best. Her childhood dream centered around her home being filled with parties. Centered around her hosting these events with her husband, to recapture a part of her life that was clearly past.

Both of her parents were gone. She had made no mention of any siblings. He appeared to be all that she had left, and yet he had seen no evidence that he did very much at all to support her emotionally.

That bothered him. Regardless of whether or not it bothered the man he had been before the accident was irrelevant to him in the moment. She was caring for him. And she clearly felt uncared for in many ways.

He felt compelled to remedy that. If he had to sit around this manor and do nothing but heal for the next several weeks he might as well focus on healing his marriage as well as his body.

It was deeper than that, too. Deeper than just a desire to right a wrong from the past.

Rose was his only touchstone. She was the only person who knew him. The only person he really knew. She was his anchor in an angry sea. And without her, he would be swept away completely.

He needed to shore up the connection between them.

He had lost himself. He could remember nothing of who he was. And from the sounds of things, their connection was much more tentative than it should be.

She was all he had. He could not lose her.

There was only one solution. He had to seduce his wife.

CHAPTER FOUR

IT HAD BEEN nearly a week since Leon's return to the manor and he still hadn't remembered anything. Rose was fighting against restlessness, hopelessness and the growing tenderness in her heart whenever she was around him.

As if that tenderness is anything new.

True. She had always felt…something for him. More than she should. He didn't care for her like that. He never had. But she could never quite stamp out that…that *hope*. That need. For someone who had been confronted with so much loss she retained rather more than a normal amount of idealism.

There was some part of her that believed steadfastly in happy endings. And being rewarded for good behavior. That was probably why she had always done exactly as her father asked. Why she had done her best to wait for Leon to come around to the idea of being her husband.

And why she had never actually sat down and told him how she felt. Better to close the door herself than have him do it.

"Don't start hoping again now. Once he remembers… everything will go back to the way it was."

She lay down on her back on her favorite settee, staring at the ornate ceiling. Then she heard heavy footsteps on the marble floors. She sat up, clutching the book she had been reading to her chest.

"Rose?" Leon strode into the room, looking much more alert and able than he had only a few days ago. He had been resting quite a bit, and had taken several meals in his room since that first night here. It seemed to have paid off.

"Just reading," she said.

"What are you reading?"

"Nora Roberts."

"I don't think I've read her. Maybe I have. I wouldn't know."

She laughed in spite of herself. "I doubt it."

"It's not the sort of thing I would usually read?"

"Unless it's business-related literature you don't strike me as the sort of man who reads."

"You don't think?"

"You're usually very confident about who you are, and how you see yourself. What do you think?"

"I think that… I cannot imagine myself going to university. But that's impossible. Being in the position that I'm in I must have gone."

"You didn't," she said, imagining that it was all right to confirm this.

But you don't think it's okay to confirm that your marriage is not quite what it seems?

She gritted her teeth and banished that thought. One thing at a time. And anyway, she intended to have this discussion with him. She intended to end their marriage. But she doubted news of a divorce would be overly welcome to him right now. Especially not when they needed to keep his condition a secret. Especially not when he would have no one else looking out for him. No one else who knew him to help him through all of this.

"Then how… I know enough to know that that is not typically how the world works." He rubbed his hand over his chin, his skin scraping against the whiskers there. The sound was…strangely erotic.

Rose had no experience with men. Not intimate experience. Beyond that single chaste kiss on their wedding day, and the strangely arousing experience of putting his T-shirt on him, she hadn't really had any physical contact with a man. Why would she? She had been waiting for Leon. Fool that she was.

As a result, she imagined she was a bit more affected by everyday things than a woman with greater experience would be. Looking at the situation with a little bit of distance she felt sorry for herself. Poor, innocent Rose quivering over whiskers.

Too bad she had no distance in the situation. She had… longing that she could do nothing about, sadness that never seemed to go away, that permeated her entire being and settled a heaviness over her chest, and a deep fear that Leon would never remember anything. Coupled with an almost equally deep fear that he would remember everything and she would have to leave this house, leave him, and move forward with her goal of independence. Of letting go of her feelings for him.

"I'm fuzzy on the details, and I'm sorry about that," she said, trying to ignore the heat in her cheeks. "All I know is that you were working for my father, for his company. In a very low-level position. You were a teenager. You had not graduated from school. Instead, you left and went straight into the workforce. You did something at the company to catch my father's eye, and from there he began to mentor you. He took a very personal interest in you, and he began to groom you to be his protégé."

"My family wasn't rich," he said, a strange, hollow

look taking over his eyes. "I know that. I'm from Greece. We were very poor. I came here by myself."

It struck her then, how little she knew about him. She knew he was Greek, that much was obvious, but she didn't know about his background, not really. She was struck then how little she knew him at all.

He had appeared in her life one day like a vapor and she had hero-worshipped him from that moment on.

That is, until she had fully realized that he would never quite conform to the fantasy she had built around him in her mind. She didn't wonder why he had married her. The perks of the union were obvious. Her father had been dying, and he wanted to see her settled. He had offered the company and the estate as incentives to Leon, and had put a time frame on the union likely to make sure the two of them gave it an adequate enough try.

All of that made sense. But she suddenly realized that she was the one who didn't make sense. What had she been hoping for? What on earth had she possibly thought would come from all of this? Who did she imagine he was? That was the problem. *All* of it was imaginary.

As she sat here in the library attempting to reconstruct who Leon was for his own sake, she realized just how much of the puzzle she was missing.

It made her feel… It made her feel small. Selfish. As if she had only ever seen him as an object of fantasy, who lived and breathed to serve her girlish dreams.

"Are you all right?" he asked.

She blinked. "Yes. Do I not look all right?"

"You look as though you have been hit across the face with a mackerel."

She tried to laugh. "Sorry. It's just… I don't actually know as much about you as I should. When confronted with the gaps in your memory I'm forced to examine the missing pieces of my knowledge."

He frowned. "I suppose I bear some part of the blame in that. If not most of it."

"I don't think that's true. I think in this case the fault is squarely mine."

"I cannot help you with it now. I don't have answers to any of the questions."

"I don't expect you to," she said, feeling rather weak and pale.

"I do know a few things," he said, squaring his shoulders, his eyes taking on a determined glitter. That made her feel more at ease. That reminded her of the Leon she had always known.

Sharp, determined, ever in command.

"That's reassuring," she said.

"I know that we are having dinner outside on the terrace tonight. And I know that it's going to be Maine lobster. Which I know is your favorite."

"How exactly do you know that? You didn't know what *your* favorite was only a few days ago."

It wasn't really because of his memory loss that she found this strange. She wasn't sure he had ever known her favorite foods.

"I am fully capable of making inquiries. Probably better than I was just a week ago. My entire life has become dependent on answers, and in part, the quality of my questions. I did my best to rustle up some members of the staff so that I could figure some things out about you."

"You didn't have to do that." She felt slightly panicky. As though she was being given a gift that was entirely unearned.

"I know I didn't. But you are my wife. Not only that, you have been taking care of me ever since the accident."

"Not entirely. We've had a nurse on call. The doctor has been in constantly. I—"

"Just knowing you were here has been invaluable." He smiled and she felt it all the way down, deep. It made her stomach tighten, made her heart flutter. Why was it always like this?

He extended his hand, his dark eyes meeting hers. She looked down at it as though it were a poisonous snake.

"I'm leading you to lobster. Not to your doom," he said.

She hesitated, feeling very much like she didn't deserve to touch him. Feeling very much like this was intended for a woman who didn't exist. The devoted wife she wasn't. The devoted wife she would be if Leon had any interest in being a husband in real life.

Or she was overthinking it. This was just dinner. This was only his hand.

She took a deep breath and wrapped her fingers around his. Lightning shot over the surface of her skin, crackling over her entire body, leaving her breathless, leaving her knees weak. She hadn't touched him since the wedding. She hadn't touched any man since then. She wasn't entirely certain she had *really* touched anyone at all.

Her father was gone. And even when he'd been here, he'd been spare on physical affection. All of her close friends, the ones she'd made in her two years of university while starting her history degree, had moved away. None of them were spending their twenties rotting in their parents' estates. They had all moved to Manhattan, London, exciting places. They were all pursuing careers, or higher education. Bigger goals than clinging to good memories. They were out making *new* memories. And until this moment, until his skin touched hers, she didn't realize how incredibly lonely she had become.

She had no one to blame but herself.

And this is why you're leaving.

She took a deep breath, trying to do her best to keep her reaction to him concealed. But then she made a terrible mistake. She looked up, her eyes meeting his, and what she saw there astonished her.

His eyes weren't blank. They weren't flat. They were… They were molten. The heat there a perfect reflection of the fire that was rioting through her core.

"Come on," he said, his voice rough.

She could do nothing but follow him. Which was terribly telling. Not just of this moment, but of the past fifteen years or so.

And once they were outside, her breath caught in her throat, all of the sensations building in her chest, making it impossible for her to do anything but stand there and tremble. He was touching her. And right before them was a beautifully appointed table set for two, a candle at the center.

It was like something that had been torn from her fantasies. Her girlish fantasies. When loving him had simply meant aspirations of sweet romance, holding hands and making sophisticated conversation.

Back before she had realized that there was much more to the connection between men and women than candlelight and hand-holding.

"Is something wrong?"

She looked at him, at his fierce expression. There was an intensity behind his eyes that she couldn't decode. All she knew was that she had waited most of her life to have him look at her like this. And for some reason he was looking at her this way now. She was… She was powerless to resist. Utterly and completely held captive by that look in his eyes.

"Nothing's wrong," she lied, making her way across the expansive terrace and taking her seat at the table.

She noticed then that Leon had a glass of water in front of his plate rather than wine. "I didn't think you were on pain medication anymore," she said.

"I'm not. But as I'm not entirely certain what my relationship is to alcohol I decided it best to continue to abstain. I seem to have done all right without it in the past week. Why start now?"

She nodded slowly. The truth was, Leon overindulged in everything. It was difficult to say what specifically he might have a problem with, and what specifically he just chose to indulge in to excess. But she was grateful that he was choosing to remain completely sober tonight. The idea of him being drunk and amnesiac made her feel far too much like the predator he had implied she might be when they had first left for the airport in Italy.

"Oh. Well. Maybe I should drink something else then."

"You're fine. It occurs to me that we've been talking rather a lot about me. I want to hear more about you, Rose. Because it isn't only myself that I have forgotten about. I don't remember anything about you."

Her heart was thundering hard, her throat suddenly dry. "I'm not sure that I'm a very interesting topic of conversation."

"I doubt there is anything more interesting to a man than the topic of his wife."

"We don't… We don't have that sort of relationship," she said, the truth stumbling out of her mouth uneasily.

"Why not?"

"I'm not sure that you are well suited to marriage."

He frowned. "Have I been unkind to you in some way?"

"No," she said, trying to dispel his fears quickly. She

was afraid that he was imagining himself to be some kind of monster when that couldn't be further from the truth. "You are independent. We do not live in each other's pockets, as you have already noticed by virtue of the fact that we have separate bedrooms. We do not often take long meals together out on the terrace. We do not often share our innermost thoughts."

"Why did you marry me?" The words were so confused, so utterly filled with disbelief. It was shocking. To hear him question why on earth she might have married him.

"I could give any number of reasons a woman would marry you. You are incredibly handsome. Successful. And as for me… I am… Well, let's not be dishonest about the situation, Leon. I am quite plain."

He frowned even more deeply. Then he reached across the table, the edge of his thumb touching the corner of her mouth. Her heart slammed hard into her breastbone, her entire body going rigid, every fiber of her being on high alert to see what might happen next. He traced the line of her upper lip, then dipped down to the lower one before sweeping his thumb up to her cheekbone, dragging it slowly across her skin.

"I will confess that my first thought was that you were plain. But as I have spent time with you, as you have cared for me… I can no longer see what I first did. The only real memory I have, the only concrete image in my mind is your eyes. You are what I *remember*, while everything else is vague impressions and hazy ideas. If it is not entirely absent altogether. Your eyes are my truth, Rose. How could I find them, or you, anything but incredibly beautiful?"

She had stopped breathing now. Any moment, she had a feeling she was going to tip sideways in her chair and lose consciousness completely. But to have him look at her like this, to have him say those things… This entire nightmare was being twisted into a dream. Perversely, she was enjoying it. Perversely, it was everything she had ever wanted. But not like this.

Still, she found she couldn't turn away. "That is… It is an incredibly nice thing to say."

"I'm stingy and arrogant, remember? I am neither generous nor particularly nice, to hear you tell it. I am not being kind when I say these words. I am being truthful. There's a limit to the sorts of truths you can tell in my position. There are very few things I know for certain. But this is one of them."

He shifted the position of his hand, cupping her face, his palm warming her. Igniting her. "You are my wife. I wish to know everything about you."

He dropped his hand away from her face, drawing it back to his side of the table. She cleared her throat nervously, shifting the cutlery on the table in front of her as a displacement activity.

"Did you go to university?" he asked.

"Yes," she said.

"What did you study?"

She shifted, feeling uncomfortable and edgy beneath his intense dark gaze. "I was a history major. As you've probably guessed, I like old things. Really, the older and dustier the better."

"Is that a jab at my age?"

She laughed. "Um. It wasn't, but that's an interesting point. No, I like the smell of books, musty pages and such. Aged velvet furniture that's always a little damp."

"Doesn't sound too appealing to me."

"No. Of course not. Your room here is all modernized."

"I like things sans dust and mold, what can I say," he returned. "So you did your history degree."

"No," she said. "I went for two years. And then I stopped."

"Why?"

"I married you."

Her answer settled uncomfortably between them. An accusation, when she hadn't meant it to be one.

"Which begs the question," he said, "that I have been dying for the answer to. How old are you?"

She fiddled even more intensely with the silverware. "Twenty-three."

"So you were twenty-one when we married."

"Twenty. I was just shy of my birthday, and we have been married a little over two years."

"That seems a bit too young."

She lifted her shoulder. "My father was dying. We both knew it. Knowing that I was safe with you, knowing that we were settled brought him a lot of joy. Neither of us wanted to deny him that."

"And then your father died and… I have been off partying. I left you here in this house by yourself with no finished degree doing…"

"You helped. When he died. You didn't just abandon me and go to parties. You supported me. You took care of so many details when I was far too emotional to do it myself."

The relief on his face touched something deep inside of her. "Well, that's something."

"And I've been organizing my family history. Our family tree, which stems back to the founding of the country, actually. So it's very rich and…you know, complicated."

"Wonderful. So I left you here to grow moldy with the old furniture you love so much. How generous of me."

"No," she said, her chest tight. Because it was the truth. Her father had died and Leon had returned to the exact lifestyle he had been living before their marriage. He had never touched her, not once, but he had continued to sleep with other women. She knew it. She wasn't blind. Gossip magazines were alight with it. The poor, sad Tanner heiress and her wandering husband. But she didn't want to tell him that. She didn't want to tell this man that.

How strange that she did not want to disappoint him with the truth about himself.

"You are not being truthful with me."

"I'm not entirely certain the truth is beneficial in this situation."

He rose from his seat and came to stand in front of her before dropping to his knees. They were eye level, and he was so close she could smell the soap on his skin, could feel the warmth coming off his body. She was seized by the desire to touch him. To close the distance between them. But she didn't. She just sat there, frozen as ever.

It turned out she didn't have to close the distance, because he was the one to do it. He reached up, cupping her cheeks with both of his hands, drawing her face down toward him. "Then we shall make a new truth. I see no reason why we cannot make a new life. You have shared with me your dreams, and I find that I like the sound of them."

"You aren't working right now. You are…housebound. I am the only entertainment you have."

His dark gaze turned stormy. "You make me sound like a child."

In some ways, he was. In some ways, he always had been. A man with a very short attention span who was constantly on to the next toy. The newest thing, the shiniest thing. As a girl she had found it exciting. His flashy cars, his sharp wardrobe, even the beautiful women he would sometimes bring to her father's parties. Until the sharp claws of jealousy had sunk deep inside her. Until she had wanted to occupy the position those women were in.

It was the moments in between that got her. That held her affection for him. The spare times when she'd caught a hint of haunted darkness around the edges of his bright smile. The times when he'd looked at her and seen down deep.

The times he'd looked at her, period, and not just past her.

"I…"

"I am not a child," he said, his voice a dark temptation she couldn't turn away from.

And before she could say another word, before she could protest, before she could even breathe, Leon had closed the distance between them. And he was kissing her like she had never been kissed before. As he had never kissed her before, since he was the only man she had ever kissed.

His lips were hot, firm and commanding as they moved over her own, his tongue a slick, sweet entice-ment as it delved deep inside her mouth, sliding against her own. Immediately, her breasts felt heavy, her core a hollow ache, wet with need for him at the first touch of his mouth to hers.

She was drowning. In this. In him. In the desire. Com-pletely and utterly at its mercy.

She wasn't even sure she cared. Because she was being swept away on a tide that she couldn't even hope to fight against. Desire dictating her every response, her every movement.

She felt… She felt ravenous for him. Completely and totally starved of the one thing she had craved for so long.

She wrapped her arms around his neck, leaning out of her chair and crushing her breasts to his chest, nearly sighing with relief as she pressed herself against him. She wanted to meld herself to him completely, wanted to get lost in this forever.

It was a sickness, a kind of madness that overtook her completely. The desire to feel his skin against hers, to have nothing at all between them. His memories didn't matter. His broken ribs didn't matter. His betrayal of their vows didn't matter. All of the hurt, all of the torture she had endured over it didn't matter.

Nothing mattered but this. The fact that she was kissing him finally.

He slid his hand down her back, pressing her more firmly against him. She parted her thighs, resting the part of herself that was aching the most for his touch up against his hardened arousal.

He growled, drawing his hand down lower to cup her rear, pressing her even more tightly to him, rolling his hips against hers.

It occurred to her then that it wasn't only alcohol he had gone a long time without. Granted, she had gone twenty-three years without this kind of sexual contact, but Leon was accustomed to more.

And it was that thought that found her pulling away from him, running her shaking hands through her hair and sitting back in her chair. "I'm sorry," she said, the words rushed.

He looked at her, frowning. "Why are you sorry?"

"You don't remember anything. You don't remember us. And you're injured…"

"This," he said, his eyes meeting hers meaningfully, "has nothing to do with memory. This is another bit of honesty, I think."

Except it wasn't. Because they didn't do things like this. Because he had never touched her before. She couldn't bring herself to voice that admission. Could not do that to what was left of her pride.

"I think it would be for the best if we held off on things like this."

"Why is that?" he asked. "Is it because you are so angry with me about something that happened before?"

"It's because I don't feel right about asking you to sleep with a stranger." It was nearly the truth.

"Everyone is a stranger to me. I'm a stranger to myself. And yet I seem to sleep in my own body every night."

"It's different. And you know it."

"Is it?"

"I think you're just…just male. And therefore would come up with any excuse for sex."

He shook his head slowly, his dark eyes searching. "You are my wife. You are not a stranger to me. And I can feel…that there is something broken between us. I know it, as surely as I know certain things about myself. I do not need a memory to know that I wish to fix that."

Her throat tightened, pressure building in her chest. "It is not entirely on you to fix it."

"I want to try."

She gritted her teeth, trying to hold her emotions in check. "Let's wait. Let's wait until you remember." The words nearly choked her, because the last thing she wanted was to wait. If they waited, he would remember his indifference. If they waited, he wouldn't want to fix what was broken. Because in Leon's eyes their marriage wasn't broken. Why would it be?

With their current arrangement he was allowed to behave as he saw fit. To do exactly what he wanted whenever he wanted with whomever he wanted. Once he remembered that their arrangement consisted of her staying home while he behaved like a man with no wife at all he wouldn't want to change a thing.

"You are not my doctor, *agape*."

"No, I'm not. But I am the one who—"

"Don't make the mistake of thinking that because I don't have my memories I'm not in full control of my desires. A man does not need a memory to know that he wants a woman. He feels that in his body. In his blood. Mine burns for you. My mind may not remember, but my body suffers no such affliction."

She drew in a deep, shuddering breath, the weight of all the restraint, of the denial pressing down on her. He was promising things that didn't exist outside of misty fantasy for her. Pleasure, satisfaction on a level she could hardly comprehend. But it wasn't for her. Not really. And she had to resist. No matter how enticing it was.

"No," she said, standing from her chair and sweeping past him, not pausing to look back at him as she walked straight into the house. She kept going. She nearly ran. All the way through the house, up the stairs, down the corridor and into her bedroom. She shut the door tightly behind her, and leaned back up against the wall.

And she couldn't help but feel she had run away from her salvation.

CHAPTER FIVE

SHE WAS BREATHING HARD, her heart fluttering in her chest like a trapped bird in a cage.

She wanted him. And this sorely tested her. All of her willpower, all of her restraint. He was offering her what she wanted on a platter. Seemingly. But she knew that as decadent, as wonderful as it all seemed, it would be poison in the end.

"It would be. It would kill me." She spoke those words aloud into the emptiness of the room. Trying to make herself believe them. Trying to force herself to feel it.

She squeezed her eyes shut tight, curling her fingers into fists. And she waited until she stopped shaking before she moved away from the wall.

When she could catch her breath she reached around and took hold of the tab on the zipper, drawing it down, feeling as though she was casting some of the weight off as she let her dress fall from her body and pool at her feet on the floor. She wandered into the bathroom, turning the tub taps on and letting the water run until it was hot.

She unclipped her bra, flinging it onto the floor, not caring where it landed. She pushed her panties down her thighs, leaving them behind, too. Then she walked back into her bedroom, digging through her closet until she found a pair of sweats, something that would entice her to stay away from Leon for the rest of the night. If she put on anything too silky, anything that might not humiliate her to stand before him in, she could not guarantee that she wouldn't go and find him later.

With that thought in mind she stared down at the pair of pajama pants in her hand, then shoved them back in the drawer, digging until she found a slightly older, slightly baggier pair. Insurance. It was what she needed.

Additional insurance came in the form of large white cotton panties that would provide more than full coverage, and handle any Leon incidentals that might occur.

She grabbed hold of an equally ancient sweatshirt and added it to her pile of clothing before heading back into the bathroom.

She wasn't foolish enough to think she would behave rationally now she'd tasted him. Wars were started over sex. The desire for it. The anger over someone else having it in a way you didn't like. Or with someone you wish you were having it with.

Sex was powerful. And she knew better than to think she was immune.

The water was hot, steam beginning to fill the air. She took a deep breath, sighing as she exhaled. Then she turned toward the counter and began to pin her hair up, slowly, methodically, trying to erase the past few moments from her mind.

"I wonder." She heard a rich, masculine voice coming from behind her and she turned. There was Leon, standing in the door, his dark eyes like black fire. "I wonder how many times I have stood here in this very place and watched you prepare for your bath like this. I have no recollection. This does not make my mind itch in any way."

Heat scorched her skin, fascination and embarrassment warring for equal place inside of her. He had never seen her naked before. No man ever had. But of course, he didn't know that. Of course, he wouldn't have any concept of just what an invasion this was.

That was her own doing. There was no one to blame for that but herself. And she still wasn't doing anything to correct it.

"An itch in your mind?" She looked around, desperately searching for a towel, something, *anything* to cover her exposed body.

"That is what it feels like sometimes. When something is familiar but I can't grab hold of it. As though I have an itch deep in my brain that I can't quite get to. But this… This is free of all of that. Perhaps because when I look at you it becomes difficult to think at all."

She swallowed hard. And she forgot to look for a towel. Forgot to be embarrassed. She was completely frozen in her tracks. It would be easy—or it should be—to move her hands strategically and offer herself some modesty. But she felt like she'd been turned into a pillar of salt. Punished for looking at him when she should have turned away.

You don't want to cover yourself. You want him to keep looking at you.

Yes, she did. As disturbing a realization as that was, she did.

Historically, people were very stupid when it came to sex. She was proving beyond a doubt that she was doomed to repeat history.

"You do say very nice things," she said, her voice thin, soft.

"Have I always?"

She shook her head. "You don't say unkind things. But…"

He took a step into the bathroom and her entire body

stiffened. "But I do not lavish you with the sort of praise you deserve. I get that sense. I get the feeling that I never adequately appreciated how glorious a sight you were." He was gazing at her openly, with no shame at all. Like this was the Garden of Eden and nudity was simply right.

"Do you even remember what women look like naked? Perhaps that's all this is. Perhaps there is a strange amount of novelty that you're contending with here." She still hadn't managed to move at all. She was standing there, completely bare, her heart pounding hard, her limbs trembling. She felt like a frightened squirrel staring down a large predator she had no hope of escaping.

You don't even want to escape. You want to offer him your neck.

She gritted her teeth, squeezing her knees tightly together, trying to tamp down the restless feeling that was growing between her thighs.

"I *do* remember what women look like naked. Oddly enough. Not one specific woman, but it is not as mysterious to me as you might think." He took another step toward her, then another. "I know that you think we should wait. But I want you to listen to me. I feel very much like what we had before this was broken. I said that to you downstairs, and I still mean it. I don't care what happened. I don't care where we were. I have a sense that you and I are the right thing. You are the woman I want. The woman I married. Whenever I lost sight of it, why I lost sight of it, it doesn't matter. If you can forgive me then I want to move forward as husband and wife. And I want to be husband and wife in every sense of the word." His voice got lower, grew rougher. "And I don't want to wait for my ribs to heal. I don't want to wait for a memory that may never come back. My life is a blank, barren field, Rose. I have… I have nothing. I have nothing but this connection to you, this need for you. Give me this. Give me something other than emptiness."

What he was offering her was a dream come true. All of her girlish fantasies come to life. It was what she had hoped would happen after their wedding two years ago. That wedding night that never actually eventuated.

Two years a wife, and she was still a virgin. Pining after a man who had held her heart as long as she could remember. It was enough to make her want to cry just thinking about it. Enough to make her want to curl up in a ball and wail for just how sorrowful a situation it was. She had wanted him for as long as she could remember, and she had been denied him. She had married him. And she had never once pushed. Not for anything. Even when she had decided that she would divorce him she had immediately rushed to his side the moment she had heard about his injury. Because what else could she do? Leon held all of her heart. There was no denying that.

It was why she had to divorce him even at the expense of the house if she wanted to retain her sanity. Because as long as she lived in hope she would never move on with her life.

And here he was, standing there, offering her hope. Offering her everything she had ever wanted to hear.

She just wasn't strong enough to say no. She had been strong, for so long, in so many ways. She had done her best to be strong for her father when her mother had died, even if he had done his best to hold it all together for her.

She had stayed strong in the face of his illness, in the face of his impending death. She had stayed strong even as he had asked her to marry Leon, so that he would know that she was protected. Even while the very thought of entering into a loveless union with the man who held every last piece of her soul killed her by inches.

She could not sacrifice anymore. Not for one more moment.

Leon was offering to make this marriage work. He wanted her to be his wife in every way. How could she deny him?

How could she deny herself?

This time, she was the one who took a step forward. Moving toward him. Her heart was in her throat, pounding, making her feel light-headed, dizzy. But even so, she took another step toward him, and then another.

He was the one who closed the distance. He was the one who ran out of patience. He wrapped his arm around her waist, pulling her tightly up against his body, a feral growl on his lips. She could feel him. All of him. His heat, his hardness, the intense thrust of his arousal up against her hip.

Oh, how she wanted him. There were no words for the depth of her desire. For the depth of her longing, her need.

It wove itself around her body, like the vines that overtook the Tanner house, creeping ever higher until it threatened to consume her. Need wrapped itself around her throat, made it impossible for her to breathe. Impossible for her to think.

"Are you afraid of me, Rose?" His voice was so soft, so tender and so full of concern, it made her own heart ache in response.

"Of course not."

"You look at me as though I am a monster of some kind."

"Not you. This thing between us. All of this. It feels like a monster. Like something that could consume us both."

He laughed, the sound rusty, hard. "Yes, I agree." He dragged his thumb along her cheekbone, his gaze filled with wonder. "Has it always been like this?"

"For me," she said, the word strangled. "For me it has always been like this."

"I think it has been for me, too."

She laughed. "You can't possibly know that."

"Of course I can. Just as I know I am generous."

"I already told you we have differing opinions on that."

"Which leads me to believe that I perhaps demonstrate the things I feel differently than people might usually. But it doesn't mean I don't feel them. This is an old feeling, Rose. I know it is. It's as much a part of me as my blood. There's nothing foreign about it. Nothing unusual. It simply is. And much like any other part of myself I'm not sure that you could remove it without destroying me completely."

"You don't say things like this," she said, feeling almost desperate to pull away now. This was too much. Because this wasn't him. Not really. This was not the kind but distant man she had always known.

The Leon that she knew did not feel this for her. If he did, he would have touched her a long time ago. If he did, he wouldn't spend his nights in bed with other women.

But she couldn't say any of that. Not in this moment. Not now. And she couldn't pull away, either. Because no matter how strong the compulsion was, it could not begin to compete with the desire to stay in his arms.

"Let's not talk," she said. "Please, kiss me."

He didn't hesitate. He lowered his head, closing the distance between them. And she ignited. All of the need, all of the desire she had felt out on the terrace was magnified now. Magnified by the feel of his large hands spanning her bare waist, of her nipples pressing against the rough fabric of his shirt. Magnified by the fact that she was utterly and completely enslaved to him now. The fact that she was not trying to fight it anymore, even for a moment.

If this was a war, she was conquered.

This was wrong. But she didn't care. She was doing the wrong thing. And she was doing it for herself. She had spent a great many years trying to do the right thing. And she had gotten nothing in return.

She wasn't afraid of being wrong. She didn't even feel guilty. She simply felt exhilaration. Freedom. Here she was in the arms of the man she had always wanted, and she would think of nothing else.

She had always imagined that the moment Leon touched her he would know that she loved him. That she would betray every part of herself if he so much as swept his hand over her cheek. But this was different. So different than how she had ever envisioned it. Because he assumed that she loved him. He also assumed that he loved her.

But because of that…there were no secrets to keep. This was no revelation for him. And there was nothing inside of herself to protect. It made her feel strong. It made her feel not quite so vulnerable.

It made her feel not so much like the neglected virgin bride she'd been.

She pressed her hands against his chest, reveling in the feel of him, in the hardness of his muscles, the evidence of his strength. Before she could think it through, before she could stop herself, she was working the buttons on his shirt, separating the fabric, brushing her fingertips over his bare skin.

She had been struck by his beauty the day he had walked into the library without a shirt. And now she was touching him.

Her fingers shook as she pressed them against his skin,

as she traced the definition of his muscles, his coarse chest hair abrading her fingertips as she continued to explore him. He was everything a man should be. But then, of course he was. Her desire for men was shaped around him. Her needs had never been generic. Her need had always been for him. Always and only.

He held the back of her head with his hand, deepening the kiss, his tongue delving deep as he tasted her slowly, leisurely. His other hand slid low to cover her bottom, his fingers pressing deep into her flesh. It was a possessive hold. It was not a hold of a man who was unsure of what he wanted. He wanted her.

It didn't matter what he had wanted in the past. This was now. And he was choosing her.

She squeezed her eyes shut tight, pouring everything into the kiss.

She didn't know what she was doing. She had no practical skill in the art of seduction. She had nothing more than her passion. And she doubted there was a woman alive who felt as passionately about Leon Carides as she did. She doubted there was a woman alive who felt this passionately about any man. This was nearly fifteen years in the making for her. And what she lacked in practical skill she more than made up for in desire.

She pushed his shirt off his shoulders, marveling at the way he was constructed. She doubted there was a man alive so perfectly formed. At least, there was no other man alive so perfectly created for her. She kept her eyes squeezed tight, did so in order to keep the tears from falling. Nerves, emotions, threatened to strangle her. This was desire like she'd never known existed. In the abstract, wanting him was something she could control.

Late at night in her bed, when she imagined being with him, when she imagined him touching her skin, she dictated the movements. She controlled how fast things went, how quickly she brought herself to completion.

In reality, she controlled nothing of what he did. And her need a blazing wildfire, burning out of control. It was terrifying. Exhilarating. Intoxicating. It was so much more than she had ever imagined it could be.

But it was moving far faster than she had anticipated. The hand that had been resting on her bottom had now dipped down between her thighs, teasing her slick folds, ramping up her need until she could hardly breathe. If he moved his hand just a little bit higher, he would push her over the edge completely. With nothing more than a simple touch, a simple kiss, she knew that she would lose her control.

And so what if she did? She was past the point of caring. In fact, she embraced it. This was what she wanted. Wild. Beyond desire. Beyond shame.

It was as though everything between them had been burned to the ground. As though they had been given a chance to start again. No one else was given this chance. They were. This was for them. This was for her. This was her chance to make a new memory of herself. Even if he did remember everything in the past, he would remember this, too.

In this moment, she could create a new image for herself. He would finally see her as a woman, because he could no longer remember her as that plain, bookish girl she'd been.

If it was that that stood between them, if it was his affection for her father, whatever it was, that was lost here. Obliterated. Gone.

There was nothing but Leon. Nothing but Rose. Nothing but the need that was sparking between them, hot and out of control.

He growled, sliding his hand down to her thigh, hooking her leg up over his hip, then the other, bringing the damp part of her up against the hardness of his arousal, sending a streak of pleasure through her body. She gasped, and he began to carry her out of the room, carry her toward the bed.

"The bath," she said, feeling dazed.

"I suppose we don't want to cause a flood," he said, depositing her at the center of the mattress and abandoning her as he went to turn the water off.

She had a moment to rethink then. A moment to gather her thoughts. A moment to flee.

She stayed where she was.

He appeared a moment later, filling the doorway, his broad shoulders, heavily muscled chest and narrow waist so utterly masculine, so completely captivating, it stole her breath.

And then there was the hard press of his erection against the front of his jeans. The absolute and complete evidence that he truly did want her.

She bit her lip, nerves threatening to swamp her.

"There's that look again," he said, his tone gentle. "Please don't be afraid of me, *agape*." He came to stand beside the bed, his hands on the snap of his jeans. "I only want to make you feel good. I want to make this a memory we share. I want... I want you to feel close to me."

She tried to speak. She tried to say that she wanted that, too. But she already did feel closer to him than she ever had. But she couldn't form the words. She couldn't make her voice work. Couldn't force anything through the tightness of her throat.

"Sometimes I wonder if you have lost your memory, as well," he said, undoing his jeans then drawing the zipper down slowly.

Her heart nearly stopped. "I haven't. It's just that... You're different. This is different."

"I am sorry." He pushed his jeans down his narrow hips, exposing his rigid arousal. He was so beautiful. So rampantly masculine. So...large.

"For what?" She managed to scrape the words past her dry throat.

"For the way I was."

He joined her on the bed then, closing the distance between them, drawing her naked body up against the length of his. His erection was hard, so very hot against her skin. It was unfamiliar. It was wonderful. He ran his hands over her curves, warm, large, soothing. She found that she wasn't as nervous now.

She just wanted. She was filled with a restless, overpowering ache that was threatening to unravel her completely. If she didn't have more of him. More of this.

"What do you like?" he asked, his voice a rich, deep whisper that whisked along her veins.

"You," she said, the deepest and starkest truth there was.

"Surely you must like something specific."

"Everything you do. Everything you are. That's what I want. It's all I've ever wanted." The admission poured from deep inside of her. From deep within her soul. And she couldn't be embarrassed.

"You are too easy on me, I think. I think you should perhaps make me grovel. I think you should perhaps make me beg." He leaned in, pressing a hot openmouthed kiss to her neck.

"I'm the one that's about to beg," she said, her voice breathless.

"There's no need. I am at your mercy," he said, "your willing slave." He kissed a line down her neck, down to the curve of her breast, his breath hot across her sensitized nipples. Then he traced the outline of one tightened bud with his tongue before sucking her in deep. She gasped, arching up off of the bed, sensation shooting through her like an arrow, hitting its target unerringly.

"You are very sensitive," he said, his voice rough. A smile curved his lips. "And do not ask how I know you are particularly. I simply do."

She had not been about to ask him anything, if only because she felt as though her voice could no longer form words. Her brain certainly couldn't muster up the amount of cells required to say anything. Indeed, sentence formation was beyond her. He had transformed her, transformed her into a creature of *feeling* and *needing*. Who could do nothing but simply wait for the next sensation to bombard her.

Still, she managed to speak. "This has only made your arrogance worse, I hope you know."

"I am a terrible trial to you," he said, a smile curving his lips. "I can see. But I feel you enjoy my arrogance."

He transferred his attention to her other breast, repeating the motion that he had done with the first, sending another direct shot of pleasure straight through her system. She shifted, parting her legs, rubbing herself against his thigh, seeking some kind of release from the pressure that was building inside her.

"So impatient," he said.

"I am," she panted. "If you could kindly move a little bit faster."

"I only have this one chance to make a memory of our first time again. If I never get my memories back this is all I will have. I intend to take my time."

He licked and kissed his way down the tender skin of her stomach, moving to the vulnerable flesh on her inner thigh before sweeping his tongue right through her slick folds. She cried out, sensation racking her body, wave after wave of release shuddering through her. And when it was over, she was panting, shaking and ready for more. Ready for everything.

"Leon," she said, feeling desperate. "I need you."

"I'm not finished," he said, lapping at her again, his fingers teasing the entrance to her body.

"I want to explore you," she said. "I want… Everything you did to me I want to do to you."

She wanted to taste every masculine inch of him. To glory over the way he was made. To revel in a fantasy long awaited. Come to scorching life finally, at long last.

"No. It is my turn."

And before she could protest he worked a finger deep inside her, continuing to tease her with his wicked tongue as he did. This sensation, the penetration was new for her. She loved it. Loved the feel of having him inside her. He added a second finger, stretching her gently as he continued to tease her clitoris with his tongue.

He couldn't know that she needed this. That she needed this introduction, this moment of preparation. And yet somehow he seemed to sense it.

Pleasure built all over again, and she found herself close to the edge once more. Needing him. Needing all of him.

"Not enough," she said, panting.

"You want me inside of you?" he asked, his voice slurred as though he had finally had that drink he'd been craving for more than a week. As though she were the alcohol that he had so long desired. As though he was drunk on her, on her body. On desire.

"Yes," she said.

He rose up, positioning himself between her thighs,

kissing her lips deeply as he tested the entrance to her body with the blunt head of his arousal. She braced herself, tensing her muscles involuntarily as he thrust all the way home. Pain lanced her, sharp and unexpected. She had known it might hurt a bit, but this was more than a little pain. But then, Leon was more than just a bit of man.

She clung to his shoulders, her fingernails digging into his skin as she tried to catch her breath. He just stared at her, his dark eyes inscrutable, unreadable. He flexed his hips, and she feared that he would pull away. Instead, he pushed back inside of her, groaning as he did.

And then they were lost. In need. In this intense, primal desire that had overtaken them both.

Pain was forgotten. Nerves were forgotten. Everything was forgotten but her desperate bid for completion. She ran her fingertips over his back, down to his strong muscled butt, back up again, sweeping over the square line of his jaw, the deep grooves around his mouth. She tilted her head to the side and kissed his neck, scraped her teeth along the tendon that was held so tight, that betrayed just how desperately he was clinging to his control. Just how close he was to losing his grip.

She could feel his muscles begin to tremble, could feel him growing closer to the edge. His own loss of control snapped hers. She cried out, arching against him, a deeper, more profound orgasm rocking her as her internal muscles tightened around him.

He thrust twice more. Hard, intense, a growl on his lips as he found his own release, holding her tightly against his body when it was all finished.

She was dazed. Storm-tossed. Completely and utterly at the mercy of what had just taken place between them. She could hardly remember her own name. And for one hysterical moment she imagined that was how Leon must feel. Wiped clean. Fresh. Remade.

There were worse things than being remade with him.

"Your ribs," she said, suddenly remembering that he was injured. She moved her hand to touch his side and he caught hold of her, his dark eyes clearer now, his expression intense.

"Tell me," he said, not moving from his position on top of her, his fingers like iron around her wrist. "How is it that my wife of two years was still a virgin?"

CHAPTER SIX

HIS WIFE WAS a virgin. There was absolutely no question about it. At least, she had been up until a few moments ago. What he didn't know was *why*.

She was beautiful, and he was incredibly attracted to her. More than that, he had married her. It made no sense at all. Although he supposed it didn't make any less sense than any other part of this situation they found themselves in.

A sense of cold dread filled his stomach and he turned toward her, his heart pounding hard. "Did you not want me? Did I force myself on you just now?"

"You know you didn't. I said that I wanted you."

"Then how is it we had never consummated our union?"

Rose looked as though she was going to curl in on herself. She moved away from him, sliding beneath the edge of the blankets, disappearing completely beneath them. "You were the one who didn't want me."

"How is that possible?"

"I don't suppose it matters how it's possible. Only that it is. And even knowing that, I said yes to you while you couldn't remember how little you wanted me. In real life—whatever you want to call it—Leon Carides does not want Rose Tanner. You didn't know that. I did." She reappeared, her face peeking out from beneath the blankets. "I'm sorry."

It took him a moment to process the words. It was taking him time to process all of this. "You are my wife."

"You keep saying that like it means anything, but believe me, Leon, it has meant *nothing* to you over the past two years."

"I want it to." He didn't know where the certainty came from, but he felt it all the same. Bone-deep and as real as anything. He had no memory, that was true. And it meant he counted on these feelings. They were all he had.

"You might not. You might not when you remember why you didn't in the first place."

"Why didn't I?"

"I don't know," she said miserably.

"Start from the beginning. Why did we get married?"

"For the house. This house. For the company you run now. And for my father. He was dying, and you were like a son to him. He loved you, Leon. And he wanted all of this to be yours. I think… I think it brought him a lot of joy to know that you would be the one taking care of me. There was no one in the entire world that he trusted the way that he trusted you."

Leon's stomach tightened. Because to hear Rose tell it her father had trusted him, had cared for him. And he had done…what with that? He had married his daughter as a formality. And then had… Rose had said much about how he often went out. The thought made him feel sick.

"Rose," he said, his tone grave. "When I go out what is it that I do?"

She didn't answer immediately, her expression mutinous. "You like to drink."

"What else?" he asked, his voice scraping his throat raw.

"You like… You like women."

Pain lanced his chest, his brain, his ribs. Everything. "I have been unfaithful to you."

"We don't have a conventional marriage. As you can see now you have never touched me. Not before this. You kissed me on our wedding day and that was it. And you told me… You told me that it didn't have to change anything. I think the offer stood for myself, as well. I think you expected I might go out and find a lover. But you are my husband, Leon, and I couldn't—"

Of course she couldn't. Rose was too sweet. So young, so innocent. He was older, harder. And he had no idea why he was the way he was. All he knew was that with everything a blank slate inside of him, without the built-in excuses, without the baggage, he was disgusted with himself.

He had been given this gift. This woman. This wife. And he had treated her with nothing but neglect.

"I want to do better," he said finally.

"What?"

"I want to do better for you. Better for us. We have a chance to change things, to make a new start." He shook his head then, his words tasting wrong in his mouth. "I suppose I have that chance. You remember everything. You know exactly who I am. You know exactly what I've done to you. And it seems the simplest thing in the world to ask for forgiveness when you can't remember your sins. I don't deserve it."

"Leon, I should've told you from the beginning about our marriage. But… It didn't seem…" She was blinking back tears now, and he hated that he was making her cry. He had a feeling he had done so more than once. "I think I didn't want you to know because I was hoping this would happen. But that was manipulative of me."

"I'm not angry. Not at you. I married you to get this

house, to get your father's company and to placate him, and what did you get?"

"Well, if we divorced after five years, I got the house." She swallowed. "But I imagine you would have wanted us to stay married so that everything would stay with you, too. Marriage is different when you aren't exactly living as a married couple. I think for you that's never been an issue."

"It is an issue to me now. And I'm not angry with you. How old am I, Rose?"

"Thirty-three," she said.

"Ten years older than you."

"That doesn't—"

"And answer me this—when you married me what did you expect would happen?"

Color flooded her cheeks and she turned away from him. "Well, frankly, I imagined that something much like tonight might happen on our wedding night."

"So I did not tell you that I intended to live my life as a single man until after you had already made vows to me."

"Yes," she said.

"Then I feel you have only been trying to claim what you rightfully are owed. And I think that we need to try and fix this. Together."

"What about when you remember? What about when things… What about when they go back to the way they were?"

"I won't lose *these* memories just because I gain the old ones. I can't imagine anything on earth changing what is between us now." He reached out, brushing his thumb over her cheek, over her impossibly soft skin. "How can I ever go back to living in the same space as you without wanting to touch you all the time? How could I possibly return to other women's beds when yours is the only one I want to be in?"

And then he leaned in and kissed her, and they did not speak for the rest of the night.

Leon appreciated the fact that his doctor had ordered him to sit out in the sun a few hours a day so he didn't end up with vitamin deficiencies, but he would much rather be in the house than sitting out on the terrace.

In the house with Rose, naked in his arms as he brought her pleasure again and again.

He was insatiable for his wife. For this woman he'd never touched before his accident. A woman he'd married and left a virgin.

He frowned. He could not understand why he'd done that. And the questions... It was concerning. Because at this point he could not imagine holding her at a distance. He wanted to hold her right up against him, skin to skin, at all times.

He was obsessed with her.

He looked out at the view of the lush grounds of the estate. He had this home. He had Rose. And yet he was never here. He had never touched her.

Instead he had gone out and slept with other women.

The idea sent a lash of shame streaking through him like the crack of a whip. Hot. Painful. But somewhere beneath the self-loathing was...concern.

Why? Why hadn't he touched her? Why had he held himself back?

"How are you feeling?"

He turned in his seat and saw Rose standing in the doorway, wearing a flowing dress with a flower pattern, teasing him with just a peek of long slender leg.

It was easy to push his questions and concerns to the

back of his mind when he could see her. As soon as he
saw her he wanted to push her dress up past her hips and
bury his face between her thighs.

It was preferable to thinking.

"Well," he said. "I can dress myself now anyway."

A wicked light danced in her blue eyes. "I would rather
undress you."

Heat flared in his gut and he pushed his previous concerns down even further. "I am glad you think that way,
agape."

She stepped out onto the terrace and he began to push
himself into a standing position, a dull pain shooting
through his midsection as he disturbed his injuries.

"Don't," she said, holding her hand out. "Just sit.
There's plenty of time for…touching later."

He frowned. "I want to touch you now."

She extended her hand and he gripped her slender fingers in his, a flash of lightning hitting him low and hard.
"How's that?"

"Not enough." Never enough. How would it ever be
enough? He might never have all the answers to who he
was. But he had her. She was his beacon. His touchstone.

She smiled and it moved places inside of him. It hurt.
As though heat was touching ice for the first time.

"Leon…"

"Why history?" he asked.

"What?" she asked, blinking.

"What made you decide to major in history?" If he
couldn't strip her naked, he would convince her to reveal
herself in other ways. She was all he had. She filled his
brain, his body, his soul. There was nothing else, and he
wasn't even certain he cared.

Why should he make an effort to know himself, in all
his filthy, broken lack of glory, when he could know her?

"Well, I like research," she said. "And if you research the past you can accomplish a lot of it in…silence. Reading. Exploring the basements and attics of old houses and libraries."

"You like to be alone?"

She frowned. "I like time to think. And…questioning texts is much…safer than questioning actual people."

He had a feeling she applied that to more than just history.

"Is that why you never said anything to me?" he asked. "About my behavior?"

She looked away from him, her pale throat contracting as she swallowed hard. "We married for the company and for the house. It never seemed…"

"That is not the only reason," he said, his voice growing rough. "I know it wasn't."

He could not have been blind to his attraction to her. And his attraction wasn't new. He was confident in that.

"It was as far as I knew," she said, her tone stiff. "For you anyway." She softened on that last part, and it made his chest ache.

He did not deserve her. He was certain of few things but that was one of them. "I do not think that's the case."

But there was something. Something that had held him back from her. Something that had kept her a virgin, and kept him away as often as possible.

Part of him wanted to know.

Most of him simply wanted things to stay as they were. Because here and now, he had her. He never wanted to let her go.

Everything went perfectly over the next few weeks. And if Rose felt a small amount of disquiet, ever present and ominous, resting in her chest, she did her best to ignore it. Leon was… He was the most caring, solicitous man she had ever known. And the sex… Well, that was much better than anything she had ever imagined she might experience. It was incredible. He was incredible. There was so much passion between them it was impossible to imagine things had ever been cold.

She felt like a newlywed. After two years.

It was a strange experience, one that made her feel like she was floating through her days. She wasn't unhappy about it. Not in the least.

Perhaps a little bit uneasy, though.

She pushed that thought down and continued on through the halls. She was looking for Leon, who had become more mobile and was beginning to wander about the estate more. He still didn't remember anything, but he was feeling much better, and he had taken it upon himself to relearn every inch of the grounds.

She imagined he was somewhere in the gardens.

This isn't real. When he remembers he's going to go back to the way he was. When he remembers, he'll be consumed with work, with desire for women who actually know what they're doing. Not sad virgins who have spent most of their lives cosseted away.

She gritted her teeth, ignoring that mean little voice. It was the source of her disquiet. And it was, unfortunately, far too accurate for her to deny.

"Ms. Tanner." The housekeeper rushed to where Rose was standing, a worried look on her face. "Someone is here to see Mr. Carides."

Rose shook her head. "That's impossible. Leon can't see anyone. We don't want anyone to know about his memory."

"It's just… It is a woman."

Rose's stomach dropped into her feet. "Is it?"

As far as she knew Leon didn't have mistresses in a traditional sense. He slept with other women, that was true, but there were none that he had a special connection with.

"A woman. A lawyer. And a baby."

Rose didn't even respond. Before she could think anything through she was running straight toward the front door, her heart pounding so hard she could scarcely breathe.

She was half expecting her housekeeper to have made everything up. For there to be no one standing at the door. For it to be empty, and everything to be the way that it was a few moments ago. Perfect, and beautiful, and not falling down around her.

The woman was beautiful. Blonde, tall, expertly made up. She was dressed simply, but effectively, every piece of clothing accentuating her coloring, her shape, and highlighting her beauty. The man next to her was grim-faced, clad in a sharp suit. And right in front of them was a car seat, the shade drawn over the part where the baby sat, concealing it from view.

"I am Leon Carides's wife," Rose said, her voice trembling. "What exactly is happening here?"

"My client has some things to discuss with Mr. Carides." It was the lawyer who spoke, the woman beside him extremely silent and pale.

"I don't know if you heard or not, but my husband was recently in a serious car accident. He's still recovering."

"Still, I imagine he will want to hear what we have to say," the lawyer said.

"I want to hear what you have to say," she said, her tone insistent.

"If you can get hold of him, and ask his permission to hear the details, I'm certain we can fill you in."

"I don't see any point in being coy about it," the woman said, crossing her arms beneath her breasts, her expression turning determined. "I want to see Leon. I want to give him his baby."

She had known what this was. The moment she'd heard who was at the door she'd known. But she still didn't want to believe it. Didn't want to believe what this woman was saying.

"I'm sorry," Rose said, asking for clarity she didn't truly need. "What?"

"His baby," she said. "The child is his, and it's time for him to take responsibility."

By the time they were all seated in Leon's office, Rose was in a daze. Leon did not look like he was faring much better. He could only stare blank-faced at the woman who was claiming to be the mother of his child. A child who was only four months old.

Rose bit back a cry of hysteria at the thought. Yes, she knew he had been with other women over the course of their marriage. But never, *ever* had she been asked to deal with the reality of it in quite such a tangible way.

The baby hadn't made a sound since arriving—it was like a little doll, sitting in the bucket seat. A girl, with a pink blanket thrown over her sleeping figure. She had dark hair, long sooty lashes that swept across her cheeks. She was beautiful. And she was Leon's. Leon and *April's*. That was the woman's name. It made Rose feel sick.

The lawyer was talking, outlining the apparent details of the agreement that Leon had previously made with April. He was sitting there, looking stoic, saying very little. Rose had plenty to say, but it wasn't the time. They were still trying to obscure the fact that Leon had no memory, difficult when he was sitting near a former lover that he clearly didn't have any recollection of. Difficult when he was sitting near a child he obviously didn't remember.

But it was all there, right in front of them. The acknowledgment of paternity, the DNA test and the agreement that April would have full custody along with a certain amount of financial support from Leon.

"I know what we agreed," April said, speaking slowly. "But I find that I'm unable to take care of her. More than that, I don't want to. I thought it would be worth it. Especially with all the money you are paying me, but I just can't. I waited for some…maternal instinct to kick in. Something that would overwhelm me and change me. I'm not changed," she said, sounding sad. Flat. "I could hire nannies, you've given me enough money for that but… I wanted better for her. I'm going to give her up for adoption. But I felt like I needed to speak to you first. I'm willing to sign over all of my parental rights to you."

"She will of course continue to collect a stipend," the lawyer added.

"Of course," Rose said, her tone brittle.

"Yes," Leon said, his tone slightly more sincere, "of course."

"If everything is in order then, Mr. Carides, we are happy to relinquish baby Isabella into your custody."

For a moment, Rose wanted to stand up and shout. She wanted to say no. To send the child out somewhere else, anywhere else but into her home. It wasn't fair. They were making a life together, her and Leon. They were trying to make their marriage work. She was the one that was supposed to have his children. Not someone else. His DNA wasn't supposed to combine with another woman's to make something so beautiful. It should be with *hers*. This should be *her* baby.

She wanted to rail against him. To rail against all of this.

And yet when she looked at the sleeping little girl all she could feel was sadness. It wasn't Isabella's fault that her mother couldn't take care of her. It wasn't her fault that her father had been careless. It wasn't her fault that her father had a wife who felt personally wounded by this indiscretion.

All of the adults in the room had made choices. Rose had chosen to marry Leon. Leon had chosen to sleep with April. April had chosen Leon even knowing he was married. Only Isabella had made no choices.

And no matter how angry she felt, she could feel no anger at the baby. Not really.

"Of course I want her," Leon said, his voice breaking.

He didn't ask Rose what she wanted. But then, she could hardly blame him. This was his child. His flesh and blood. How could she ask him to do anything but take her into his home? And how could he ever leave the decision up to anyone else? He couldn't. She understood that.

She was still angry.

But she said nothing. She said nothing at all while Leon and April signed the paperwork. Paperwork that didn't include Rose, because why would it? She wasn't a parent to this child. She was only Leon's wife. Why would she matter at all?

"Thank you," April said, her tone hushed. "This isn't my proudest moment."

Rose didn't care at all about the other woman's pride. She found herself short on sympathy.

Leon did not seem to suffer a similar affliction. "You're doing what you think is best," he said. "You should be proud of that."

The other woman tilted her head. "You seem different," April said. "Not that we know each other all that well."

"I stopped drinking," he said, his tone grave.

"Maybe that's it."

Then April turned her focus to Rose. And Rose really wished she hadn't. Rose would rather disappear into the ornate wood paneling on the wall. She wanted to hate the other woman. But when she saw the exhaustion in her eyes, a deep sadness that her flippant *I don't want this* tried to disguise, she simply couldn't. "I'm sorry," April said, her words directed at Rose.

"There isn't anything to be sorry for," Rose said, surprised by the fact that she meant them at least a little bit. "Leon has to answer for his own actions—you don't. *You* didn't make vows to me."

"Well, I think he was trying to keep all of this away from you. But I didn't feel right about putting her up for adoption without..."

"I understand. I'm glad that you came to us." She wasn't sure it was true. But it was the right thing to say.

Without another word, April and her lawyer walked out of the office. April didn't look back again, not at Leon, not at Rose, and not at the child that was still safely buckled up in her car seat.

Rose felt like a small pink bomb had been detonated in the middle of them. They had been making things work. Things had been changing. Things had been different. But the simple fact was that no matter whether or not Leon could remember the past, the past existed. It was so tempting to believe that a clean slate was possible. That because his memories were changed, his actions had, as well. But this was incontrovertible evidence to the contrary.

"We don't have any supplies for a baby," Leon said finally, breaking the silence between them.

"That's what you're going to lead with?" Rose asked, hearing in her tone the fragile nature of her mental state.

"What do you want me to say? I have no memory of any of this. Obviously I knew about the child, Rose—I signed those documents. That is my signature. I signed away the rights to my child."

"A child you had with another woman during our marriage."

"Yes," he said, his tone fierce. "Though it is no surprise to you that I was sleeping with other women."

"It does surprise me," she said, her voice rising along with the hysteria in her breast, "that you had a child with someone else. That's quite the secret to keep."

"I find I am more distressed by the fact that I clearly wanted nothing to do with Isabella."

"Well, I imagine you wanted to avoid this scenario."

"What kind of man does that?" Leon asked. "What kind of man pays a woman off to keep a child out of his life?"

"You," Rose said, not caring if she was cruel. Not caring if her words cut. "Apparently you do."

"I'm starting to think I know nothing about myself at all," he said, his voice hollow.

But she didn't feel sorry for him. She refused.

"The feeling is mutual," she said.

Rose turned on her heel and stormed out of the office, doing what she knew was about the cruelest thing she could. She left Leon alone with his thoughts. And with his child.

Leon stared down at the sleeping baby in the car seat, emotions rolling through him like storm clouds, pressure building inside him. Who was he? What sort of man kept his wife ensconced in a manor house in the country, leaving her a virgin for two years while he lived his life as though she didn't exist?

What sort of man brought a baby into the world and wrote an agreement making it completely clear he never wanted to see her?

He gathered from the paperwork that he had never set eyes on his daughter. He gathered he hadn't even known the gender of the child.

Weariness stole through him, and a darkness rolled through him like clouds covering the sky.

What did you do when you found out you were a monster? Because he had to be a monster. There was no other explanation. Real men did not abandon their children like this. They did not pay to make their own flesh and blood go away.

He didn't know if he had ever held a baby. He had certainly never held this one.

Suddenly, he found himself dropping down to his knees, his heart pounding so hard he could scarcely breathe. He looked at the little girl, sleeping there in the car seat. So tiny, so perfectly formed. Abandoned by the only parent she knew, brought to stay forever with the man who had signed her away as though she was an unwanted object he didn't want cluttering up his home.

"I am sorry," he said, his voice raw, strange. "I am sorry for the man I was. But I will not abandon you. Not now. I will fix this. I will be the father you deserve. I will be the man that both of you deserve."

He didn't know how long he stayed like that, sitting on the floor in front of her, simply staring. But eventually, she began to stir, a plaintive, high-pitched wail on her lips as she came fully awake. Her eyes open, bright blue, not at all what he expected, glaring at him as though he was her enemy. Then the tears started to fall down her angry red face and panic flooded through him.

He picked up the car seat, wincing as pain from his ribs shot through him.

He had to find someone. Anyone. He did not want to pick her up. He was afraid he would break her. He had no memory of how to hold a child. Perhaps he had never known how.

"Rose!" He made his way out of the office and through the halls. "Rose, I need you."

Rose emerged from the library, her face pale, her eyes red.

"What is it?"

"The baby is crying."

"Yes," Rose said, crossing her arms, "she is."

"I do not know what to do."

Rose stayed right where she was, her feet planted firmly on the floor. "I'm not sure what you want me to do about it."

"*Help* me."

She still didn't move. Then finally, as Isabella's cries continued to fill the air, Rose's expression softened. "I'm not going to help you. But I will help her." She crossed the space between them, stopping in front of him. "Put her seat down."

He complied, and then Rose knelt down, beginning to work the harness that kept the baby strapped in.

She undid the seat belt and plucked the baby up from the seat, cradling her tiny body close to her chest. It made something inside Leon's own chest tighten. Made it almost impossible for him to breathe. There was something about all of this that was familiar and foreign at the same time. Something that filled him with a terrible sense of dread that made it feel as though his insides were slowly turning to ice.

He found himself completely rooted to the place he was standing. He couldn't move forward. He couldn't turn away.

"She might be hungry." A tear slipped down Rose's cheek and he despised himself. The two women in his life were here in front of him, weeping, and he could do nothing to stop any of it. He didn't know how. He didn't know how to comfort a baby, and he found himself somewhat terrified by the sight of her. He didn't feel he deserved to try to offer comfort to Rose. Whom he had betrayed.

"Are you all right?" It was the wrong thing to ask. He knew the moment he spoke the words. And it was confirmed by the way her mouth flattened. By the way her eyes cooled.

"I don't know how to take care of a baby. I don't know what to do. This isn't what I want," she said, her voice breaking.

There was no response for that. It didn't exist inside of him. He wondered what he would have said if he was in possession of his memories. He wondered how he would respond to this. How he would respond to her.

"First I will send out some of the staff to buy supplies," he said. He didn't know what would come next. He realized the way he had begun that sentence implied that he had a list of actions to take. But he could barely wrap his mind around the one.

"That would be good," she said, her tone stiff. "Please just…take her." She took a step forward, thrusting the baby into his arms. He took her, cradling her close. He could do nothing but stare down at her, marveling at the intense shot of fear that gripped him. As though she were a man-eating tiger and not a small girl.

When he looked up, Rose was gone.

And Leon was left alone with his daughter.

CHAPTER SEVEN

Rose felt like she was made of pain. She'd spent the entire day curled up in her bed, a lump of misery that could not be moved. She was assuming that Leon had seen to taking care of Isabella's needs. She felt guilty for the assumption. But not quite enough to move from her position in her bed.

It wasn't as though she had any experience with babies. None of her friends had them yet. She was an only child, and she had never done babysitting or anything like that when she was growing up.

She couldn't offer him any help. The house was full of staff. He would figure something out.

She ignored the crushing weight that thought brought. She didn't know how she was supposed to sort through this. She didn't know how she was supposed to forgive this.

But she had shared herself with him. As much as she had loved him before he'd touched her, she had only fallen deeper since they'd started sleeping together. Since she'd started to hope again.

The door to her bedroom opened and she sat up, clutching her blanket to her chest, in spite of the fact that she was fully clothed. "What do you want, Leon?" she asked, not bothering to moderate her tone as Leon walked into her room, slamming the door behind him.

"Are you going to stay angry with me?"

"Probably," she said.

"There is nothing that I can do about this. There is nothing I can do to turn back time."

"And there's nothing I can do to erase how horrible this feels. I just don't understand. I don't understand how you could do something like this."

He exploded then. Every bit of the rage she imagined had been simmering inside of him since his accident, since his memories had been ripped from him, pouring from him. "I don't know why I would do something like this, either, Rose. I have no memory of any of it. No memory of what reasoning there could have possibly been. Why was I not in your bed? Why did I turn my own child away? I don't know the answer to these questions. Everything is gone. It's a black hole inside me. I can never reach the bottom of it. I can't seem to see anything around me. These are the consequences of my actions, and I understand that. I understand that I'm not innocent because I don't have answers. But it doesn't make this any easier."

She gritted her teeth. Fighting against sympathy. Fighting against any kind of understanding. She held on to her anger like it was a lifeline, and she refused to release her hold. "It doesn't make it easier for me, too. It simply means that I can't even rail against you the way I want to. All it means is that I can't get an answer out of you. No matter how hard I try. Though I doubt you would give me one even if you could remember. That's just how you are. You have been kind to me in the past. But I've been clinging to those memories like they have anything to do with the man you became."

"And who is that?"

"A bored, cynical playboy with a drinking problem. A man who has been given *everything*, and seems to feel *nothing*." She took a deep, shaking breath. "You're a brilliant businessman, but you're a terrible husband. You don't love anyone but yourself, Leon. And it has been like that for a very long time."

He seemed stunned by her outburst. Stunned by her words. Well, that made two of them. But it was true. It was everything that she had buried down deep inside herself. Even deeper than the love she felt for him. When she had talked herself into divorcing him, she hadn't used anger to make the decision.

She had latched on to a kind of world-weary practicality. Forcing herself to face that if after two years they didn't have a real marriage they never would. She hadn't allowed herself to feel anything like the sadness that bloomed deep inside her now. Nothing like the rage that burned hot beneath it.

She was allowing herself to feel it now.

"I was wrong. There is no excuse. The reasons don't matter. I was wrong, and I'm very sorry that I hurt you. I'm sorry that I hurt April. That I had any part in hurting Isabella. I am *sorry*." His words were raw, genuine. But she couldn't find it in herself to care.

"It changes nothing. What good does *sorry* do? Can you give me back the last two years of my life? Can you give me back my heart? I am so tired of you holding my heart. I am a fool. I am the fool who has loved you for the last fifteen years, and you never deserved that."

"I feel you're probably right. That I never have deserved for you to have any feelings for me at all."

"I am right," she said, conviction burning in her words. "You didn't deserve my father's affection, either. The world has been kind to you. I imagine the first time anything tragic ever happened to you was when that other car crossed the centerline in Italy."

He closed the space between them, reaching down to where she was on the bed, wrapping his arm around her waist and pulling her up against him. His dark eyes blazed down into hers. "I deserve all of that," he said, his voice low, soft. "All of that and more. Give me your anger, *agape*. Let it out."

"I hate you," she hissed. "As much as I ever thought I loved you. How dare you do this to me? I did nothing but live my life trying to please people. I was the daughter that my father required. I took care of him after my mother died. I never let him see how I used to cry. I never let him know how badly I missed having a woman in my life. I never let him know how lost I was all through junior high and high school. How lonely I was. Because I didn't want him to worry. I agreed to marry you for his peace of mind, even though I knew you didn't love me." She took a gasping breath. "And I never let you know how much it killed me when you went out with other women. I simply accepted what you handed to me. I licked the crumbs that you threw me off the floor, because I am such a sad, pathetic creature. But I am not *your* creature anymore."

He reached up, sifting his fingers through her hair, holding her head steady, staring down at her. "You cannot possibly hate me more than I hate myself."

"Of course I can," she spat. "I wish you could feel this." She pressed her hand to her chest. "I wish you could feel exactly what you did to me."

Tears burned her eyes, her heart pounding, her entire body trembling. She felt desperate. Desperate to make him understand exactly what she felt inside. Her heart was like shattered glass, the shards working their way into her skin, burning, aching.

She wanted him to feel this. She wanted him to understand. This man who had always seemed so charmed to her. So together. Who seemed to get everything he wanted from life, who seemed to be denied nothing.

Who made her want with every deep, desperate part of herself. Who made her want him even now as she burned incandescent with rage over his actions.

She wrapped her arms around his neck, tilting her face upward as she rose up onto her tiptoes and claimed his mouth with hers. She kissed him with all the anger inside her. She poured all the hatred, all the rage that she had just professed straight into him. Hoping it would burn all the way down. Hoping it would destroy him slowly the way that it was destroying her.

She sobbed helplessly even as she parted her lips, thrusting her tongue deep into his mouth. She hated herself. Almost as much as she hated him. For wanting him even now. For needing to be comforted by him even though he was the one who had caused her all of this pain.

But if it was so easy to turn it off, she would have done it a long time ago. If she could simply decide that she didn't want him, decide that she didn't love him, things would be so much easier.

If she could transfer it all to him, exorcise it from her body, everything would be simpler. She would be free. *Finally.* Instead of feeling like there were chains wrapping around her wrists, around her neck, pulling ever tighter. Binding her to a man who could never give her what she needed. To a love that could never give back to her.

She moved her hands, curled her fingers into the fabric of his shirt, holding tightly to him as she continued to kiss him. He pulled her forward, taking a step back, bringing them up against the wall. Then he flipped their positions, her shoulder blades pressing into the wood paneling.

She slid her hands down to his chest, felt his raging heartbeat beneath her fingertips. She couldn't stand these clothes between them. Couldn't stand secrets between them. Couldn't stand lies, even lies that were lost in the dark spaces in his mind.

She couldn't erase those other things. But the clothes, she could do something about.

She tore his shirt from his body, followed by his jeans, and all the while, he made quick work of what she was wearing. Soon they were both naked, pressed skin to skin, as though they were trying desperately to connect. Trying desperately to get beneath everything between them so they could find some way back to each other.

His desperation matched her own. His pain did, too.

Whatever Leon might have felt about any of this at another time, it hurt him now. That didn't absolve him. Not even close. But it satisfied her. Deep down in the meanest part of her, the part of her that wanted him to hurt, too.

She pulled her mouth away from his, angling her head and scraping her teeth along the side of his neck. He growled, grabbing hold of her chin and straightening her head, leaning in and kissing her before nipping her lower lip.

She returned the favor. Sinking her teeth into his skin before soothing him with her tongue. He moved his hands down her body then, cupping her bottom, pressed her tightly up against his hardened length. She arched into him, seeking oblivion. Seeking satisfaction.

He shifted, moving his hand down, grabbing hold of her thigh and lifting it up over his hip before testing her readiness. Then he thrust up deep inside her, both of them groaning as he filled her.

It wasn't a gentle coming together. It was fiery. Intense. It was rage, it was need. It was a kind of broken hopelessness that wound its way through the air around them, impressed itself on their skin.

When all was said and done they had something to contend with that neither of them knew how to handle. Once the desire between them was extinguished they would have to find a way to move on from this moment. Find a way to handle the child that was now in their life, in the center of their marriage.

Find a way to either repair this betrayal or go their separate ways.

But right now, there was this. Right now, they had each other. And she clung to him. Held tightly to his shoulders as he pushed her to the heights. As he shattered her completely beneath his touch.

She arched against him, crying out as she found her release, and he let out a hoarse growl as he found his own, spilling himself deep inside her.

And when it was over, when her heart rate returned to normal, she released her hold on him, sliding down the wall and sinking to the floor, allowing misery to overtake her completely.

Leon found himself dropping to his knees next to Rose. He wrapped his arms around her, holding her against him as she wept. She cried because of him. Because of the pain that he had heaped upon her. He held her, even though he had no right. Even though she would be better off with a stranger.

It seemed inappropriate to try and heal a wound that he had caused. Although perhaps there was no one else who could do it. Perhaps it was right really. To pour himself into atoning for his sins.

"I'm sorry," he said, the words feeling frustratingly hollow.

He wished he knew everything he was sorry for. He wished he could give them more weight by being aware of each and every transgression he'd committed against her. He didn't need to know what they were to know that he was sorry, but he wanted to list them. Wanted to feel the full weight of them. And he couldn't. Just another in the long list of growing frustrations.

He wanted to answer for his sins. He couldn't even name them.

He wanted to understand why he had betrayed the woman in his arms. Why he had abandoned the little girl sleeping in the crib in the room down the hall. He wanted answers, and his own mind refused to give them.

He was the only one who knew these things. He couldn't tell himself.

"I'm sorry," he said again, because he had no other words.

"This isn't what I wanted," she said, miserable, broken. "It wasn't my dream to raise a child you had with another woman." She drew in a shuddering breath. "I wanted to have your baby. I wanted you to love me."

"Rose…"

"I sound like a child throwing a tantrum," she said, her voice hollow. She drew her arm across her face, wiping in her tears. "It doesn't matter what I wanted. All that matters is what we have. You have a baby."

"I want her," he said. He did. In spite of the ice block that seemed to grow larger inside his chest every time he looked at her. The fear. The uneasiness.

He had a feeling that even if he was in possession of all of his memories, coming into the care of a tiny baby would frighten him. But with nothing, with no background, with no reference for things like this, he was chilled to his bones.

"I know," she said, her throat tight. "And I couldn't ask you to do anything different. She's your daughter."

"But you don't want her."

"No. That isn't it. I... I've known about you sleeping with other women, Leon. It has always been in tabloids. On gossip websites. It's the world's worst-kept secret. Everyone knows that you aren't faithful to me. Everyone knows that you married a little homebody who can't keep up with you. Who isn't as beautiful as the other women you see." She swallowed hard. "But this... Looking at the evidence of the fact that you were with other women... Knowing that someone else got something I wanted so desperately... It's different. It isn't something I can just brush off."

"I understand that."

"But it isn't Isabella's fault. She hasn't done anything wrong. She's so tiny and helpless, and her mother abandoned her... I can't face the idea of abandoning her. I can't."

"I care about you. You are...the only memory I have, Rose. The one who has been there since I opened my eyes and came back to the world a man with no memory. And I am very sorry for my behavior. But one thing I know... beyond anything... If you feel like you will be angry with Isabella, in any way, if any of your feelings about what I have done might spill onto her...then it would be best if we worked out a different arrangement."

It made his chest feel like it was cracking to say it. But his daughter would always have questions about what had happened to her mother. And if Isabella had to live in a house where her presence was resented he would never be able to forgive himself. He doubted he would forgive himself for any of this anyway. But for his sins, he had to do something to make it up to Isabella.

He waited. He waited to see if Rose would be angry. She would have every right to be. But it didn't change the truth and what he said. She had every right to be angry. She had every right to punish him. She had every right to leave. But he had to protect Isabella.

"You mean I shouldn't be involved with her if I can't treat her like my own child."

He shook his head. "I can't ask for a promise quite like that. I only mean if you find it impossible not to resent her. If you cannot be in the same room with her. Those things... I deserve them. But she doesn't."

"I know." She blinked. "I feel like I'm being scolded. And you're the one who deserves to be scolded."

"I'm not trying to scold you. It's just... This kind of beginning... If I don't make up for what I did to her then what future does she have? I signed my rights away. And now I've taken them back, but only because her mother has abandoned her. I never want her to feel like she was a child unwanted by so many. I don't want her to be wounded beyond repair because the adults in her life were too selfish, too broken, to see beyond themselves."

Rose nodded. "I understand. She's just a baby. I'm not angry at her. It was hard for me to look at her. It was hard for me to hold her." Another tear slid down her cheek. "Because I wish she were mine." She pulled away from him, leaning back against the wall, drawing her knees up to her chest. "I wish that things had been different. If they had been, then she very well could have been mine."

"I can't fix the past. I can't even guarantee the future. I can only try and fix what we have now. She can be ours. And I don't say that lightly. I don't say it expecting that you can drop every last piece of baggage you're carrying because of this. I don't say it as though it's a magical fix. But she is here. And so are we. I still... I want to make this work with you."

"Sometimes I feel like you're just going to keep asking impossible things of me," she said, sounding weak, sounding reduced.

"Someday I hope you're able to ask something impossible of me, Rose." He leaned in, cupping her cheek. "And I pray that I am able to rise to the task."

"I want to try." Rose nodded. "For both of us. For all of us. I want to try. Where is she?"

CHAPTER EIGHT

OVER THE NEXT few weeks things seemed to progress slowly with Rose and Isabella. They employed a nanny—a married, grandmotherly sort, at Rose's request—who helped care for Isabella during the day. Though Leon tried to assume as much responsibility as he could. It was just that given the state of things, he wasn't sure he entirely trusted himself. What if he forgot some essential bit of information regarding the care and keeping of babies that everyone else knew? Or, more likely, what if he had never possessed it, but didn't know enough about himself to ask the appropriate questions?

Employing someone to assist had seemed the best option. He could hardly ask Rose to interrupt her life to care not only for him, but for his child.

Still, Rose was beginning to take some charge of Isabella on her own. When Isabella cried, Rose was often the first to move to comfort her.

Seeing them together made his chest feel like it was being torn in two. Earlier today Rose had been standing by the window, Isabella held tightly to her chest as she stared out at the garden below.

It had been like looking at something much clearer than a memory—especially since he had none that extended beyond the past few weeks. But it hadn't been wholly reality, either. It was a window into a life he didn't truly possess. Something the two of them didn't really have.

In that moment it was easy to believe this was his wife and child, and they had nothing but love between them.

Rather than the dark, tangled mass of lies and betrayal that wound itself around them like a vine covered in thorns. Thorns that wrapped themselves tightly around his gut, making it hurt every time he breathed.

He rubbed his hand over his face and eyed the bar on the other side of his bedroom. It was stocked with alcohol, evidence of the man he'd been before, he imagined. A man who had a drink as he brushed his teeth in the morning and at night.

A man who had sought oblivion with tenacity.

He laughed bitterly, the sound echoing in the dimly lit room. He had his oblivion now. And with it, he found no peace.

Improvement only described the relationship between Rose and Isabella. *Improvement* did not apply to his relationship with Rose. She would not touch him. She would barely talk to him.

He had imagined—erroneously, as it turned out—that after he had held her in his arms while she wept in her bedroom that she might continue to seek out an intimate relationship with him. That was not the case. She scarcely made eye contact with him unless she absolutely had to. She very solicitously inquired about his well-being, never asking about his memories, as she assumed—rightly— that if there were any change he would let her know.

But she didn't look at him the way she had. Those blue eyes, that only real, organic memory in his mind, had changed. They were icy. Angry. Or, on the very worst of days, completely blank. This woman had loved him. And he had destroyed that love.

There were no fresh starts. It was easy to buy into the idea that they'd had one here. That just because he didn't remember what he had done those things didn't exist. But his consequences had now reached their home. Consequences that didn't care whether or not he remembered committing the sin.

That fresh start had always been a lie. He was not a new man, reborn from the fiery wreckage of his accident. He was the same old man. A man who had betrayed his wife, a man who—according to Rose—loved no one but himself. A man who had abandoned his child. He was that man. With Isabella here it was impossible for him to absolve himself in the way he had been attempting to before her arrival.

There was no absolution. He just had to find a way to move ahead. To move ahead desiring the new things that he desired. Carrying the sin on his shoulders, a weight he would try to bear as best he could. A weight he would try not to put on to Rose.

He wanted to walk on, caring for Rose in the deep, real way he had come to. To try to make her care for him again.

He had a feeling he would have to work hard to earn her affection. As it had taken such a massive betrayal to destroy it in the first place.

It was late now. He would have to worry about these things another day.

He crossed the room and got into his empty bed, feeling a deep ache and loss over the fact that Rose wasn't in here. Not because he would go to bed without an orgasm—though he was not thrilled about that prospect—

but because of the reasons she wasn't here. Because of the distance between them that it represented.

But even with that regret looming over him it didn't take long for him to drift off.

He woke with a start. The baby monitor he had plugged into the wall was nearly vibrating with the sounds of Isabella's rage. She was crying in the middle of the night, which she had never done before. Something was wrong. Both he and Rose had baby monitors in their rooms, he knew that. They had decided that given the size of the house it was the wisest thing to do. But he was going to have to be the one to go and handle his daughter.

He could hardly expect Rose to get out of bed at this hour to deal with a baby that she scarcely wanted.

He made his way out of the bedroom, but each and every step he took down the hall he found his feet grew heavier. A strange, terrified sensation grabbed hold of his chest, freezing his heart, freezing his lungs. He didn't know what was happening to him. His face was numb, his fingertips cold. His mouth tasted something like panic, which was strange, since he wasn't entirely certain panic had a flavor.

The baby wasn't crying anymore. He couldn't hear her. He could hear nothing but the sound of his own heart beating in his ears.

He suddenly felt like he was walking down two different hallways. One in a smaller house. An apartment. And the one he was actually standing in. This was a new feeling. A strange one. The feeling of existing in two places at once, in separate moments of time.

And he realized suddenly, that this was a memory.

The second memory. Second only to Rose's eyes.

It was a foreign sensation. And it was still entirely nebulous. He couldn't grab hold of it, couldn't force it to play out. It simply existed, hovering in the background of his mind, wrenching his consciousness in two.

He tried to catch his breath, tried to move ahead. It took a concerted effort. Perhaps this was what happened to someone with amnesia when their memory started to come to the surface. Perhaps it was always terrifying and foreign. Always immobilizing. If so, then the process of recovering his memories was going to be the death of him. Because this nearly stopped his breath.

He continued to walk, battling against the icy grip of foreboding that had wrapped its fingers around his very soul. He had no idea what he was afraid of. Only that this was fear, in its purest, deepest sense.

The image of the past imposed itself over the present again. Just as he walked into her room, he saw Isabella's crib, and he saw another crib, as well. Smaller, not so ornate. There was no puffy swath of pink fabric hanging down over a solid wood frame. This one was simple. A frail, fragile-looking frame in a much smaller room.

He took another step forward, and found himself frozen again. Isabella wasn't making any sound. And he was afraid to look into her crib.

Suddenly he felt as though he was being strangled. He couldn't breathe. His throat was too tight, his chest a solid block of ice. He was at the mercy of whatever this was— there was no working his way through it. There was no mind over matter. He didn't even know the demon he was fighting, so there was no way to destroy it.

He was sweating, shaking, completely unable to move.

And that was how Rose found him, standing in front of Isabella's crib like a statue, unable to take another step. Terrified of catching a glimpse of his child.

That was what was so scary. He didn't want to see

her lying there in the crib. He didn't know why. He only knew that he couldn't face the sight of it.

"Leon?" Her soft voice came from behind him, and he couldn't even turn to get a look at her. "Is everything all right with Isabella?"

"She isn't crying," he said, forcing the words through lips of stone.

"Did she need anything?"

"I don't know."

He heard her footsteps behind him, and then she began to sweep past him and he grabbed hold of her arm, pulling her back. "No," he said, the word bursting from him in a panic.

"What?" she asked, her blue eyes wide, terrified.

"You can't… You can't go to her."

"What's wrong with you?"

"I'm having a memory. It hurts and I can't… I can't move."

She examined him for a long moment, the expression on her face shaded. "I can." She pulled herself free of his hold and moved forward to the crib, reaching down and plucking Isabella up from inside of it.

Terror rolled over him in a great black wave, and he forgot to breathe, bright spots appearing in front of his eyes.

Then Isabella wiggled in Rose's hold and suddenly he could breathe again.

He took a step forward, and the crib mattress came into full view. It was empty, because Rose was holding Isabella. But yet again, he was seized with the sensation that he was standing in two different places. That he was looking inside a different crib.

He stopped. Closing his eyes he let the images wash over him, along with a dark wave of grief that poured over him and saturated him down deep. It was so real, so very present, so overpowering he felt as though he would never smile again.

And then, it wasn't the same. He wasn't seeing images superimposed over reality. He was just remembering.

Michael didn't wake up for his feeding like he normally did. The silence was what had woken Leon out of his sleep. Amanda wasn't awake. It was all right—Leon didn't mind going and checking on his son.

He walked down the hall quickly, making his way to the nursery. And from there, the vision in his head seemed to move in slow motion. He could remember very clearly being gripped by a sense of dread the moment his son came into view.

And then he reached down to touch his small chest, finding him completely unresponsive.

There was more to that memory. So much panic. So much pain and desperation. He tried to close it all out. Tried to prevent it from playing through to its conclusion. There was no point. Nothing would change the outcome.

And nothing would fill the deep dark hole that was left behind in his soul. The pit that he dumped all of his excess into.

He waited, bracing himself. Wondering if other memories would pour forth in a deluge, overtaking him completely.

As intense as it was to remember anything at all, he would have welcomed more memories. Would have begged for more if the option were available to him. Anything other than being left here with this, and this alone.

He no longer had only empty blackness in him. No, the blackness had been filled. It had been given substance. It had been given form.

Grief. Loss. Death.

Emptiness—he could see now—was a blessing in contrast.

He didn't question whether or not this memory was real. Didn't question if it belonged to him or to someone else.

It was real, and it was part of him. He knew it down to his marrow. It was such a strange thing to have this memory, with a great gulf between it and the present.

To have the image of that child back in his past so clear in his mind with this child right in front of him.

Suddenly, his legs began to give way and he found himself sinking down to the floor.

"Leon?" Rose's voice was filled with concern.

She placed Isabella back in her crib and turned to him, dropping down to her knees in front of him, placing her hands on his cheek. "Leon," she said, her tone hard, stern, as though she was trying to scold him back to the present.

His breathing was shallow, his face cold. He despised this. Being so weak in front of her. And that realization nearly made him laugh in spite of the pain, because it was always fascinating to simply know something about himself even when he didn't know why it was true.

There was nothing fascinating about any of this, though. Nothing good about this memory. He wished it could have stayed buried. Of all the things to return to him, why had this returned?

"Michael," he said. It was all he could say.

"What?"

"I had a son. His name was Michael."

Saying that brought back more memories. Amanda. Finding out she was pregnant. The fear. The joy. They had been young, but there was enough love between them to hold it all together.

Until that light had been extinguished.

"What?" Rose asked again, the word hushed.

"I just remembered. I walked in here and I remembered everything about him."

"What happened to him?"

He looked up at her, his chest so tight he could hardly breathe, the words like acid on his tongue. "He died."

Rose looked at her husband, shock and horror blending together, making it difficult for her to process his words. Difficult for her to do anything but sit there in frozen silence as his words cut into her like broken glass. She could feel every bit of pain in them, all of his trauma, his agony.

"You can't have had another child. That isn't possible," she said.

"Do you not know about him?"

"How would I know?"

"I don't know anything about my life, Rose. I don't know what you know about me. I don't... I don't have any idea who I am. Not really."

She swallowed hard. "I didn't know about this." She kept her voice soft, even.

She was angry with him. She had been angry with him from the moment the revelation about Isabella had come to light. She didn't know what it meant for them. What it meant for their relationship, for their future. But she couldn't withhold comfort now. Not now when he looked like a man in the throes of fresh grief.

"Can I tell you?" he asked, his voice tinged with desperation. "Can I tell you before I forget it?"

"You won't forget."

He reached out, grabbed hold of her arm and held her tight. "Someone else has to know. I lost this. I lost the memory of him. Who else knows about him? If I don't tell you… Who else will know?"

She nodded slowly. "Tell me about him."

"Amanda and I were sixteen when we met. We were far too young to have a child. Far too young to have any idea of what we were getting into. And yet that was where we found ourselves. I had come to the United States a year earlier, by myself. I'd managed to find some sponsorship, to enroll myself in school. That was where I met Amanda. Her parents were not impressed that she started a relationship with a broke Greek boy who barely spoke English and lived in his own apartment. No parental supervision."

"I can imagine," Rose said, her voice muted.

"Their concerns were founded. She got pregnant. But we were young and in love, so I imagined that whatever challenges we might face as a result we could overcome." He cleared his throat. "It was us against everyone. And we fought hard. She had a boy—we named him Michael because I wanted him to have an American name. I wanted him to have his place here in this country that I was beginning to love."

He let out a long, slow breath, and leaned back against the wall. "It is amazing. I'm remembering all this now. It is so simple, but there are other things…"

"You still don't remember everything."

He shook his head. "No."

"Tell me the rest of the story," she said.

It had a terrible ending. She already knew that. But it was his story. A blank space filled in not only in Leon's own memory, but in hers, as well. She didn't know about his life before he came to work at her father's company. Didn't know how he had come to this country. She didn't know who he was. All of these little revelations that were coming to light were more and more proof. Beginning with Isabella, ending with this.

The man she thought she loved was a construct of her imagination. A man she had imagined Leon might be.

But of course, she had been so young when she had first formed feelings for him. In her mind, he had sprung from the earth fully grown and handsome, perfect and kind.

A man created to dash away her tears when she had been stood up for prom. A man designed especially to stand at the head of an aisle in a church, looking beautiful and perfectly pressed in his tuxedo as he took her hand and faced her, making beautiful vows to her that she had taken straight to her heart, because she had allowed herself to believe they had come from his.

Now she was seeing the truth of it. He was a man comprised of struggle, of pain. A man who had lived a life full of happiness, loss and untold grief before she had ever met him.

What a shortsighted fool she had been. What a silly little girl.

"Her family would have nothing to do with her or the baby," he said. "I told her I would take care of her. I told her that I had come here to make my dreams come true, and I would make hers come true, as well. She continued to go to school in the few months after Michael was born. I got a job working in the mailroom at Tanner Investments. I paid close attention to the way everything worked, and I started offering suggestions on various different stocks and patterns I was noticing to anyone who would listen. Your father heard about this and allowed me to shadow a few of his best employees while I continued to see to my duties in the mailroom. I thought… I thought it was the key to changing our lives. To giving Amanda everything I promised."

"I doubt there are very many people on earth who could have accomplished what you did," she said, her voice husky.

"But my business accomplishments aren't really the point of the story. Interesting though they might be." He let out a heavy breath. "Michael died of SIDS in January. He was almost three months old. I have never felt… I am not a man who accepts life. I left Greece, I left my parents, such as they were. I had every confidence that I could make a way for myself here. I believed with great conviction that if I set out to make a home with Amanda, to make a life with her, that we could. And I promised my son that he would want for nothing. And then I walked into his nursery and he was gone." His words were thick, labored as he fought against emotion. "And there was no fighting that. It was too late. Too late. He was gone before I ever knew he struggled. There was no bargaining, no negotiation to be done. I have never felt so helpless. I have never been so aware of the finality that exists in life. Because I was so young and I simply didn't believe rules applied to me. Here I was beating the odds at work, finding my way in this country, but there was nothing that could be done for my son. I was not too special, too strong, or too clever to be defeated by death." His shoulders sagged. "I couldn't help Amanda through her grief, not when I was so lost in my own. Not when I wanted to disappear into each and every new job opportunity that presented itself. A chance to change something. A chance to control something. Of course it wouldn't bring Michael back."

He cleared his throat. "I came home one day and she was gone. I never looked for her. I didn't want a girlfriend anymore. I didn't want someone to care for me. I didn't want to care for them." He closed his eyes and a single tear rolled down his lean cheek. "What kind of father cannot protect his son? If I accomplish all these things, earn money in unimaginable quantities, improve my station in ways others would see as impossible… What does it mean if I allowed my little boy to die?"

"Leon… You didn't let him die. It was a tragic thing." Emotion was creeping over her, threatening to choke out her words. This was his grief, and yet she felt as though it was a part of her. "It was something you couldn't have prevented no matter what."

He dragged his hand over his face. "I suppose there should be comfort in that. And yet I do not see any. I see only the futility of being at the mercy of fate."

"I'm not sure it's fate. Life is a series of unpredictable things. Beautiful. Terrible. Some are direct consequences for our actions, and others don't make sense. They aren't payments or punishments. They simply are. But the measure of it is what we do after. Those are the things that you can control."

"And what have you controlled? What have you controlled in your life, Rose?" His words were hard, cynical. He sounded much more like the Leon she had spent the past two years married to than he had over the past few weeks.

"Nothing." She blinked back tears. Tears of frustration, of sorrow. Tears because everything about this situation hurt, and no one was left undamaged. "I went along with everything my father wanted from me because I had the idea that if I did he might be happy. That was how I chose to deal with the loss of my mother. I thought you would be my reward. But I'm realizing something."

"What is that?" he asked, his voice sounding rung out, scraped raw.

"Another person can't be your reward. Because they're

yet another thing you can't control." She laughed, but nothing was funny about it. "A person isn't cake. They can't just exist to be a treat for you. They have their own baggage. Their own needs and desires. And it wasn't until just before your accident that I started to fully realize that you weren't just going to magically become that reward I felt I deserved. And it wasn't until this that I... Leon, I didn't know about your son. I'm embarrassed to admit how little I know about you. I expected you to be something for me, *only* for me. And I never realized that whatever you were, as broken and debauched as it was... maybe you needed to be that for yourself. For your own pain. I never... I never once considered that."

It didn't fix the past. It didn't make her trust him. It didn't really even make her forgive him. But understanding that he had suffered a loss greater than any she could possibly imagine did help cast him in a new light. It helped explain some of his behavior. His drinking.

It didn't remove the deep wound from her heart. There was no magic here. Only grim understanding that didn't do a thing to revive the scorched earth that surrounded them.

"I was afraid when I came in here," he said, not addressing what she had just said. "I was afraid that she would be..."

"She's fine," Rose said, knowing that the assurance was empty.

Because she knew what he would always see. She knew what he would always fear as he approached the crib.

And she knew then with absolute certainty why he had signed away his parental rights to Isabella.

"That's why," she said. "It's why you didn't want her."

"If you had asked me what love was after my accident

I would have told you… I don't know. But if you ask me now… Love is pain, Rose. It is a hope that blooms with no thought for what might lie ahead. No cares about what could go wrong. And that makes it all the more painful when it's cut away. Devastating. I didn't want this. I didn't want to do this again."

"She's here now," Rose said. And as hard as it had been for her to accept Isabella, she couldn't imagine sending her away. It was a process. There was no getting around that. For Rose, there had been no magical maternal bond between herself and this little baby. But there was something growing in her chest. Blooming, just as he had described it. The beginnings of love.

And protectiveness. She felt that, too. The desire to prevent Isabella from feeling unwanted. Unwanted by Leon or herself.

"Yes," he said, "she is."

"You can't send her away."

"I never said I would," he responded.

"It's my turn to be fearsome about it," she continued. "Things are changing. You are changing. The more memories fall into place, the more you're going to become who you were. And if you think that your original reasoning can stand in light of that—"

"I don't," he said, pushing himself up from the floor, beginning to pace the length of the room.

"And if you do? If you do then I'm going to fight you. Every step of the way. No more secrets. We can't afford to have any between us. This is our life." She was making a stand, a stand she wasn't entirely certain she wanted to make. A commitment. "I want to be a family."

"I don't know if I can promise that."

"You will promise it. You will, or I'm going to have to fight you. For this house. For her."

"You couldn't win a fight against me. As you've already explained if you do not stay married to me for three more years you don't get the house. And as for Isabella... Biologically she's mine. You don't have a right to her."

She was remembering now. Remembering all the ways he could be so impossible. So arrogant. It had been easy to forget because the Leon of the past few weeks had been held at a disadvantage. But this was the man she had always known. Strong. Driven. Occasionally ruthless.

He had done nothing but reveal vulnerability over the past weeks. And she could tell he was fighting now to reclaim these traits.

"So what, then? What is it you want?"

"You will remain my wife."

"And you think you will continue to live as you did? Only instead of abandoning me alone in the manor you'll leave Isabella here, as well?" She stood, closing the distance between them. "That would be in keeping with your past behavior. Shut away the women that cause you grief, that might get in the way of your good time."

"It is not so simple, and you know it. Especially now that you know about Michael."

"Love scares you. *You*, big bad Leon Carides. It terrifies you, and you run from it."

"Only a fool isn't afraid of a lion, Rose. Even I know well enough to be afraid of things that can be fatal."

She was pushing too far. She knew it, but she couldn't help it. "I know you've suffered loss. I know you've suffered pain. But it doesn't give you the right to put other people through hell while you protect yourself."

"You spend your whole life hiding in this mansion, hiding yourself behind the convenient lies you tell yourself, little girl. Hiding in books. You think you know pain because you lost your parents. I buried my *child*. Do not lecture me on pain. Do not lecture me from your safe little nest. You know nothing. Nothing at all."

He turned on his heel and walked out of the nursery, leaving Rose there alone with Isabella.

She debated going after him, but decided against it. She turned and walked to the crib, leaning over the side, letting her knuckles drift over the soft skin of the baby's cheek.

She knew more about Leon now than she had before walking into the nursery. She had a piece of who he was. An explanation for why he was. And yet she felt no closer to him than she had before. If anything, she felt like there was a greater distance between them.

She was beginning to believe that they would never be able to bridge this divide.

The more reality crept in, the more it filled this space between them, the more impossible it seemed they could ever find their way back to each other.

He was not her reward. She thought of everything they had. A broken marriage, loss, pain. She couldn't see the reward in any of it.

She looked down at Isabella again. Maybe there were no rewards at all. Maybe there was simply life. And what you chose to do with it.

"I don't know that my father ever knew what to do with me," she whispered into the silence of the room. "But I loved him anyway. He loved me, too. He didn't know how to show it, but he did. You see, much like your father he lost someone he loved very much. My mother. I think it becomes difficult after that to show love."

She only realized just now, talking to an infant who didn't understand a word she was saying, that it was the truth. Her father was more comfortable with work, with

Leon, because it was simpler than love. Taking a protégé on, helping him succeed…it cost less than loving.

Love was so terribly expensive. And she was only fully grasping that now.

"I loved your father," she continued, a hot tear slipping sown her cheek. "But he's never loved me. That hurts. It makes me want to curl into a ball and never love anything ever again. But I think you're going to need someone to love you. I will. I'll love you like no one has ever hurt me. We didn't choose this. And you certainly deserve better than me. But it's time for me to start making some choices. It's time for me to stop waiting. I choose you, Izzy."

She swallowed hard past a lump that was rising in her throat. "I don't know what your father will do. I can't… I can't make him into the man I want him to be. I can only be the woman I want to be. I can only try to be the mother you deserve. I don't know how to be a mother. I barely remember my own. But I know what I missed having. I can give you those things. He's right about one thing—I do hide. Well, I'm not going to hide anymore."

CHAPTER NINE

THE MEMORIES OF his son had begun to fade back into the past. Shifting from a fresh, sharp grief back into a tender bruise. When they had first hit him they had been as fresh as if it had occurred yesterday, rather than sixteen years earlier.

It had taken him a couple of days to stop reliving it. To stop being hit with fresh realizations.

His son would be a man now, had he lived. Or, at least, on his way to it. He wondered if he had dealt with these realizations on and off in the ensuing years, or if the drinking, the women, were all a part of making sure he *didn't* have these realizations.

He had found that his ability to care for Isabella had suffered. He had avoided her. A behavior he was in no way proud of. But there was no pride in any of this. There was no reason. It was just pain. Pure, unmitigated.

Ever present.

Because, though it didn't hurt to breathe today, the reality still existed in the background. It was part of who he was, this loss. A wound that time might ultimately heal, but one that had most definitely left a scar.

He walked into the study where Rose spent most of her time, where he knew she was cataloging her father's books, and other pieces of his extensive collection. He was surprised to see that there was a little pink bassinet placed next to her chair. She was idly jiggling it as she hummed and took notes, something about the multitasking particularly maternal. Causing a shock wave of emotion to rock him.

"I owe you an apology," he said, the words even shocking him. He hadn't realized that was what he was going to say before he said it.

"Please don't tell me you have more surprises. A bunch of mail-order brides who have just arrived ordered prior to your memory loss? A stable of horses? Gambling debts." She snapped a finger as though a brilliant idea had just occurred to her. "A passel of racing ferrets."

"No," he said, moving deeper into the room, taking his seat on the settee near her chair, keeping a distance between himself and Isabella's bassinet. "Remember when I lectured you on how you needed to treat Isabella?"

"Yes, I believe I do. As I was naked and in the middle of an emotional meltdown. Those moments tend to stand out in your mind."

"It was easy for me to say that to you. That you would have to treat Isabella as your own or remove yourself from the situation."

She arched a pale brow. "Well, I'm delighted that it was easy for you to say. It was not easy for me to hear."

"I imagine not."

"Regardless, it was the right thing for you to say. And I knew it, even then. She's innocent. She has nothing to do with the poor decisions the adults in her life have made. She doesn't deserve to carry anyone's resentment. I might have a right to my anger, but I have no right to direct it at her."

"That is incredibly mature and clear-sighted of you. But I had no right to say it to you. I didn't understand how heavy baggage could be, Rose. Emotionally, I might as well have been a child. Not now. I understand how difficult overcoming anything can be. I'm not sure I have overcome anything of importance."

"Except for the vagaries of the immigration system, poverty and a lack of education?"

"Full points to me for that. However, emotionally speaking... I was in no position to lecture you."

"Is this an honest to goodness apology?" she asked, her blue eyes wide.

"Yes."

"I feel like you owe me one for the other day, too."

"Don't get overly hopeful."

Isabella began to fuss and Rose swiftly put down her notebook, bending down to pick the baby up out of the bassinet, holding her close to her chest. "I feel like Isabella is hopeful she will be getting fed soon."

"Do we...call the nanny for that?"

"No. Elizabetta is out for the day. You're acting like Isabella hasn't been here for the past few weeks. The only thing that has changed is you. You were feeding her. You were taking care of her. Before you remembered."

"The memory is what prompted my apology. It's easy to see things as simple and uncomplicated when you haven't experienced anything."

"I have a news flash for you. Isabella doesn't care about your pain. She's an infant. She cares about herself. More to the point, about being held, being fed and sleeping. She doesn't care if you're struggling." Rose made no move to get up. "Her bottle is on my desk in the warmer. Get it for me."

This was a new Rose than he had previously experienced. She was being imperious; she was not being careful with him, or tiptoeing around his mental state. He found he rather liked it. A few nights ago in the nursery had been like a trial by fire. It had been painful, excruciatingly so, but it had also brought out a fire in him that had been missing.

Arguing with Rose had felt… Not normal. It occurred to him then that they never argued. They hadn't, before his accident. He was sure about that. That was easy because they barely spoke. Still, he felt more alive when he was butting up against her. Perhaps it recalled the way that he was in his job.

Whatever the reason, it felt like a return to being a man and not just an invalid.

Of course, he felt a lot like a man when Rose kissed him. When she touched him. But she seemed interested in doing none of those things now. So if necessary he would accept fighting as a substitute.

"The longer you stand there the louder she'll scream," Rose said.

He moved toward the bottle warmer, plucked the bottle out of it and handed it to Rose. He was careful to maintain his distance from Isabella.

Rose put the bottle in the whimpering baby's mouth; Isabella made a few grateful sounds as she latched on. Then Rose stood, leaning toward him, "I think you should take her."

He took a step back, his stomach tightening. "I don't think I should."

"You can hold me at a distance all you want, Leon, but you can't do it to your daughter. You dropped your defenses when you remembered your past. You came in and apologized to me, and that was nice of you, but I don't think it was the right thing to do. If you're not going to fight for her, then I'm going to do it. I made a promise. Not for you, not for your sake, but for hers. I promised her that I was going to love her like she was my own child, that I was going to fight for her, and I am. Even if I have to fight you."

He simply stood, staring at her.

"She's a baby. Not a bomb," she insisted.

He had to disagree with that. He knew better than just about anybody that grief was a unique kind of bomb. One that detonated deep inside of you and left wounds that no one else could see. Left shrapnel embedded deep in your soul that you couldn't simply remove.

Children. Your own children had the very greatest ability to damage you simply because of the immediate and intense love they commanded. The protectiveness. That was almost worse than anything else. The need to protect. The gut-rending terror when you failed.

"She is so soft," he found himself saying. "So very vulnerable. I find it…terrifying. I wish I could remember more of myself. I wish I could remember more of my years. As it is, the strongest things are the loss of my son, and the presence of my daughter."

"That must be difficult. You're right. I don't understand that. I don't understand what it's like to lose a child. It must be… I don't pretend to understand what you're feeling. I won't. But what I do know is that Isabella is here. She needs you now. If you fail her it's because you choose to."

He tasted the strange metallic tang on his tongue, similar to the all-encompassing panic he had felt in Isabella's nursery a couple of nights ago.

"She's here," Rose continued. "She's here, and you've had this accident that might have killed you. This accident that's giving you a chance to change. What's the point of it if you don't take it?"

He reached out slowly then, taking his daughter into

his arms, relishing the feel of her soft, warm body against his. She was very alive. Perhaps not something that most people would think about their children. But something he would never take for granted.

"You are right," he said slowly, never taking his eyes off Isabella. He could see himself in her face. In her dark, sharp eyes and her sullen mouth. It was a miracle. To see yourself in a child. Which he was not entirely certain he had appreciated the first time around. But he had been young, and he had not been touched by loss. A baby had been an accident that they were working to contend with. *This* baby was not planned, either. But this baby was a miracle. A miracle he had never thought he'd get a chance to experience again. "I gave this away. I was going to give this up."

"You were afraid," she said simply.

"Do not defend me. I don't deserve it. I was taking the easy way. Perhaps I was afraid because of my experience with Michael, but I'm certain that not wanting to disrupt our marriage came into play. Not for your feelings. For my own comfort. For the protection of my ownership of the company."

She looked away. "You're so certain of that?"

"Like I am about so many things regarding myself. I am certain about this, too. Regrettably so."

"Change it then."

"A fresh start would've been much easier. But that isn't what we have, is it?"

"No. It isn't. But we do have a second chance. You got another chance to live. You have another chance with Isabella."

As she said that, he realized he wanted those things. And along with it, a second chance with her. Though he wasn't sure he had the right to ask for it.

And he noticed she hadn't listed it.

He had been so determined to try to fix things between them when he couldn't remember what it was he'd done. But once his sins had come to full, horrifying light, he had given her space.

He was through with that. He was through with allowing her to sit back and take her time as she decided what to do with him. He had decided.

He would be the father that Isabella needed. He would withhold nothing from his daughter even with what he remembered.

And he would be a faithful husband to Rose.

Those blue eyes that had once looked at him with so much affection were cloudy now. They were guarded. He would not rest until she looked at him the way she once had.

He was not a man who failed at what he set his mind to.

By dinnertime Isabella was safely in her nursery, but Rose was nowhere to be found. She had spent the past couple of days avoiding him, but he had always imagined that had he looked for her, she would be easy to find. That was not proving to be the case.

It was eternally frustrating. If he could remember even one thing about her, about the past, then perhaps he might have better luck figuring out where she slipped off to at the estate.

He closed his eyes, picturing the grounds. He had walked all over them in the weeks since his accident. He had nothing else to do.

There were great lawns, a maze comprised of hedges and a few little alcoves with benches and flowers.

Roses.

There was a rose garden that she went to. It was the garden that her mother had planted when Rose was a little girl. That was where she went.

He walked straight out of the house and down a winding, narrow path, closed in with foliage on either side. It was…exhilarating to have figured this out. To know something about his wife. To realize that somewhere inside of him he did hold knowledge about her. Thoughts about her. Feelings.

As frustrating as it was not to be able to connect more dots, knowing this now was a high unlike any he'd experienced in his recent memory.

Possibly in any memory, but with him it was very hard to say.

The little alcove came into view, a running fountain, large mature rosebushes that were in bloom. And seated on a carved stone bench in front of a bush with crimson roses was the namesake of the flower itself.

She looked up when he came into the clearing, a startled expression on her face.

"I thought I might find you here."

Her mouth dropped open. "You did?"

"Yes. I was thinking about you. And where you might be. And I remembered this garden. Your mother planted it for you. After you were born. Roses were her favorite flower, and that's why she named you Rose. And after she got sick she left this for you."

"I didn't know you… I didn't know you knew anything about me."

He drew closer to her, kneeling down slowly on the ground in front of her, the dew from the grass soaking into his pants. He looked up at her, something about the position familiar, something about the moment echoing in his mind.

He could see her blue eyes, full of sadness, tears tracking down her cheeks as he looked up at her from his position. Here in this spot. In this very garden.

He lifted his hand, cupping her cheek, mimicking what he had done back then. He slid his thumb along her cheekbone, his heart pounding hard.

"This is where you always go when you're upset." He didn't move his hand from her face, and she didn't pull away.

She just stared at him, her cheeks turning a darker shade of pink. "How do you know that?"

He never took his eyes from hers. Those eyes. Eyes he had seen just before his accident. The only memory in his mind when he had woken up in the hospital.

"Prom night," he said, the words coming at the same time as the memory. Just as it had been back in the nursery.

"What?"

"Your prom night."

"I didn't know you remembered that," she said. "What I mean is… I didn't even know you remembered that when you…remembered everything else."

"I do. Your date stood you up."

"My date was a joke to begin with. Nobody wanted to go to the prom with me. I was so weird. And bookish… And afraid of everything."

"You don't seem so scared to me. Not anymore."

She turned her face away from his. "I definitely can be," she said, her voice soft. "I have been. Afraid of my own shadow. You were right when you said I was hiding here."

"I was angry when I said that."

"Yes. But just because you were angry doesn't mean you weren't right."

"We all hide," he said. "We just do it in different ways. I should know."

"What else do you remember?" she asked, her tone hopeful.

"We danced."

Those two simple words opened up a torrent of feeling inside of him. They rocked him. Utterly. Completely.

It was as if the clouds had rolled away revealing an inky, clear evening filled with sparkling stars. And he could see it all clearly.

More than that. He could feel it.

He had gone to the rose garden because he knew she would be there. Because he knew that her date hadn't arrived. And she had been there, crumpled on the bench, sobbing as though her heart was broken.

He had always seen Rose as a girl. Sweet, young. But when she lifted her head and he saw her tear-streaked face, saw the deep sadness inside of her, he saw something more.

And when he had lifted her from her seat and pulled her up against his body, leading her into a dance, he had felt something that terrified him. She was a woman. Not a girl anymore. And he could no longer play off the connection that he felt to her.

Rose. So quiet and serious. Every smile felt earned, every laugh hard-won. And he had lived to earn those things.

He had lived to make those blue eyes sparkle.

He had never wanted to make her cry. And he would bet most of his considerable fortune that he had made her cry more tears than almost anyone else on earth.

"I remember," he said. "I remember coming here. And I held your hand, and it was so soft. And I pulled you up against me and held you close. And you were so beautiful. You were too young for me. But that didn't stop me from wanting you."

She gasped, pulling away from him.

"Did that ruin a nice, innocent memory? I have a way of ruining things. I think we've proven that."

"Nothing is ruined for me," she said, her tone hushed. "I wanted you, too."

"Thank God I didn't know. I fear I would have taken unforgivable advantage of that. I'm not a good man, Rose."

"You are. You *are* a good man… It's just that you've been hurt…"

"How do you defend me? Even now, how do you defend me? If anyone has seen absolute proof that nothing in me is good, that everything I am is deceitfully wicked, it's you. I have been an unfaithful husband. I have been… I have not even been a husband. I was a better friend to you back then."

She shook her head. "What do you want me to say, Leon? Do you want me to say that I think you're terrible? That you've hurt me so deeply I don't know if the wound will ever heal? Do you want me to say that I don't know if I can ever trust you?"

"Yes. Yes, because it's what I deserve."

"But I don't know if it's true. And I won't know, unless we try. I won't know until time passes."

"Time. Bloody, stupid time. I don't have any affection for it at all. What has it given me? It has taken more from me, that's for sure." He laughed hollowly. "Most people grow better. If my memories are any indication I have done nothing but get much, much worse. Until I became nothing altogether."

"That isn't true. The memory that you're having now? The memory of my prom night? It's one of my favorites.

Out of all of my memories. And that started out as the worst night… Someone who has the power to take a terrible moment and make it amazing… He can't be all bad."

"Yes, well. While you were wallowing in teenage heartbreak I was imagining pushing your dress up your thighs and burying myself inside of you. And I knew you were a virgin, Rose. I didn't particularly care one way or the other."

"Do you think my imagination was pure?" she asked, raising one eyebrow. "You have no idea how badly I wanted to kiss you."

"I wanted to do much more than kiss you," he ground out.

"I wouldn't have said no."

"I would've hated myself forever."

Her father had brought him through the darkest time in his life. Another piece locked into place. Yes, her father had known about Michael. Leon had confided in him one day at the office. That was the beginning of him taking an interest in Leon.

And he had been the most important person in Leon's world. Rose was a close second. He'd met her when she was a child, and she had delighted him immediately. Realizing she was a woman had been a problem. That night after her prom, he had gone and found a woman at a bar and exercised his sexual frustration with her. Random hookups to keep himself from making any move toward his mentor's innocent daughter.

Because the simple fact was, there was nothing he could offer Rose. She would want love. She would want a husband who could care for her as a husband should. She would want children. He wanted none of those things. He had tried for a family as a young man, and had lost too greatly to ever consider it again.

Rose was so new. So completely untainted by the world that he didn't want to touch her with any of his darkness.

And so he had resisted any pull to her. Any attraction to her. He had buried himself in other women. In alcohol. In all of the usual vices that he used to help himself forget unpleasant feelings.

But one day, his mentor had called him into his office. And he had told him that he was ill. That he was dying. That there was nothing that could be done. Rose was so young; she had always been so protected. And he felt he had failed her as a father. That he hadn't been there for her when she needed him. He had expressed deep, terrible regret to Leon. How he had held her at a distance because of the way he had grieved his wife.

And now, he would never have a real chance to make up for it. He wouldn't be here when she needed him. He wouldn't be here to greet any grandchildren.

He was leaving her, and he wanted to know that she would be cared for.

That was when he had asked if Leon would marry Rose.

He closed his eyes. And he was lost in a memory.

Their wedding day.

She walked down the aisle toward him, her lithe figure displayed to perfection by her designer wedding gown. He took her hand, her father formally giving her to Leon's care.

His throat dried, his heart pounding in his chest. He had spent years denying his forbidden attraction to Rose. Years pretending it didn't exist. And now here she was, being given to him as a wife. He could do whatever he wanted with her. He could finally give in to the fantasies. To the desires that he had always tried to keep in check.

And then it was time to kiss her. He pushed back her veil, revealing her face. Those beautiful blue eyes.

He leaned in, pressing his lips to hers, expecting it to be simple. Expecting to maintain control. She was young and inexperienced, and he'd been with more women than he could count.

But the moment their lips touched, he'd burst into flames.

He was lost in it. In her taste. In her touch. Lost in a way he couldn't remember ever being. And something began to swell in his chest. Something began to shift and change.

And when he had pulled away, he realized he was no freer to have Rose now than he had been before the wedding. That look on her face, that look of sheer joy. Of desire, of… Of love. He could never hope to pay back the wealth that she offered in that look. The deep, rich capacity for caring and emotion that he could see in those beautiful eyes was something he knew he would never be able to match.

And afterward, Rose had gone to their honeymoon suite. And he had not joined her.

He had gotten drunk. So drunk that there would be no chance of finding his way to her. So drunk that there would be no chance he would give in and have her in a moment of weakness.

And she had never come to him. She had never said anything.

Had never begged him to come to her bed. So he had let himself believe it was for the best. That he was making the right choice.

It wasn't until her father had died that he had taken another woman into his bed. He had convinced himself that it was for the best. He had found a brunette. One with dark eyes that would remind him nothing of his wife. But when he had taken her, he hadn't been able to look at her. He had used her. In addition to betraying his wife he had used the other woman.

But just as he had done with feelings, just as he had done with all finer emotions, he continued to sear his conscience until it felt nothing. Until picking up another woman was simply a matter of course, and he could no longer feel any guilt over it. Until he could convince himself that it was nothing more than a game. Until he could force the desire he felt for Rose into the background.

"Why didn't you say anything to me?" he asked, when the torrent of memories finally stopped flowing so freely.

"What do you mean?"

"You wanted me. You wanted a real marriage. After I didn't come to you on our wedding night why didn't you say anything to me?"

She laughed, a hollow, bitter sound. "You can honestly ask me that? Remembering my prom night and the way my date stood me up? I waited for you. But you didn't come. And I would've rather died than ask you why. A man should *want* to be with his wife. She shouldn't have to beg him."

He felt as though he was being torn in two. Regret consumed him. Threatened to overwhelm him completely. The degree to which he had wounded her cut him deeply. The realization of all he had done a destructive force inside of him.

He could say nothing. He had apologized and apologized. It felt empty. It didn't feel enough. At every turn there was new evidence of the way he had harmed her. The ways in which he had betrayed her. He had no words. They were empty. They were fruitless. He could remember making her laugh and smile. Saying all the right things to her. But when it came right down to it he had never done the right things.

He reached up, curving his hand around the back of her head, drawing her down for a kiss. He had no words in him. But he could show her. He could show her what was inside of him.

And if it burned them both alive, he would happily be consumed in the flames.

CHAPTER TEN

HE REMEMBERED.

Those were the words that echoed in Rose's mind as she gave herself over to Leon's kiss.

He remembered that night. And he had wanted her, too.

Somehow, in the years in between that dance and this moment here in the garden, things had taken a terrible turn. Or perhaps, the real problem was that wanting wasn't love. At least, not for a man like Leon. And nothing less than love would ever entice a man to abandon a life of hedonism.

In many ways, that hurt worse than total indifference.

She realized then that it had been very easy to imagine that the real issue was that he felt no attraction for her. As painful as that was, she had imagined that one day she could perhaps make him see her as a woman. That all she had to do was change his feelings and he would look away from other women and turn to her forever.

Now she was faced with the simple truth that he had been attracted to her. It just hadn't been strong enough. He had been attracted to her, and he had resisted her.

It made her ache inside. It made her feel hollow.

But at the same time she wanted to lose herself in this kiss. In this moment. What did it matter what had come before? What did it matter what came after? If she could go back in time to when she was eighteen, sitting here crying, desolate over being abandoned by her date, and grab even one scrap of courage to take hold of what she wanted—to take hold of Leon—she would do it.

She had lived so quietly. So timidly.

She had not gone to him on their wedding night and begged for him because she'd been so afraid of rejection. Because she'd been afraid to face the truth outright, and had preferred instead to cling to hope, no matter how small and hazy it might be.

Where was her reward?

She didn't want to live that way anymore. She wanted to mess up her hair, mess up Leon's suit. She wanted to scream. She wanted to take everything that was on offer and please only herself.

She wanted to change him inside. To affect the kind of landslide that he had triggered inside of her years ago. To leave him altered, to leave him completely and utterly changed for having touched her.

She didn't know if there was anyone in the entire world that was true of. If she had done a single thing to change anyone at all. She was pale, kind of hanging in the background and committed to being inoffensive. Doing her best to keep her head down, doing her best not to be tormented by her peers. Doing her best not to unsettle her father in any way, or cause him any grief.

She was afraid that if she was too loud, if she laughed too much, she would make him sadder. That she would only make him miss her mother that much more.

And the one time she had tried to step outside of that, the one time she had accepted a date at school, it had all blown up in her face.

So she had gone back into hiding. But it had done her

no earthly good. She had gone back into hiding, putting her head down, hoping that someday she could convince Leon to care for her, too.

But why would anyone care for a pale little crustacean hiding inside a shell? One that didn't even act like it wanted to see the sun.

But she did now. She wanted to have the warmth of it bathe her bare skin. Here and now out in the garden she wanted the sun to touch her skin; she wanted Leon to touch her skin. And who cared about the consequences?

She had nothing to lose. She had given him her heart years ago and had never gotten it back. She had already been broken by him, broken into tiny pieces so many times it was a miracle she hadn't been blown away by the breeze.

She wouldn't be. She resolved that then and there.

She would become more. She would be filled. With her own desires. With him. She would be too substantial to blow away. Too substantial for anyone to ignore.

She kissed him back. And like every kiss that had come before it, there was nothing simple to it. It tasted of years of longing, of missed opportunity, of grief and pain. But there was hope, too. Hope for more. Hope for absolutely everything, because the alternative was to exist in silence.

She unbuttoned his shirt, pushing it from his shoulders, baring his chiseled body to her gaze. She placed her fingertips at the center of his chest, moving her hand over his heated skin.

"Nothing is ever as good as you think it's going to be," she said, her throat tightening as she skimmed her touch down over his abs. "Fantasy is limitless. It's also painless. You direct everything. You control all of the movements. Your very own composition." She took a deep breath, inhaling his scent. "Reality doesn't have a place in it. It's like walking in the stars. Knowing that you can't fall back down to the earth."

A rough growl rumbled in his chest. "You make it sound beautiful."

"It's been most of my life. Safe and secure, dreams without consequences." She pressed against the firm heat of his skin. "You never sweat. You never get dirty. You never get injured." She leaned in, pressing her lips to his angular jaw. "And you never reach the heavens. Why walk in the stars when you can go so much higher?"

"Because you might fall," he responded.

She nodded. "I might. We both might. I don't care anymore."

She tilted her head, claiming his lips with hers. It was as reckless, as intense as she was. She vibrated with it. Her need, her desire, coursing along her veins. She raised her hands, grabbing hold of his face, holding him to her as she attempted to quench the thirst that only he could satisfy.

She let her hands drift down to his belt buckle, and that was when she found the control wrenched away from her completely. He growled, reached down and gathering fistfuls of her dress, pushing it up over her hips before tugging it up over her head.

That left her in nothing more than a lace bra and wispy panties, outside in the waning light. She never would have imagined she might do something like this. Ever.

But Leon made her crazy. And she didn't really mind.

She was full with her feelings for him. With her need. Desperate for release.

"Fall with me," she said.

"It might hurt."

She leaned in, pressing her lips to his. "Then we'll be bruised together."

"My main concern is breaking you."

"I think we're already both a little broken." She wrapped her arms around his neck, splaying her hands over his back. "Maybe that's why we fit so well."

"Just a couple of jagged pieces." He brushed his thumb over her cheek. "Except I fear I'm the one who broke you."

She fought against the dry, stinging press of tears putting pressure on the backs of her eyes. Denying this would be easy. Absolving him would be. She wanted to. For his conscience, if for no other reason. But he had broken her. Or at least, he had broken her heart. More times than she could count.

"I think I needed to be broken," she said finally. "So that I would finally start fighting."

She nipped his bottom lip, an echo of what she had done the last time they were together. When they had fought, and they had made love, and she had cried. That day she had been completely broken in her bedroom. Destroyed as she faced the realization that her husband had betrayed her.

Destroyed as she realized she didn't possess the capacity to be eternally patient. That perhaps she couldn't be eternally forgiving. That, perhaps, in light of that she and Leon couldn't make a future together.

But now she felt like it might be different. Now they were out here in the sunlight together. And it really did feel new. Not because the past was a blank slate. Not because they were starting over. But because they were walking forward.

Because the secret things had been dragged out into the light, and while some of them had proved to be monsters, now that she could see them, she could see how to fight them. Now that she had decided she would stand up and fight.

"You're going to fight me?" he asked, grabbing hold of her hair, tugging her head back so that she was forced to meet his gaze.

"I don't think I could win. In terms of brute strength I'm most definitely outmatched." She fought against his hold, not minding the little pinpricks of pain that dotted her scalp as she did. She pressed her lips to his chest, scraping his nipple with her teeth.

He jerked beneath her touch, growling like a feral beast. Appealing to the wild thing in her. "You plan to use other weapons then?"

She looked up at him, and she smiled. She felt powerful. More powerful than she ever had in all her life. She felt his muscles shift beneath her touch and she scraped her fingernails across his abs, scoring his skin lightly.

His expression was that of a man carved from stone, his entire body gone rigid beneath her touch. Suddenly, she was overcome with a desire to taste him. With the need for it.

She leaned in, tracing a line down the center of his abs, tasting salt and skin and Leon. She was starving for him. She didn't know how she would ever get enough.

She had been with him when he didn't have memories of who she was. She had been with him when she was angry. But this was different. This was different in every way.

This time, when she put her hands on his belt buckle, he didn't pull them away. This time he let her undo his belt, let her pull the zipper on his pants down, exposing himself to her. The breath rushed out of her lungs, desire replacing it.

She leaned in, flicking her tongue over the head of his arousal. He stiffened, grabbing hold of her hair again, pulling her away from him. "Don't," he said, his words hard.

"Why not?"

"I don't deserve that."

"Life isn't about what we deserve. Sometimes it's just about what people want to give. Or don't. You were never my reward, Leon. And I'm not yours. This isn't a reward. But it's what I want. I want to taste you. I want to be filled with you. Let me."

She took him deep into her mouth then, his harsh groan of pleasure washing over her as she slid her tongue down his length.

He clung tightly to her as she continued to pleasure him. As she gratified herself. Because she made him shake. Because he wanted this. Because he wanted her. Because there was a time when he had not wanted her enough to take her, when he had been able to resist.

But that time wasn't now.

She tasted him until his thighs began to tremble, until his whole body was shaking with pleasure. And then, just as he was about to lose control completely, he pulled her away. He stripped her of the rest of her clothes and laid her down in the grass, the sun washing over her skin.

He kissed her deep, hard, kissed her as he thrust deep inside her, joining his body to hers. There was a rock just beneath her shoulder blade, and it dug into her skin. She knew it would leave a mark. But it was perfect in a way. Because this wasn't gentle. It wasn't clean. It would leave a mark deep down in her soul, and she felt like her skin should bear the evidence of it, too.

She wrapped her legs around his lean hips, urging him to go deeper, to go harder.

His each and every thrust sent a shock of pleasure through her, and she refused to remain silent about it. She encouraged him, told him just how much she wanted him. Just how good he was.

She gasped as her climax washed over her, shuddering out her pleasure as it consumed her completely.

And as she lay there with him, naked, unashamed, exposed in the sunlight, she knew she could never go back to the way things had been. She knew she could never go back to being invisible.

Right here in this place where her love for him had been cemented, she'd found something new. Love for herself. A need to have more than a quiet, nonconfrontational existence.

Even the way she was planning to leave him had been too easy. Because even leaving him possessed no risk. Kept her hidden.

Kept her from revealing just how much she cared for him.

But here and now it was all laid out in the open. And she wasn't ashamed.

He rolled over, cupping her cheek. "It's time for dinner. That is actually why I came to find you," he said, his voice gruff.

"I guess we had dessert first," she said.

He laughed. Genuine. Real. Balm for her soul. "I guess we did." He pulled her close, his hands drifting over her curves, his touch hotter than the sun. "We should probably go in."

"I don't want to," she said. "I want to run away into the mountains. And then we won't have to do anything. It won't matter what you remember, or what the papers say. You can grow a beard and chop wood."

"Would you like me to grow a beard and chop wood?

I could. But I don't think we should move to the mountains."

"Why not?" she asked, pretending to sound tragic.

"Because our home is here. Our family is here."

His words tapped into a well of longing that expanded in her chest. Deep. Intense. So very needy it stole her breath. "You're right," she said. "It is."

"I take it you want to…try?"

She knew what he meant. To try for a marriage. To try and be a real family. "Yes," she said. "Yes, Leon. I do."

This vow was deeper than those she'd spoken at their wedding. Because then, she hadn't known all they would face. Hadn't known how he might hurt her. How he would heal her. Then, she hadn't truly known how deeply she could care. She hadn't known how much it might cost.

But it was the cost that made it valuable. It was the cost that made her *yes* matter.

When they walked back into the house, it was the first time it felt like theirs. And it was the first time she truly felt like Leon's wife.

Leon's memory continued to improve over the course of the next few weeks. Filling in gaps that had previously been vacant. And it was a good thing, too. Because it was time for him to get back to work. He could no longer leave his company unattended and expect that it would thrive. He was in the business of investments, and he knew well just how fraught the market could be. Truly, it was a miracle that everything had been left standing in his absence.

He was beginning to do a little bit of work from home, and he hadn't destroyed anything. Now that he was certain he wouldn't break things simply by touching them, he was beginning to feel a similar level of confidence in his dealings with Rose. Though he was slightly less confident on that score. She was so beautiful. Fragile, and easily bruised much like her namesake. He wanted no part in harming her in any way.

At least, no more than he already had.

Those memories, the memories of how he had treated their marriage, were the most difficult to reconcile.

He still couldn't remember April, Isabella's mother. Couldn't specifically remember dealing with her when she had told him about her pregnancy. He could only make assumptions. He was consigning a certain amount of memories to that file. Memories he would simply have to forget ever existed.

He knew enough now to function as Leon Carides. He knew enough to see to his work. To be a father. And to be a husband. He didn't need anything else.

Rose walked into the studio space that they were beginning to share more often than not. He was holding Isabella as he sought to work on his computer. He had missed so much time with her, he liked to make it up when he could.

"I thought I might find the two of you in here."

"I'm never anywhere else," he responded.

She smiled, her expression almost sad. "That's going to change. Soon you'll be going out and going to work. Probably traveling again."

He frowned. "Yes. I was thinking about that. I see no reason why you and Isabella can't travel with me. I know you've been working to archive your father's writing. To compile your family history. But surely once you have a good amount of that digitized you can start to travel away from the manor."

"Yes. I don't see any reason why I can't." The offer made her glow; the response made him warm in his chest.

"Well, that's settled then. Of course, this is assuming that you aren't sick of me."

"Not even a little bit," she said, treating him to a smile that he knew down in his bones he didn't deserve.

"I have also been thinking about the fact that we never did have a party here in the manor. I know it isn't Christmas. But I will be returning to work. I'm going to need to put on a strong face. Of course, most of the world doesn't know about the exact effects my accident had. But I am going to have to put on quite a show to restore confidence in my abilities as an investor. Beyond that... there is the small matter of introducing Isabella as part of our family."

The look of pain on Rose's face stole any warmth that had just lodged itself in his chest a moment ago. "Of course we will," she said, her tone practical.

"It is a necessity. But of course, the world will not believe that you secretly gave birth to a child. I'm going to have to confess my indiscretions."

She nodded slowly. "And I suppose I'll stand behind you like a dutiful wife as you make the claim."

"You do not have to stand behind me. You can stand in the crowd and throw rotten fruit if you like."

She shook her head. "No. I'm not going to do anything that would cast you or our family in a negative light. No, we can't hide the truth. Obviously, Isabella isn't my baby. And, honestly, if we tried to maintain that fiction it would only come crashing down around us later. Nothing is going to stop April from coming forward if she sees the potential opportunity for a payday. She didn't seem like a terrible person, but she did seem like a woman who might find herself in desperate straits eventually. We don't want to open ourselves up to that. The truth is the only way forward."

It had been true for the two of them; of course it would continue to be true for their family.

"I agree. We will release a statement, but quietly. After our party."

"You want to have a party?"

"Yes. With my beautiful wife by my side. A statement. Of my commitment both to you and to the business. A show of how things are changing after the accident."

"I see. And what will you tell the public?" she asked.

"Simple. I will tell them that you nursed me back to health. I will tell them that my brush with death caused me to reevaluate some things. And that I have changed. All of these things are true."

"Yes. Just leaving out the part about the amnesia."

"I feel that amnesia is best left unmentioned."

"That is probably true. First of all, I doubt very many people would believe it," she said, wrinkling her nose.

"We are rather like a bad soap opera, aren't we?"

She crossed the space, coming to sit down beside him, and pressed kisses on his cheek. "With a little bit less tragedy, I hope," she said.

"One can only hope."

"Then, I suppose we are going to be very busy planning a party," she said.

"Or rather, the staff will be. I would rather keep you busy with me."

Rose smiled. "That can be arranged."

CHAPTER ELEVEN

PUTTING ON FORMAL dresses never did end well for Rose. That was why she was unaccountably twitchy and deeply uncomfortable as she zipped up the crimson gown, smoothing the silky fabric, watching the weight conform to her figure. First there was her prom. Then there was her wedding. And now this.

It made her feel a deep sense of encroaching doom. It made her feel so uneasy she could hardly breathe.

She looked at her reflection. At the wide-eyed woman staring back. She was expertly made up, shadow highlighting the blue of her eyes, her lips a deep crimson.

But she still saw plain, bookish Rose. Who would have to go downstairs and stand next to Leon, who couldn't be called plain or bookish in any circumstances.

She took another breath. It would be fine.

This was different. This was their first party as a married couple. This was a symbol of Leon's commitment to moving forward with her. This was their new beginning. And yes, eventually, they were going to have to deal with the fact that they had to tell the world about him having a child with another woman. But, for tonight, they would just have their party. For tonight, Leon would show off his improved health, and they would stand together, truly a couple for the first time in the eyes of the world.

She took a deep breath, looking down at Isabella, who was in the small bassinet that was currently in the room she shared with Leon. The baby was sleeping, and Elizabetta would be upstairs to ensure that she was taken care of during the party.

Still, it was Rose's first instinct to stay hidden up here with the baby. Mostly because she was used to hiding. Used to staying out of the spotlight. Out of the way.

She was used to watching from upstairs. She was definitely not used to being down in the party.

"Well," she said fiercely to her expression. "Tonight you are."

The bedroom door opened and Leon walked in. Her heart slammed against her breastbone, her mouth going dry. He looked beautiful in his perfectly fitted suit, all traces of the vulnerable, confused man she had spent the past couple of months caring for erased. This was the Leon she had always known. Confident. Suave. Perfectly at ease in any situation he might be dropped into.

"Rose," he said, his dark gaze intense. "You look… I don't have words. There is nothing that will do you justice."

She felt her skin heating all over. "Thank you."

"Shall we?" He extended his arm, and she looped hers through it. Then they continued downstairs together.

The ballroom was already full of guests, men who looked exquisite in their tuxedos, women who were resplendent in their gowns. That earlier insecurity that was vibrating over her body grabbed hold, worked its way beneath her skin.

He had said there were no words for her beauty, and yet there were so many women in here who possessed a much richer, deeper beauty than Rose did.

The kind of women he used to prefer to her.

He had spent nearly two months with her as his only lover. Surely these other creatures, rare hothouse flowers—that were nothing like the common garden variety of bloom that she was—held greater appeal.

Perhaps that was why he had no words. Because she was simply plain.

At some point, she scolded herself, tightening her hold on him, *you have to trust him.*

Yes, at some point she would. But it was difficult. Not because he hadn't proved himself to be loyal over the past couple months. Simply because these months were like something out of a dream. And when it all came down to it, he had not offered her the most important thing. He had promised commitment. He had promised it several times over. But he had never offered feelings. He had never offered love. That concerned her.

Attraction was one thing. It was most certainly real. At least between the two of them. At least…for her.

What would happen when that changed? What would happen if she were to become pregnant with his child? If her body changed? What would happen when she aged? Would his feelings change along with her appearance?

She pushed the thought firmly into the back of her mind. She was not going to focus on anything like that. She wasn't going to doubt him. Not now, not when he had given her nothing to doubt.

A man in a perfectly cut suit, with a beautiful woman on his arm, crossed the space between them. The woman was visibly pregnant, although her bump was neat and small, making her look rather serene and elegant. And she was very much in love with her companion.

"Carides. It is good to see that you're unharmed."

She could see by the relatively blank look on Leon's

face that he was not entirely certain of who he was speaking to.

"We haven't met," Rose interjected. "I'm Rose Tanner. I'm Leon's wife."

At that, the man's beautiful companion blinked. "Nice to meet you," she said. "I'm Charity. Charity Amari. This is my husband, Rocco."

"Charmed," Rocco said, reaching out and taking her hand, pressing his lips to her skin.

She could see something change in Leon's expression. "The last time I saw you was just before my accident," he said.

"Yes," Rocco said. "I'm glad to see you weren't killed. Though I did find myself a little bit irritated with you as you did such a good job of charming my wife."

Rose looked at Charity, then down at the baby bump. Charity laughed. "That is definitely my husband's doing," she said. "Not yours. I was not as charmed as Rocco feared I might be. But since I was feeling rather uncharmed by him at the time, he had cause for concern."

"My own fault," Rocco said. "But all is well now. As it seems to be with the two of you."

"Yes," Leon said, taking a step toward Rose and wrapping his arm around her waist. "One thing my accident showed me was that I was taking my wife for granted. I will not do so anymore."

Rose couldn't help herself. She turned to look at her husband. "Why?"

He frowned. "Why what?"

"Why won't you take me for granted?"

She knew what she wanted to hear. She didn't know why she was pressing for it now. But it was too late to turn back.

"Because, *agape*. You're very important to me."

"Why?" she insisted.

"Oh, dear," Charity said. "I do think you might be in a bit of trouble, Mr. Carides."

"That is nothing new," Leon said, his tone smooth. Clearly, he was no longer uncertain of how he knew the Amaris.

"Well, I suggest you find a way to fix it," Rocco said. "I'm glad that I did."

The two of them turned and walked away, and left Rose alone with Leon.

Jealousy was like a fire-breathing dragon inside of her. "Would you care to explain to me exactly how you know her?"

"Jealousy, Rose? You know perfectly well that I committed sins before my accident. That has been made abundantly clear. But if you suspect every woman we come into contact with—"

"I have every right to suspect her. We've been living in a dream world, Leon. Everything between us has been so easy. Because we've been here alone."

"We have not been alone. If you will recall we had a visit from one of my former mistresses. And it has not been easy. As you will also remember she came to give me my child."

"I have not forgotten."

"You think so little of me that you think you have cause for concern just because other women are parading themselves in front of me?"

"When have you earned anything else?" She despised this small, mean part of her that was lashing out at him now. It was all of the insecurity. Roiling inside of her like a beast.

He shook his head. "I haven't. But at some point, you will have to allow me to try without constant suspicion."

"Just answer my question."

"I met Charity at an event the night of my accident. She was firmly and fully besotted with the man she has now married. She had no interest in me."

"But you tried to see if she might?"

"Mostly to make Rocco angry. I find him insufferable."

"You remember him now."

When Leon had a memory, it tended to come in waves. She wondered which other memories would be visiting them tonight. She should have known there would be new memories. After all, they would be encountering people he had interacted with in the life that extended beyond the one they had created here in the manor. This truly had been a cosseted existence, one she hadn't fully appreciated until now.

Now she was sharing him with the world. This man who had become so essential to her. She had always cared for him, but now that they had become intimate it was different. Now he felt like he was a part of her. And allowing other women to look at him, allowing them to get anywhere near him… It was much more difficult than she had anticipated it might be.

There were women here who would remember what it was like to be with him. Who would remember what he looked like naked. And he would have similar memories of them.

She really hadn't appreciated how hard that might be.

"Do you remember anyone else?"

"Is that a rather snappish way of asking if I have ex-lovers here?"

"Yes," she said, her voice near to a hiss.

"You have certainly changed, Rose. You used to be much more biddable."

"New things you're starting to remember?"

"Yes."

"Who knew this party would be such a treasure trove."

He grabbed hold of her arm, stopping her from walking away, turning her toward him. Then he reached out, gripping her chin between his thumb and forefinger. "What we have has been good. Do not ruin this."

"How can you accuse me of being in any danger of ruining it? I'm not the one who took lovers during our marriage."

"No. That was me. I am the one who took lovers during our marriage. I did not hide it. I am ashamed of it. I am also the one who cannot change the past. And so, *agape*, I would ask that if you wish to be in a marriage with me you allow me to move on from the mistakes that I have made. For if you never allow me to be more than that, then how will I ever transcend it?"

"It's on me now?" she asked, her tone icy.

"If you want to be with me," he responded. "If I can never be anything to you but the man who betrayed you then I don't see how we can move forward."

His words hit her square in the heart. "I'm sorry."

She had been nervous from the moment they had arrived down here at the party. She wasn't acting like herself. And it wasn't fair to him.

"Can you tell me what the problem is?" His voice was tender, his eyes soft. It made her feel terrible.

"We don't need to have this discussion now."

"I fear that we might. Especially as you seem so very upset with me."

"I'm not upset with you. But… I can't forget the fact that you were happy to sleep with every woman in this room except me for the past two years. And yes, that makes me a little bit insecure. And it's much easier to be angry at you than it is to feel that insecurity."

"You are exaggerating. I did not sleep with every woman in this room."

"Oh, really?"

"A third of them. Maybe. And that's being generous."

She laughed, in spite of herself. "All right. So maybe I'm being a little bit overdramatic. It's just… It's hard for me to believe this is real. Everything has changed so much. You've changed so much. And I suppose I'm afraid that you'll wake up and everything will change back."

He tipped his head to the side, his dark eyes glittering with intensity. "I'm not asleep, Rose. I'm not going to wake up from anything."

She nodded slowly. "Okay. I think I understand that. But it isn't as though there is a guideline for dealing with things like this."

"Yes. Sadly, the *So Your Spouse Has Amnesia* handbook has been out of print for quite some time."

"It really is a shame. Women like me could use some guidance."

"Well, I'm all out of guidance. Why don't we dance?"

He took her hand and led her out into the middle of the dance floor. Rose allowed herself to be swept into his arms. For a moment, she felt like she was lost in one of her childhood dreams. The ballroom was ornately decorated, the music swirled around them. Her husband, so strong, so impossibly handsome held her close. And when he turned her, she could see straight through the ballroom doors, up to the top of the stairs where she used to sit, crouched and watching as her parents did the very same thing.

Finally, she was a part of this life that she had dreamed of for so long. She felt like she was standing in a dream.

And she knew there was only one thing that would make it even more perfect. The one thing that was causing the trouble tonight.

It was a risk. She knew it was. But she was ready to take it. Here, lost in this beautiful moment that seem to be comprised almost entirely of stars, she felt as though she could never fall down to the ground. And if she did, surely he would catch her.

"Love," she said, her voice soft. "It's the lack of love that's concerning me. I love you. I love you so much, Leon, and I want very much for you to love me, too. That's what I need to be certain. That's what I need to trust. Love."

He went stiff beneath her touch, his black eyes taking on a hollow quality.

The world as she knew it fell away, the stars burning out. And Rose fell down to earth.

CHAPTER TWELVE

LEON WAS LOST in a memory that he had tried very hard to keep at bay. It was the look in Rose's eyes that had done it. That earnest sincerity. It was imagining that that had propelled him forward during his discussion with April a little more than a year ago. He had been imagining what Rose might look like when he told her he had gotten his mistress pregnant. Because it had *absolutely* occurred to him to fob the child off on his wife. After all, he was never home. He wasn't intimate with Rose. But surely she wanted a baby.

That thought had stopped him short. Because there was no way the baby could be in his house and he could keep himself from forming an attachment to it. He knew well enough that babies had a way of crawling beneath your skin. Of overtaking you completely. And of ripping your heart out when loss invaded your beautiful family.

"I'm pregnant, Leon. And I'm not going to get an abortion. So I don't know what you want to do about it. But I can't raise the baby without support—"

"I'll pay you. Whatever you need. But I'm not going to take care of the child. If you need support putting it up for adoption, that's up to you. Otherwise, I'm more than happy to set up funds so that you can make sure that you are both cared for."

There was one thing he knew for certain. He could not undertake raising another child. He had never, ever intended to put himself through that ever again.

He hated himself for being so irresponsible. For putting himself in this position. But he was a man with money. And he could pay to make it go away. There was no reason on earth he would ever have to see the baby. He could pretend it had never happened.

And so he had established the paperwork, come to an agreement on the amount and promised to give April full payment once paternity had been established. He had never seen the child. He had been notified of its birth, and he had asked that she not tell him whether it was a boy or a girl.

He'd wanted to know nothing about it.

But the night of his baby's birth, he had gone and gotten as drunk as he could remember ever getting. There wasn't enough alcohol on earth to drown out the pain. And he had wished more than anything that he might find solace in Rose's arms. Because there was something about her that had always seemed like home. Something about her that had always seemed like she might be the resting place he had wished for his entire life.

And it had been all the more reason to stay away from her. He had found another woman. A woman whose face he couldn't even remember. And that had been so much the better because she hadn't been special. He didn't deserve special.

He snapped back to the moment and Rose was still staring at him, her blue eyes filled with concern. With pain.

"What did you say?" he asked.

"I love you. And I want for you to love me back."

He could see the truth in her blue eyes, and it was all

too harsh. Too clear and bright. It was everything he'd always feared.

That honesty. Real, and deep. Reaching out for him. Asking for it in return.

He realized it then, as he stared back at her. She was everything pure and true, and she always had been. While he was a lie. Down to his very core.

He did nothing, not a single thing, with a shred of honesty. He lied to everyone. To his wife, his mistresses, himself.

No wonder he had lost his memories so easily. No wonder they had slipped away into the darkness with such ease. They were nothing.

He was nothing.

His mind was full now, but his hands were empty, and she wanted him to give her something that he…he simply couldn't.

He released his hold on her and began to back away. Then he turned, walking out of the ballroom, straight out into the entryway of the house, and out the front door. A summer shower was pouring down, large drops of water splashing on the paved drive. He looked around, desperate for escape. Desperate for reprieve.

"Leon!"

He turned, and saw Rose standing there in the doorway, her pale petite silhouette backlit by the golden light coming from inside the house. He knew right then she was everything he had ever dreamed of. She was warmth. She was light. She was home. And he could reach out and take none of it.

"No," he said, his voice rough.

"Leon, don't go."

"We cannot do this."

"Like hell we can't." Rose picked up her dress, holding

the red silky fabric balled up in her fist as she made her way down the steps, and out into the rain. It fell across the gown, leaving dark splotches on it, as though she were bleeding out right there in front of him.

A wound for his every word.

He had hated himself. Hated himself for a long time, for a great many things, but he'd never hated himself more than he did in this moment.

"I can't," he bit out. "And there is the final piece of my memories. I can't love you. That's why I never touched you. That's why I was never supposed to. That's why it was better for me to spend the past two years warming the bed of every woman who would have me, rather than ever touching you. Because for all my sins, Rose, I never intended to hurt you."

"But you did hurt me. You always hurt me. From the moment you agreed to marry me and then never touched me you hurt me. So it's too late to pretend that you had any kind of self-sacrificing notion when you married me. You might have felt guilty, but surely you must've known you were going to hurt me."

"I thought…" he ground out, the rain splashing down his shirt, sending trickles of cold water down his skin. He didn't care. "I thought," he continued, "that I might be able to have you. I thought perhaps I could condemn my conscience to hell and have what I pleased. I wanted you, Rose, make no mistake. Were it only down to attraction I would have had you on your back when you were eighteen, as I already told you. But it was more than that. Your father trusted me, and I knew that I could never give you what you would want."

"And you thought you knew what I wanted?"

"Yes. You want this. You want love. You want things that I can never, ever give. You would stand there and tell me that I'm wrong? Even as you prove me right? You cannot do that."

"But things have changed. You have Isabella… You have *me*. Surely…"

"I remembered," he said. "I remembered when we were in there. When April came to me to tell me she was pregnant. If only my reaction were one half so steeped in grief as I imagined. I did not want the responsibility. I couldn't bear it. My life was perfect. I was a carefree bachelor with everything I wanted. Never mind the fact that I actually had a wife. You were a wife that I never had to see, a wife that I never had to speak to. Out of sight, out of mind. I had established for myself a perfect life. And, while I considered taking the child and giving her to you to raise, since I certainly wasn't going to get you pregnant, I decided in the end that perhaps you wouldn't take so kindly to that."

"Leon…"

"It started with grief, Rose. It definitely did. But it twisted me into a cold, selfish man, and by the time I rejected my own child that was the only thing that was driving me. I lost the capacity to love. I felt no sadness signing away the rights to my flesh and blood. Do you think I once mourned the fact that I wasn't in your bed? Do you think I felt even the tiniest sliver of guilt when I took another woman into my arms in spite of the vows that I spoke to you? I didn't. I could pledge faithfulness. I know that I can. I don't want the things that I did. I find that I'm satisfied with you. Love? I don't love anything. I'm never going to love you."

The words poured from him, a toxic kind of black ooze that covered everything it touched. He hated himself. He hated her even more for asking this of him. For making him hurt her. For making him destroy this beautiful thing that they had built between them. But he couldn't love her. He couldn't.

Already, there was Isabella. And he loved her in spite of himself. Perhaps, she would even love him in spite of himself. But…when he looked at Rose, when she demanded love from him, there was nothing but fear. Loving Isabella… Loving Rose… If he did that and he lost them, it would bleed him dry. There was no way he could ever endorse such a thing.

"Leon, I know you love me."

"No," he said, his tone final. "I don't."

"But these past few months…"

"When we began a physical relationship it was when I had no memory. I had no idea who you were. I had no idea who I was. But I know now. I am simply a man too scarred, too damaged to ever care for anyone. I am not the man you wish I was. I'm not even the man I wish I was. I can promise you faithfulness, but I cannot give you love."

"A promise doesn't mean anything without love."

"Then that is your decision," he said. "I cannot make you change your mind."

"So you're telling me I should simply believe you? With nothing else but your word?"

He saw it then. The chance to do the right thing. For the first time in too many damn years. He met her gaze, watched the rain pour down her beautiful face. And he memorized her. Memorized every slope and curve of her face. Memorized that exact color in her eyes, and deeper, the way they looked at him now. With hope. With love.

One last moment before he drove it all into the ground.

"You are right not to trust me, Rose. Very few things matter to me less than the truth. I know who I am now. I'm Leon Carides. I was a boy in Greece who hated his impoverished life and lied his way into the US. Who seduced a girl from a nice family and promised to care for her, and instead devastated her existence. Who married his mentor's daughter with no intention of ever honoring his vows. Who had a child with a lover whose name he barely knew and was so comfortable piling deceit on yet more deceit he thought nothing at all of concealing it from the world. From his *wife*. I don't even know what the truth is. Much less love."

"I want to show you," she said, the light still shining in her eyes.

"But I won't be able to see it," he said.

"I told you once that you asked the impossible of me. And you said—" her voice broke "—you said someday I could ask you for the same. And that you would try. Why won't you try?"

Something broke inside him. Or maybe it was already broken. Maybe now he just remembered that it was. "Because I don't want to."

And with that, he extinguished it. Finally. With that, she turned and left him, standing alone in the rain.

She left him there with all of his memories, all of his pain.

And he simply stood there, and longed for that moment when the only thought in his head had been Rose.

When they had simply been the truth. And there hadn't been a single lie in him.

He had loved her then.

He realized that now. When everything else had fallen away, he had loved Rose. There had been nothing to stop him then. When he was clean, and new. There had been only him, only her, and loving her had been both instant and simple.

But with each new memory that crowded in, each new

wound reopened, he'd found love pushed further and further away. Until it was out of his reach.

Until he envied a man lying broken in a hospital bed without a single memory beyond his wife's blue eyes.

Rose couldn't face going back into the party. Instead, she turned, leaving Leon standing there in the rain, and ran. She didn't realize quite where she was running to until she found herself in the rose garden. She knelt down in front of the stone bench, not caring that her dress was getting soaked. Not caring that it was getting dirty. She laid her head across the hard, cool surface and allowed her tears to mix with the drops of water that were falling from the sky.

She felt hollowed out. Hopeless. She felt utterly and completely alone.

She shivered, cold and panic washing over her in equal measures.

This was the thing she feared the most. Being alone. Demanding so much that the person standing before her would decide she wasn't worth it. It was why she had never demanded her father pay attention to her. Why she had never done anything but play the part of meek, solicitous daughter.

Why she had never once commanded Leon treat her more like a wife, rather than like she was invisible. Why it had taken her so long to get to the point of asking for a divorce.

Why she had preferred a divorce, *running*, to asking him to be her husband. To asking for what she wanted. Because she had been afraid that if she did he would prove that he truly didn't think she was worth the effort. And then she would have to know, not just suspect deep down that there was nothing about her that grabbed hold of anyone tight enough to incite change.

Her father had been so lost in his grief over his wife that he had not been able to pull out of it for the sake of his daughter. Leon, on the other hand, had drawn him out in a way she never had. Perhaps it was their matching grief. She could easily see that now. At the time, she hadn't realized the loss that Leon was contending with.

Still, at the time it seemed very much like there was something missing in her that other people seemed to possess. A spark that she just couldn't seem to ignite inside of herself.

And now, she had finally tried. She had finally demanded the impossible.

He hadn't been able to give it. Not to her.

She lifted her head, raising her face toward the sky, not caring as the droplets landed on her skin, rolling down her face. She could feel something expanding inside her chest—anger, desperation. She could feel herself expanding, changing. Perhaps because she was out here alone. Perhaps because she was no longer trying to shrink herself, contort herself to fit someone else's view of who she was.

It was so easy for her to imagine she wasn't worth it. That she didn't have what it took to inspire passion in someone. But who knew her? Did anyone? She had spent so long being quiet. Not making demands. How would anyone know what she wanted? How would anyone know that she was worth it?

She had never once behaved as though she was worth it. She had hidden herself away, made herself quiet. Made herself pale. And it had been easy, earlier in the rose garden when Leon was looking at her, when he was kissing her, to imagine that she could be loud. In that space, with his permission. But it was much harder when he had been looking at her with cold, dispassionate eyes. When he wished she would shrink again, and not ask quite so much. That had been the true test.

The test of whether or not she had the strength to be heard. Whether or not she could stand her ground and ask for these things when someone else said they didn't want to give them.

She realized finally that even if Leon didn't think she was worth it, even if her father had never thought she was worth it...*she* thought she was.

She realized it with a rush of absolute certainty and strength. How could she be a mother to Isabella if she taught her that a woman should twist and contort and bend endlessly in order to accommodate other people in her life?

She didn't want that little girl to bend, not even once. The world should bend around her, because she had value that was beyond estimation.

But Rose would never be able to teach her that if she didn't live her own life in that way.

So she got up off the ground.

She spread her arms wide, still facing the heavens, water cascading down her body. Her dress was soaked, probably ruined. Her marriage was ruined.

Her life was not.

Her life would be what she made it. She wanted love. She deserved love. She did not deserve to tiptoe around musty halls hoping for attention. She did not deserve to spend her entire professional life continuing to pour into her father's legacy. She deserved to create her own.

She did not deserve to have her love defined by Leon. To have him put limitations on it. Because she deserved to give it to someone who loved her back.

God knew, he would probably always have her love. That was the simple truth. She had loved Leon Carides from the moment she had first seen him and she very seriously doubted that that would change. But the way she responded to it had to.

Her only real concern was how this would affect her relationship with Isabella. She truly had grown to love the baby as her own. But then, Leon *did* love his daughter. And he wanted her to have a mother. They could come to an agreement, on that she was confident.

But she would have to leave this house behind. This thing she had been clinging to for so many years. This place that had held memories and dreams that she had so longed to live over and over again.

Tonight she had lived a dream. A fantasy. She had attended one of those beautiful parties in this wonderful home, but it hadn't fixed anything.

It was surreal, standing there, living out a scene you had always desired to be a part of, then realizing that there were no answers to be found. There were only more questions. It hadn't magically brought her happiness. Because love had still been missing. And so it hadn't mattered.

In the end, the only answer she had truly received was that it was time to grow up. It was time to stop living in the past. It was time to stop wishing that old fantasies would become a new reality.

It was time to move forward, knowing that she deserved it.

Whether or not Leon ever believed it.

She believed it. And that was all that mattered.

CHAPTER THIRTEEN

IF THERE WAS one thing Leon Carides was well acquainted with it was grief.

It was a truth about himself he was certain of as he sat on his bedroom floor, his back pressed against the wall, staring into the darkness. This feeling was old. It was familiar. A yawning cavern that was desperate to be filled.

And fill it he had done, for years. With alcohol, with sex. With work.

But here he was, sober, desiring no woman besides the one who had left him, with no choice but to allow grief to roll over him in waves. That experience was new.

It didn't take a genius to figure out why he had spent so many years avoiding the emotion. It was desolate and raw. It forced him to examine every dark space inside of him and acknowledge the fact that in many ways he was severely lacking.

Yes, he had defied the odds. Defeating poverty, climbing up the ranks in business... But it was empty. In the end, all of it was empty. What had it accomplished? What had it done for him?

All of that money and he had not been able to buy himself a soul. He had not been able to banish fear.

He had been so afraid that he had denied the existence of his own child.

He stood up suddenly, ignoring the rush of blood that made his head swim. He walked to his bedroom door, slowly making his way into the hall. Terror, his old friend, gripped his chest as he walked down the hall toward his sleeping daughter's room. Memories from the past mingling with the present as they often did in this situation.

He pushed open the door to the nursery and walked inside, fear and love wrapping itself around his heart in equal measure. He put his hand on Isabella's little back, breathing out a long, slow sigh of relief as he felt her warmth beneath his palm. As he felt her small heart beating, her back rising and falling with each indrawn breath.

He could have wept with relief. Every time.

And suddenly, a barrage of images flashed through his mind. But they weren't memories. They were visions of the future. Of Isabella growing up. Walking, going to school, dating. Driving. Going away to university.

The thousands of ways he would never be able to protect her. He would never be free of this terror that resided in his chest. Not where she was concerned. She was too precious to him. And the world around them was too uncertain.

Love would always carry this terrible weight.

He reached down and picked up his sleeping child, cradling her closely to his chest. She made a small, squeaking sound as she nuzzled deeper into him. He placed his hand over the back of her head, relishing the feel of her softness, the sweet scent that was unique to new life. He had never thought he would have this again. He hadn't wanted it.

The cost of it. There was no way to calculate it. It could tear you apart in a thousand different ways. With worry, with grief, with loss.

But this moment… In this moment he thought it might be worth all of it.

Something so valuable would never be free. It would never be without cost or risk.

He sat down in the rocking chair in the corner of the nursery, something he had not done with Isabella before. He had done it with his son, all those years ago. Sat and rocked him endlessly, singing songs that were probably inappropriate because he hadn't known any lullabies. Because he had been a seventeen-year-old father.

A small smile tipped his lips up as he began to rock Isabella.

Such a beautiful soul his son had been. He never let himself think of him. He'd buried this. This grief. This love.

But he knew for certain that if he never allowed himself to feel pain, he would never experience anything true. The past sixteen years of his life were a testament to that. The buzz from drinks faded, the pleasure from meaningless sex lasted only a few moments. None of it was real. It was all too *easy*.

The real things, the true things…they were quiet. They were darkened nurseries, sleepless nights. Vows that bound you to another person for life. They were simple. They were hard.

Babies, and beautiful women with blue eyes.

They were the impossible things.

And the most important.

It had been so easy to coast through life, as long as he wasn't allowing himself to remember what it was to feel. Ironically, he had to lose all of his memories to feel. To remember what it was to feel.

He had to get past the lies so that he could experience something true.

He had told Rose he was hollow inside. He had told himself the same. That he couldn't love her. He had told himself that from the moment he had begun to see her as a woman. He had prevented himself from touching her because he knew that once he did she would touch him, deeper than he ever wanted anyone to go. That she would reach down deep, all the way to his scarred soul and try to force him to feel again.

He knew what love was. That was the problem. He also knew what it cost.

But now he was sitting here, having lost Rose. Having hurt her. It didn't matter if he had intended to avoid feeling things for her... It was too late. He had felt things for her from the moment he'd taken her into his arms on the night of her prom.

And that was why when he had run from her, he had run so hard.

He was still running. All these years later.

"I think it's time to stop."

Leon had established a meeting with her so that they could discuss custody. She hadn't seen him for a week. She hadn't seen Isabella, either, and the loss of both of them ate at her like a vicious beast.

She was miserable. This bid for independence, for self-worth, had a high cost. And she was still on the fence about whether or not it would be worth it in the end.

As she walked into the manor, a wave of sadness washed over her. But it wasn't memories of her childhood that made her ache for this place. It was memories of her time with Leon. Of her time with Isabella.

The family she wanted to make, the real family, not a fantasy or a vague dream. The family she could have if she was just willing to take something less than love.

But if she took something less now, then she would always take something less. She had proved that for the past twenty-three years.

She blinked, continuing on up the stairs, and to Leon's office. This was like submitting to torture. But for Isabella, it was worth it.

When she walked in, Leon was sitting behind the desk. She just stood there, staring at him for a long moment. As if somehow looking at him now could get her through the rest of her life.

The sad thing was, she would see him again. She would see him hundreds of times. Thousands of times. But she wouldn't touch him. She wouldn't have him. Isabella bonded them together. Prevented her from walking away completely.

She looked away from him. "All right. I hope that we can see to all this as civilly as possible."

"Why would you have concerns about my civility?"

"Maybe it's mine that I'm worried about," she said.

"You have always been perfectly civil."

She looked back at him. "Yes. And I'm through with that. I'm tired of blending into the wood paneling of this old estate. I'm tired of trying to be accommodating to you. Just as I was accommodating to my father. I'm tired of waiting around for things to happen simply because I'm so quiet. Because I'm so good."

"You aren't quiet or good at all," he said, his voice frayed. "If you were you would still be here with me."

"Yes. Warming your bed as you saw fit and getting out of your way when you decided you wanted to warm someone else's."

"When did I ever say I wouldn't be faithful to you? You were the one who decided you couldn't believe me."

He cleared his throat. "But that is not what we're here to discuss."

"We're here to discuss custody," she said, swallowing hard.

"No," he said. "I lied. I asked you to come here because I wanted to give you something."

She blinked rapidly. "What?"

"Only everything." He pushed a stack of papers over the desk toward her, then stood. "The house. The company. Everything. It's yours. There are no conditions. You love this house. And the company should always have been yours."

"But you can't… Our marriage means it's yours. I left you, which means I'm the one who forfeits it."

He shook his head. "Your father told me to take care of you. And I failed at every opportunity. At every turn. I told myself I was protecting you by staying away from you, when I was, in fact, protecting myself. Ensuring I could have everything I wanted at no cost to me."

"But…"

"This is your home. Your history. Your legacy. I never want you to feel as though you have to be with me to have it. I never want you to feel as though I kept on taking from you. Not after what I took already. Though… Rose, I swear I will be faithful to you. If you would have me."

"No," she said, taking a step back. "I can't. I can't put myself through it."

"I am giving you everything! And my word. Why do you not believe me?"

"It wasn't about believing you. It was about believing in myself. What would you say if Isabella wanted to marry a man who didn't love her?"

He looked as though he had been punched in the face.

"I would tell her to stay far away from any man who didn't see her as the treasure that she is."

"And you would ask me to take less?"

"Yes. I would have. Not because I think you deserve less, Rose. But because I wanted you. I wanted you and I didn't want to have to give everything to have you. From the very beginning."

"What are you talking about?"

"I told you that when we danced together the night of your prom I wanted you. But what I didn't tell you was how much deeper it went. Because I didn't want to acknowledge it to myself. I didn't want to admit it."

"What are you saying exactly?"

"I'm a coward. I told you I didn't know how to love. I wished that I didn't. For so many years I wished that I didn't." He swallowed hard, his Adam's apple bobbing up and down. "I did. I could see it in your eyes, every time I looked at you. And… Dear God, Rose, you have no idea how much I wanted to reach out and claim that. To claim you."

He hadn't moved. He was still standing behind his desk, the large expanse of furniture between them. And she was still standing there, frozen, unable to take the chance. Unable to make the move. For fear of rejection.

Just *rejection*. She had been running scared for so long for fear of something that wasn't even fatal.

She looked at Leon, and she understood. For the very first time, she understood. It wasn't rejection he feared. It was loss. Loss he had experienced on such a keen, deep level. He had lived his entire life in avoidance of feeling that kind of pain ever again.

"And then I thought… Rose, I thought that if I married you, perhaps I could put my feelings for you in a separate compartment. Perhaps I could have you without truly having you. Without being changed by you. That was why I didn't come to you on our wedding night. Because I figured out very quickly that could not be. When I kissed you, the world turned upside down. It inverted beneath my feet, and I knew that if I were to ever put my hands on you, if I were ever to join my body to yours I would never be the same. And I had been... I had been changed by love already. I have been broken by it."

"I know," she said, her tone hushed.

"No. I don't think you do. I don't think you really understand what I'm trying to say. Because I didn't truly understand it. I had to be reduced to nothing so that I could understand exactly what I was. So I could understand what I was running from. When everything was removed, there was nothing but the truth. There was nothing but you. And I... I loved you easily. When there was no past... It was so simple to love you."

Her throat tightened, her chest feeling like a heavy weight was settled over the top of it. "Please don't. Please don't torment me with this. With the fact that you loved me when you didn't remember—"

"I'm not trying to torment you. I want you to know the truth. All these years... All this time... It was the broken things that kept me from you. It was the damage in my soul. But there was one part of me that recognized you from that first moment. That recognized you were my truth. That you were life. But I ran from it. Because I was afraid of what it would do to me to want again. To hope again. To love again. And when I woke up in that hospital bed I didn't have fear. I had you. And I was free to have you."

"But now you remember again. So all of it was for nothing."

He slammed his hand down on the top of his desk,

knocking over an hourglass, the glass clattering against the wood. "No. It was for *everything*. Because before, I had kept myself protected. Before, I had prevented myself from touching you out of a sense of self-preservation. So while I had the fantasy of what it might be like to have you, I didn't have the knowledge. But I have it now. When all of the fear was removed I claimed you. And I can't forget that." He put his fingertips on the side of the hourglass, turning it back onto its end. "I think I forgot myself sixteen years ago, not two months ago. I lost myself in grief." He looked up at her. "I do not want to forget again. I do not want my destruction to be the legacy of my son who I love so very much. I do not want the man I have been to be my legacy."

She struggled to take a breath, struggled not to hope. "It doesn't have to be."

"I will always be afraid. I will always be afraid of losing you. I will always be afraid of the dangers that lurk around every corner when it comes to Isabella. Because that's what it is to love. But it's only a small part. Loss is only great when love is great, and I had allowed myself to forget how truly great love was. I would not even allow myself to remember Michael with any sense of joy. It is difficult. It is difficult to remember something you lost. But he was beautiful. And I should remember him that way. I should remember my time with him that way."

"Leon… There is no right way to deal with such a thing."

"There are wrong ways. Marrying a woman, wishing to possess her without actually caring for her, betraying her… Betraying your marriage vows, that's the wrong way. I have been such a coward," he repeated. "And you… You were brave. You stood out there in the rain and you demanded more for both of us. I was the one who could not give that to you. But I asked you to come here today not to discuss custody, and not even to sign over the house and Tanner Investments."

"Really?" The word was soft, strangled.

"I asked you to come here today because I needed to ask the impossible of you one more time."

Hope, joy and pain washed over her in equal measure. "It doesn't hurt to ask."

"I am a man with nothing. Being with me will give you nothing. The house is yours. The company is yours. I have nothing to offer you but myself, and it is a sorry offering indeed. This place is yours. You could have me thrown out for trespassing, erase my name from the door at Tanner Investments as though I were never there. The power is yours. But I need to ask this. Please forgive me. Please give me a second chance."

She swallowed hard, using every ounce of her strength not to launch herself over the desk and throw herself into his arms. "Why? Why should I give you a second chance now?" She was trembling. Inside and out. "The house, the company. None of that means a damn thing, you foolish man. I was ready to leave it all. I don't want it. The only thing that matters is your heart. Are you prepared to give the impossible back to me?"

He rounded the desk, moving to stand in front of her, taking her hand in his, his dark eyes blazing into hers. "No," he said, "no, I'm not."

Her heart sank down into her stomach. "Oh."

"Because loving you was *never* impossible. And you should never have felt as though it was."

A rush of breath escaped her lips. "I'm sorry, you're going to have to be a little bit more explicit."

"I love you, Rose. When everything inside of me was

a lie, you were the truth. When I knew nothing, I knew you. When I lost touch with everything, with the man I was, the man I wanted to be, you brought me back home. I loved you, but I was afraid to embrace you. And I love you now, without fear. Without reservation."

She was trembling. Shaking from her core. She could scarcely breathe, scarcely speak. But one thing was certain. No matter the pain they had endured together, no matter who owned the house, no matter how she'd been hurt by his rejection...

Her love for him remained.

"Tell me more," she said.

"I love you," he ground out. "And I am terrified to my soul over it. It is why I ran from you, so far and so fast. It's why I'm giving you all of these things...my possessions, because I feel too unequal, too empty to offer only myself. I am a sinner, Rose. Some would say beyond redemption. Perhaps they are correct. Perhaps I have no right to ask for love, not after what I've done. But I am. Because I have to. As certainly as I have to breathe to live, I have to love you. And beg for your love in return."

A tear slid down her cheek, the clouds parting in her soul and allowing a shaft of light to shine through.

Hope.

It was brighter than fear. Brighter than anger. Stronger than pain. It flooded her, warmed her. And she knew that this was the moment. When she stayed safe, but wounded, hiding in the dark.

Or when she stepped into the light and embraced forgiveness. Redemption. Love.

There was no question. Because all she had ever wanted was there, in the light. And all she had to do was reach out and take him.

"Oh, Leon, I love you, too." She wrapped her arms

around his neck, kissing him on the cheek, the jaw, the corner of his mouth. "I really do."

"Why do you love me?" he asked, the words raw and tortured.

She traced his features with her fingertips, memorized his face. "That is the hardest and easiest question. Sometimes I think my love for you simply walked in right along with you, that very first day you came to Tanner house. That in that moment it lodged itself in me, and I have never been free of it since. But it's more than that. Deeper. You always saw me. Who I could be. Not just the small, mousy creature I felt like. And you challenged me. In a lot of ways I wish you hadn't. And in the years since, in this moment, it has become a choice. One I have made knowing you, all of you. Your perfections and your broken edges. It is more precious because of that. More real. More costly and more special than you'll ever know."

"I know you have no reason to trust me."

"That isn't true. Because for all your sins you didn't lie to me."

"Except for the marriage vows."

"Yes. That was wrong of you. Though given the circumstances…you were not given much choice but to marry me out of your loyalty to my father." She cleared her throat. "I never went and asked you for what I wanted. You know, before your accident, I was going to ask you for a divorce."

He took a step back. "You were?"

"Yes. I thought I was being brave. I thought I was moving on with my life by separating from you. But the simple fact is I was just running. I either hid, or I ran. But I certainly never asked you for what I wanted."

"Ask me," he said, his voice raw as he gathered her back into his arms. "Ask me now."

"Be my husband. In every sense of the word. Love me. Love our children, and in that I include Isabella. Be faithful to me."

"I swear it," he said. "With all of the memories of my grief, all of the memories of my sins, with the man I have been and the man I hope to be, I swear it. I will be your husband, I will forsake all others and I will do it happily. I will choose love over fear, every day. And some days I know it will have to be a choice, a very purposeful choice, but I swear to you that I will come to you when it threatens to overwhelm me."

"So will I. I'm not going to stay silent when I want something from you. I'm going to tell you."

"Good."

"I might make your life a living hell."

He cupped her cheek, skimming his thumb over her cheekbone. "The only living hell I can imagine is a life without you. I know what love costs, Rose. I know it better than most. And I choose it anyway. I choose you." He leaned in, kissing her lips lightly. "When I say that I love you it is with the knowledge of what that might cost. When I say that I love you, you can trust that it's real."

"I do," she said, her lips brushing against his as she spoke.

Rose remembered clearly being told that Leon's survival was a miracle after the accident. And it was. But here in her home—their home—safe in his embrace, she understood that survival wasn't the true miracle.

It was living.

EPILOGUE

LEON REMARRIED ROSE the following year. It was entirely different to that first wedding three years earlier. When a pale, young bride had walked toward him, unsure of what exactly she was getting herself into.

Giving herself to a man she knew didn't love her.

Things had changed. He had changed.

Today, when Rose walked down the aisle toward him, it wasn't in a heavy veil that concealed her face from him. Today, she had her hair loose, with a crown of pink flowers adding a pop of brightness to her pale blonde beauty.

Her dress was simple. Long and flowing, swirling around her feet. She looked like an angel. And if anyone would have asked, he would have said that Rose Tanner was, without a doubt, his angel.

She had saved him. From his grief. From loneliness. And most especially from himself.

This time, when he took her hands in his and made vows, they were vows he had written himself. Vows that came from his heart, not from tradition. Not from anyone else.

"Rose, I made promises to you once before. But they were empty. I didn't keep them. I spoke the words, but I didn't make vows. But now…now I'm making vows. You're the reason my heart beats. You're the reason I live. The reason I love. I promise you my life. I promise my love and my fidelity. I know there is no happiness for me outside of this, outside of us. I spent years taking you for granted. I spent years squandering what we could have had. I was given a precious gift, and I was far too lost to truly appreciate it." He tightened his hold on her hands. "But now I know. I have seen death, Rose. And I have lived it. A sort of survival that isn't living at all, just breathing. But you…you are life. My life. My breath. My truth."

When they had finished speaking their vows, Rose turned and took Isabella from the arms of her maid of honor, holding the little girl—who was growing far too quickly for Leon's taste—close. "I promise to love you, too," she whispered. "We're a family."

Leon took hold of his daughter's hand. "You both have me. My heart. Always."

Later, there was cake, and there was dancing. And a very cranky Isabella had to be taken back to the house by the nanny.

But Leon and Rose stayed, until the very last song. He held her tightly against him, letting the music wrap itself around them.

The whole world, all of the people, the past and everyone in it, fell away.

And all he could see were Rose's blue eyes.

* * * * *

CAPTIVATED BY THE GREEK

JULIA JAMES

For carers everywhere - you are all saints!

CHAPTER ONE

Nikos Parakis twisted his wrist slightly to glance at his watch and frowned. If he wanted to make his appointment in the City he was going to have to skip lunch. No way could he fit in a midday meal now, having delayed leaving his Holland Park apartment—his base in the UK—in order to catch a lengthy teleconference with Russian clients. He'd also, on this early summer's day, wanted to get some fresh air and brief exercise, so had dismissed his driver and intended to pick up a taxi on the far side of the park, in Kensington High Street.

As he gained the wide tree-lined pavement he felt a stab of hunger. He definitely needed refuelling.

On impulse, he plunged across the road and headed for what appeared to be some kind of takeaway food shop. He was no food snob, despite the wealth of the Parakis banking dynasty at his disposal, and a sandwich was a sandwich—wherever it came from.

The moment he stepped inside, however, he almost changed his mind. Fast food outlets specialising in pre-packed sandwiches had come a long way in thirty years, but this was one of the old-fashioned ones where sandwiches were handmade on the spot, to order, constructed out of the array of ingredients contained in plastic tubs behind the counter.

Damn, he thought, irritated, he really didn't have time for this.

But he was here now, and it would have to do.

'Have you anything ready-made?' he asked, addressing the person behind the counter. He didn't mean to sound brusque, but he was hungry and in a hurry.

The server, who had her back to him, went on buttering a slice of bread. Nikos felt irritation kick again.

'She's making mine first, mate,' said a voice nearby, and he saw that there was a shabbily dressed, grizzled-looking old man seated on a chair by the chilled drinks cabinet. 'You'll 'ave ter wait.'

Nikos's mouth pressed tight, and he moved his annoyed regard back to the figure behind the counter. Without turning, the server spoke.

'Be with you in a sec,' she said, apparently to Nikos, and started to pile ham onto the buttered slice before wrapping the sandwich in a paper serviette and turning to hand it to the man. She pushed a cup of milky tea towards him, too.

'Ta, luv,' the man said, moving to stand closer to Nikos than he felt entirely comfortable with.

Whenever the man had last bathed, it hadn't been recently. Nor had he shaved. Moreover, there was a discernible smell of stale alcohol about him.

The man closed grimy fingers around the wrapped sandwich, picked up the mug in a shaky grip and looked at Nikos.

'Any spare change, guv?' he asked hopefully.

'No,' said Nikos, and turned back to the server, who was now wiping the sandwich preparation surface clean.

The old man shuffled out.

The server's voice followed him. 'Stay off the booze, Joe—it's killing you.'

'Any day now, luv, any day…' the man assured her.

He shuffled out and was gone, lunch provided. Presumably for free, Nikos supposed, having seen no money change hands for the transaction. But his interest in the matter was zero, and with the server finally free to pay him attention, he repeated his original question about the availability of ready-made sandwiches—this time most definitely impatiently.

'No,' replied the server, turning around and busying herself with the tea urn.

Her tone of voice had changed. If Nikos could have been bothered to care—which he didn't, in the slightest—he might have said she sounded annoyed.

'Then whatever's quickest.'

He glanced at his watch again, and frowned. This was ridiculous—he was wasting time instead of saving it!

'What would you like?'

The server's pointless question made his frown deepen.

'I said whatever's quickest,' he repeated.

'That,' came the reply, 'would be bread and butter.'

Nikos dropped his wrist and levelled his gaze right at her. There was no mistaking the antagonism in her tone. Or the open irritation in his as he answered.

'Ham,' he bit out.

'On white or brown? Baguette or sliced?'

'Whatever's quickest.' How many times did he have to *say* that?

'That would be white sliced.'

'White sliced, then.'

'Just ham?'

'Yes.' Anything more complicated and he'd be there all day.

She turned away and busied herself at the preparation surface behind her. Nikos drummed his fingers on the counter. Realising he was thirsty, he twisted round to help himself to a bottle of mineral water from the chilled drinks cabinet against the wall.

As he put it on the counter the server turned round, sandwich prepared and wrapped in a paper serviette. She glanced at the bottle and Nikos could see she was mentally calculating the combined price.

'Three pounds forty-five,' she said.

He had his wallet out already, taking out a note.

'That's a *fifty*,' she said, as if she'd never seen one before.

Perhaps she never had, thought Nikos acidly. He said nothing, just went on holding it out for her.

'Haven't you anything smaller?' she demanded.

'No.'

With a rasp of irritation she snatched it from him and opened the till. There was some audible clinking and rustling, and a moment later she was clunking his change down on the countertop. It consisted of silver to make it up to a fiver, a single twenty-pound note and twenty-five individual pound coins.

Then she raised her gaze to Nikos and glared at him.

And for the first time Nikos looked at her.

Looked at her—and *saw* her.

He stilled completely. Somewhere inside his head a voice was telling him to stop staring, to pick up the ludicrous heap of coins and pocket the note and get the hell out of there. Get a taxi, get to his meeting, get on with the rest of his life and forget he'd ever been hungry enough to step into some two-bit sandwich bar patronised by alcoholic down-and-outs.

But the voice went totally and entirely unheeded.

Right now only one part of his brain was functioning. The part that was firing in instant, total intensity with the most visceral masculine response he had ever experienced in his life.

Thee mou, but she was absolutely beautiful.

There was no other word for her. In an instant Nikos took in a face that was sculpted to perfection: high cheekbones, contoured jawline, straight nose not a millimetre too long or too short, wide-set eyes of startling blue, and a mouth… Ah, a mouth whose natural lushness was as inviting as a honey-drenched dessert…

How the hell didn't I notice her straight away?

But the question searing through him was irrelevant. Everything right now was irrelevant except his desire—his need—to keep drinking her in. Taking in the incredible impact her stunning looks were having on him. His eyes narrowed in their instinctive, potent perusal of her features, and he felt his response course through him.

He was not a man who had been deprived of the company of beautiful women in his thirty-odd years. As the heir to the Parakis banking dynasty he'd become accustomed to having the hottest girls making a beeline for him. And he knew that it wasn't just the Parakis millions that drew them in. Nature, for whatever capricious reason, had bestowed upon him a six-foot frame—which he kept in peak condition with rigorous and ruthless physical exercise—and looks that, without vanity, he knew women liked. Liked a lot.

The combination had proved highly successful, and his private life was plentifully supplied by any number of keen and eager females only too happy to be seen on his arm, or to keep him company in bed. Given that, therefore, it would have been perverse of him not to have chosen those females who were of the very highest calibre when it came to their appearance.

And this woman, who had drawn his attention so rivetingly, was most definitely of that elite calibre.

His gaze worked over her, and as it did so another realisation struck him. She wasn't wearing a trace of make-up and her hair—blonde, from what little he could see of it—was concealed under some kind of baseball cap. As for her figure—although she appeared to be tall—she was clad in a baggy T-shirt that bore the legend 'Sarrie's Sarnies' and did less than nothing for her.

Hell, if she looked this good stuck in this dump, dressed in grunge, what would she look like dressed in designer labels?

For a moment—just a moment—he felt an overriding desire to put that to the test.

Then, in the next second, he crashed and burned.

'If you want a piece of meat, try a butcher's shop!'

The server's harsh voice cut right through Nikos's riveted attention to her physical attributes.

A frown of incomprehension—and annoyance—pulled his brows together.

'What?' he demanded.

Her face was set. Absently Nikos noted how looking angry actually made her even more stunning. Her cerulean eyes flashed like sapphires.

'Don't give me that,' she snapped. 'Now, take your change, *and* your damn sandwich, and go!'

It was Nikos's turn to experience anger. His face hardened. 'Your rudeness to a customer,' he said freezingly, 'is totally unacceptable. Were you one of *my* employees you would be dismissed instantly for taking such an attitude to those whose custom pays your wages.'

For answer, she put the palms of her hands on the counter—Nikos found himself noting how well shaped they were—and braced herself.

'And if I worked for *you*—which, thank God, I don't—I would be suing *you* for sexual harassment!' she bit back. Her eyes narrowed to slits. '*That's* what I meant by wanting "meat", sunshine!'

Nikos's expression changed. The hardness was still in his eyes, but there was something else, too. A glint that, had the stunning but inexplicably bolshie female facing him been one of his acquaintances, she would have known sent a crystal-clear message.

'Since when is it illegal to admire a woman's beauty?' he riposted silkily.

To prove his point he let his gaze wash over her again. Inside him, the visceral reaction she'd aroused so powerfully warred with the irritation he'd felt ever since his hunger had hit him—an irritation that her hostility and rudeness had elevated to outright anger. He wasn't sure which emotion was predominant. What he *was* sure of, though, was that right now his overpowering desire was to rattle her cage…

'If you *want* to go round ogling women like *meat*, then you should damn well wear sunglasses and spare us the ordeal,' she shot back.

Nikos felt yet another emotion spark through him. Almost unconsciously, he found himself starting to enjoy himself.

One arched eyebrow quirked tauntingly. 'Ordeal?' he asked limpidly.

And then, quite deliberately, he let his gaze soften. No longer assessing. More…caressing. Letting her see clearly that women who received his approbation most definitely did not regard it as an *ordeal*…

And before his eyes, to his intense satisfaction, he saw a wave of colour suffuse her clear, translucent skin. Her cheeks grew stained and her gaze dropped.

'Go away,' she said. Her voice was tight. 'Just...*go away*!'

He gave a low laugh. *Game, set and match—thank you very much.* He didn't need any further confirmation to know that he'd just effortlessly breached her defences...got right past that bolshie anger barrier and hit home, sweet home.

With a sweeping gesture he scooped the pile of coins into his pocket, together with the solitary twenty-pound note, then picked up his ham sandwich and the bottle of water.

'Have a nice day,' he said flippantly, and strolled out of the sandwich shop.

His irritation was gone completely.

As he emerged he saw the down-and-out, Joe, leaning against a nearby lamppost, wolfing down the sandwich he had been given. On impulse, Nikos reached into his jacket pocket, jingling with all the pound coins she'd landed him with.

He scooped up a handful and proffered them. 'You asked about spare change,' he said to the man, who was eyeing him.

'Ta, guv,' said the man, and took the handful eagerly, his bloodshot eyes gleaming.

His grimy hands were shaking, and Nikos felt a pang of pity go through him.

'She's right, you know,' he heard himself telling the man. 'The booze *is* killing you.'

The bloodshot eyes met his. They were not gleaming now. There was desolation in them.

'I know, mate...'

He pulled his gaze away and then he was off again, shuffling down the street, pocketing the money, shoulders hunched in defeat. For a moment Nikos's eyes stayed on him. Then he saw a taxi cab approaching along the High Street, with its 'For Hire' sign illuminated. He flagged it down and flung himself into the back seat, starting to wolf down his ham sandwich.

His own words to the down-and-out echoed in his head. *'She's right, you know...'*

His jaw tightened. Damn—she was, too. And not just about that wretched alcoholic.

Finishing his sandwich, he lifted his mobile phone from his inside pocket and pressed the speed-dial key for his London PA. She answered immediately, and Nikos gave her his instructions.

'Janine, I need to have some flowers delivered...'

Mel stood, palms still pressed into the surface of the counter, and glared after the tall retreating figure. She was mad—totally hopping mad. She hadn't been this angry since she couldn't remember when.

Damn the arrogance of the man!

She could feel her jaw still clenching. She hadn't liked him the moment he'd walked into the shop. The way he'd spoken—not even waiting for her to turn around to him, just making his demands as if she was some kind of servant. Underling. Minion. *Lackey.* The insulting words marched through her head.

She'd tried for her customary politeness while she was finishing Joe's sandwich, but then she'd caught the way the damn man had looked at Joe—as if he was a bad smell. Well, yes, he was—but that wasn't the point. The point was that Joe was in a bad way, and for heaven's sake *anyone* would have felt pity for the guy, surely? Especially—and now her jaw clenched even more—especially a man whom life had so obviously *not* treated anything *like* as grimly as it had poor old Joe.

That had put her back up straight away. And from then on it had just got worse.

The whole monosyllabic exchange about what kind of sandwich he'd wanted replayed itself in her head, followed by—oh yes—his dropping a fifty-pound note down in payment. Mel's mouth tightened in satisfaction. Well, it had given her particular pleasure to dump all those pound coins on him by way of change.

Boy, it had riled him—she had seen that immediately. Trouble was…and now her expression changed yet again, to a mix of anger and something else quite entirely…he had had that comeback on her…

Right through her body she could feel the heat flush. It was running right through her—through every vein, right out to the tips of her fingers—as though someone has tipped hot water into her. And to her own mortification she even felt glorious heat pooling in her core, felt her breasts start to tingle with traitorous reaction.

Oh, damn! Damn, damn, damn!

Yet she couldn't stop herself. Couldn't stop the memory—instant, vivid and overpowering—of the way he'd looked at her. Looked *right* at her. Looked her over…

Meat, she said desperately to herself. *As if you were a piece of meat—that's how he looked at you. Just as you told him.*

She fought to call back the burst of satisfaction she'd felt when she'd rapped that out at him, but it was impossible. All that was possible now was to go on feeling the wonderful flush of heat coursing through her. She fought it down as best she could, willing it to leave her—to leave her alone—just as she'd told him to go, just *go away…*

She shut her eyes, sighing heavily—hopelessly. *OK—OK*, she reasoned, *so face it*. However rude, arrogant and obnoxious he was, he was also—yup, she had to admit it—absolutely, totally and completely drop-dead *devastating*.

She'd registered it instantly—it would have been impossible not to—the minute she'd turned round with Joe's sandwich to see just who it was who'd spoken to her in such a brusque, demanding fashion. Registered it, but had promptly busied herself in making Joe's tea, pinning her eyes on pouring it out and ladling sugar into it the way Joe needed it.

But she'd been conscious of that first glimpse of Mr Drop-dead Devastating burning a hole in her retina—burning its way into her brain—so that all she'd wanted to do was lift her gaze and let it do what it had been trying to do with an urgency she still bewailed and berated.

Which was simply to stare and stare and stare…

At *everything* about him.

His height…his lean, fit body, sheathed in that hand-tailored suit that had fitted him like a glove, reaching across wide shoulders and moulding his broad chest just as the expanse of pristine white shirt had.

But it wasn't his designer suit or even his lean physique that was dominating her senses now.

It was his eyes. Eyes that were night-dark and like tempered steel in a face that was constructed in some particular way that outdid every male she'd ever seen—on-screen or off. Chiselled jaw, strong nose, tough-looking cheekbones, winged brows and always, *always*, those ludicrously long-lashed, gold-flecked eyes that were lethal weapons entirely on their own.

That was what she'd wanted to gaze at, and that was what had been searing through her head all through their snarling exchange.

And then, as if a switch had been thrown, he'd suddenly changed the subject...

More heat coursed through her as the physical memory of how he'd looked at her hit her again. Turning the blatant focus of his male reaction on her like a laser beam. One that had burned right through her.

The slow wash of his gaze had poured over her like warm, molten honey—like a silken touch to her skin. It had felt as though he were caressing her, as if she could actually feel his hands shaping her body, his mouth lowering to hers to taste, to tease...to arouse.

All that in a single sensual glance...

And then, when she'd been helpless—pathetically, abjectly helpless—to do anything other than tell him—beg him—to leave, what had he done? He'd *laughed*! Laughed at her—knowing perfectly well how he'd got the better of her, how he'd made a cringing mockery of her defiance.

The colour in her cheeks turned to hectic spots as anger burned out that shaming blush he'd conjured in her.

Damn him!

Fuming, she went on staring blindly out through the shop door. She could no longer see him. With a final damning adjuration to herself to stop thinking of him, and everything about him, she whirled around to get on with her work.

Washing up had never been so noisy, nor slicing bread so vicious.

CHAPTER TWO

'DID YOU HAVE those flowers delivered?'

It was the first question Nikos found himself asking as he returned to his London office after his meeting that afternoon. He did not doubt that his PA had complied, for she was efficiency itself—and she was used to despatching flowers to the numerous assorted females that featured in his life when he was in the UK.

But not usually to females who worked in sandwich bars...

Mouthy, contrary females who gave him a hard time...

Possessed of looks so stunning he still could not get them out of his head...

He gave a shake of his head, clearing the memory and settling himself down at his desk. There really was no point thinking about the blonde any more. Let alone speculating, as he found himself wanting to do, on just what she might look like if she were dressed in an outfit that adorned her extraordinary beauty.

How much more beautiful could she look?

The question rippled through his mind, and in its wake came a ripple of something that was not idle speculation but desire...

With her hair loosened, a gown draping her slen-

der yet rounded figure, her sapphire eyes luminous and long-lashed...

He cut the image. She'd been a fleeting fiery encounter and nothing more.

No, he thought decisively, switching on his PC, he'd sent flowers to atone for his rudeness—provoking though *she'd* been—and he would leave it at that. He had women enough to choose from—no need to add another one.

He flicked open his diary to see what was coming up in the remainder of his sojourn in London. His father, chairman of the family-run Athens-based investment bank, left that city reluctantly these days, and Nikos found himself doing nearly all the foreign travel that running the bank required.

A frown moved fleetingly across his brow. At least here in London he was spared his father's wandering into the office to make one of his habitual complaints about Nikos's mother. The moment Nikos got back to Athens, though, he knew there would be a litany of complaints awaiting him, while his father indulged himself and offloaded. Then—predictably—the next time he saw his mother a reciprocal litany would be pressed upon him...

With a sigh of exasperation he pushed his interminably warring parents out of his head space. There was never going to be an end to their virulent verbal attacks on each other, their incessant sniping and backbiting. It had gone on for as long as Nikos could remember, and he was more than fed up with it.

Briskly, he ran an eye down the diary page and then frowned again—for quite a different reason this time.

Damn.

His frown deepened. How had he got himself involved in *that*? A black-tie charity bash at the Viscari St James Hotel this coming Friday evening.

In itself, that would not have been a problem. What *was* a problem, though, was that he could see from the diary that the evening included Fiona Pellingham. Right now that woman was *not* someone he wanted to encounter.

A high-flying mergers-and-acquisitions expert at a leading business consultancy, Fiona had taken an obvious shine to Nikos during a business meeting on his last visit to London, and had made it strikingly clear to him that she'd very much like to make an acquisition of *him* for herself.

But for all her striking brunette looks and svelte figure she was, as Nikos had immediately realised, the possessive type, and she would want a great deal more from him than the passing affair that was all he ever indulged in when it came to women. And that meant that the last thing he wanted to do was to give her an opportunity to pursue her obvious interest in him.

He frowned again. The problem was, even if he didn't go to this charity bash she'd somehow put into his diary, Fiona would probably find another way to pursue him. Plague him with yet more invitations and excuses to meet up with him. What he needed was to put her off completely. Convince her he was unavailable romantically.

What he needed was a handy, convenient female he could take along with him on Friday to keep Fiona at bay. But just who would fit that bill? For a moment his mind was totally, absolutely blank. Then, in the proverbial light-bulb moment, he knew exactly who he wanted to take. And the knowledge made him sit back abruptly and hear the question shaping itself inside his head.

Well, after all, why not? You did want to know just how much more beautiful she could look if she were dressed for the evening...

This would be a chance to find out—why not take it?

A slow smile started to curve his mouth.

Mel was staring at the cluttered table in the back room behind the sandwich bar. She didn't see the clutter—all she saw was the huge bouquet that sat in its own cellophane container of water, its opulent blooms as large as her fists. A bouquet that was so over-the-top it was ridiculous. Her eyes were stormy.

Who the hell did he think he was?

Except that she knew the answer to that, because his name came at the end of the message on the card in the envelope pinned to the cellophane.

Hope these make amends and improve your mood.

It was signed 'Nikos Parakis.'

Her brows lowered. So he was Greek. It made sense, now she thought about it, because although his English accent had been perfect, his clipped public-school vowels a perfect match with the rest of his 'Mr Rich' look, nevertheless his complexion had a distinctly Mediterranean hue to it, and his hair was as dark as a raven's wing.

Even as she thought about it his image sprang into her vision again—and with it the expression in those dark, long-lashed eyes that had looked her over, assessing her, clearly liking what he saw...

As if he was finding me worthy of his attentions!

She bristled all over again, fulminating as she glared at the hapless bouquet of lilies. Their heady scent filled the small space, obliterating the smell of food that always permeated the room from the sandwich bar beyond. The scent made her feel light-headed. Its strength was almost overpowering, sending coils of fragrance into her lungs. Exotic, perfumed…sensuous.

As sensuous as his gaze had been.

That betraying heat started to flush up inside her again, and with a growl of anger at her own imbecility she wheeled about. She had no idea where she was going to put the ridiculously over-the-top bouquet, but right now she had work to do.

She was manning the sandwich bar on her own because Sarrie himself was on holiday. She didn't mind because he was paying her extra, and every penny was bankable.

As she returned to her post behind the counter, checking what was left of the day's ingredients and lifting out a tub of sliced tomatoes from the fridge, she deliberately busied herself running over her mental accounts. It stopped her thinking about that ridiculous bouquet—and the infuriating man who'd sent it to her.

OK, so where was she in her savings? She ran the figures through her head, feeling a familiar sense of satisfaction and reassurance as she did so. She'd worked flat-out these last twelve months, and now she was almost, *almost* at the point of setting off on her dream.

To travel. To leave the UK and see the world! To make a reality of all the places she'd only ever read about. Europe, the Med, even the USA—and maybe even further…South America, the Far East and Australia.

She'd never been abroad in her life.

A sigh escaped her. She shouldn't feel deprived because she hadn't travelled abroad. Gramps hadn't liked 'abroad.' He hadn't liked foreign travel. The south coast had been about as far as he'd been prepared to go.

'Nothing wrong with Bognor,' he'd used to tell her. 'Or Brighton. Or Bournemouth.'

So that was where they'd gone for their annual summer holiday every year until she was a teenager. And for many years it had been fine—she'd loved the beach, even on her own with no brothers or sisters to play with. She'd had her grandfather, who'd raised her ever since his daughter and son-in-law had been killed in the same motorway pile-up that had killed his wife.

Looking back with adult eyes, she knew that having his five-year-old granddaughter to care for after the wholesale slaughter of the rest of his family had been her grandfather's salvation. And he, in return, had become her rock—the centre of her world, the only person in the entire universe who loved her.

When she'd finished with school and started a Business Studies degree course at a nearby college, she'd opted to continue to live at home, in the familiar semi-detached house in the north London suburb she'd grown up in.

'I'd be daft to move out, Gramps. Student accommodation costs a fortune, and most of the flats are complete dumps.'

Though she'd meant it, she'd also known that her grandfather had been relieved that she'd stayed at home with him.

It hadn't cramped her social life to be living at home still, and she'd revelled in student life like any eighteen-year-old, enjoying her fair share of dating. It hadn't been until she'd met Jak in her second year that things had become serious. He'd taken her seriously, too, seeing past her dazzling looks to the person within, and soon they'd become an item.

Had she been in love with him? She'd discovered the answer to that at the end of their studies. Not enough to dedicate her life to him the way he'd wanted her to.

'I've got a job with the charity I applied for—out in Africa. I'm going to be teaching English, building schools, digging wells. It's what I've always dreamed of.' He'd paused, looking at Mel straight on. 'Will you come with me? Support me in my work? Make your life with me?'

It had been the question she'd known was coming— the question she'd only been able to answer one way. Whether or not she'd wanted to join Jak in his life's work, it had been impossible anyway.

'I can't,' she'd said. 'I can't leave Gramps.'

Because by then that was what it had come down to. In the three years of her being a student her grandfather had aged—had crossed that invisible but irreversible boundary from being the person who had raised her and looked after her to being someone who now looked to her to look after *him*. The years had brought heart problems—angina and mini-strokes—but far worse than his growing physical frailty had been the mental frailty that had come with it. Mel had known with sadness and a sinking heart that he had become more and more dependent on her.

She hadn't been able to leave him. How could she have deserted him, the grandfather she loved so much? How could she have abandoned him when he'd needed her? She had only been able to wait, putting her own life on hold and devoting herself to the one relative she'd possessed: the grandfather who loved her.

The months had turned into years—three whole years—until finally he'd left her in the only way that a frail, ill old man could leave his granddaughter.

She'd wept—but not only from grief. There had been relief, too—she knew that. Relief for him, that at last he was freed from his failing body, his faltering mind. And relief, too, for herself.

She hadn't been able to deny, though it had hurt to think it, that now, after his death, she was freed of all responsibility. Her grandfather had escaped the travails of life and by doing so had given Mel her own life back—given back to her what she wanted most of all to claim.

Her freedom.

Freedom to do what she had long dreamt of doing. To travel! To travel as she'd never had the opportunity to do—to travel wherever the wind blew her, wherever took her fancy. See the world.

But to do that she needed money. Money she'd been unable to earn for herself when she'd become her grandfather's carer. Yes, she had some money, because her grandfather had left her his savings—but that would be needed, as a safe nest egg, for when she finally returned to the UK to settle down and build a career for herself. So to fund her longed-for travels she was working all the hours she could—Sarrie's Sarnies by day, and waitressing in a nearby restaurant by night.

And soon—oh, *very* soon—she'd be off and away. Picking up a cheap last-minute flight and heading wherever the spirit took her until the money ran out, when she'd come back home to settle down.

If she ever did come back…

Maybe I'll never come back. Maybe I'll stay footloose all my life. Never be tied down again by anything or anyone! Free as a bird!

Devoted as she had been to her grandfather, after years of caring for him such freedom was a heady prospect.

So, too, was the looking forward to another element of youth that she had set aside till now.

Romance.

Since Jak had gone to Africa and she'd stayed behind to look after her grandfather romance had been impossible. In the early days she'd managed to go on a couple of dates, but as her grandfather's health had worsened those moments had become less and less. But now... Oh, now romance could blossom again—and she'd welcome it with open arms.

She knew exactly what she wanted at this juncture of her life. Nothing intense or serious, as her relationship with Jak had been. Nothing long-term, as he had hoped things would be between them. No, for now all she craved was the heady buzz of eyes meeting across a crowded room, mutual desire acknowledged and fulfilled—frothy, carefree, self-indulgent fun. *That* was what she longed for now.

Her mouth curved in a cynical smile and her eyes sparked. Well, that attitude should make her popular. Men were habitually wary of women who wanted more from them—they were the ones who didn't like clingy women, who didn't want to be tied down. Who liked to enjoy their pick of women as and when they fancied.

The cynical smile deepened. She'd bet money that Nikos Parakis was a man like that. Looking her over the way he had...

As she started to serve a new customer who'd just walked in she shook her head clear of the memory. She had better things to do than speculate about the love life of Nikos Parakis—or speculate about anything to do with him at all.

Soon his extravagantly OTT flowers would fade, and so would her memory of the intemperate encounter between them today. And eventually so would the disturbingly vivid memory of the physical impact he'd made on her, with his dark, devastating looks. And that, she said to herself firmly, would be that.

'What kind of sandwich would you like?' she asked brightly of her customer, and got on with her job.

'Pull over just there,' Nikos instructed his driver, who duly slid the sleek top-of-the-range BMW to the side of the road to let his employer get out.

Emerging, Nikos glanced along the pavement, observing for a moment or two the comings and goings at the sandwich bar and wondering whether he was being a complete idiot for doing what he was about to do.

He'd reflected on the decision on the way here from the Parakis offices, changing his mind several times. The idea that had struck him the day before when faced with the prospect of enduring an evening of Fiona Pellingham trying to corner him had stayed with him, and he'd reviewed it from all angles several times. But he'd found that whenever he'd lined up all his objections—she was a complete stranger, she was bolshie, she might not even possess an evening gown suitable for the highly upmarket Viscari St James—they'd promptly all collapsed under the one overwhelming reason he *wanted* her to accompany him on Friday evening.

Which was the fact that he could not get her out of his head.

And he could think of nothing else except wanting to see her again.

The same overwhelming urge possessed him again now—to feast his eyes on her, drink her in and feel, yet again, that incredible visceral kick he'd got from her. Anticipation rose pleasurably through him.

He glanced at his watch. It was near the end of the working day so she should be shutting up shop soon—these old-fashioned sandwich bars did not stay open in the evening. He strolled towards the entrance, pushed the door open with the flat of his palm and walked in. There was only one other customer inside, and Nikos could see he was handing over his money, taking his wrapped sandwich with him.

Serving him was the blonde, bolshie, bad-attitude total stunner.

Instantly Nikos's eyes went straight to her and stayed there, riveted.

Yes! The affirmation of all that he'd remembered about the impact she'd had on him surged through Nikos. She was as fantastic now as she had been then. Face, figure—the whole package. Burning right into his retinas, all over again.

Oh, yes, definitely—most definitely—this was the right decision to have made.

'Here's your change,' he heard her say to her customer as he paused just inside the door. Her voice was cheerful, her expression smiling.

No sign, Nikos noted with caustic observation, of the bolshiness she'd targeted *him* with. But what he was noticing more was the way that her quick smile only enhanced the perfection of her features, lending her mouth a sinuous curve and warming her sapphire eyes. He could feel his pulse give a discernible kick at the sight of her smile, even though it wasn't directed at him.

What will it feel like when she smiles at me? he wondered to himself. But he knew the answer already.

Good—that was what it would feel like.

And more than good. *Inviting...*

But just as this pleasurable thought was shaping in his brain he saw her eyes glance towards the latest person to come in—himself—and immediately her expression changed. She waited only before her customer had quit the shop before launching her attack.

'What are *you* doing here?' she demanded.

Nikos strolled forward, and it gave him particular satisfaction to see her take a half-step back, defensively. It meant she felt the need to raise her defences about him—and *that* meant, he knew with every masculine instinct, that she was vulnerable to him—vulnerable to the effect he was having on her. The effect he *wanted* to have on her.

He had seen it in her eyes, in the way they had suddenly been veiled—but not soon enough to conceal the betraying leap of emotion within.

It was an emotion that was as old as time, and one he'd seen before when he'd deliberately let his gaze wash over her, making his own reaction to her beauty as tangible as a caress...

And, veiled though it had been, it told him all he needed to know. That in spite of her outward bristling towards him, behind that layer of defence, she was reacting to him as strongly, as powerfully, as he was to her.

And once again he felt satisfaction spread through him at the knowledge that she was as reactive to him as he was to her—as powerfully attracted to him as he was to her—oh, yes, most definitely.

His eyes flickered over her again. He felt an overwhelming urge to drink her in, to remind himself of just what it was she had that so drew him to her. That extraordinary beauty she possessed was undimmed, even in these workaday surroundings and even clad as she was in that unprepossessing T-shirt. She had made not the slightest adornment to her natural beauty by way of make-up or styling her hair—most of which was still concealed under that unlovely baseball cap.

'I wanted to see you again,' he told her, coming up to the counter.

She stood her ground—he could see her doing it—but her figure had stiffened.

'Why?' she countered, making her expression stony.

He ignored her question. 'Did you get my flowers?' he asked. He kept his voice casual, kept his own eyes veiled now—for the time being.

'Yes.' The single-word answer was tight and...unappreciative.

An eyebrow quirked. 'They were not to your taste?'

Her chin lifted. 'I bet you don't even know what they are. I bet you just told your secretary to send them.'

His mouth indented. 'I suspect they will be lilies,' he answered. 'My PA likes lilies.'

'Well, send them to *her* next time!' was the immediate retort.

'But my PA,' he returned, entering into the spirit of their sparring, 'was not the one I needed to apologise to. And besides...' his dark eyes glinted '...*she* wasn't the one whose mood needed improving.'

It was deliberate baiting—and unwise, considering he wanted her to accept his invitation for the evening, but he couldn't resist the enjoyment of sparring with her and it got him his reward. That coruscating sapphire flash of her eyes—making her beautiful eyes even more outstanding.

'Well, they *didn't* improve my mood,' she snapped back. 'And you standing there doesn't either. So if that's all you came here to say, then consider it said.'

'It isn't,' said Nikos. His expression changed as he abandoned the sparring and became suddenly more businesslike. 'I have an invitation to put to you.'

For a moment she looked stupefied. Then, hard on the heels of that, deeply suspicious. 'What?'

'I would like,' Nikos informed her, 'to invite you to a charity gala this Friday night.'

'What?' The word came again, and an even more stupefied look.

'Allow me to elaborate,' said Nikos, and proceeded to do so.

His veiled eyes were watching for her reaction. Despite her overt hostility he could see that she was listening. Could see, too, that she was trying not to look at him. Trying to keep her eyes blank.

Trying—and failing.

She's aware of me, responsive to me—she's fighting it, but it's there all the same.

It flickered like electricity between them as he went on.

'I find,' he told her, keeping his tone bland and neutral, so as not to set her hackles rising again, 'that at short notice I am without a "plus one" for this Friday evening—a charity gala to which I am committed.' He looked at her straight on. 'Therefore I would be highly gratified if you would agree to be that "plus one" for the occasion. I'm sure you would find it enjoyable—it's at the Viscari St James Hotel, which I hope you will agree is a memorable venue.'

He paused minutely, then allowed his mouth to indent into a swift smile.

'Please say you'll come.'

Her expression was a study, and he enjoyed watching it. Stupefaction mixed with deep, deep suspicion. And even deeper scepticism.

'And of course, Mr Parakis, you have absolutely no one else you could possibly invite except a complete stranger—someone you told to her face you'd sack if she were unfortunate enough to be one of your hapless minions!' she finally shot at him, her head going back and her eyes sparking.

He was unfazed. 'Indeed,' he replied shamelessly. 'So, if you would be kind enough to take pity on my predicament and help me in my hour of need, my gratitude would know no bounds...'

A very unladylike snort escaped her. 'Yeah, right,' she managed to say derisively.

'It's quite true,' he answered limpidly. 'I *would* be extremely grateful.'

'And I'd be a complete mug to believe you,' she shot back.

Nikos's expression changed again. 'Why? What is the problem here for you?' His eyes rested on her, conveying a message older than time. 'Do you not know how extraordinarily beautiful you are? How any man would be privileged to have you at his side—?'

He saw the colour run out over her sculpted cheekbones. Saw her swallow.

'Will you not let me invite you?' he said again. There was the slightest husk in his voice. It was there without his volition.

Mixed emotions crossed her face. 'No,' she said finally—emphatically.

His eyebrows rose. 'Why not?' he asked outright.

Hers snapped together. 'Because I don't like you—that's why!'

He gave a half-laugh, discovering he was enjoying her bluntness. 'We got off to a bad start—I admit that freely. I was hungry and short-tempered, and you gave me a hard time and I resented it.'

'You spoke to me like I was beneath you,' she shot at him. 'And you looked down your nose at Joe—wouldn't give him a penny even though you're obviously rolling in it!' She cast a pointed look at him. 'Your wallet was stuffed with fifties!'

'Did you expect me to hand a fifty over to him?' he protested. 'And for your information I gave him a handful of all those pound coins you dumped on me.'

Mel's expression changed. '*What?* Oh, God, he'll have just gone off and spent it on booze.' Her eyes narrowed. 'Did you really give him money?'

'Ask him next time he comes in for a free sandwich,' said Nikos drily. 'So…' his voice changed '…are you going to take pity on me and accept my invitation?'

She was wavering—he could tell that with every male instinct. *She wants to accept, but her pride is holding her back.*

'You know,' he said temperately as her internal conflict played out in her betraying gaze, 'I really am quite safe. And very respectable, too. As is the Viscari St James Hotel and the charity gala.'

'You're a complete stranger.'

'No, I'm not. You know who I am—you addressed me by name just now,' Nikos countered.

'Only because you put your name on the card with those flowers—and *they* were an insult anyway.'

'How so?' Nikos's astonishment was open.

The sapphire flash that made her beauty even more

outstanding came again. 'You can't even see it, can you?' she returned. 'Sending me a ludicrously over-the-top bouquet and then having the gall to tell me to improve my mood—like you hadn't caused my bad mood in the first place. It was just so...so *patronising*!'

'Patronising? I don't see why.'

Mel's screwed her face up. Emotion was running like a flash flood through her. She was trying to cope with seeing him right in front of her again, just when she'd been starting to put the whole encounter of the previous day behind her, and trying urgently to suppress her reaction to seeing him again. Trying *not* to betray just what an impact he was having on her—how her eyes wanted to gaze at him, take in that sable hair, the incredible planes and contours of his face—and trying not to let herself fall head first into those dark eyes of his...

She was trying to use anger to keep him at bay—but he kept challenging it, eroding it. Throwing at her that ludicrous invitation which had stopped her dead in her tracks—an invitation which was as over-the-top as that vast bouquet had been.

'Yes,' she insisted, 'patronising. Mr Rich and Lordly sending flowers to Poor Little Shop Girl!'

There was a moment's silence. Then Nikos spoke. 'I did not mean it that way.' He took a breath. 'I told you—I sent them with the intention of making amends once I realised I had been rude to you—in more ways than one.'

He avoided spelling out what he was referring to, but he knew she was thinking about it for he could see a streak of colour heading out across her cheekbones again.

'But if you want me to apologise for sending the flowers as well, then—'

She cut across him. 'No, it's all right,' she said. She tried not to sound truculent. OK, so he hadn't meant to come across as patronising. Fine. She could be OK with that. She could be OK with him apologising to her. And she could be fine with him giving money to Joe, even if he *would* just go and spend it all on alcohol.

But what she *couldn't* be fine with was what he was asking her.

To go out with him. Go out with a man who set her pulse racing, who seemed to be able to slam right past every defence she put up against him—a man she wanted to gaze at as shamelessly, blatantly, as he had looked at her.

What's he doing to me? And how? And why am I being like this? Why can't I just tell him to go so I can shut the shop and never see him again and just get on with my life?

And why don't I want to do that?

But she knew why—and it was in every atom of Nikos Parakis, standing there across the counter, asking her why she didn't want to go out with him.

'Look, Mr Parakis, I don't know what this is about—I really don't. You set eyes on me for the second time in your life and suddenly you're asking me out for the evening? It's weird—bizarre.'

'Let me be totally upfront with you about why I'm asking *you*, in particular, to come with me on Friday evening,' he answered.

His eyes were resting on her, but not with any expression in them that made her either angry, suspicious or, worst of all, vulnerable to his overwhelming sexual allure.

'I'm in an awkward situation,' he said bluntly. 'Whilst in London I find myself committed to this charity gala tomorrow night, at the Viscari St James. Unfortunately, also present will be a woman whom I know through business and who is, alas, harbouring possessive intentions towards me which I cannot reciprocate.'

Was there an edge in his voice? Mel wondered. But he was continuing.

'I do not wish to spend the evening fending her off, let alone giving her cause to think that her hopes might be fulfilled. But I don't wish to wound or offend her either, and nor do I wish to sour any future business dealings. I need a…graceful but persuasive way to deflect her. Arriving with my own "plus one" would, I hope, achieve that. However, the lady in hot pursuit of me knows perfectly well that I am currently unattached—hence my need to discover a sufficiently convincing partner for the evening to thwart her hopes.'

His expression changed again.

'All of which accounts for my notion that inviting a fantastically beautiful complete stranger as my "plus one" would be the ideal answer to my predicament,' he finished, keeping his gaze steady on Mel's face.

He paused. His eyes rested on her with an unreadable expression that Mel could not match.

'You fit the bill perfectly,' he said. And now, suddenly, his expression was not unreadable at all…

As she felt the unveiled impact of his gaze Mel heard her breath catch, felt emotion swing into her as if it had been blown in on the wind from an opened door. He was offering her an experience she'd never had in her life—a glittering evening out with the most breathtakingly attractive man she'd ever seen.

So why not? What are you waiting for? Why hesitate for a moment?

She thought of all the reasons she shouldn't go—he

might be the most ridiculously good-looking and most ludicrously attractive man she'd ever seen, but he was also the most infuriating and arrogant and self-satisfied man she'd ever met.

But he's apologised, and his self-satisfaction comes with a sense of humour about it, and he's given me a cogent reason for his out-of-the-blue invitation...

But he was a complete stranger and could be anyone.

I know his name—and, anyway, he's talking about a posh charity bash at a swanky West End hotel, not an orgy in an opium den...

But she had nothing suitable to wear for such a thing as a posh charity bash at a swanky West End hotel.

Yes, I have—I've got that second-hand designer evening gown I bought in a charity shop that was dead cheap because it had a stain on it. I can cover the stain with a corsage...and I can make the corsage from that over-the-top bunch of lilies he's just sent...

But she ought to be working—she made good tips on a Friday night at the restaurant.

Well, I can work an extra shift on Sunday lunchtime instead, when Sarrie's is closed...

One by one she could hear herself demolishing her own objections against accepting Nikos Parakis's invitation. Heard herself urging on the one overwhelming reason for accepting it.

A little thrill went through her.

She was about to start a new life—her *own* life. She would be free of obligations to anyone else. Free to do what she wanted and go where she wanted. Free to indulge herself finally!

And when it came to indulgence what could be more self-indulgent than a gorgeous, irresistible man like the one standing in front of her? It was just too, too tempting to turn down.

If anything could herald her new life's arrival with the sound of trumpets it must surely be this. So why not grab the opportunity with both hands?

Why not?

'Well,' she heard him say, one eyebrow quirked expectantly, 'what's the verdict? Do we have a deal?'

Her eyelids dipped briefly over her eyes and she felt a smile start to form at her mouth.

'OK, then,' she said. 'Yes, we have a deal.'

CHAPTER THREE

MEL TWISTED AS best she could, but it was no good. She couldn't possibly see her full length reflection in the tiny mirror she'd got propped up on top of the filing cabinet where Sarrie kept the accounts.

Well, it didn't matter. She knew the dress suited her because she'd loved it from the moment she'd first seen it in the charity shop. It was the prize piece in the collection she'd been scouring charity shops for over the last year, putting together a cut-price but stylish wardrobe for her foreign travels.

The dress was silk, but in very fine plissé folds, which made it ideal for travelling as she could just twist it into a roll for packing. The colour suited her perfectly, she knew, because the pale blue was shot with a deeper hyacinth-blue, with a touch of lilac to it that set off her eyes. And its simple folds suited her preference for unfussy, 'no bling' styles.

With the reassurance of its designer label she knew she could go anywhere in it—even the Viscari St James. She'd looked up the hotel on Sarrie's PC and had whistled. It had a cachet that was way, way beyond any place she'd ever set foot in. But that was hardly surprising—for the internet had also revealed to her that Nikos Parakis was the scion of the Parakis banking dynasty—a

Greek-based outfit that seemed to be rolling in it to the tune of *zillions*.

And he came slumming along into a humble sandwich bar! she thought with mordant humour. No wonder he'd been so outraged at her lack of awed deference.

But, to his credit, he had at least apologised, and she'd draw a line under it. Now, she realised, she was simply looking forward to seeing him again. Would they still spar with each other?

She found a smile quirking her lips at the prospect... And, of course, at the prospect of feasting her eyes on the paean to male gorgeousness that was the very, *very* gorgeous Nikos Parakis.

Eyes glinting in anticipation of the treat that she knew this evening would be, she picked up the little satin clutch bag that went with her dress. Time to get going. Nikos had told her a car would collect her, and it was nearly the specified pickup time now.

She stepped outside on to the pavement, carefully locking up as she went and dropping the keys into her clutch, aware of a sleek, chauffeured car humming quietly and expensively at the kerb. She headed purposefully towards it, getting used to the unaccustomed feel of high heels and long skirts and her hair being loosened from its usual workaday tied-back plait.

As she approached the car the driver got out, tipping his cap to her in salutation, and from the very male expression in his eyes she knew she looked good enough for the evening ahead.

And for the man who was making it possible.

A little flutter of happy anticipation went through her as she got gracefully into the car when the door was held open for her. It had been so, so long since she'd gone out at all for the evening—and never like this, in such luxury and elegance.

The flutter came again, and she settled back happily to enjoy the chauffeured car, with its soft leather seats, its wide footwell lined with dove-grey carpet, and its fittings all in polished marquetry, as she was driven to her glamorous destination—and to the breathtakingly devastating man who awaited her there.

Her wonderful new life of freedom was just beginning, and this gorgeous, *gorgeous* man was just the person to start it off for her.

Nikos strolled up to the bar and placed his order. He did not sit down—merely propped one forearm on the gleaming mahogany surface, rested his foot on the brass rail and glanced around. The resplendent Edwardian-style bar just off the equally resplendent lobby at the Viscari St James was a popular watering hole for the well heeled. Many, like him, were in tuxedos, gathering for the evening's main function—the charity gala.

His mood, as he glanced around, was mixed. Happy anticipation filled him—his driver had phoned a while ago to inform him that he was en route, and soon— very soon—he was going to see just how even more fantastically beautiful his date for the evening looked in evening dress.

But he also felt a momentary doubt assail him. Would she possess the kind of attire that was appropriate for the Viscari? Perhaps he should have offered to help in that department? Then he quashed the thought—he was pretty sure that any such offer, however well intentioned, would have got shot down as 'patronising'. No, if having nothing to wear had been a problem she'd have said so.

He barely had time to take a first mellowing sip of his dry martini, directing another sweeping glance around the room, before he stilled.

She was walking into the bar area.

His eyes went to her immediately—it was impossible for them not to. Dimly, he was aware that he was far from being the only male whose eyes had gone straight to her. *Thee mou*, but she could turn heads!

And as for any concerns that she might not possess the kind of dress that was suited to a venue like the Viscari St James...they evaporated like a drop of water on a hot stove.

She looked stunning—*beyond* stunning.

Finally he could see just what nature had bestowed upon her, now untrammelled and unconcealed by her workaday appearance as it had been so far.

She was tall and slender, but with curves that went in and out in all the right places that were perfectly enhanced by the elegant fall of the ankle-length gown she was wearing. Its style and colour were perfect for her—a blending of delicate shades of blue and lilac. Her shoulders were swathed in soft folds of the multi-hued material, and the décolletage was draped but not low-cut. A creamy white corsage nestled in the drapery, and Nikos's mouth gave a quirk of amusement. He was pretty sure the corsage originated from the bouquet of lilies he'd had sent to her.

As for her hair—finally he could see what he'd wanted to see of it, freed from that obnoxious baseball cap. It was everything he could have wanted, loosened and swept back from her face, caught to one side with a mother of pearl comb before curving around one shoulder in a long, lush golden fall.

And her face— *Ah*... Nikos thought, satisfaction running through him with an even greater intensity. He had thought her stunningly beautiful when she'd had not a scrap of make-up on, but now, with her luminous eyes deepened, their lashes lengthened, her cheekbones delineated and her mouth, like a ripe damson…

He stepped forward, his smile deepening.

She saw him immediately—he could tell. Could tell, too, that the impact he was making on her was everything he'd wanted. His sense of satisfaction intensified again.

Her eyes widened with telltale revelation as she made her way towards him. And as she came up to him for the first time Nikos could detect a dent in her air of self-assured composure. Two spots of colour burned briefly but revealingly in her sculpted cheeks.

His eyes were warm upon her. 'You look fantastic,' he breathed.

His compliment drew a new expression from her face.

'I rather thought that was the idea,' Mel said.

Her voice was dry. But she needed it to be. She needed it to be because as her eyes had alighted upon Nikos Parakis she had felt a kick go through her that she had not intended to feel. If he'd looked drop-dead gorgeous before, in his handmade suit, now, in a handmade tux, he looked ten times more deadly.

And as for the sensation going through her now, as his dark gold-flecked eyes worked over her… She could feel awareness shooting through her, sky-high. Urgently she sought to quell it, to stay composed and unruffled.

Nikos's smile deepened. 'What can I get you to drink?' he asked.

'Sparkling mineral water is fine, thank you,' she managed to get out, without sounding too breathless.

He glanced at her. 'Do you not drink alcohol?'

'Oh, yes,' she replied, more easily now, glad to find her voice sounding a little more normal. 'But I assume there will be wine with dinner, so I don't want to make a start on it yet.'

'Very wise,' Nikos murmured, and relayed her order to the barman.

Then he turned his attention back to his date for the evening. A date, he suddenly realised with a sense of confusion, whose name he had absolutely no idea of!

Up to now, in his head, she'd simply been the stunning blonde in the sandwich shop. He blinked for a moment. Then, to his relief, he realised that of *course* he knew her name. It had been emblazoned on that unlovely T-shirt she'd been wearing in the sandwich bar.

The barman placed a glass of iced sparking water on the counter. Nikos picked it up and handed it to her. 'There you go, Sarrie,' he said, with a smile.

She took it, but stared at him. 'Sarrie…?' she echoed.

Nikos frowned slightly. 'You prefer not to be called that?' he checked.

She gave him a look. 'Well, no, actually—because it's not my name. *Sarrie*,' she elucidated, giving him another look—one that reminded him of their first sparking encounter, 'is the name of the guy who owns the sandwich bar—hence "Sarrie's Sarnies." *My* name,' she informed him, 'is Mel.'

She paused minutely.

'Do you require a surname? Or is that a complete irrelevance because after all,' she said lightly, 'our acquaintance is going to be terminated after tonight?'

Nikos found himself frowning. *Was* their acquaintance gong to be terminated after tonight? Was that what he intended?

Do I want this to be the only time I spend with her?

Did he really want this incredible, fantastic-looking, stunningly gorgeous blonde who was making his senses reel to be with him only for one single evening?

As his eyes flickered over her he knew what his body wanted him to answer—oh, yes, indeed! No doubt about that in the slightest. But it wasn't just his body responding to the overwhelming physical attraction he felt for this fantastically beautiful woman.

What was she like as a person? As an individual? Oh, he knew she could stand up to him—stand her ground and spark verbal fire with him—but how much more was there to her than that?

Time to find out…

He smiled a warm, encompassing smile. 'Mel,' he asked her, 'don't you realise yet that I want to know a lot more about you than just your surname?'

To his distinct satisfaction he saw once again that telltale colour run fleetingly over her sculpted cheekbones. He let his gaze have the effect he wanted, and then deliberately let it soften as he relaxed against the burnished mahogany surface of the bar.

Her colour was still heightened when she answered him. 'Well, it's Cooper—just in case you should need to know. Like when you introduce me to this woman you want me to keep at bay for you.'

There was an acerbic tinge to her voice, but Nikos ignored it.

I would want her here tonight even if Fiona Pellingham were a hundred miles away.

The knowledge was sure in his head—the certainty of it absolute. Mel Cooper—so fiery and so fantastically beautiful—was a woman he wanted to know more about. *Much* more.

'So, tell me, Mel Cooper,' he said, 'first of all how do you come to be working in an establishment rejoicing in the name of "Sarrie's Sarnies"?'

Deliberately he kept his tone light, with mild humour in it. He could see her recovering her composure. The slight stain of colour ebbed. She took a sip of water from her glass. Her voice, when she spoke, had lost its acerbic tone and he was glad.

'Sarrie Silva is the uncle of a friend of mine, and he offered me the job,' she explained. 'The pay isn't bad, and I actually enjoy the work.' No need to tell him that in comparison with looking after her grandfather day in and day out for years *any* kind of alternative work was bliss. 'And best of all he lets me use the back room as a bedroom, so I effectively live there.'

Nikos's eyebrows rose. 'You *live* in the back room of a sandwich bar?'

'Yes, it's rent-free—and in London that counts for a hell of a lot,' Mel answered feelingly.

'How long have you been living like that?' Nikos asked.

'Nearly a year now. Ever since I had to move out of my childhood home.'

Nikos frowned. 'Why did you have to do that?'

'It was after my grandfather died. I'd…looked after him…' She could hear her voice twist, feel her throat tighten, feel the familiar grief at his loss ache within her, and hurried on. 'When I lost him…' the twist in her voice was more pronounced, though she tried to cover it '…I decided I'd rather rent out the house, because that would give me some steady income.'

'But you became homeless?' Nikos objected.

She gave a quick shake of her head, smiling now. 'That

didn't matter, because it was only ever going to be temporary. I'll be off abroad soon,' she explained.

She said it deliberately. It had occurred to her as she spoke that it would be prudent to make it clear to Nikos Parakis that she was going to be out of London very soon. His words to her after she'd made that jibe at him just now echoed in her head.

'Don't you realise yet that I want to know a lot more about you than just your surname?'

Echoed dangerously...

Dangerously because all she wanted to do was enjoy this evening, enjoy the lavish luxury of her surroundings and keep as tight a lid as possible on the totally predictable effect Nikos Parakis was having on her female sensibilities.

Definitely time to make it clear that she was not hanging about in London for long. This evening was nothing more than an unexpected and most important a one-off treat—one she would enjoy, make the most of, and then consign to memory. And Nikos Parakis with it.

His dark eyebrows had come together when she'd mentioned going abroad.

'Where are you thinking of travelling to?' he asked.

'No idea,' she replied insouciantly, taking a sip of her water. 'Spain, probably—wherever I can get a cheap flight to.'

He looked slightly startled. 'You have no destination in mind?'

'Not really. I just want to travel—that's all. So any place is as good as another.' Her voice changed. 'Wherever I go it will be an adventure.'

Nikos took another sip of his martini. 'Where have you travelled so far in your life?' he asked.

'Nowhere. That's the whole point,' Mel replied.

There was emotion in her voice—Nikos could hear it. He could also see the enthusiasm in her face…the excitement. Could see, too, how it made her eyes sparkle, lighting up her face. Enhancing her stunning beauty.

It was a beauty, he knew, from all his long-honed masculine experience, that would cause total havoc amongst the entire male population of the world once she was out in it. Probably too much havoc…

'Are you going with friends?' he asked.

Behind his innocuous question he knew another one lurked. *Are you going with a boyfriend…?*

But of course she wasn't. If she were, she wouldn't have accepted his invitation tonight, would she?

The knowledge that she was unattached gave him satisfaction. More satisfaction than her answer to his question.

Mel shook her head. 'No, just solo. I'm sure I'll make friends as I go.'

'Well, be careful,' he found himself warning her. 'There are parts of the world where solo travellers—let alone female ones—are not advised to go.'

Her mouth tightened. 'I can look after myself.'

Nikos's expression was wry. 'Yes, I know,' he said, his voice dry. 'You can go twelve rounds verbally—no problem. But…' He held up a hand. 'All the same, stick to tourist areas—that's my advice.'

For a moment it looked as if she was going to argue the point, for he could see the warlike sparkle in her eyes. Then it subsided.

'OK, OK…' Mel temporised. 'I'll hire a bodyguard and lug him around with me—I get the picture,' she said, in a deliberately resigned voice.

'An excellent idea,' Nikos murmured, humour in his eyes. 'I can recommend a first-class firm offering the kind of close personal protection which I have, on occasion, engaged myself.'

Mel's expression changed. 'Good grief—are you serious?'

Nikos nodded. 'There are some…let us say *restless* places in the world, where it is advisable to have someone riding shotgun beside you.'

Her eyes widened. 'Why do you go to such places?'

'I do business there,' he answered drily. Then, at the questioning and indeed wary look in her eyes, he went on swiftly. 'And, no, before your fervid imagination carries you away, I am *not* an arms dealer. I am a very boring and tediously respectable banker,' he informed her.

'Yes, I know,' she admitted. 'I looked you up. Just in case,' she said dulcetly. 'Though of course,' she went on, allowing herself a provocative glance at him, 'I didn't think bankers *were* very respectable these days…' She paused, quirking an eyebrow questioningly. 'Or should that be *respected*?'

'Ouch!' said Nikos. He took another mouthful of his martini. 'Given the sorry economic state of the world, and the role that reckless lending by the banks has played in that, I can appreciate your scepticism. *However*,' he stressed, 'what banks *should* be doing— what I strive to do myself—is *aid* business recovery. Primarily for the Parakis Bank in Greece, which has been so badly hit by recession, but also in other parts of the world, as well.'

She was looking at him with an interested expression—no dumb blonde, it seemed—and the knowledge gladdened him.

He went on with his explication. 'The Parakis Bank is an investment bank, and we have always strived for genuine partnership with our clients—which means we take a financial hit if they lose money. It also means we have to choose clients very carefully—reckless, over-ambitious companies run by greedy, lazy people who want only to enrich themselves are not on our books. I look for clients who have a passion for the sector they are in, who understand the global trends in their markets and know where opportunities lie—who have worked hard to build their businesses so far, and who simply need a loan to get them to the next level, which is what we provide, to our mutual benefit.'

He smiled at her.

'So, have I convinced you that not all bankers are evil incarnate?' His voice was infused with wry humour.

Mel looked at him. 'It *sounds* persuasive,' she conceded.

'And are you persuadable?' he pressed.

His stance had changed subtly, and so had his tone. She heard it and broke eye contact, making herself glance away briefly, then looking back again. There was a subtext going on, she knew. One that had nothing to do with the banking industry.

She flashed a smile at him. Deliberately coruscating. Deliberately calling him on his challenge.

'Sometimes,' she said.

She let the ambiguity hang in the air. He wanted subtext—she could do subtext. Or so he could think if he wanted. Which it seemed he did. She saw long eyelashes dip over his dark expressive eyes.

'How very reassuring,' he murmured, and again Mel knew the subject was not banking or finance.

She made a face, abandoning her pose of ambiguity.

'Well, you knew that anyway, didn't you? I mean, you persuaded me to turn up here tonight,' she exclaimed, in a half-exasperated tone.

'And how incredibly glad I am that I did,' he answered, his voice openly warm. 'Or I would have missed out on having the most beautiful woman in London on my arm and being the envy of every male here.'

There was humour in his voice, too, and Mel gave a laughing shake of her head at the over-the-top compliment.

'Yeah, yeah…' she said with good humour, playing down his over-the-top compliment. Even as she spoke, though, she could feel a little thrill of gratification go through her that he had given it.

She drained the last of her mineral water and replaced the glass on the bar. 'So…' she changed the subject '…do we actually get to eat tonight? It might sound weird, considering I work in a sandwich shop, but I never get time for lunch and I'm totally starving.'

'Excellent,' said Nikos. 'The food here is outstanding—even when you're dining *en masse* as we shall be doing—so a hearty appetite is a distinct advantage.' He threw an assessing glance at her slender figure. 'I do hope you're not the type of woman who considers two lettuce leaves a feast?'

Mel laughed again. 'Not tonight, I promise you,' she assured him.

'Excellent,' he said again. 'In which case, shall we go through? I see people are beginning to make a move.'

He set his own empty martini glass on the bar and with the slightest flourish proffered his arm to Mel with a very small bow.

'Sounds good,' she said, and hooked her hand over his sleeve. 'Lead me to the food!'

Long lashes swept over dark, dark eyes, not quite hiding the glint within. 'I am yours to command,' Nikos murmured, and started to escort her forward.

Mel cocked her head at him. 'You might live to re-gret that rash offer,' she riposted, a smile audible in her voice.

Deep within the dark eyes that glint came again. 'I regret nothing about you whatsoever, Mel, I do assure you,' was his murmured answer.

She gave a low laugh and felt in excellent humour, for tonight was turning out to be even more enjoyable than she'd hoped it would be—and it wasn't because of the fancy venue and the chance to dress up to the nines, much as she appreciated both of those factors.

No, it was the man at her side who was giving her that buzz—as if she'd already drunk a glass of cham-pagne and it was fizzing in her veins. The man whose strong arm was beneath her lightly resting hand, whose tall figure was at her side, and whose long-lashed, dark glinting glance was making her heart beat that entic-ingly bit faster...

Careful! a voice in her head was whispering, low, but urgent. *You're only with him for a single evening—re-member that! So enjoy the next few hours, enjoy Nikos Parakis—his gorgeous looks, the sparky fun you're hav-ing with him—then walk away and put it in the mem-ory box.*

She heard the voice—listened to it and knew it was telling her the truth. But as she walked out of the bar on Nikos Parakis's arm she could still feel her heart beat-ing just that bit faster than it had ever done before...

CHAPTER FOUR

'OH, MY WORD!' Mel's exclamation was instantaneous and audible.

'Impressive, isn't it?' murmured Nikos.

'And then some.'

Mel was gazing around her at the ballroom of the hotel, now filling up with other guests taking their places for the evening. The room was quite a sight, its opulent *fin de siècle* Edwardian decor of gilding and gold satin drapery enhanced tonight by an array of damask-covered tables, each adorned with its own candelabrum and floral arrangement, as well as the glitter of crystal and silver.

Nikos led her forward. It felt good to have her on his arm. Good for multiple reasons. The main one, he reminded himself, was that having a fantastic-looking female on his arm was exactly what he'd planned for this evening to keep Fiona Pellingham at bay. But he was also increasingly aware, with every minute he was spending in Mel's company, that even without the other woman's presence here tonight, he would still want Mel with him.

Thee mou, what man wouldn't want this golden-haired goddess at his side? What man wouldn't desire her…?

'I think that's our table—just over there,' he murmured, pulling his thoughts to heel, indicating their places with a slight nod.

As they approached he realised that one of the several guests already seated was the woman whose presence had inspired him to make his choice of partner for this evening. Fiona Pellingham had turned her dark brunette head towards him and was levelling her dusky gaze at him with an intensity that made him even more glad of Mel at his side.

'That's her, isn't it?' he heard Mel say out of the corner of her mouth in a low voice. 'The pesky female who's got the unrequited hots for you?'

'Alas, yes,' Nikos replied. 'And it would seem,' he went on, his voice low, too, 'that she has taken exception to your presence.'

Fiona's gaze was, indeed, gimlet-eyed, and Nikos could see that his arrival with Mel on his arm was *not* what the other woman had wanted to see.

'What a pity,' Mel returned.

There was a sweet acidity in her voice now, and Nikos glanced at her.

'Don't let her put you down.' he said, with sudden warning in his voice.

A shaft of concern went through him. Fiona Pellingham was a high-flying career professional in a top job—and she hadn't got there by being sweetness and light to others…especially to other women.

But his concern was unnecessary.

'I wouldn't dream of it,' Mel assured him sweetly, and Nikos was instantly reminded of just how unputdownable Mel could be. He should know!

As they joined their table the other men present got to their feet and Nikos greeted them. He knew one or two professionally, and Fiona introduced the others. His greeting to Fiona was urbane—and hers, he noted observantly, was unruffled: a manner that did not go with the assessing expression in her eyes when they turned to the fabulous blonde beauty on Nikos's arm as he introduced his dinner partner.

'Hi,' said Mel casually, with a dazzling smile.

With not the slightest sign of apprehension she settled herself down at the table in one of the two remaining spaces. Nikos took his place beside her, opposite Fiona. He could see that the other males present were taking in Mel's fantastic looks, despite the presence of their own partners.

A waiter glided up to the table and started the business of pouring wine and water, while another circled with bread rolls.

Mel shook out the stiff linen napkin at her place and draped it over her lap. Then she dug into the basket of warm bread rolls and helped herself.

'I skipped lunch,' she said cheerfully, and reached for the butter dish, where tiny pats of butter floated in iced water.

She busied herself tearing the bread roll in half and applying butter to it while all around her the rest of the party started to chat. The conversation was mostly about how they knew or knew of each other, and that, Mel realised, was through their work—which was, not surprisingly, all to do with finance, corporate stuff and the City in general.

She tucked into her roll and with half an ear listened to the chit-chat. With the other half she took the measure of the female whose intentions towards Nikos Parakis she was here to block.

Fiona Pellingham was very, very attractive, with her svelte, chic brunette looks enhanced by a clearly top-end designer evening dress in deep ruby-red. Mel had quickly assessed that Fiona was very much put out about her own presence.

The other two women present were not in Fiona's league looks-wise, but they were dressed elegantly for the evening and had the appearance of being long-time partners of the men they were with.

Everyone, Mel decided, seemed perfectly amiable members of their own class and background—which was about a thousand times more privileged than her own. But so what? She wasn't picking up hostility from anyone except Fiona, and she was being accepted for what she was: namely, Nikos Parakis's 'plus one' for the evening.

While the others chatted away in their well-bred tones, talking about the City, business and the financial world in general—which Mel found out of her league, but interesting for that very reason—she settled down to make the most of what was clearly going to be a gourmet meal.

A delicious-looking salmon terrine proved as smooth and light as she could want. It was washed down very nicely, she discovered, with the crisp, cold Chablis that was served with it.

She was just setting down her glass, enjoying the delicate bouquet, when she realised she was being directly addressed.

'So, what line are *you* in, Mel?'

It was the man sitting next to Fiona who had addressed her. The question had been politely asked, and Mel saw no reason not to answer in the same way. At her side, though, she could sense that Nikos had gone on the alert, ready to intervene. But she ignored him.

'FMCG,' she replied easily. 'Food retail. I've been

researching market segmentation and seasonal versus time-of-day product-matching against predicted demand.'

'Interesting,' her questioner responded. 'Are you with one of the big retail analysts?'

Mel shook her head. 'No, this is independent research—directly customer-facing.'

Beside her, she could swear she heard Nikos make a noise in his throat that sounded distinctly like a choke.

'What will you be doing with the data?' This from one of the others around the table.

'Oh, it will go to my client to support his expansion strategy,' she answered airily.

'And is that something that the Parakis Bank will be funding?'

Fiona's voice was superficially sweet, but Mel could hear the needles in it.

Before she could reply, though, Nikos's voice interceded. 'I'd have to wait until turnover reaches an appropriate level,' Mel heard him say. His voice was dry.

She turned to him, her eyes glinting. 'I'll hold you to that,' she said lightly.

Then, deciding that Sarrie's business expansion plans—let alone her own role in his business—had better not get any more probing right now from all these high-powered City folk who dealt in turnovers of millions of pounds, she changed the subject. Time to disarm Fiona...

'Nikos was telling me,' she said, directly addressing the other woman, 'what a rising star you are, and how much you've achieved.' She made her voice warm and her smile genuine.

A slightly startled, but gratified expression crossed

Fiona's face. 'Well, it's been hard work,' she acknowledged.

There was a definite thaw in her voice now—Mel was sure of it. She pressed on.

'How real is the glass ceiling in the City?' she asked, and widened her question to include the other two women there. 'You seem to be unhindered by it.' She went back to Fiona and let her approbation show in her face.

'It does take determination to break through it,' Fiona replied.

One of the other women nodded in agreement. 'And not having babies,' she exclaimed feelingly.

'The dreaded "mommy track".' Mel grimaced. 'It's still the ultimate dilemma, isn't it, for women? Career versus family.'

Just as she'd hoped, the conversation took off along the well-trodden path of whether high-flying women could have babies without jeopardising their careers and she left them to it. It was a vigorous debate, with one of the female guests strongly defensive about the 'mommy track', and Fiona and the other woman saying bluntly that families would just have to wait.

At Mel's side, she felt Nikos lean closer in to her.

'FMCG?' she heard him query heavily. One arched eyebrow was lifted interrogatively.

Mel turned to him and smiled sweetly. 'Fast-moving consumer goods—surely you know *that*, Nikos?'

His dark eyes glinted. 'And so do you, it seems.' His voice was dry now, with a hint of surprise in it.

Mel's gaze was limpid. 'Yes, the knowledge came courtesy of my degree in Business Studies,' she murmured. 'Oh, don't tell me you thought I was just a little blonde bimbo, Nikos, sweetie?' she mused.

The glint which was so becoming familiar to her showed in his eyes. 'Only if I feel like living dangerously,' he replied, the resigned humour in his voice audible.

Mel shot him a flashing smile of approval. 'Smart guy,' she said, with a quirk of her mouth.

'You know, I'm beginning to think I *am*. Inviting you tonight was the smartest thing I've done in quite a while,' Nikos replied, and there was something in his voice that told Mel he wasn't talking about her brainpower any more.

A tiny ripple of heat went down her veins.

Careful! The voice inside her head was sharp, and instant.

She was grateful to hear herself addressed by someone else. The question came from Fiona.

'And where do you stand yourself on the "mommy track"?'

Mel answered without hesitation. 'I'm afraid I'm pretty much indelibly focussed on personal goals and priorities at the moment,' she said, not elaborating to say that travel and globetrotting were those personal goals and priorities—not building a glittering career in FMCG data analysis. 'So right now,' she added feelingly, 'I'd definitely say I don't want a baby. Of course,' she allowed, 'I'm nowhere near your level, and never likely to be, so the whole "mommy track" thing wouldn't be the issue for me as it is for you.'

Again, her compliment on Fiona's high-powered career was well-received by its target. Mel could almost see her preening.

'Mind you,' she went on, 'there is another tricky issue that female high-flyers hit, which is the shortage of suitable partners for you in the first place. It's a pretty brutal truth that men "date down"—I mean, look at *me*. Here I am, a humble retail analyst, and I get to hang out with a guy whose family own a *bank*!'

'So how *did* you?' The needles were back in Fiona's voice.

Mel smiled disarmingly. 'Oh, Nikos can be so very... *persuasive* when he sets his mind to it,' she purred, in an outrageously over-the-top style, clearly meant to be humorous, that drew a laugh from the other guests.

Even Fiona smiled, and Mel was glad. She didn't blame the other woman for setting her sights on Nikos Parakis. She wouldn't have blamed *any* woman for doing so. With or without a bank in his family, Nikos was the kind of man that every female in town would make a beeline for.

And go weak at the knees over.

Like I'm doing?

The darting question—warning?—came before she could stop it.

At her side she could hear his deep tones take up the conversational baton.

'You've no idea how hard I had to work to get Mel here,' Nikos was saying lightly. 'In the end I think it was this venue that swung it for her.'

'It's certainly fabulous,' she agreed warmly, glancing around once more at the opulent ballroom.

'All the Viscari hotels have this level of cachet,' one of men commented. 'Something that sets them apart from the common run of luxury hotels.'

'Oh, yes, absolutely,' enthused his partner. 'I think my favourite so far has to be the one in Florence.'

The conversation moved into a lively discussion about just which of the ultra-luxurious Viscari hotels was the very best of all, and Mel left them to it.

The main course was being served, and she got stuck in with definite enthusiasm. The lamb melted in her mouth, and the Burgundy washed it down to perfection.

'To think I was going to turn this down,' she murmured sideways to Nikos.

He turned his head to glance down at her. 'Enjoying yourself?'

'Oh, yes,' she breathed. 'You know, I could definitely, *definitely* get used to this.'

Something flickered across his eyes. 'Well, enjoy…' he murmured, and reached for his wine glass.

Mel found she was lifting hers, too. There was a clink as the rims met together.

'To all my good ideas, Mel,' he murmured, and his eyes were like dark, melting chocolate.

Except that the melting sensation seemed to be inside her as he spoke.

She took a mouthful of the wine, hoping it would steady her, then got back to focussing on the gourmet food she was eating. That, at least, was a safe thing to do.

Beside her, Nikos's long lashed eyes rested on her averted face. There was speculation in his gaze. As if he were asking himself a question.

A question that had the dazzling beauty that was Mel Cooper at its heart.

Mel sighed luxuriously and leant her head back against the soft leather headrest of the car seat. 'This,' she announced extravagantly, 'has been the best evening *ever.*'

Nikos, sitting beside her in the back of the chauffeur-driven car, turned his head towards her and smiled. 'I'm glad you enjoyed yourself,' he replied.

'Definitely,' she assured him, turning towards him.

Their eyes met. Mel could see, even in the dim light of the car's interior as it made its way through the nearly deserted streets of London long after the midnight hour, that there was an expression in them that made half of her want to pull her own gaze away immediately, because that was the most prudent thing to do, and half of her want to go on letting her gaze entwine with his.

For a moment she almost let her gaze slide away—then didn't. The evening was going to end very soon now, and she was going to make the most of the short time left.

Make the most of Nikos.

He was just too damn gorgeous for her to do anything else.

It was a thought that had been forming all evening and now, with the end fast approaching, cocooned in the privacy of the car, she let herself indulge in the last luxury of gazing at him, drinking him in. She could feel the wine she had drunk with dinner filling her veins, could feel its effects upon her, but she didn't care. Right now it seemed good—*very* good—just to enjoy the moment.

'That's a pretty definite vote of approval,' Nikos said. His mouth quirked.

She tilted her head slightly. She must remind herself of just why Nikos had taken her with him this evening. Not for her own sake, but to serve as a foil against another woman's unwanted attentions. It would be sensible not to forget that. Especially when they were alone together in this confined space, with the driver behind his screen and the anonymous streets beyond.

'Do you think Fiona will try and pursue you again?' she asked.

The quirk deepened. 'Hopefully not.' The dark eyes were veiled as his long lashes swept down momentarily. 'Not now you've introduced her to Sven.'

Mel gave a gurgle of laughter. 'He's not called *Sven*,' she remonstrated. 'He's called Magnus—and anyway his name doesn't matter. Only that he's a Viking hunk and runs some trendy Nordic telecoms company, which means that Fiona can consider him dateable.'

'Let's hope he considers *her* dateable. It was *you* he was chatting up when you disappeared off to the powder room,' Nikos retorted.

There was, he realised as he spoke, a discernible bite in his voice. Seeing Mel walk back to their table with the 'Viking hunk' at her side had sent a primitive growl through him. Only when she'd made a point of introducing the Viking to Fiona and leaving them to it had the growl subsided.

'I let him—precisely because I wanted to hand him over to Fiona,' Mel riposted. 'I felt genuinely bad, cutting her out—she needed a consolation prize.'

'Well, I hope Sven keeps her busy—and away from *me*,' he replied.

'Happy to have been of use.' Mel smiled with exaggerated sweetness.

'And I'm *very* grateful to you, I assure you...'

There was a husk in Nikos's voice as he spoke—she could hear it. Could feel it vibrating deep within her. The humour of a moment ago was gone, and suddenly the breath was tight in Mel's lungs.

She knew she had to break that gaze holding her motionless like this, making her breathless, but it was impossible to move. Impossible to breathe. Impossible to do anything other than just sit there, her head turned towards Nikos, feeling him so close, so very, *very* close to her...

Then she realised something had changed. The car

had stopped moving. She jerked forward, jolting her gaze free to look out of the passenger seat window.

'We're here,' she said. Her voice sounded staccato.

Breaking that compelling, unbreakable gaze had freed her. Freed her to get out of the car, go back into Sarrie's sandwich bar and bid farewell to the evening. Farewell to Nikos Parakis.

A terrible sense of flatness assailed her. The evening was definitely, *definitely* over. The flatness was crushing. Her brief encounter with Nikos Parakis was at an end.

The chauffeur was opening the passenger door for her and, gathering her skirts, she made herself get out. The night air seemed chilly…sobering. As if all the fizz had gone out of everything. She knew that the alcohol in her bloodstream was exacerbating her reaction, but the knowledge didn't help counter it.

Nikos followed her out, giving a brief dismissive nod to the driver, who got back into his seat at the front of the car.

Mel painted a bright smile on her face. 'Thank you for a fabulous evening,' she said. 'I had the best time ever. I hope Fiona is now duly convinced that she doesn't stand a chance with you, and focusses on her Nordic telecoms hunk instead,' she rattled out.

In a moment the evening would truly be over. Nikos would bid her goodnight and she would get the sandwich bar keys out of her bag and go inside. Nikos would get back into his chauffeur-driven car, and go off to his fancy apartment, back to his glittering, luxurious life filled with tuxedos and five-star hotels and champagne.

She'd go back to making sandwiches. And to booking a flight on a budget airline, heading for the Spanish *costas*.

She waited for the customary little thrill of anticipation that always came when she thought about her future life—but it didn't come. Instead an unexpected chill of despondency sifted through her. How could something that only a few hours ago had been her sole burning ambition now seem so…*un*burning?

Because a few hours ago I hadn't spent the evening with Nikos Parakis!

Had she sighed? She couldn't tell. Could only tell that she was making herself stretch out her hand, as if for a brisk farewell handshake. A handshake to end the evening with before she walked back into her own life.

'Thank you,' she said again. 'And goodnight.'

She would do this neatly and briskly and they would go their separate ways. He to his world, she to hers. They had been ships that had bumped briefly into each other and were now back on course to their original destinations. And that was that.

You had fun—now it's over. Accept it. Accept it graciously and go indoors.

Right now.

And stop looking at him!

But she could not stop staring at him, or gazing into his ludicrously gorgeous face and imprinting it on to her memory.

She felt her hand taken. Steeled herself to give the brisk, brief handshake that was appropriate. Nikos Parakis wasn't a date—this whole evening had been a set-up…nothing more than that. She'd done what she'd been asked to do, had had a wonderful time herself, and now it was time to bow out.

So why did she feel so damn reluctant to do so?

She could feel the blood pulsing in her veins, feel her awareness of his searing masculinity, his ludicrous good looks, as she stood on the bleak bare London pavement at two in the morning, the night air crystal in her lungs. She seemed ultra-aware of the planes and contours of his face, the dark sable of his hair, the faint aromatic scent of his skin and the shadowed darkening of his jaw.

Why, oh, why was she just stuck here, unable to tear herself away, while she felt the warm, strong pressure of his hand taking hers? He was folding his other hand around hers as well, drawing her with effortless strength a little closer to him. Looking down at her, his long-lashed eyes holding hers just as effortlessly as she gazed helplessly up at him.

'Goodnight—and thank you for coming with me this evening.' There was a husk in his voice that belied the prosaic words.

Her hand was still enclosed in his and she was standing closer to him now. So close that she could feel her breasts straining, as if she wanted only to press forward, to bind herself against the strong column of his body. She longed to feel that sheathed muscled strength against the pliant wand of her own body, to lift her mouth to his and wind her fingers up into the base of his neck, draw that sculpted mouth down upon hers…

It shook her…the intensity of the urge to do so. Like a slow-motion film running inside her head, she felt her brain try to reason her way out of it. Out of the urge to reach for him, to kiss him…

It had been so, so long since she had kissed a man— any man at all. And longer still since she had given free rein to the physical impulse of intimacy. Jak had left for Africa long ago, and since then there had been only a few perfunctory dates, snatched before caring for her grandfather had become all-consuming.

And now here she was, gazing up at a man who was

the most achingly seductive man she'd ever encountered, wanting only to feel his mouth on hers, his arms around her.

As if he heard her body call to him he bent his head to catch her lips, and his mouth was as soft as velvet. As sensuous as silk.

Dissolving her completely.

She moved against him and felt her breasts crushed against his torso, that strong wall of steely muscle. Her other hand lost its grip on her evening bag. It fell to the ground, letting her freed hand do what it so wanted to do—to slide beneath the fall of his tuxedo jacket, her fingers gliding around his back, strong and smooth and so, so warm to her touch.

Her eyes fluttered shut as she gave herself to a slow, velvet kiss that seemed to lift her right off her feet, that absorbed every part of her consciousness. Gave herself to the sensuous caress of his lips on hers. Assured, expert, arousing…he knew exactly how to glide and tease and coax her lips to part for his, to deepen the kiss with skilled touch until he had everything of her he sought.

How long he kissed her for she didn't know. She knew only that her fingers were pressing into his back, holding him fast against her, and that her hand, still crushed in his, was being held in the valley of her breasts, whose peaks were taut against his chest and beneath whose surface her heart was beating like a soaring bird.

His mouth let hers go and he was looking down at her—at her parted lips, her dazed eyes, her heated cheeks. His face was unreadable, but there was a shadow somewhere deep in the dark pools of his eyes… There were words he wanted to speak—but he kept silent…

How long she stood there, just gazing at him, overwhelmed by his kiss, she couldn't tell. Something ran between them. She could not quite tell what, but she would not let herself read that wordless message. Would only, with a breathy little catch in her throat, step back from him, separating their bodies.

Then, with a jerky movement, she bent her knees and scooped up her evening bag, made her fingers open the clasp, extract her keys. She focussed on movement, focussed on stepping towards the door, unlocking it, opening it. When she was half inside, she turned.

He hadn't moved. He was still standing there, watching her. Behind him, his car purred silently at the kerb. It would take him back to his world and she would never see him again.

There was a sensation of tightness in her chest suddenly, as if breathing were impossible. Her eyes rested on his outline one last time.

'Goodbye, Nikos,' she heard her own voice say, softly now. Then she turned away, heading towards the back room.

The evening was over now. Quite over.

Outside on the bare pavement Nikos went on standing for a while, motionless. Then, with a sudden jerky movement of his body, he turned on his heel and got back into the car.

It moved off along the deserted road.

In his head, that wordless message hung.

It was a message he did not want to hear—never wanted to hear. Had spent his life blocking out.

A message that challenged all the precepts by which he lived his life.

CHAPTER FIVE

WITH A YAWN, Mel set the tap running to fill the hot water urn and started her routine preparations for opening up the sandwich bar. But her thoughts were a million miles away, remembering everything about the evening before. It filled her head as if she were there again, reliving it all. Reliving, most of all, that melting goodnight kiss from Nikos…

For a moment—just a moment—she experienced again that sense of questioning wonder she'd felt as they'd gazed into each other's eyes. Then, with an impatient shake of her head, she shook it from her. For three long years she'd had no romance in her life at all—no wonder she was feeling overwhelmed, having been kissed by an expert kisser like Nikos Parakis!

Her mouth gave a wry little twist. He'd have acquired that expertise by kissing scores of females in his time. Kissing, romancing and moving on. Keeping his romances simple—transient. Avoiding serious relationships.

Well, she could sympathise. Right now, with freedom beckoning, that was the way *she* saw things, too—no commitments, no complications. Just enjoying light-hearted, fun-time romance if it came her way…

She made a face as she set croissants to warm. Well,

it wasn't going to come her way courtesy of Nikos Parakis—that was for sure. He'd kissed her goodnight and headed back to his own life. He hadn't wanted anything more of her than that single evening.

She paused in the act of reaching for a packet of butter from the fridge.

What if he had? What if he'd asked for more?

Like feathers sifting through her mind, she felt again that moment when he'd finished kissing her—when they'd parted but had still simply been looking at each other, their eyes meeting. A message had passed between them...

A message she hadn't been able to read—*wouldn't* read.

She shook her head, clearing the memory. What did it matter anyway? Nikos was out of her life as swiftly as he'd come into it and she wasn't going to be seeing him again. That melting goodnight kiss was what she'd remember of him—the final icing on the *amuse-bouche* that had been the evening she'd spent with him.

And in the meantime she had a loaf of bread to butter.

Nikos was running. Running fast. But not fast enough. He upped the speed on the treadmill, his feet pounding more rapidly as his pace picked up. But he still could not outrun the memory in his head.

The memory of his kiss with Mel.

It kept replaying in his head...the feel of her mouth, soft and sensuous beneath his, that taste of heady sweetness in her lips...and it was still doing so now, back in Athens, over a week later. He was still remembering the words he had not spoken—the words he'd come so close, so very, *very* close to murmuring to her...

*Don't let the evening end now—come back with me—
come back and stay the night with me...*

But, as they'd drawn apart, as he'd finally relinquished her mouth, her soft, slender body still half embraced by his, she'd gazed up at him with that helpless,
dazed expression in her beautiful eyes and the words
had died on his lips. That wordless, unspoken message
that had flowed between them had been silenced.

He knew why.

To have invited her to stay the night with him would
not have been fair to her. He did not know her well
enough to risk it—after such intimacy she might expect
of him what he could not, *would* not give. He could not
offer her anything other than a brief, fleeting romance.

Oh, he was no Lothario, getting a malign pleasure
out of rejecting women after they'd fallen for him. He
would far rather they *didn't* fall for him. Far rather they
shared his terms of engagement. His short-term view.

Because the best relationships were short-term ones.
He had ample personal evidence of that. His jaw tightened. And ample evidence that those who did not ad-
here to that view ended up in a mess. A mess that had
fallout for others, as well.

Like children.

He knew only too well, with bitterly earned self-
knowledge, that was why he did not risk long-term relationships. Because they could become a trap—a trap
to be sprung, confining people in relationships that became prisons. Prisons they were incapable of leaving.

His expression darkened. That was what had happened to his parents. Locked in a destructive relationship that neither of them would or could relinquish. A
macabre, vicious dance he'd had to watch as a boy. Still
had to watch whenever he spent time with them and saw

them gouging at each other like two wounded, snarling animals trapped in the same locked enclosure.

Why the hell they hadn't divorced years ago he could never fathom. Whenever he'd challenged either of them as to why they'd stuck together they'd both turned to him and said, 'But it was for *your* sake we stayed together. So you would have a stable home. There's nothing worse than a child growing up in a broken home.'

He gave a choke of bitter laughter now. If that had been their reasoning, he wasn't grateful for it. He'd headed for university in the USA with relief, then found his own apartment once he'd graduated and come back to take his place at the family bank.

He was still trying to avoid their recriminations about each other. He left them to it. Heard them out, but did not really listen. Got back to his own life as quickly as he could. Took up with women who would never be like his mother, would never turn him into a man like his father. Women who understood, right from the off, that while he spent time with them he would be devoted to them—but when that time ended he'd simply move on. When it came to the goodbye kiss, goodbye was what it meant.

Would Mel have understood that?

That was what he did not know—had not risked asking that night in London. Which was why he had to put that evening behind him, that kiss behind him—why he had to stop remembering it.

But that was what seemed so impossible, however hard he tried.

The treadmill slowed, coming to the end of its programme, and he stepped off, heading for the weights. But even as he pumped his muscles he could still feel the memory of Mel in his arms, feel the sensual power of that amazing kiss. It haunted him wherever he went, whatever he did.

Back at work, he made yet another determined effort to move on. Keeping busy must surely help. His diary for today was full, and tomorrow morning he was flying to Geneva. Then he was scheduled for Frankfurt, and after that there was some banking conference somewhere he was due to speak at. Where was it being held? Somewhere long-haul, he thought. New York? Atlanta? Toronto? Was that it?

But as he clicked on the link a completely different venue sprang up on his screen.

Bermuda.

An offshore banking haven, only a couple of hours' flight off the US East Coast, and best of all a sub-tropical paradise. He'd been before on business, but always on his own. The beautiful island just cried out for spending more time there, R&R—and not on his own...

The thought was in his head before he could stop it. Instantly he sought to eject it, delete it, but it was no good. It was there, indelible, right at the front of his mind. He knew exactly who should be with him on such a break—exactly who it was he wanted there.

Instantly he summoned all the arguments against it—the arguments that had stopped him whispering the words he'd wanted to whisper to Mel—but they were being drowned out. Drowned out by a cacophony of counterarguments.

She longs to go abroad—anywhere in the world. Bermuda would be perfect for her. It's not the kind of place she'd ever get to on her own—not the place for budget backpacking tourists—but with me it would be possible. I could show her a place she would otherwise never see.

It was a brilliant idea—just brilliant. And now it was in his head he could not obliterate it. It would not be silenced.

He stared out over his office, his thoughts churning. Overwhelming him with their power.

Why do I assume she would want more from me than a simple holiday romance? Why do I fear she would want something deeper, more lasting? Why not ask her and see? After all, she told me she wanted to see the world, travel everywhere—does that sound like a woman who wants to tie me down or get involved in a heavy relationship?

Even as he thought it alarm snatched at him. When had she said she was leaving London? Setting off on her travels? She might already be in Spain for all he knew.

The thought was like a blow. If she were gone, how would he ever find her?

She could disappear completely and I'd have no clue where she was!

Without realising it he'd reached for his phone. Urgency impelled him, overriding everything else. Only one thing filled his head—Mel, as she'd been that evening, so fantastically beautiful, so soft and ardent in his arms, the sweetness of her mouth, the honey of her lips.

I won't let her disappear from my life. Not without seeing whether I can't persuade her to come with me!

His secretary answered the phone instantly. Mood soaring, he gave her his instructions.

'Cancel Geneva and Frankfurt. Book me to London tomorrow instead.'

'Sarrie, here are the accounts for while you were away. I think they're looking quite good. I made a few tweaks to the menu, and tried out a few new things. I think they've worked.'

She'd added more boxed salads for diet-conscious customers, and sourced a scrumptious organic carrot cake for when they fell off their diets, keeping careful tabs on costs, sales and profits.

A sudden shaft of memory assailed her—of how she'd spun that impressive-sounding line about FMCG customer-facing research at that charity do, surrounded by all those high-flying career women. She hadn't meant it seriously…it had just been to amuse Nikos…

No. No thinking about Nikos.

No remembering that evening. And no remembering that devastating goodnight kiss.

This time tomorrow I'll be in Spain, and if I want romance I'll set my cap at some sultry Spaniard. That will take my mind off Nikos Parakis.

It had better.

Because so far nothing was taking her mind off him and everything was reminding her of him—even packing for Spain. When she'd refolded the evening gown she'd worn for him memories had rushed back into her head—memories of how he'd gazed at her when she'd glided up to him in the hotel, how he'd smiled at her, how at the end of that wonderful, fabulous evening he'd taken her into his arms to kiss her…

Stop it. Just…stop it. It's over, he's gone, and he's not coming back into your life.

That was what she had to remember. That was what she had to think about.

Not about the way he kissed me…turning me inside out and back again…

Most of all not wishing there had been more than just a single kiss…

If he'd kissed me again—swept me off my feet—if I'd gone with him—

No, she must not think of that—definitely, *definitely* not that!

And anyway—she dropped a clanging reality check down through her hectic thoughts—he *hadn't* kissed her again, had he? And there'd been no sweeping her off her feet, had there? No, he'd just kissed her goodnight and gone. The evening had ended and her brief, fleeting acquaintance with Nikos Parakis had ended, too.

Time for her to move on. To put Nikos Parakis out of her head for once and for all.

She heard the shop door open and, leaving Sarrie in the back room with the accounts and her packed suitcase, went through to serve their latest customer.

And froze.

'Hello, Mel,' said Nikos Parakis.

Emotions surged within her. Mixed emotions. Fighting each other. One emotion—the rational one that went with her head, that went with her packed suitcase, her airline ticket to Spain and her new life—was dismay. Just as she was finally on the point of leaving London, making a new start, putting him and their brief, intoxicating encounter behind her, *this* had to happen.

But that emotion didn't last. Couldn't last. It was flooded out by a far more vivid one.

Nikos was here—right here—just the other side of the counter, half a metre away and exactly as she remembered him. Tall, ludicrously, ridiculously good-looking, with his sable hair and his olive skin, and his eyes…oh, his eyes…all dark and velvety, with lashes you could sweep floors with. And the look in them was turning her stomach inside out.

The rush of emotion was unstoppable, palpable. Her face lit. She couldn't stop it.

'Nikos!'

The long lashes swept down over his dark, gold-flecked eyes. 'I'm glad you're still here,' he said.

She bit her lip. 'I'm flying off tomorrow morning,' she said. Did her voice sound breathless? She didn't know—didn't care. Knew only that her heart had started pounding, her pulse racing. Nikos Parakis—no longer just a memory of a fabulous evening, a goodnight kiss to remember all her life—was here, now, right in front of her in real, glorious flesh.

He smiled, and the tug of his mouth was doing things to Mel's stomach that it shouldn't—but did all the same.

'Then I've arrived just in time,' he said.

She stared. 'In time for what?' she asked automatically.

He changed his stance, became relaxed somehow. It made Mel aware all over again of the long, lean length of him, of the way the jacket of his suit fitted like a glove across his shoulders, the way his silver-buckled leather belt snaked around his narrow hips, the way the pristine white of his shirt moulded the strong wall of his chest. She felt the force of his physical impact on her assailing her senses like an onslaught of potent awareness…

'In time to ask you something,' he elucidated.

There was an expression in his face now that Mel could not read. Truth to tell, she could not do anything other than gaze at him, feeling her heart-rate soaring in her chest.

The intensity of emotion inside her kicked once more. He was speaking again. Saying something that knocked the breath out of her. Stilled her completely.

'Would you…?' Nikos said, the eyes resting on her veiled suddenly, she realised, even though they met hers. 'Would you consider a…detour…before you head for Spain?'

There was a husk in his voice as he put the question to her. The question he'd cancelled his engagements for, flown to London for. He'd driven straight here from Heathrow and walked into Sarrie's Sarnies to invite this fantastically beautiful woman, whom he could not get out of his head, to come to Bermuda with him.

Seeing her again, now, he wanted to hear only one answer to the question. Just seeing her in the flesh had slammed the truth of that into him with the full force of a tangible impact. He'd felt a kick go through him—a stab of exultation. Desire had coursed through him like a flash flood.

Would she accept what he was offering her? Share a few weeks with him, no more than that, before she headed off on her travels and they went their separate ways?

His eyes rested on her and his brow quirked. She was looking at him. Was it with a wary expression in her luminous blue eyes?

'I don't understand…' she said.

He elucidated. 'I'm due to speak at a conference in Bermuda next week. I was wondering…' his long lashes dipped over his eyes as he studied her reaction '…if you'd like to come with me?'

She didn't answer—not for a full second. She'd gone very still. Then her expression changed.

'Don't tell me Fiona Pellingham is going to the conference, as well?' she asked.

Mel's voice was dry. But her emotions, whirling around inside her, were not dry at all—they felt as if they were in a spin cycle, like turbulent laundry. Was

Nikos *really* standing there asking her to go to Bermuda with him?

He shook his head immediately. 'Nothing like that,' he assured her. His expression changed. 'This is just for you and me.'

She was staring at him still. 'Why?' she asked.

'Why?' he echoed. Then he smiled. 'Because, Mel Cooper, I can't get you out of my head—that's why. One kiss,' he told her, 'was not enough.' He paused. '*Will* you come with me?'

He could see her face working—see the emotions flitting through her gaze. He took a breath. Before this went further he had to speak—anything else would not be fair.

'A holiday, Mel—that's what I'm asking you to share with me. A holiday—fun, relaxation, good times. With each other. A few weeks in the sun. On a beautiful island which,' he said, 'I suspect is probably not on your itinerary but which, I do promise you, you *will* enjoy.' He paused. 'What do you say?' he asked.

She was silent still.

His voice changed. 'Mel, we can't deny the charge between us—it would be pointless to do so. So let's not deny it. Let's have some time with each other—a holiday—and then…' He took a breath. 'Then you go off on your travels, as you planned, and I… Well, I go back to banking. Nothing more demanding than that.'

He watched her take it in. It had been uncomfortable to spell it out, but he knew he'd had to. He wanted no deceit, no false expectations, no hope for anything more of himself than he could give her.

She'd gone very still again. She was resting her eyes on him, but not, he thought, really seeing him. It was as if she were absorbing what he'd said to her. What was behind what he'd said.

He fixed his eyes on her, waiting for her answer. Then she spoke. There was less strain in her voice now, but her tone was serious for all that.

She lifted her chin, looked right at him. 'Nikos... You gave me, without doubt, the most glamorous evening of my life. And you don't need me to tell you that that goodnight kiss would have won you a gold medal.'

The slightest tinge of humour infused her voice, and then it was gone again.

'But I really, *really* should say no to you now. It's the sensible thing to do. To say thanks, but I'm going to Spain tomorrow. I'm never going to see you again.' She closed her eyes for a moment, then opened them again. '*That's* what I've got to say to you.'

She meant it—meant every word. Of course she did. It was the only sensible thing to do. Nikos Parakis was temptation personified. How could he not be? But even with what he was offering her—a no-strings romance, a couple of weeks in the sun, in a place she'd never be likely to go to herself—she felt the ripple of danger go through her.

She'd melted like chocolate at a single kiss—what would she be like after a fortnight with him? And after a lot more than a kiss.

You melted because you haven't been kissed for years and the man who kissed you is a world champion kisser!

Her thoughts ran on...hectic, whirling around in her head...

Don't you deserve something like this? Something thrilling and wonderful and fantastic, with a man like Nikos? He's offering you exactly what you want now—a carefree, no-strings holiday romance. A few weeks of bliss and fun. Fabulous while it lasts—and unregret-ted when it's over.

His expression had changed. She didn't quite know how, but it had. He was looking at her still, but there was a glint in his eye—a gleam of humour and of ex-pectation.

'And are you?' he asked. His voice was limpid, his eyes lucent. '*Are* you going to say that? Say goodbye to me again?'

Mel looked at him. Heard the confidence in his voice and knew the reason for it. Knew, too, what the sensi-ble answer was—but why *should* she be sensible now? Her life was her own from now on—she could make decisions that maybe weren't sensible, but so what? *So what?*

A flutter of emotion went through her. She took it for excitement. Seized it. If a single evening with Nikos had been an *amuse-bouche* before the banquet that was to be her new life of freedom, and his melting kiss the icing on that *amuse-bouche*, then a holiday with him—and all that entailed—would be the most fabulous *entrée*.

The flutter of emotion came again. Oh, it was defi-nitely excitement. And why not?

Nikos was a gorgeously irresistible male—why should she resist him? They both wanted the same thing from each other—so why not take it?

He was quirking an eyebrow at her, waiting for her answer. A smile was curving his mouth…his eyes glinted in the sunlight.

She took a breath, lifted her chin. *Yes*, she would do it!

Her mouth split into a dazzling smile.

'So,' she said, 'when are we going?'

CHAPTER SIX

'I CAN SEE IT,' Mel's voice sounded excitedly. 'There—just coming into view!'

Nikos leant sideways in his seat, peering out of the porthole. 'So it is,' he said.

Mel gazed entranced as the deep cobalt sea beneath changed colour to a paler blue. The curving shoreline was fringed with a clear reef line, changing the colour of the sea yet again, turquoise in the lee of the little bays, with foam from the ocean swell catching on the rocks of the reef.

Could this really be happening? Could she really be gazing out over the western Atlantic, flying in a plane and descending to a subtropical, reef-fringed island far below?

She'd barely had time to say goodbye to Sarrie, her face flushed and her eyes as bright as sapphires with excitement as she'd seized what Nikos was offering her. And now here she was, Nikos beside her, as the plane descended to the tiny island below.

She could see houses and gardens and palm trees now, closer and closer, and then there was the tarmac of the runway and they were touching down.

'We're here!' she exclaimed.

Nikos grinned. She was reacting like a kid, but he

could see why. Hell, he was pretty damn ecstatic himself. Here he was, his hopes utterly fulfilled, with Mel beside him, coming away on holiday with him—and she was everything he'd remembered about her. Even more beautiful... His gaze softened as it skimmed over her.

Deplaning was swift, and so was Immigration.

'It's so *British*,' exclaimed Mel, looking at the large portrait of the Queen that graced the immigration hall.

'It *is* British.' Nikos smiled. 'An Overseas Territory—the last outpost of Empire. But most visitors are Americans, because it's so close to the Atlantic seaboard. You can get here from New York in a couple of hours—short enough for a weekend.'

When they left the small airport building a chauffeured car was waiting for them. Mel spent the journey with her face pressed almost to the window, gazing at the scenery as they left the airport and started to head south.

'It will take a good forty minutes or so to reach the hotel, and we should get a good sunset there—the hotel is right on the beach,' Nikos told her.

He was thinking ahead rapidly. With jet lag, and Mel not being used to dealing with it, she would probably need an early night. He'd booked adjoining rooms at the hotel because he didn't want to rush her, or appear crass, and he knew—reluctantly—that a romantic evening tonight might not be on the cards.

He continued with his tour-guide speech. 'We're bypassing the capital, Hamilton, although the old capital, St George's, is a must-see while we're here. It's one of the oldest European settlements in the New World. Most of the island south of Hamilton is covered by villas, as the land mass is so small here, but there are botanical gardens, and a few small agricultural plots. Of all things, Bermuda is famous for its onions.'

Mel laughed. 'It's all so incredibly *pretty*,' she said, gazing out over the stone-built houses, many of them painted in pastel shades of pink and pale green and yellow, set in lush tropical gardens with palm trees, hibiscus and vivid bougainvillaea. 'The houses have funny roofs—sort of stepped tiles.'

'It's to catch rainwater and channel it down into underground cisterns,' Nikos explained. 'There are no rivers here—the island is volcanic in origin, and the big harbours to the west are the remnants of an ancient caldera. So rainwater is essential. The island is lush, but the rainy season is only for a few months in the winter. Overall, the island is very fortunate. There are occasional hurricanes, but by and large it's clement all year round.'

Mel glanced back at him. 'Shakespeare is said to have used it as his inspiration for Prospero's magical island in *The Tempest*,' she said.

'Maybe he did. It was known to Europeans by then, and St George's was settled early in the seventeenth century. It was a dangerous place, though—the surrounding reefs are full of the wrecks of unfortunate ships.' He quirked an eyebrow at Mel. 'Do you fancy trying diving while we're here?'

Her eyes widened. '*Can* we?'

His smile warm and embracing. 'Mel, we can do anything and everything while we're here. This is our time together, and I really, *really* want you to have the time of your life.'

He did, too. It would be a joy and a pleasure to give her the holiday of her dreams—and he would take pleasure in *her* pleasure. Take pleasure—oh, such pleasure—in her altogether. Mel in his arms, his embrace, his bed…

Right now, life was very sweet indeed. This was set to be a great holiday—

'Oh, this is so *beautiful*.'

Mel's exclamation came from the heart. Sun was pouring over the breakfast terrace at the hotel, dazzling on the azure sea beyond. Palm trees waved in a deliciously light breeze, and canvas parasols shaded the breakfast tables.

Mel gazed about her, fizzing with excitement and wonder. Bermuda, the fabulous hotel, the glittering blue sea, the heat, the palm trees, the vivid exotic flowers tumbling everywhere over walls, the glimpse of a sparkling marble pool a few steps beyond the terrace—they were all real. No dream, no mere photo in a travel brochure, but all, *all* real.

And real, too, was the man standing beside her. Inside the fizzing champagne of excitement in her veins she felt her blood gave a kick, shooting adrenaline through her system.

Nikos was right here, beside her. She'd grabbed the strong, warm hand he'd held out to her and run off with him, winging across the wide Atlantic to land here, on this beautiful, gorgeous island in the sun.

She turned and grinned at him. 'It's just absolutely fantastic!' she exclaimed. 'I can't believe I'm really here.'

'Believe it,' Nikos assured her, his eyes smiling as they rested on her. Drinking her in.

Her long golden hair was caught back with a scarf, but the breeze was blowing it into a halo around her head, and her face was alight with pleasure as she gazed around, eyes wide. His breath caught at her beauty.

And the hotel was perfect—tucked away on a promontory overlooking the long, reef-fringed south shore beaches to the east and a calm, sheltered bay to the west, perfect for sailing. The accommodation was low-rise, pastel-painted cottage-style rooms, all with sea views.

'Is this where your banking conference is going to be?' she asked Nikos.

Nikos shook his head. 'No, that's taking place at one of the much larger, more modern hotels, closer to the airport.' He reached for the jug of chilled orange juice that a server had just placed on the table with a smile. 'I'll take a taxi there on the day I have to speak.' He glanced at Mel. 'Do you want to come along?'

She gave him a mischievous smile. 'I wouldn't miss it for the world,' she assured him. 'Seeing you in your natural environment.'

He made a slight face. 'My natural environment?' he echoed. 'Is that what you think?'

She looked at him. 'I don't know,' she answered. 'I don't know you well enough, Nikos.'

Her voice was sober suddenly, her expression uncertain. Did she *want* to know Nikos? Did it matter to her who he was? Wasn't he just a fantastic, gorgeous man whose company she enjoyed and who could melt her with a kiss? Wasn't that enough for her?

He reached across the table with his hand, just grazing her cheek with his fingers. The gesture was soft, fleeting. Reassuring.

'There is no rush,' he said. 'We're here to enjoy ourselves.'

The smile was in his eyes, on his lips. She nodded, relaxing now. He saw it, and was glad.

'Speaking of which...' He took a mouthful of freshly squeezed orange juice. 'What do you want to do after breakfast?'

Mel's answer was immediate. 'Hit the beach!' she enthused. 'I can't wait to get into that water. It's like something out of a travel brochure.'

'Great idea,' he agreed. 'The beach it is. We'll laze the morning away—and very possibly the afternoon, too.'

Which was exactly what they did.

After a leisurely breakfast, with Nikos regaling Mel with all he knew about Bermuda, they went back to their rooms to change into beach clothes. As she let herself into her room Mel knew she was grateful to Nikos for being sufficiently sensitive to the impulsive nature of their holiday together and reserving separate rooms.

Yes, she knew—oh, she most *certainly* knew—what she had committed herself to, but to have arrived last evening, jet-lagged as she'd been, and to have been thrust into the immediate intimacy of sharing a room—a bed—would have been too...too... Well, too awkward, really.

And definitely too rushed. When they came together—a little frisson of excitement shimmered through her at the thought—it would be when they were relaxed, comfortable with each other, and with a wonderful sense of anticipation having been built up during the day and heightened to heady passion in the evening...

Then he'll take me in his arms, kiss me as he kissed me before. But this time...oh, this time it will not be goodbye...it will be the very opposite.

Nikos and me, embracing, entwining, his mouth on

mine, his body clasped by mine, only passion and de-sire between us...

She gave her head a quick shake to clear the image.

Yes, well, that was for later. For now, she had to change into her new swimsuit, which would be christened in the turquoise waters of Bermuda.

Another little quiver of disbelief went through her as yet again the realisation of just where she was impacted. How absolutely gorgeous it all was.

Hurriedly she slipped into her swimsuit, pulling a long, loose, semi-transparent cover-up over her head and pushing her feet into flip-flops. She grabbed her beach bag and headed outdoors via the private patio, separated from Nikos's by a low grey stone wall that could be hopped over in a second.

Nikos was already waiting for her, lounging back in one of the terrace chairs at the little dining set provided. He got to his feet, and Mel's breath caught.

Board shorts in deep cobalt-blue hugged lean hips, and his torso was moulded by every square centimetre of a white short-sleeved top bearing a fashionable surfing logo. And he was sporting wrap-around sunglasses that made her want to drop her jaw gormlessly open and gaze at him.

It took a moment for her to realise that he was returning her stare. She couldn't see his eyes behind the opaque sunglasses, but that was just as well, part of her registered. The other part was trying hard to ignore the insistent fact that beneath the veiling of her cover-up and the sheer material of her swimsuit her breasts were shamelessly engorged, following an instinct that was as powerful as it was primeval...

I want him.

The stark, visceral words sounded in her head almost audibly as she stood, rooted to the spot.

'Ready for a hard day's beach-lounging?' Nikos smiled at her, the corners of his sculpted mouth crinkling.

Mel took a breath. 'All set,' she said with determined lightness, and they headed down the path that would take them to the beach below.

A line of white sunbeds had been set out along the pale sand that was already too hot to walk on. A beach steward ushered them to a pair with a little table in between them, a parasol overhead for shade, and towels draped over the foam mattresses, with more neatly folded at the end of each lounger. They settled themselves down, and the steward enquired if they would like refreshments from the beach bistro.

'OJ and sparkling mineral water, please.'

Mel smiled. How blissful just to give a request like that and know that two minutes later it would be served to her as she relaxed back on her lounger, gazing out over the sea, feeling the warmth of the day like a cocoon around her.

'This,' she announced feelingly, 'is absolute bliss.'

'No question,' agreed Nikos.

He reached across the space between their respective sunbeds and took her hand. It was an instinctive gesture, and he was hardly aware of doing it—except that the moment his fingers wound into her hers he knew it felt right.

Mel turned to look at him, then smiled. A warm, wide smile that seemed to encapsulate everything about what they had done—run off here, to this beautiful island in the sun, to have time to themselves, to have the affair that both of them wanted to have. He knew that with absolute certainty.

He gave a deep sigh of contentment and looked out to sea again. Beside him, Mel gave an echoing sigh—and then a wry little laugh.

'It's just so gorgeous,' she said, 'to lie here with absolutely nothing to do except relax on the beach. I feel utterly idle.'

Nikos turned his head to glance at her. 'That's the general idea of a holiday,' he said, amused.

She gave a semi-shrug. 'Well, I'm not used to holidays.' She glanced away, towards the brilliant azure sea glinting in the morning sunshine, then back to Nikos. 'I've waited just *so* long to start my real life—to travel as I've longed to do—that now I am I can't quite believe it. I keep feeling I should be working.'

The focus of Nikos's gaze sharpened slightly. 'Tell me,' he asked, 'why do you feel so strongly that you should be working all the time?'

He cocked an interrogative eyebrow at her, but his voice was merely mildly curious.

Mel's expression changed. Became thoughtful. But also, Nikos thought assessingly, became guarded.

'Habit, really, I suppose. Like I say, I'm not used to holidays. Not used to having time off.'

'I seem to remember you said you did waitressing in the evenings, after the sandwich bar had closed?' Nikos recalled. 'How long did you keep that kind of double shift going? It can burn you out in the end, you know.'

He sounded sympathetic, but Mel shook her head. 'Oh, no, that wasn't a problem. I was working for myself—building up my bank balance to fund my getaway. It was a joy to work, to be honest, in comparison with looking after my grandfather. *That* was—' She broke off, not finishing.

What word would describe that period of her life? Only one—*torment*. Absolute torment…

Torment to watch the grandfather she'd loved so much become more and more frail, in body and mind. Torment to be the only person who could look after him—the only person he wanted to look after him—so that she could never have a break or even the slightest amount of time to herself.

He was looking at her curiously now, and she wished she'd kept her mouth shut.

'Was he ill?' Nikos asked. Again, his voice was sympathetic.

'Yes,' she said tightly. 'His mind went.'

'Ah… Dementia can be very hard,' acknowledged Nikos.

A kind of choke sounded in Mel's voice as she answered. 'I was raised by my grandfather after my parents died when I was very little—they were killed in a car crash. My grandfather took me in to stop me going into care. That's why, when he needed care himself, it was my…my turn to look after *him*, really.'

Her voice was tight, suppressed. She didn't want to talk about this—didn't want to think about it, didn't want to remember.

Nikos was frowning. 'Surely you didn't have to cope single-handed? There must have been help available? Professional carers on call?'

Mel swallowed. Yes, there had been help—up to a point. That hadn't been the problem. It was hard to explain—and she didn't want to. Yet somehow, for some reason—maybe it was her release, finally, from the long years of caged confinement at her grandfather's side as he made the slow, dreadful descent into dementia and eventual death—she heard the words burst from her.

'He didn't want anyone else.'

Her voice was low, the stress in it audible to Nikos.

'He only ever wanted me—all the time. He couldn't even bear to let me out of his sight, and he used to follow me around or get distressed and agitated if I just went into another room, let alone tried to go out of the house. He'd wander around at night—and of course that meant that I couldn't sleep either...not with him awake and wandering like that...'

Her voice was shaking now, but still words poured out of her, after all the months and years of watching her grandfather sink lower and lower still.

'It's what the dementia did to him. He was lost in his dark, confused mind, and I was the only thing in it he recognised—the only thing he wanted, the only thing he clung to. If I tried to get a carer from an agency to sit with him he'd yell at her, and he'd only calm down when I was back in the room again. It was pitiful to see. So no matter how exhausting it was, I just couldn't abandon him—not to outside carers—nor put him into a nursing home. How *could* I? He was the only person in the world I loved—the only person in the world who loved *me*—and I was absolutely adamant I would take care of him to the end.'

Her expression was tormented.

Nikos's voice was quiet, sombre. 'But the end did come?' he said.

She swallowed the hard, painful lump in her throat. 'It went on for three years,' she said, her voice hollow. 'And by the time the end came he didn't know me—didn't know anyone. I could only be relieved—dreadful though it is to say it—that he was finally able to leave his stricken body and mind.'

She shut her eyes, guilt heavy in her heart.

'I'd started to long for the end to come—for his sake, and for mine, too. Because death would finally release him—' She swallowed again, her voice stretched like wire. 'And it would finally release me, too…let me claim my own life back again.'

She fell silent—horrified by what had poured out of her, shutting her eyes against the memory of it, haunted by the guilt that assailed her. And yet she remembered that terrible, silent cry of anguish at the captivity his illness had held her in.

She'd never said anything of her anguish before—never said anything of those heartbreakingly difficult, impossible years she'd spent as her grandfather's carer. And yet here she was, spilling her heart to a man who was little more than a stranger still…

Beside her, Nikos had stilled as he heard her out. Now, slowly, instinctively, he reached across for the hand that she was clenching and unclenching on her chest as she relived those tormented years she'd spent at her ailing grandfather's side. She felt his palm close over her fist, stilling her.

'You did your very best for him,' he said quietly. 'You stayed with him to the end.'

He took a breath, the tenor of his voice changing.

'And now you deserve this time of freedom from care and responsibility.' His voice warmed and he squeezed her hand lightly, then let it go. 'You deserve the most fantastic holiday I can give you.'

She felt her anguish ease, and took a long, deep breath before opening her eyes to look at him.

'Thank you,' she said, and her eyes were saying more than mere words could.

For a moment their gazes held, and then Nikos deliberately lightened the mood. He wanted to see her happy again.

'Tell me,' he said, 'would you like to take a boat out sometime?'

Her expression lit as she followed his cue. Glad to do so. Glad to move away from the long, dreadful years that were gone now. Her grandfather, she hoped, was in a far better place, reunited with his long-lost family. And she was free to live her own life, making her own way in the world, enjoying her precious, fleeting youth untrammelled by cares and responsibilities. Revelling in all the new experiences she could.

Like skimming across the brilliantly azure sea that lay before her.

'Yes, please! I've never been on a boat.'

His eyebrows rose. 'Never?'

She shook her head. 'No, never,' she confirmed. 'My grandfather didn't like the water. It was as much as he'd do to go on seaside holidays when I was a child. He would sit in his deckchair, in long trousers and a long-sleeved shirt, and wish he were elsewhere while I played, merrily building sandcastles and splashing around in the freezing cold English Channel.'

She spoke easily now, far preferring to remember happy times with her grandfather. Then her expression changed again.

'When I was older I used to gaze across the water and long to see what was on the other side.' She smiled. 'And now I know. It's *this*—this blissful, gorgeous place.'

Instinctively she reached for his hand, squeezing it lightly. 'Thank you,' she said. 'Thank you for bringing me here. I shall treasure the memory of this all my life!'

Nikos lifted her hand and grazed her knuckles lightly,

so lightly, with his mouth. Little flurries of electricity raced along her skin at his touch.

'It is my pleasure to bring you here,' he said, the husk audible in his voice.

Mel could feel desire pool in her stomach. Then, with a little laugh, she dropped his hand.

'I can't resist the water any more,' she cried, and got to her feet. She peeled off her cover-up and glanced down at Nikos. 'Last one in is a sissy!' she taunted wickedly, and hared across the hot sand to where the azure water was lapping at the beach.

She ran right into the water, which was blissfully warm to the skin, and plunged into its crystal-clear embrace. Behind her she heard a heavier splash, and then Nikos was there, too, grinning and diving into the deeper sea like a dolphin, surfacing again with his sable hair slicked back and water glistening like diamonds all over his broad muscled shoulders and torso.

'Not going to get your hair wet, then?'

It was his turn to taunt, and with a toss of her locks Mel mimicked his dive into the gently mounded swell and swam underwater, to emerge further out to sea, almost out of her depth. She trod water while Nikos caught up with her in two powerful strokes.

'This is glorious!' she cried exuberantly. 'The water's so warm it's like a bath!'

His grin answered hers and he dived again. Exuberance filled him as he surfaced for air some way yet further out. Mel swam to him and her eyelashes were glistening with diamond drops of water. Her slicked-back hair emphasised the perfection of her sculpted features. How incredibly beautiful she looked.

Without conscious thought, he caught her shoulders and pressed a swift, salty kiss on her mouth. Not with passion or desire, but simply because—well, because he wanted to. It lasted only a second and then he was away again, powering through the blue waters of the warm sea.

Mel came racing after him in the same exuberant mood. That sudden salty kiss had meant nothing—and everything. A joyous salutation to the playful pleasure of being in the warm, embracing sea, bathed in glorious bright sunshine, with fresh air and water spray and absolutely nothing to do except enjoy themselves. And enjoy each other...

The afternoon passed in as leisurely and lazy a fashion as the morning until, with the sun lowering, they made their way up the winding paths towards their rooms. Mel's skin felt warm and salty, and a sense of well-being filled her.

'A good first day?' Nikos asked.

'Oh, yes,' Mel assured him. She gave a sigh of happiness and went on walking. The day might be over but—a little thrill went through her—the night was only just beginning...

And what the night would bring was what she longed for: Nikos in her passionate embrace.

The little thrill went through her again.

The process of transforming herself from beach babe to evening goddess took Mel some considerable time.

'Take as long as you want,' Nikos had assured her, his eyes glinting. 'I know it will be worth the wait.'

Nearly ninety minutes later she checked herself out in front of the long mirror on the wardrobe door.

As she did so a memory fused in her head of the way she'd tried to inspect her appearance in Sarrie's back room, with nothing more than a hand mirror.

I had no idea that I'd be here only a couple of weeks later—here with the man I was meeting up with that night!

A sense of wonder went through her. And as she let her gaze settle on her reflection she felt wonder turn to gladness. She looked *good*.

She was wearing another find from her charity shop hunts—this time a sleeveless fine cotton ankle-length dress in a warm vermilion print, with a scoop neck that hinted at a décolletage without being obvious. Her jewellery was a simple gold chain, hoop earrings and a matching bangle, her footwear low-heeled strappy sandals comfortable to walk in but more elegant than flip-flops. She'd left her hair loose, held back off her face with a narrow hairband, so that it fell in waves around her shoulders. Her make-up was light, for she knew her face was flushed from the sun, protected though her skin had been all day.

Slipping her arms into the loose, evening jacket that went with the dress and picking up her bag, she headed out—ready for the evening ahead. Ready for all the evening would bring her—and the night that would follow…

When Nikos opened the door of his room to her soft knocking the blaze in his eyes told her that her efforts had been more than worthwhile, and she felt the blood surge in her veins. Her pulse quickened with her body's response to him as she gazed in appreciation at his tall, lean figure, clad now in long linen chinos and an open-necked cotton shirt.

He guided her forward through the warm, balmy night, along the oleander-bordered path up towards the main section of the hotel, where they would be dining, and she could catch the spiced warmth of his aftershave mingling with the floral tones of her own perfume, giving her a quivering awareness of his presence at her side.

The same awareness of him remained with her all through dinner, which was taken on the same terrace where they had breakfasted. The tables were now decked in linen, adorned with tropical flowers, with silverware catching the candlelight and the light from the torches set around the perimeter.

She felt as light as gossamer, floating in a haze of happiness to be here now, like this, with this man, in this gorgeous place, eating food that was as delicious as it was rare, beautifully arrayed on the plate, melting in her mouth, washed down with crisp, cold wine.

What they talked about she hardly knew. It was the same kind of easy, casual chat they had indulged in all day. About Bermuda, the sights they would see as they continued their stay, its history... They talked about films they had seen and enjoyed, about travel, all the places Nikos had been to that Mel was eager to hear about. Easy, relaxed, companionable. As if they had known each other for ever.

Yet underneath, beneath their relaxed conversation, Mel knew that a current was running between them. Another conversation was taking place and it was signalled to her in every raised beat of her heart, every swift mingling of their eyes, every movement of his strong, well-shaped hands as he ate or lifted his glass.

She knew she was keeping that conversation beneath the surface of her consciousness—knew that it was necessary to do so. For otherwise she would not be able to function in this social space. Yet the knowledge that it was shared with him, that just as she was constantly aware of *his* physical presence—the way his open-necked white shirt framed the strong column of his neck, the way his turned-back cuffs emphasised the leanness of his wrists—so he was aware of her, too—of *her* physical being. The way the candlelight hollowed the contours of her throat, caught the glint of gold in her earrings, burnished the echoing gold of her hair.

They were both aware of the courtship being conducted—silently, continually, seductively. Aware, with a growing, subtle assurance, of just how that courtship must find its completion…that night.

And so it did.

As they rose from the table eventually—the candles burnt low, almost the only couple left out on the terrace—without thinking she slipped her hand into Nikos's as they strolled back into the interior of the hotel. It seemed the right thing to do. The obvious thing.

His warm, strong fingers closed around hers and it felt right, so right, to let it happen. To walk beside him, closer this time, her shoulder sometimes brushing against his, her skirts fluttering around her legs, catching against him. From inside the hotel they could hear the low sound of a piano being played somewhere.

'Would you like another coffee? Or a drink in the lounge?'

'Only if you would,' she answered, glancing at him.

His eyes caught hers. 'You know what I want,' he murmured. 'And it isn't to be found in the piano lounge.'

There was humour in his expression, in his eyes. But his voice, when he spoke next, was serious.

'Is it what *you* want, Mel? Tell me truly. If it isn't, then you must say now. Because, to be honest…'

Now the humour was back again, and she could hear a touch of self-mockery, too, and was warmed by it.

'I'm not sure I've got the strength of mind or character to walk you back to your room and not come in with you—'

She glanced up at him, with a similar self-mocking wry humour in her own eyes. 'I'm not sure I've got the strength of mind or character to stop you coming in,' she told him. 'In fact...' She bit her lip. 'I strongly suspect I'd yank you inside my room even if you were being strong-minded—'

He gave a low laugh, and Mel could hear the relief in it. The satisfaction. She gave an answering laugh as they headed off through the gardens, back towards their rooms, towards what both of them knew would happen now...

There was a pool of darkness nearby, where the light of the low-set lamps that lined the stone pathway did not reach, and she felt him draw her into it with a swift, decisive movement. His hand tightened on hers and the other drew her round to face him. He was close... so close to her.

She felt her heart give a little leap and that electric current came again, sizzling through her body. She could not see his expression, but she knew what it was... what it must be...what hers must be. He was dim against the night, against the stars...

Unconsciously, instinctively, she lifted her face to his. His free hand slid to cup her throat, to tilt her face higher. She felt the smooth, gliding pressure of his fingers—their warmth, their sensuous touch. Felt her heart beating wildly now, her breath catch.

He was standing with his legs slightly apart, a dominating male stance, one hand still gripping hers, the other fastened to her with a strong, sensuous hold, the pad of his thumb on the delicate line of her jaw.

His long dark lashes dipped low over his eyes, glinting in the starlight. 'Well, if that's your attitude...' his voice was low and husky, and it made her bones weaken '...I'd better not disappoint you, had I?'

For a moment—just a moment—he delayed, and the pad of his thumb moved to her mouth, gliding leisurely across her lips. Her bones weakened further and her pulse quickened. With every fibre of her being she wanted him to kiss her...wanted to feel the warm pressure of his mouth...wanted the sweet taste of him...

'Nikos...'

She must have murmured his name, must have half closed her eyes, waiting, longing for his mouth to swoop and descend, to take hers in its silken touch.

His fingers wound in hers and his thumb slipped away now, his fingers touching at her throat, her jaw, gentling, caressing. And then finally...finally...his mouth descended to hers. Kissing her softly, sweetly, sensuously.

Endlessly.

She folded into him. A gesture as natural, as instinctive as the way her mouth opened to his. She wanted to feel the fullness of his kiss, the full bliss of it, as every part of her body dissolved into it.

Beneath the glint and glitter of the stars, in the soft, warm air, with the perfume of the night-scented flowers the susurration of the cicadas all around, his kiss went on and on. Claiming her, arousing her, calling forth from her all that she would bestow upon him that night, telling of all that he would give to her.

When his lips finally left hers she felt as if she was still in his embrace—as if she were floating inches off the ground and as if her heart were soaring around like a fluttering bird. He led her down the path to his room and then they were inside, in the cool, air-conditioned dimness. No light was needed—only the pale glow from the phosphorescence of the open sea beyond the windows.

He took her into his arms again, slipping his hands around her slender waist, cradling her supple spine as she leant into him, offering him her mouth…herself.

His kiss deepened, seeking all that it could find, and she offered all that she could give, her lips moving beneath his, her mouth opening to his in a rush of sweet, sensuous bliss. She could feel the blood surge in her veins, the heat fan out across her body, as she leant into him to taste, and take, and give, and yield.

She could feel him gliding the jacket from her shoulders, his warm hands slipping down her bared arms, and then she was pulling away from him slightly, and in a single fluid movement lifting the dress from her body, shaking her hair free of its band, giving a glorious, breathless laugh of pleasure, of anticipation.

As Nikos's eyes feasted on her she stood there, clad only in bra and panties, and a heady recklessness consumed her. Wordlessly she slipped the buttons of his shirt, easing her hands across the strong, warm column of his body. He caught her hands, his breath a rasp in his throat, and then he was folding her arms gently back, using the same movement to haul her against him, his mouth dipping to the soft, ripe swell of her breasts.

She gave a little gasp, feeling her nipples engorged against the straining satin of her bra. A low laugh came from him as his hands glided up the contour of her spine to unfasten the hooks that were keeping his mouth from what it sought to find. She felt her bra fall to the ground, felt his lips nuzzle at her bared breasts delicately, sensually, teasing and tasting until she gasped again in the sheer, trembling pleasure of it.

Her head fell back, her eyes fluttering closed, and an unconscious movement to lift her breasts to him overwhelmed her. A growl of satisfaction came from him and then he was scooping her up, lifting her as if she were a featherweight, carrying her across to the wide, waiting bed and lowering her down upon it.

She lay upon its surface, breasts still engorged and peaked, her eyes wide as she gazed up at him. Swiftly he discarded his own clothes, and then, with a groan, came down upon her. His weight crushed her, but she gloried in it—gloried in his questing mouth that now roamed her body, his hands likewise, exploring and caressing and arousing such that if the world had caught fire that very hour she would have burned in the flames that were licking through her now.

Her breath quickened, her pulse racing as she clutched his strong, hard shoulders, feeling her body yielding to him, feeling his glorious, piercing possession of her that felt so right, so incredibly, wonderfully right, nestling in the welcoming cradle of her hips. She felt the fire intensify within her, consuming her, until in a final conflagration she heard herself cry out, heard his answering cry, and felt a pleasure so intense it filled her entire being, shuddering through her, shaking and possessing her, on and on and on…

Until the quietness came.

Their bodies slaked, they held each other with slackened gentleness, beside each other, loose-limbed, embracing.

She sought his mouth. A gentle, peaceful kiss. He kissed her back, then grazed her forehead with a kiss, as well. His eyes were soft in the dim light.

There were no words—there did not need to be—only the gradual slowing of their racing hearts, their hectic pulse subsiding now. He drew her to him, his arms around her, hers around him, and with a little sigh she felt sleep take them.

CHAPTER SEVEN

'So, WHAT WOULD you like to do today? Anything on Bermuda you haven't seen yet?'

Nikos smiled encouragingly at Mel. They were breakfasting on Nikos's patio, gazing out over the aquamarine waters of the bay, as calm as a mill pond at this time of day. Breakfasting together like this had become the rule in the days since they'd arrived, after rising in a leisurely fashion, both of them having awoken to yet more arousal after a night of searing passion.

Hastily she reached for her coffee, hoping it might cool her suddenly heated cheeks. Time to focus on the day's activities—yet another wonderful, blissful day of self-indulgent holidaymaking.

In the week they'd already spent on Bermuda they'd covered nearly all the sights.

They'd toured the historic Nelson's Dockyard at the far west of the island, where British men-of-war had once dropped anchor, and which now welcomed massive cruise ships, disgorging their passengers to throng the myriad little cafés and craft shops.

They'd taken the ferry from the dockyard across to the island's bay-lapped capital, Hamilton, lunching on the sea front and exploring the shops. They'd gone to the old capital of St George's in the north of the island, with its white-painted little houses, art galleries, churches and museums.

And they'd been out to sea—Nikos had taken her sailing in the bay and further afield, and they'd enjoyed a sunset champagne dinner on a sleek motor yacht chartered to sail them around the island. He'd hired a dive boat, which had hovered over the reef for Nikos to dive with the instructor, leaving Mel content to snorkel on the surface, glimpsing long-sunk wrecks rich with darting fish, and the scary but thankfully harmless purple jellyfish that trailed long tentacles in the water deep below her.

Mel had wanted to see and do everything, had been excited and thrilled by even the simplest things— whether it was wandering through the beautiful gardens around the hotel, or pausing for coffee at a little Bermudian coffee shop overlooking one of the beautiful pink sand beaches. She was just revelling in being in this beautiful place, in the company of this fabulous man…

This is the most fantastic holiday romance that anyone could ever wish for.

Again she felt heat fan her cheeks. Nikos was so sensual and passionate a lover she was blown away by it. Never had she realised how incredible it could be when two people gave themselves to each other up to the very hilt of passion. How in the moment of union their bodies could pulse with an intensity, an explosion of sensual overload that wrung from her a response she had never felt before.

Jak had been a careful lover, and her memories of him were fond and grateful, but Nikos—ah, Nikos was in a league of his own. All the promise…all the shimmering awareness of the irrepressible physical attraction that had flared between them right from their first intemperate encounter…had exploded on their first night together. And now, night after night, when he took her in his arms, skilfully caressed her body to melting, she felt transported to a level of sensual satiation she had never known existed. And it was Nikos who took her there…

Will there ever be anyone in my life like him again?

The question was in her head before she could stop it. And so was the answer.

How could there be? How could there be anyone like him again—how could there be a time like this ever again in her life?

A little quiver went through her, but she silenced it. She had come away with Nikos with her eyes open—knowing he wanted only a brief, passionate affair and nothing more. Knowing that that was exactly what she wanted, too. A fabulous, gorgeous, breathtaking *entrée* in the feast of freedom that was to be her new independent life.

Nikos was for the wonderful, wonderful *now*, and that was how she was going to enjoy him—how she was going to enjoy their time together, night after night, day after day.

Speaking of days…

'We still haven't done the Crystal Caves,' she said. 'Could we visit them today?'

'Why not?' Nikos answered with lazy complaisance. 'We can take the hotel launch around to Hamilton, do a spot of shopping, have lunch and take a taxi on to the caves.'

His eyes rested on her warmly. How right he'd been

not to let her fly off to Spain and disappear on her travels without him. Instead he'd brought her here, romanced her and made love to her, and he was with her day in, day out.

Satisfaction filled him—more than satisfaction. Contentment.

He wondered at it. It just seemed to be so easy to be with Mel—so natural, so absolutely effortless. Conversation was easy with her. They still sparked off each other, just as they had right from the first, but now it was always humorous, easygoing, mutually teasing each other, but with a smile. And it was as easy *not* to talk as it was to talk. They could wander or lie on sun loungers or watch the sunset in happy silence.

Yes, being with Mel just seemed to…*work*. That was the only way he could explain it.

Not that he wanted to analyse it, or find words to describe being with her. No, all he wanted to do was enjoy this time with her. Enjoy it to the full. In bed and out.

And that gave him an idea—a very good one, now he came to think of it.

He glanced at his watch. 'I think the hotel launch leaves every hour to make the crossing to Hamilton. Do you want to make the next one? Or would you prefer to skip it and we could take an early siesta, maybe?'

He threw her an encouraging look.

Mel gave a splutter of laughter. She knew perfectly well what he meant. And sleep would *not* be involved!

'Early siesta? It's barely gone ten in the morning!' She got to her feet, stooping to whisper to him, 'You're insatiable—you know that? Honestly. Come on.' Her voice was bracing now. 'If we get going we can get the next launch.'

'So keen to go shopping in Hamilton?' It was Nikos's turn to sound teasing.

She gave another splutter of laughter. 'No. I don't need a thing—my bathroom's chock-full of complimentary toiletries.'

Nikos smiled indulgently. 'So easily pleased...' he said fondly.

'Well, I am!' Mel riposted. 'Everything...' she waved her arms expansively, taking in the whole resort and the island it was on '...is brilliant.' She turned a warm gaze on Nikos. 'And *you're* the most brilliant of all.'

He reached to stroke her sun-warmed bare arm. 'That's the right answer,' he laughed. 'I am *definitely* more brilliant than complimentary hotel toiletries,' he finished feelingly. 'And if you really, *really* insist...' he gave an exaggerated sigh '...I shall deprive myself of our...er...siesta...until after we get back from these Crystal Caves you're determined to drag me to.'

'Oh, you'll *love* them,' she assured him with a playful thump. 'They're a marvel of nature, the guidebook says. Limestone caves with pools and walkways all illuminated like something out of a fairy tale. What's more...' she glanced at him with a determined look in her eyes '...we won't need a taxi—you can get there by bus from Hamilton. I think we should do that—I'd love to see Nikos Parakis on a humble bus.'

He laughed, and they finished off their breakfast companionably, in harmony with each other and with the day ahead.

Gratitude for all that she had been given ran through Mel like circling water. So much. This fabulous place, this fabulous time—and this fabulous man who had given it to her and was sharing it with her.

* * *

The Crystal Caves were as breathtaking as she'd hoped from their description in the guidebook, and after their visit they headed back to their hotel and some time on the beach.

As the sun lowered, though, Nikos got to his feet.

'You stay on down here for a while,' he told her. 'I need to head back to my room—check over my speech for tomorrow.'

'Oh, my goodness—is it the conference already?' Mel asked, surprised.

'I'm afraid so. But, like I've said, I'm only putting in a single day there. Then we can get on with the remainder of our holiday.' He smiled.

Her eyes followed him as he made his way along the beach. A little frown furrowed her brow. Halfway— they were halfway through their holiday already. Nikos had said 'the remainder'—that was a word that had a tolling bell in it, pointing towards the end. The end of their time together. The end of their romance.

She felt a little clenching of her stomach.

The end.

Her gaze slipped away, over the sea beyond. Her frown deepened, shadowing her eyes. Theirs was a holiday romance—a brief, gorgeous fling—and holidays always came to an end. But it would also mean a start to her independent travels—her footloose, fancy-free wandering—going where she wanted, when she wanted, tied to no one and bound to nobody...

Not even Nikos.

It's what I want—what I've planned. What I've always intended.

The reminder sounded in her head—resolutely. Determinedly. Silencing anything else that might be trying to be heard.

* * *

The conference hall was packed with delegates in business suits, and Mel had to squeeze into a space at the rear. But from there she still had a good view of Nikos on the podium. But it wasn't his discourse on sovereign debt or optimal fiscal policy that held her gaze. Oh, no.

It was the way his bespoke tailored business suit moulded every long, lean line of his fit, hard body. The way his long-fingered hands gestured at the complex graphs displayed on the screen behind him. The way his expression—focussed, incisive, authoritative, as befitted a man who had responsibilities she could not dream of—would suddenly give a hint…just a hint…of the humour that could flash out so beguilingly.

So she sat and gazed, spellbound and riveted, until his Q&A session had ended and the audience was dispersing for lunch.

She didn't join him—this was his world, not hers—instead making her way to the poolside bistro. The area was busy, but after her lunch she found an empty sun lounger in the shade and settled down to leaf through a magazine, content to while away the afternoon until Nikos was finished with the conference.

A voice nearby interrupted her. 'Hi—didn't I see you in the conference hall before lunch?'

The American-accented voice was female, and friendly, and it came from the next lounger along. Mel looked towards the woman, taking in an attractive bikini-clad brunette, a few years older than her, with an extremely chic hairstyle and full eye make-up.

The woman smiled. 'Wasn't that last speaker something? The foreign guy with his own bank—total *dish*!' Her dark eyes sparkled appreciatively.

There was an air of shared conspiracy, an invita-

tion to agree with her, and Mel found herself smiling
in wry agreement.

Taking it as consent to keep chatting, the woman
continued. 'Are you here as a delegate yourself? Or a
spouse?'

'Well, not a spouse—just…um…a "plus one." I guess
you'd call it,' she answered, not sure whether she should
mention that she was the 'plus one' of the 'dish'… 'What
about you?' she asked politely.

'Oh, my husband's a banker,' the woman said. 'John
Friedman of Friedman Hoffhaus,' she added, looking
expectantly at Mel.

Mel gave an apologetic shake of her head. 'I'm afraid
I'm very ignorant of the banking world,' she answered.

'Oh—so who are you the "plus one" of?' the woman
asked curiously.

Mel's expression changed again. 'Well, actually…
um…it's the "dish",' she said apologetically.

Immediately the woman's eyes sparkled. 'No *way*!
My, oh, my—you are one lucky, *lucky* lady! Mind
you…' she nodded in tribute to Mel's blonde beauty
'…I can see how you pulled him. The thing is, though,'
she went on airily, 'how are you gonna *keep* him? Men
that rich *and* young *and* good-looking are hard to hog-
tie. You're going to have to have a watertight "get him
to the altar" strategy to be his *permanent* "plus one"!'

Mel looked uncomfortable, not wanting to elaborate
to a stranger on the fact that she and Nikos were simply here together on holiday and weren't an established
couple—and that she was in no need of a strategy to
'hog-tie' him.

Not that Nikos was the kind of man to get hog-tied
anyway.

For an instant so brief it wasn't measurable in time

a flicker of emotion went through her—but what that emotion was she could not tell. Did not want to...

The other woman was talking again. 'Maybe you'll find yourself pregnant,' she said, and now there was an openly conspiratorial look in her eye. 'That's what happened to me—worked like a dream.'

She glanced towards the shallow end of the pool, where Mel could see a preschooler splashing about, with a young woman—presumably his nanny—playing with him.

Mel was thankfully spared the necessity of responding to such an untoward comment by a server gliding by, offering coffee. She took one, and so did the woman, who now introduced herself as Nyree, eliciting a reciprocal if somewhat reluctant response from Mel.

She was relieved when Nyree Friedman changed the subject to that of shopping opportunities, for which she considered Bermuda inadequate, which led to her regaling Mel with the delights of New York for that purpose, and giving a little cry of disbelief when she discovered that Mel had never been there.

'Oh, but you *must*! Tell the dish you absolutely *have* to go from here,' she urged.

Not waiting for an answer, she chattered on, and Mel was happy enough to leave her to it. Nyree Friedman was chatty and convivial, but Mel had to conclude she was something of an airhead.

She didn't seem to be much of a devoted mother, either, for she was perfectly happy to leave her little boy's nanny to do all the entertaining of her son. Cynically, Mel presumed that the child had served his purpose in 'hog-tying' his wealthy banker father for Nyree. It was a depressing thought.

Their mostly one-sided chat about Nyree Friedman's

fashionable, affluent Manhattan lifestyle was finally brought to an end by the emergence of Nikos from the conference. He strolled up to Mel.

'There you are…' He smiled. Then his glance swept sideways to take in her partner in conversation, who had stopped mid-sentence, her eyes wide with open appreciation at the arrival of 'the dish.'

Her dark eyes sparkled. *'Hi…'* she said warmly, holding out a languid, perfectly manicured hand. 'I'm Nyree Friedman. I heard your presentation this morning—it was *fascinating*!' she breathed. Her expression was blatantly admiring.

There was a tug at the side of Nikos's mouth as he shook the extended hand—but briefly, Mel was glad to notice. No lingering contact with the attractive brunette…

'Well, I can only hope your husband was just as taken by it,' he replied drily.

Clearly, Mel realised, he knew perfectly well who Nyree Friedman's husband was—even if he'd never met his wife before.

Nyree's gaze was visibly eating Nikos up. Out of the blue Mel felt a dagger's blade of possessiveness go through her. Sharp and piercing. For an instant she wanted to grab Nikos and drag him away—and slap Nyree down at the same time, for daring to make eyes at him.

The intensity of the emotion shocked her. No *way* did she want to feel possessive about Nikos. Hadn't he told her right from the start that possessiveness was exactly what put him off a woman? The reason he'd asked her out that very first evening had been to ward off Fiona Pellingham's possessive intentions. No, possessiveness—from either of them—wasn't what their deliberately brief time together was about, she reminded herself sharply. Possessiveness had no place at all in a fun but fleeting holiday romance such as theirs was.

To her relief, Nikos's attention was back on her, and his eyes were sending a silent question that echoed his verbal one.

'I'm all done here now, Mel,' he told her. 'So if you're ready to go we can head off? Unless,' he went on politely, his glance taking in Nyree again, 'you want to stay longer?'

His tone was polite, but Mel knew he didn't want to stay on longer here at this huge, crowded hotel. He'd already told her he wasn't going to be attending the conference dinner that evening, and she'd been glad. She wasn't going to have him for much longer, and she didn't want to share him for any of that time if she didn't have to.

'No, I'm good to go,' she said. She looked across at Nyree, who was looking rueful. 'It was lovely to meet you,' she said brightly, getting to her feet.

'Well, we must meet up in New York!' Nyree said promptly. Her flirtatious gaze went back to Nikos, then changed as it moved past him. 'John,' she said imperiously, 'persuade this gorgeous man to bring his girlfriend to New York. She's never been—can you believe it?'

The man approaching was clad in a business suit, like Nikos, but he was a good twenty years older, thought Mel, and unlike Nikos very overweight.

He nodded at Nikos, then addressed Mel. 'Has my wife let you get a word in edgeways?' he asked with heavy humour. 'She does like to dominate the airwaves.'

It was said humorously, but Mel could detect underlying irritation at his wife's garrulity.

'It's been very…interesting,' Mel said politely.

John Friedman laughed again, a little too heavily, and then his attention was drawn to the small figure hurtling towards him.

'Dad! Dad!' he was calling out excitedly. 'Come in the pool!'

Mel watched him hug the pool-wet boy and ruffle his damp hair.

'I can't wait!' his father assured him. 'But I need to get changed first, OK?' His eyes went to his wife, who was still lounging back on the recliner. 'Will *you* spend any time with our son in the pool?'

There was a clear jibe in the question, and it drew an acid response from his wife.

'And wreck my hair? Don't be ridiculous. Besides, it's time for cocktails.'

'It's too early for cocktails—especially for *you*,' John Friedman said immediately. And pointedly.

Nyree's mouth thinned mutinously and it looked as if she was going to make an angry retort. To Mel's relief—for witnessing this marital acrimony was uncomfortable—Nyree's husband had turned to Nikos.

'You made a persuasive case in there,' he said, very much banker-to-banker now. 'Maybe we should discuss some potential mutual opportunities?'

'I'd be glad to,' Nikos said promptly.

'Good.' John Friedman nodded. 'Get in touch next time you're in New York.'

'Make it *soon*!' Nyree enthused, her gaze fastening greedily on Nikos again.

Nikos gave a non-committal smile and took Mel's hand, squeezing it meaningfully. He wanted out, she knew. And so did she. For all their superficial politeness, the atmosphere was uncomfortable, and the tension between Nyree and her husband was palpable. But they said goodbye politely, even though Mel could hear regret in Nyree's voice, and saw her eyes linger on Nikos.

As she and Nikos moved away Mel could hear Nyree start up. 'Oh, my God, John—your suit is soaking wet! Why do you let the boy maul you like that? It's ridiculous. You make far too much fuss of him.'

Her husband's voice cut across her. 'One of us needs to. You won't—so I do. I'm his father. And do you *have* to try and flirt with every man you see—even when they're obviously not interested in you?'

Mel grimaced as they got out of earshot, heading through the hotel grounds to pick up a taxi at the front. 'Eek—not a happy marriage, I think. Nor a great start for that little lad of theirs, I fear.'

There was an edge to Nikos's voice as he replied. 'No, indeed.' His expression was set. That barbed exchange they'd been witness to had been all too familiar. The sniping, the acid tones, the mutual accusations and complaints… He'd grown up with them. They weren't any easier to witness in other couples any more than between his own parents.

Mel cast him a curious, slightly guarded look. There'd been a lot in the suppressed way he'd said that.

He caught her glance and made a rueful face. 'Sorry, but they just remind me of my own parents. All smiles and bonhomie to others, but with each other constant tension and backbiting. Absolutely everything becomes a verbal skirmish.'

She gave him a sympathetic smile. 'It sounds very… wearing,' she said, trying to find a word that wasn't too intrusive into what was, she could tell, a sensitive issue for him.

He gave an unamused snort. 'That's one word for it,' he said. 'Two people locked together, hammering away at each other and making themselves and everyone else miserable.'

Mel looked concerned. 'Why on earth did they ever marry each other, your parents?' she asked.

'Would you believe it? They were infatuated with each other,' he said sardonically. 'My mother was the catch of the season—the belle of every ball—and every man was after her. She kept them all guessing, playing them off against each other, but my father ended up winning her because she was bowled over by him.'

His voice twisted.

'Then I came along and everything went pear-shaped.' He gave a hollow laugh that had no humour in it. 'My mother hated being pregnant—as she constantly tells me still—I ruined her figure, apparently. And my father stopped paying her the attention she craved. And then—worse—he felt jealous of the attention she gave me when I was little, so he started straying. That incensed my mother even more than his neglecting her, and the whole damn thing just spiralled downwards until they reached a point where they couldn't even be civil to each other.'

His mouth thinned to a tight, taut line.

'They still can't be civil to each other, all these years later. They've bad-mouthed each other for as long as I can remember. Not a good word to say about each other and expecting *me* to side with each of them. Yet they absolutely refuse to admit failure and divorce—it's beyond ghastly.'

Mel kept the sympathy in her voice. 'I used to feel very sorry for myself when I was young, not having parents, but who knows which is worse? No parents—or parents who make your life a misery growing up?'

'Yes, tough call,' acknowledged Nikos, terse now, after what he'd bitten out at length.

Where the hell had all that come from?

He found himself wondering why he'd made any reference to his bumpy childhood and warring family. It wasn't a subject he discussed with others. It was too deep, too personal. Too painful. But with Mel it had seemed...natural.

He sought for a reason for his embittered outburst.

Maybe it's because she didn't have it easy either, growing up with only a grandfather to look after her, missing a mother and father. Maybe that's why it's easy to talk to her about such things...

But he didn't want to think about his endlessly sparring parents and their utter insensitivity to anyone except themselves—their refusal to acknowledge the fact that their marriage was a failure and they should have ended it years ago. He'd washed his hands of both of them and left them to it.

Deliberately he took a deep breath to clear his clouded thoughts. He wouldn't spoil his time with Mel by thinking about his parents—let alone pouring it out to her again the way he just had. No, it was far more pleasant to know that he was here, with a woman like Mel at his side, making the most of this carefree time together.

With the conference over there was nothing more to do on the island except enjoy themselves. Revel in the passion that flamed between them and relish the absolute leisure and relaxation they had, day after golden day.

It doesn't get better than this...

The words shaped themselves inside his head and he knew them to be true. Had he ever enjoyed himself more in his life than he was doing now, with Mel? It was just so *good* being here with her. Oh, the sex was beyond fantastic—no doubt about that—and he'd always known it would be. But it was so, *so* much more than just the sex.

It's the being with her that's so good. Just every day—over meals, on the beach, sightseeing...just everything.

Right now, he thought, *I'm a happy man.*

It was a good feeling.

As they settled into the taxi, setting off for their own quiet hotel, Nikos gave a sigh of relief. 'I'm glad to get out of here,' he said. 'Now we can get back to the rest of our holiday.'

'A week to go,' said Mel lightly.

Her words drew a frown across Nikos's brow. A week—was that all? It would go by in a flash, as this last one had. His frown deepened. A week wasn't enough...

Rapidly, in his head, he ran through his diary. Was there anything critical the week after next? Offhand, he couldn't think of anything. And if there was nothing absolutely critical...

The idea that had struck him was obvious—and inspired, of all things, by the warring Friedmans.

He voiced it over dinner, having checked his online diary to confirm his assumption.

'Tell me,' he said as they settled down to their evening meal, which they were taking at the beach bistro, to refresh their spirits after the day's busyness, 'are you tempted at all by the idea of going to New York?'

Mel's face lightened. She'd been thinking along just those lines herself. Going to New York would surely be something to look forward to after this fabulous time with Nikos had ended, wouldn't it? And she needed something to look forward to...

'Oh, yes,' she said. 'It would make sense, being so close to Bermuda. If I can get a cheap flight, and find a cheap tourist hotel in Manhattan, then—'

Nikos interrupted her. 'What do you mean?' he demanded, his buoyant mood altering immediately.

There was an edge to his voice she found unaccountable. She looked at him, confused.

'Why do you talk about cheap flights and tourist hotels?' he went on, in the same frowning tone.

It was her turn to look confused. 'Well, I have to make my savings go as far as they can—'

'Not when you're with *me*,' he contradicted. His expression darkened. 'Unless for some reason you don't *want* to see New York with me?'

If she hadn't known better she might have read accusation in his voice. But accusation was so inexplicable it couldn't possibly be that.

'Nikos, that's a daft question,' she replied, in a rallying humorous tone.

But he was not mollified. 'Then what is making you talk of going there on your own?' he demanded.

She looked at him uncertainly. 'When you invited me to Bermuda, Nikos, you told me it would just be for a couple of weeks—around the conference,' she said.

He gave a dismissive shrug. 'So we make it longer. That's all. I've checked my diary and I can bring forward some meetings in New York scheduled for the following month. By extending our stay on Bermuda we can go straight from here to New York. Plus,' he finished, 'I could take up John Friedman's invitation—I dare say it would prove very useful to me.' He looked across the table. 'So, let's do it—shall we?'

His voice was expectant. But Mel's expression did not lighten in return.

'Nikos, I'm not sure it's a good idea—'

His brow darkened. 'Why?' His question was blunt.

Her eyes slid away, out over the dark expanse of water beyond the beach. She wanted to put into words her reluctance, and yet it was hard to do so. Hard because shooting through her, making a nonsense of reluctance, was an arrow of sheer exhilaration that seemed to be penetrating to her very core.

He wanted to stay longer on Bermuda, to take her to New York! Wanted to spend more time with her! Wanted not to kiss her goodbye and wave her off out of his life!

She felt the force of it—felt its power.

And it was that that gave her pause.

I came with him for a holiday romance—that's all. A couple of weeks with Nikos—a glorious, fantastic, fabulous entrée in the banquet of my new life of travelling, of freedom and self-indulgence—that was what this holiday was supposed to be. All that I planned it to be.

A holiday romance was something she could accommodate. Indeed, she'd envisaged fun-filled, lighthearted holiday romances as being an integral part of her new free life. Making up for the lost years of enforced celibacy, for the absolute lack of romance in her life while she'd cared for her grandfather.

But when did a holiday romance turn into something more?

If she let Nikos take her to New York what would come afterwards? He would still go back to Athens, wouldn't he? Still kiss her goodbye...

Her mind sheered away. She didn't want to think of that. Didn't want to think about anything except what she had now—their time together here in Bermuda. Their holiday romance...

Beautiful—and brief.

Her eyes swept back to him, found his resting on her, dark and stormy-looking.

'Why?' he asked again. 'Why is going to New York with me not a good idea?'

He would not let it go. Why was she saying such a thing? Weren't they having a fantastic time here in Bermuda? Why not keep going with it?

We're so good together.

That was what was in his head all the time. Simple, uncomplicated and true. There was no reason for her to be unenthusiastic about him going to New York with her. She wanted to go there—he wanted to go there with her. What was the problem?

He wanted her to answer so that he could dispose of her objections. But at that juncture the waiter arrived with their food, and as he left them Mel determinedly changed the subject.

He could see the ploy for what it was—a way to stop him grilling her—and he accepted it. There were more ways to persuade her than by out-arguing her...

That night, as he took her in his arms, he put into their lovemaking all the skill and expertise that lay within his command, deliberately drawing from her a consummation that left her shaking, trembling in his arms—left him shaking, trembling in hers.

Finally, sated and exhausted, they drew apart and lay beside each other, their bodies sheened with perspiration, their breathing hectic, the echoes of their shared ecstasy still burning between them. He levered himself up on his elbow, smoothing back her damp hair, gazing down into her wide eyes.

'Come to New York with me...' he whispered.

His lashes dropped over his eyes, his mouth dipped to graze her lips, parted and bee-stung from his passion.

'Come to New York with me…' he whispered again.

Surely she must be persuaded now? Surely she must not want what was between them to end before it needed to? And it did not need to—not yet. They did not have to part—they could keep going—keep going to New York and who knew how far beyond? Who knew how long this romance would last? All he knew was that he had no intention—none at all—of letting it go a single moment before he was ready.

But she didn't answer him—only let her eyes flutter shut and rolled herself into his waiting embrace. And he closed her against him, hugging her tight, so tight, against the wall of his chest.

In her head she could hear his voice—so low, so seductive, so tempting…

Come to New York with me…

In her body, deep in the core of her, she could feel the hectic pulse ebbing slowly, leaving only the incandescent afterglow of passion. She felt her breathing ease, her heated skin start to cool. But in her heart there was a tightening.

There was one thing she must say to him—only one thing. The sensible thing.

He was nuzzling at her ear, his breath warm, his touch sweet.

'Come to New York,' he murmured, coaxing and caressing. His mouth moved from the delicate lobe of her ear, grazing along the line of her jaw. 'Come to New York,' he said again.

She could feel his mouth break into a smile suddenly, and his arms tightened around her.

'Come to New York,' he said, and she could hear the

laugh in his voice. 'Because I'll go on asking you until you give in and say yes.'

He was kissing her eyelids now.

'Give in and say yes… Give in and say yes. You know you want to.'

He was laughing, and so was she, and suddenly, out of nowhere, she couldn't fight it any longer.

'*Yes!* OK—I give in! I'll come to New York with you!' Her capitulation was complete.

He gave a low, triumphant rumble and she was grinning, too, half shaking her head and then kissing him. Oh, what the hell? She hadn't been sensible at all. But she didn't care—couldn't care—not now…

Wrapping his warm, strong body against her, she wound herself tighter into his embrace. She felt a singing inside her. *She was going to New York with Nikos*— their holiday would be longer, their time together would be longer, there were still more glorious days to come.

CHAPTER EIGHT

'Is THAT YOU guzzling rum cake again?' Mel's voice was humorously indignant.

'Just testing it for quality,' Nikos assured her, licking his fingers after eating a slice of the cake that was the speciality of the island.

'Yes, well, if you test much more of it there'll be none left,' she riposted, removing the cake tin from him and placing the lid firmly back on top. 'I'll keep this in *my* room, I think.'

Nikos laughed. 'We can always go to Nelson's Harbour and restock.'

'We'll need to if you keep eating it like that.'

She dropped a kiss on his head before stepping over the dividing wall between their patios and heading indoors. Emerging again, she saw Nikos was pulling on his shirt. Despite the rum cake, his pecs and abs were still spectacularly honed.

Mel felt a ripple of desire go through her. But this wasn't the time to indulge in a siesta—not least because it was only just after breakfast and they were about to head to the beach.

As they stretched themselves out on their beach loungers, just above the tide line so that the spray from the waves breaking exuberantly into airy foam on the soft pale gold sand could cool their sun-heated bodies, lying on the beach seemed especially blissful.

But that, she knew with a squeezing of her heart, was because their days here were finally running out...

Then they'd be off to New York—for their last, final few days together.

And then goodbye...

Finally, goodbye.

Despite the heat of the beach a sudden draught of cold air seemed to be playing around her body. She fought it back.

But it's not the end of the holiday yet! I've still got time with Nikos.

And yet it was precisely the fact that she'd felt that cold draught that caused her concern.

I shouldn't be so eager to stay with him—I shouldn't be clinging to our time together like this. It isn't what I intended at all. I should be excited at the prospect of going on to see the rest of America—exploring all the places I've only ever read about or seen on films or TV. I shouldn't be wanting to go on being with Nikos all the time—I shouldn't...

But the problem was she *did* just want to go on being with Nikos. Here on Bermuda. In New York. And be-yond...

For a moment she tried to force herself to imagine exploring the USA on her own—but her mind had gone blank. Beyond New York there seemed to be nothing at all...

Dismay filled her. This was not good—not good at all. For so long she'd thought and dreamt of nothing but being footloose and fancy-free, going where she wanted, when she wanted, making her own way across the world, free as a bird… Yet now there seemed to be only a blank ahead of her.

The time would soon come when they would go their separate ways—she to see the rest of America, he to head back to Athens, to his life. Their holiday together over.

The chilly draught came again.

She didn't want to think about it—didn't want to face it. Didn't want to think that in just a few days' time it would all be ending.

But what—what will be ending?

That was the question she shied away from answering.

'Mel—bad news.'

She turned abruptly, halting in the action of fastening her packed suitcase. Nikos was standing in the open French windows of her room. He was frowning, phone in hand.

'What's happened?' she asked, alarmed.

Their extended time on Bermuda had finally ended, and now they were due to head off to New York.

Mel could not deny that she'd given up on those ambivalent feelings she'd had about his determination to take her to America for a final few days together—she didn't even try. There was no point. They were going there now, and that was that. They were booked and packed. Any moment now their bags would be collected and the hotel car would take them to the airport for their late-morning flight to New York. So it was too late to question why she was so uneasy about it all—wasn't it?

'I'm going to have to change our plans,' Nikos said, his voice short. 'We have to head back to Europe. Something's cropped up and I can't get out of it—I'm really sorry.' He gave an annoyed sigh. 'New York is off the cards—I'm getting us booked on the evening flight direct to London, and then we'll need to drop down to Athens straight away...'

She was staring at him. Just staring.

He came up to her, slid his phone away and put his arms loosely around her waist.

'I'm really sorry,' he said again, apology in his eyes. 'But on the other hand...' he dropped a light kiss on her nose '...you'll get to see Athens instead of New York.'

She stepped away from him.

'Nikos—'

There was something in her voice that made him look at her.

Emotions were shooting through her like bullets. What had she just been thinking? That it was too late to be so uneasy about extending her time with Nikos yet further? Her expression twisted. Suddenly out of the blue, with a phone call that had changed.

'Nikos, I can't come to Athens with you.' The words fell from her lips.

It was his turn to stare. 'Why not?' There was blank incomprehension in his voice.

'Because...because I'm going to New York. Because seeing the USA is what I've planned to do.' She swallowed. 'I know you were going to be with me for a couple more days in New York, but I'm...I'm going on, Nikos. The way I planned.'

His face was taut. 'Change your plans. See Athens instead. Didn't you say you wanted to go "everywhere"?' he challenged. 'You haven't even set foot in Europe yet.'

She shut her eyes. She could hear a kind of drumming in her ears.

I thought I'd have a few more days with him...just a few more days...

But that wasn't going to happen. It was over—right now.

Because of course she couldn't go to Europe with him—it was out of the question. Just out of the question.

'Nikos—no. I can't.'

'You can't *what*?' he said, the words cutting into the space between them.

He could feel emotion starting to build in him, but he didn't know what it was. Knew only that the woman he wanted with him was saying she couldn't be with him...

'I can't just...just tag along with you to Athens. What *as*, for heaven's sake? Here, we've been on holiday, but if you go back to your home city—well...what will I be doing there with you? What *am* I to you there?'

How can I have nothing more than a holiday romance with you if we're not on holiday?

He was staring at her, his eyes dark, his expression darker.

She had to make him understand.

Something had changed in his eyes. 'What had you in mind?' he said.

His voice was dry. As dry as the sand in a desert.

It was her turn to stare, not understanding what he was saying—why he was saying it. Emotion was churning away inside her and she felt a sense of shock—shock that the moment she'd thought would be deferred for a few more days was upon her. Right now.

Then he was speaking.

'Mel, I was clear with you from the start, wasn't I?' she heard him say. 'Before we came here? I never fed you a line—you knew the score with me from the start. Don't expect anything more than that.'

His voice was flat, unemotional. Had she read more than he'd intended into his saying they needed to head for Athens? He hoped not—he really hoped not.

Because 'anything more' is not how I live my life. I've seen where 'more' can take people—how it can screw things up...screw people up...

His mind sheered away from familiar thoughts, familiar reactions. Things he didn't want to associate with Mel—not Mel.

I just want what we have now—because it's good... so good—and I want it to go on just the way it is. I don't see why it can't, but why can't she see that, too? Why can't we just go on the way we are? Not question things the way she's doing now?

Mel's face worked. 'Nikos, I don't expect anything more of you than what we've been having.' She swallowed, making her voice lighter. 'Which is the most fantastic holiday that anyone could ever imagine. A holiday that…' She swallowed again, and this time there seemed to be something in her throat as she did so, though she didn't know what. 'That is over,' she finished.

The expression in his eyes changed. Had she seen a flash of emotion? And if she had, what had it been?

For a moment she thought it might have been relief.

Or had it been regret?

Well, whatever it was, it didn't matter. All that mattered now was…was…

A strange, hollow sense of emptiness stretched inside her.

All that matters now is saying goodbye...

She made herself move—walk up to him, loop her arms around his neck. He was standing stock-still, all muscles tensed.

'Nikos, I have had the most fantastic time with you,'

she told him, steeling herself to say what must be said right now—days before she'd thought she would be saying it. She smiled at him, made herself smile, because smiling at this moment was suddenly very necessary to her. 'But…'

She let him go, stepped away again. She took a breath. It was painful, somehow, to draw breath in and out of her lungs, but she had to do it. Had to say goodbye to him.

'It's come to an end, Nikos,' she said. 'I'm sorry we're not getting our…our bonus time in New York, but… well…' she gave a little shrug with muscles that did not want to move '…there it is. All holidays end. So has ours.'

That was all the time they'd planned to have with each other—nothing more. So why was he glowering at her the way he was, his expression rejecting what she was saying to him?

She bit her lip, hating what was happening but knowing there was no alternative.

This has come too fast—I'm not ready…not prepared—

Out of nowhere panic boiled up in her chest, suffocating her. She had to fight it down. Had to make herself speak to him in a tone of voice that sounded reasonable.

'I'm sorry this has just happened so fast like this— but, oh, Nikos, we always knew this moment would come. Whether now or in a couple of days in New York it doesn't matter much. We mustn't make a big deal of it—it *isn't* a big deal and it mustn't become one.'

There was a plea in her voice now—even she could hear it. But who was she pleading with? Him—or herself? Well, she mustn't think about that. Mustn't think about anything except making herself reach for her nearby handbag, clutch it to her.

He was still standing there, motionless. His face was frozen, as if turned to stone.

Why is it like this? Why? It shouldn't be hard to say goodbye and get on with my own life. It just shouldn't!

'Nikos, I'm going to take the hotel shuttle to the airport—make that New York flight on my own. I know the London flight isn't till this evening, so there's no point you setting off now. And...and I don't want to say goodbye at an airport...'

I don't want to say goodbye at all.

The words were wrung from inside her, but she ignored them—she had to.

'I don't believe you're doing this.'

That deep, accented voice. But no longer flat. No longer edged. Just—harsh.

'It's for the best. It really is,' she heard herself say.

She picked up the handle of her suitcase, backing towards the door. As she yanked it open she paused. Looked at him one last time.

For some strange, inexplicable reason he looked out of focus. Blurred.

She blinked, trying to clear her vision. Trying to keep her voice the way it had to be—the only way it could be when a holiday romance came to an end. 'Have a good flight back,' she said.

She smiled. Or thought she did. She wasn't sure.

She wasn't sure of anything at all except that she had to manoeuvre her suitcase out onto the path that ran along the back of their rooms. A hotel buggy was waiting there, ready to take both of them up to the hotel for the airport shuttle. Now it would only take her.

She let her suitcase be hefted up, clambered onto the seat herself. Nerveless...numb. Her chest was bound with steel bands, her vision still blurred. The afternoon heat pressed down on her like a crushing weight.

The buggy glided off, taking her away.

In Mel's room Nikos stood very still.

The room was empty. Quite empty.

Emotion sliced through him. He stopped it. Meshed himself together again. Made himself walk towards the house phone and pick it up, speak to the front desk to request, in tones that were curter than he would normally use to a member of hotel staff, that he be booked on the London flight that evening. Then he put the phone down. Stared about him.

She'd gone. Mel had gone. That was the only thought in his head. She'd waved him goodbye and walked out.

And he couldn't believe it. Just could…not…believe it.

In the space of a few minutes he'd gone from having Mel with him to not having her.

She walked out on me. She just walked out on me!

The slicing emotion came again—vertically from the top of his head right down to his feet. Slicing him in half, as if each side of his body would keel over separately. Destroying him.

Breath ravaged his lungs as he drew air into them, hauling the two sides of his body back together again by raw strength of will. He was in shock, he knew. Recognised it with the part of his mind that was still capable of functioning, which was somewhere deep inside him, somewhere very remote, it seemed. Shock was all there was to him right now. And the disbelief that went hand in hand with it.

The ringing of the house phone made him jolt. Automatically he picked it up, listened as he was told his flight had been booked, automatically gave his mono-syllabic thanks before hanging up.

He walked out through the French windows he'd walked in through only minutes earlier. When his world had been completely different...

When Mel had been in it.

But now Mel was gone.

Oh, God, she's gone.

The emotion came again, like a sweeping knife, head to foot—and this time it severed him in two com-pletely...

Mel was standing in bright sunlight, heat beating down on her bare head. The view was beyond all imagining.

The great chasm in the earth a few metres beyond her was a full ten miles wide at this point, she knew—one of the greatest natural wonders of the earth. But as she stood at the rim of the Grand Canyon she could not feel its grandeur, nor its wonder. All around her tourists were milling, exclaiming, taking photos, grouping and regrouping, but still she stood, gazing out over the contorted rocks that cascaded down into the belly of the earth, where far below the Colorado River snaked along the almost subterranean base of the canyon.

She was taking part in an organised day tour from Las Vegas, having flown in from Washington, where she'd gone after New York. She'd assiduously visited every landmark on the tourist trail, determined to miss absolutely nothing.

Determined to fill every moment of the day with oc-cupation. With busyness and fulfilment.

Determined to show that she was living her life to the full, seeing the world and all its wonders as she had planned and hoped so much to do.

Determined *not* to let herself remember the brief, glorious introduction to that new life of hers that she had had courtesy of Nikos.

It had been good—brilliant—fantastic—fabulous. But it had only ever been supposed be a glittering, gorgeous introduction to her new life of hedonistic freedom after long servitude. Travelling on her own, going where she wanted when she wanted, footloose and fancy-free, answerable only to herself—that was what her new life was supposed to be about.

So she must not stand here and think of Nikos. Must not stand here and see only him in her mind's vision, not the jaw-dropping stupendous splendour of the Canyon.

And above all she must not—must not, *must not*— let that most dangerous and fatal thought creep into her head: *If only he were here with me, standing beside me now, and we were seeing all this together... If only he were seeing everything with me...*

Seeing everything with her...

If only he'd been with her in New York, seeing the sights with her as they'd planned. The Statue of Liberty, Central Park, the Empire State Building. And then in Washington, seeing all the historic monuments there, and then—oh, then the complete contrast of Las Vegas...so gaudy and garish and such ridiculous tacky *fun*!

In her head she could hear him laughing with her, murmuring to her, could feel him sweeping her into his arms, kissing her senseless and carrying her off to their bed to find passionate, burning rapture in each other's arms.

Oh, the longing for him was palpable, the yearning all-consuming. There was an ache inside her...she wanted him with her so much...

But he wasn't with her. Would never be with her again. They would never stand beside each other seeing the wonders that the world had to offer. Never sweep each other into their arms again.

So she must get used to it. Must accept it. Must simply stop letting thoughts like that into her head. Such uselessly tormenting thoughts…

She must simply go on standing there, staring blindly, vacantly out over this chasm in the earth. While inside her there seemed to be a chasm almost as vast.

CHAPTER NINE

'So, HOW WAS BERMUDA?'

It was a casually asked question, and not one that should have made Nikos tense instantly. He made himself return an equitable reply.

'Not a bad conference,' he said.

'Nice venue, too.' His acquaintance smiled. 'Did you manage to add on any holiday time?'

Somehow Nikos managed an answer, and then ruthlessly switched the subject. Whatever he talked about, it wasn't going to be his time in Bermuda. It wasn't even something he wanted to *think* about.

That desire was, of course, completely fruitless. He thought about Bermuda all the time.

And Mel. Always Mel.

Mel laughing, head thrown back, glorious blonde hair rippling. Mel gazing at him with that expression of amusement, interest—desire. Mel melting into his arms, her mouth warm and inviting, her body clinging to his, ardent and eager...

Then he would slam down the guillotine and make himself think about something else. Anything else. Anything at all.

Work was what he mainly thought about. Lived and breathed. He'd become a powerhouse of focussed, relentless dedication to the business of the bank. Deal after deal after deal. Tireless and non-stop. Rising early and working late.

He was back to working out a lot, too. Muscle mass glistened…heart and lungs purred like the engine of a high-performance car. Sinews were lean and supple like a honed athlete. It was essential to keep his body occupied.

Because his body had a mind of its own. A mind he could not allow to function—not in the slightest. A mind that made every cell in his honed, taut body crave another body—a body that was soft and satin-smooth and sensuous as silk. Flesh to his flesh…

He still wanted her.

The irony of the situation was not lost on him. He was the one who'd wanted nothing more than a temporary affair. Had wanted only a holiday romance with Mel.

But no one had said how long the holiday had to be, had they? No, they hadn't. Or *where* it had to be. It could just as easily have been here in Greece. Mel had never seen Greece, and showing her the glories of the ancient ruins, the beauty of the islands and mountains, would have entranced her.

But she'd turned it down. Turned down spending more time with him. Gone off on her travels just the way she'd always planned to.

That was what was so galling now. That the very thing that had once reassured him that she would accept the temporary nature of her romance with him was now twisting back to bite him!

Bite him hard.

The door of his office swung open and his father

strode in from his adjoining office, his expression angry, as it so often was, Nikos thought with a silent sigh.

'Do you know what your mother has done now?' his father demanded. 'She's taken herself off to Milan. She says it's because she's out of clothes—*ha!* That woman could open a fashion store with her wardrobe. But I know better. She's in a ridiculously unnecessary sulk—just because she's taken it into her stupid head that I'm having an affair with another woman.'

Nikos's mouth tightened. *Oh, great, that was all he needed.* His father sounding off to him about the latest behaviour of his wife and how it irritated him.

'And are you?' he replied bluntly.

His father waved a hand impatiently. 'Do you blame me?' he demanded, his voice aggrieved. 'Your mother's impossible! Completely impossible! She's taken off at just the most inconvenient time. We are *supposed* to be joining Demetrius Astarchis and his wife on their yacht tomorrow! Now what am I supposed to do?'

'Take your mistress instead?' his son suggested acidly.

'Don't be absurd. They're expecting your mother and me. She should be there—Demetrius and I do a valuable amount of business with each other. If nothing else, your mother should realise that the only reason she can run riot in couture houses is because of the effort I put in to keep the coffers full. She owes me *some* loyalty!'

Nikos forbore from pointing out the obvious—that loyalty was a two-way street, and keeping a mistress was not the way for his father to win his wife's. But he also knew, with weary resignation, that his mother's poisonous tongue couldn't have done a better job of driving away her husband than if she'd changed the locks on the house.

He'd never heard a conversation between them that didn't involve his mother making vicious little digs at his father all the time…or sweeping sabre strokes of bitter accusation.

He looked at his father now, standing there angrily, filled with self-righteous indignation at his wife's errant behaviour, and felt an immense exasperated irritation with them both.

'Is that what you came in to tell me?' he asked tightly, having no intention of being drawn into witnessing any further diatribes by his father against his mother.

'I wanted to check over the Hong Kong trip with you,' his father said, still ill-humoured, 'and warn you that if your mother hasn't deigned to return before you go I'll have to go and fetch her home. I'm not having her roaming around Europe, bad-mouthing me to everyone she knows. And I'm not leaving her in Milan on her own too long either—catching the eye of some predatory male!'

He gave his son a withering look.

'Not that your mother has any looks left—she's not aged well,' he said sourly. 'Which is another reason,' he finished defiantly, 'for me to find something more agreeable to look at than her crow's feet.'

Nikos forbore to add oil to burning waters by reminding his father that his mother was equally and vocally critical of her husband's jowly features and increasing paunch. Instead, all he said was, 'I've got the meetings in Hong Kong all set up. Take a look.'

He found he was glad he had a trip to the Far East coming up—it might help take his mind off his own miseries. Though it didn't do him any good to realise that he was already thinking how much he'd have loved to show Hong Kong to Mel.

We could have flown down to Malaysia after-wards, Thailand, too, and Bali—even on to Australia, maybe.

And from Australia they could have taken in New Zealand—and beyond that the verdant jewels of the South Pacific islands…

He tore his mind away. Why torment himself? Why think about holidays he would never have with Mel? All she'd wanted from him was a brief few weeks on a single island. Nothing more than that…

'Good,' his father was saying now. He glanced at his watch. 'I must go—I'm having lunch with Adela.' He paused. 'I might not be back afterwards…'

Again, Nikos deliberately said nothing.

Not even as his father headed back to his own office, adding, 'And for God's sake don't tell your mother. That's all I need.'

What you need, thought Nikos grimly, *is a divorce.*

But that wouldn't happen, he knew. His parents were locked in their bitter, destructive dance, circling round each other like snarling dogs, biting at each other constantly.

That's why I've stayed clear of long-term relation-ships. So I'll never get trapped in an ugly, destructive relationship the way my parents have.

Moodily, he jackknifed out of his chair, striding across the office to stare out over the streets of Athens below. Thoughts, dark and turbid, swirled in his mind.

He didn't want to be here, staring out over the city of his birth, working himself senseless, just to block his mind from thinking about what he *did* want—which was to be somewhere utterly different.

With Mel.

He shut his eyes, swearing fluently and silently inside his head. He was off again, thinking about Mel—wanting her…wanting her so badly it was a physical pain.

But she was gone—gone, gone, *gone*. She had walked out on him and she'd been *right* to walk out on him—that was what was so unbearable for him to face. Mel had done exactly what would have happened anyway, a few days later—ended their affair. It had been just as he had planned it to be—transient, temporary, impermanent.

Safe.

Safe from the danger he'd always feared. That one fine day he'd find himself doing what his father had just done—walking in and snapping and snarling, berating and bad-mouthing the woman he was married to.

His eyes opened again, a bleak expression in them. He could hear his father's condemnation of his mother still ringing in his ears. Together or apart, they still laid into each other, still tore each other to pieces. The venom and hostility and the sheer bloody nastiness of it all…

They couldn't be more different from the way Mel and I were together…

Into his head thronged a thousand memories—Mel laughing, smiling, teasing him with an amused, affectionate glint in her eye at his foibles—him teasing her back in the same vein,—both of them at ease with each other, companionable, comfortable, contented…

Contented.

The word shaped itself in his head. He'd used it in Bermuda—trying to find the right word to match his feelings then.

Contented.

That had been the word—the right word…

Me and Mel. Mel and me.

Because it wasn't just the passion that had seared between them—incandescent though that had been— it was more, oh, so much more than that.

His mind went to his parents. They were always complaining about each other, with lines of discontent, displeasure, disapproval around their mouths, with vicious expressions in their eyes when they spoke to each other, spoke of each other to him.

Nothing, *nothing* like the way he and Mel had been.

He felt his body tense, every honed muscle engaging, as he stared out of the window—not seeing what was beyond the glass, not seeing anything except a vision of Mel's face. Beautiful beyond all dreams, but with an expression that was far, far beyond beauty to him. She was smiling at him, with a softness in her eyes, a warmth—an affection that reached out to him and made him want to reach out to her. To cup her face and drop a kiss on the tip of her nose, then tuck her hand in his, warm and secure, and stroll with her, side by side, along the beach, chatting about this or that or nothing at all, easy and happy, *contented*, towards the setting sun…

All the days of my life…

And into his head, into his consciousness, slowly, like a swimmer emerging from a deep, deep sea, the realisation came to him.

It doesn't have to be like my parents' relationship. I don't have to think that will happen. Mel and I aren't like that. We're nothing like that. Nothing!

He could feel the thoughts shaping inside his head, borne up on the emotion rising within him. If that were so, then he could take the risk—*should* take the risk— the risk he had always feared to take. Because never had he met a woman who could take that fear from him.

As if a fog had cleared from his head, taking away the occluding mist that had clouded his vision all his life, he felt the realisation pierce him.

Mel can—Mel can lift that fear from me.

That was what he had to trust. That was what he had to believe in.

What we had was too good—far too good to let go of. Far too good to cut short, fearing what it might become in years to come. I refuse to believe that she and I would ever become like my parents. I refuse to believe that the time we had together—that brief, inadequate time—couldn't go on for much longer. Not weeks, or months—but years...

His breath seemed to still in his lungs.

All my days...

For one long, breathless moment he stood there, every muscle poised, and then, as if throwing a switch, he whirled around, turned on his heel and strode back to his desk. His eyes were alight—fired with determination, with revelation, with self-knowledge.

She might not want him—she might be halfway around the world by now—she might turn him down and spurn him, go on her laughing, footloose way, but not before he found her again and put to her the question that was searing in his head now. The question he had to know the answer to...

Snatching up the phone on his desk, he spoke to his secretary.

'Get me our security agency, please—I need to start an investigation. I need—' he took a hectic breath '—to find someone.'

The plane banked as it started its descent into Heathrow. Mel felt herself tilting, and again the sensation of nausea rose inside her. She damped it down. It had started when they'd hit a pocket of turbulence mid-Atlantic, but they would be on the tarmac soon—then she'd feel better.

Physically, at least.

Mentally, she didn't feel good in the slightest. She felt as if a pair of snakes were writhing, fighting within her—two opposing emotions, twisting and tormenting her. Her face tightened. Her features pulled taut and stark. She had an ordeal in front of her. An ordeal she didn't want but had to endure. Had to face.

This wasn't the way it was supposed to be.

A holiday romance—that was all she'd ever intended Nikos to be. A brief, glorious fling—then off on her travels as she'd planned for so long. Happy and care-free. On her own.

Travels had turned out to be nothing—to be ashes—without Nikos at her side to share them with.

It wasn't supposed to have been like that…

Missing him so much…

Missing him…missing him all the time—wherever she went, wherever she'd gone. Just wanting to be with him again. Anywhere in the world…so long as it was with him…

How could she have been so unbearably stupid as to walk out on him? He'd asked her to go with him to Athens and she'd refused.

I could have had more time…more time with him…

Yet even as the cry came silently and cruelly within her she heard her own voice answer the one inside her head—even more cruel.

How much more time? A week? A month? And then what? When the holiday romance burned itself out? When he finally didn't want you any more because all he wanted was an affair...? Nothing permanent. Nothing binding between them.

She heard again in her head his warning to her that horrible, horrible morning in Bermuda when she'd walked out and gone to the airport to fly to New York alone.

'What had you in mind? I made it clear, right from the start, that I was only talking about a few weeks together at the most...'

A hideous, hollow laugh sounded inside her. A few weeks? Oh, dear God, now she had the means to be with him, to keep him in her life, for far longer than a few weeks...

A permanent, perpetual bond between them.

Her features twisted.

No, it wasn't supposed to have been like this at all.

I wasn't supposed to fall for him.

She swallowed the nausea rising in her throat again.

I wasn't supposed to get pregnant...

CHAPTER TEN

NIKOS EXITED THE brand-new office building, heading for the car that waited for him at the kerb. He glanced up at the sky between the tall serried ranks of modern office blocks in downtown Hong Kong. The clouds had massed even more, and the humid air had a distinct chill to it. The wind was clearly rising. The local TV channel had been full of news of an impending typhoon, speculating on whether it would hit the island or not.

Back at his hotel, he noticed that the typhoon warning notice had gone up a level. His mouth set. He still had more meetings lined up, but they might have to be postponed if the weather worsened. Once a typhoon hit in force the streets would be cleared of traffic, the subway shut down and the population kept indoors until it was safe to go out again.

From his suite at the top of the towering hotel, with its view over the harbour, he could see the grey water, choppy and restless, and watched frowningly as ocean-going ships came in from the open sea beyond to seek shelter from the ferocious winds that were starting to build. The way things were going, it was more than likely his flight back to London would be cancelled.

Frustration bit at him. The last thing he wanted

was to be stuck here in Hong Kong with a typhoon threatening!

He forced himself to be rational. He'd set the security agency he used for personal protection to the task of tracking down the woman he *had* to locate—and that would take time. Even as he thought this a memory darted with piquant power—the memory of his first evening with Mel, bantering with her about how she should take a bodyguard with her on her travels to keep all predatory males away from her...

How long ago that seemed—and yet also as if it were only yesterday...

Automatically, he checked his mobile and email—still nothing from the agency. With a vocal rasp, he got stuck back into his work yet again.

Patience—that was what he needed. But he wasn't in the mood to be patient. Not in the slightest.

The tube train taking Mel into the City, towards the London offices of the Parakis Bank, was crowded and airless. She felt claustrophobic after the wide-open spaces of America, and she was dreading the ordeal that lay in front of her.

She should have phoned first, she knew, but she hadn't been able to face it. Nikos probably wasn't even in London now—why should he be? But maybe she could talk to his PA, find out where he was, how best to get in touch with him. At worst she could leave the painfully written letter she'd got in her bag. Telling him what she had to tell him...

She'd written it last night, rewriting it over and over again, trying to find the right words to tell him. The right words to tell him the wrong thing. That their holiday romance had ended in a way that neither of them could possibly have foreseen. That neither could possibly have wanted.

Yet even as she thought it she could feel emotion rising up in her—feel the conflict that had tormented her since her first shocked and disbelieving discovery of what had happened. Conflict that had never abated since—that was going round and round and round in her head, day and night.

What am I going to do? What am I going to do?

The train glided to a halt at another station and the doors slid open. More people got off. Then the doors slid shut and the train started forward again, out of the lighted platform area and back into yet another tunnel. Stop, start, stop again, start again—over and over. And still the words went round and round in her head.

What am I going to do? What am I going to do?

She was pregnant, with an unplanned baby, by a man who had only been a holiday romance. That was the stark truth of it.

It was the very last thing she had ever thought would happen.

She heard her own words, spoken so casually, so confidently, at the charity dinner Nikos had taken her to—their very first date.

'Right now, a baby is definitely not on my agenda.'

All she'd wanted was the freedom to indulge her wanderlust—finally, after so many years of looking after her grandfather. She hadn't wanted more ties, more responsibilities.

Other words cut into her mind. Not hers this time. Nikos—talking as they'd walked away from that mismatched couple at the conference hotel. Telling her bitterly how his parents had become warring enemies.

'When I came along everything went pear-shaped.'

That was what he had said. Showing her his scars—his fears. His determination never to risk what had happened to his parents happening to him.

And now, thanks to her, that was what was facing him.

Her features twisted and emotion stabbed at her like a knife…a tormenting, toxic mix of dismay, fear, doubt and fierce, primitive protectiveness…

What am I going to do? What am I going to do?

Round and round the question circled in her tired, exhausted brain, with no answer at all.

The train pulled into yet another station, and with a start Mel realised she should have changed lines at the previous one. Hastily she pushed her way off, pausing on the platform to look around for directions to the line she needed. As she was staring about the large lettering on the advert plastered to the curved wall in front of her suddenly caught her eye.

Pregnant? Unsure?
Overwhelmed? Confused?

Her gaze focussed instantly, and the words below resolved themselves into sense in her brain.

Talk to us in complete confidence for help to find your way forward.

Beneath was the name of a charity she had been vaguely familiar with in her student days, but had never had need to pay any attention to.

Until now.

She stared, repeating the words of the advert inside her head. *Unsure…overwhelmed…confused?* Dear God, she was all of those, all right. Her eyes drifted to the address given on the advert, registering that it was nearby.

Her grip tightened on her suitcase and with a jerk she started to head towards the escalators.

Oblivious of the quietly dressed man doing likewise a little way behind her...

Fifteen minutes later she was seated, hands clenched with tension, in a consulting room at the charity's walk-in offices.

'You really should take longer to think this through.' The woman talking to Mel spoke with a warm, sympathetic, but cautious tone.

'I *have* thought it through—I've thought it through over and over again...ever since I found out I was pregnant. It's the only thing I've been thinking about.'

Mel's voice was stressed. She had poured everything out, tumbled and conflicted and anguished, and the trained counsellor had listened quietly and attentively. Then she had spelt out to Mel the options that were available—the choices she could make.

As Mel had listened she had felt her heart grow heavier and heavier at the answer to the question that was tormenting her—that had tormented her ever since she had stared, disbelieving, at the blue line on the pregnancy test kit.

She looked across at the counsellor, her expression strained, but there was a resolve in her eyes that had not been there before.

'My mind is made up,' she said. 'That's my decision. My baby—my responsibility for what happens.'

She got to her feet. Once more a slight wave of nausea bit at her, and she swallowed it down.

The counsellor had stood up, too.

'I am always here,' she said, her voice kind, 'if you

feel you want to discuss this further…talk things through again.'

But Mel shook her head. 'Thank you—but, no. I know what I'm going to do.' She gave a difficult smile. 'Thank you for your time. It's been…' she took a breath '…invaluable. You've helped me to reach the answer I needed to find.'

She held out a hand, shook the counsellor's briefly and made her way back out on to the street. Her pace, as she headed off, was determined. Resolute. But her tread felt as heavy as her heart.

As she headed back to the tube station she got out the letter she'd written so painfully the night before. Tearing it in two, she dropped it in a litter bin. Then she went back down into the Underground. This time taking the direction away from the City.

Away from Nikos's offices.

There was nothing to tell him now. Nothing at all.

Her mind was clear on that.

Finally the writhing snakes that had tormented her had ceased their endless conflict.

Her baby was hers and hers alone.

And as she sat carefully down on a seat in the tube train her hand crept to her abdomen, spreading across gently. Protectively.

Nikos threw himself into his first-class seat on the plane as they boarded in Hong Kong, relief filling him. Finally he was on his way back to Europe. The typhoon had hit, just as he'd feared, and all flights had been cancelled. Now, though, the delayed flights were resuming and he was headed for London.

But he still didn't know where Mel was. His investigators had drawn a blank—and in a way he wasn't surprised. Because how *did* you locate someone who was one of thousands of tourists?

He'd told the agency about the sandwich bar she'd worked in, in case that might help. Maybe her former employer could shed some light on where she was right now? Hadn't Mel said that Sarrie was the uncle of a friend of hers?

And there was a possibility that she might be traceable by checking out the former address details of anyone with her surname who had died the previous year in North London, to see if they could locate the address of her late grandfather's house. If they could, then maybe the estate agents handling the tenancy had contact details for Mel?

With a shake of his head, Nikos waved away the glass of champagne being proffered by the stewardess in First Class, oblivious of the admiring look the attractive brunette had thrown his way. He was oblivious to all females now. Only one in the world mattered to him—the one he was trying to find—the one who was somewhere…wandering the face of the earth…

What if she's met someone else by now?

That was the fear that bit at him—gnawed at him in the night, when his body ached for Mel to be in his arms…

But he wouldn't let himself think like that—he wouldn't. He would hang on to the purpose he'd set for himself: he would find her and put to her the one thing he needed to say.

The one thing it was most vital to him that she knew.

Some twelve hours later Nikos strode out of the long-haul terminal at Heathrow. His car was humming at the kerb and he threw himself in, barely greeting his driver. Flicking open his laptop, he loaded his emails.

A surge of triumph welled in him—there was the email he'd been longing to see.

It was from his investigators and it was headed with the magic words: Subject located.

Yes! He all but punched the air even as his finger jabbed at the screen, opening the email. His eyes seized on the words and he started to read.

And then, inside his head, all hell broke loose.

Mel stepped out on to the pavement, hefting her suitcase out over the doorstop of the flat she had been staying in. It felt heavier than it had used to feel. Maybe the weakness she felt was to do with early pregnancy? Her mind was a blank—it was the only way she could keep going.

She'd booked a flight from Luton to Malaga, and now she had to get to Luton. But first she had a medical appointment. At a clinic that the counsellor at the pregnancy advisory charity had recommended to her and then made an appointment with.

The appointment letter was in her hand and she stared at the address again, trying to decide whether to take a bus or make for the Underground. The bus would be slower, but it would avoid her having to lug her suitcase down the tube station escalators.

She opted for the bus—she'd have enough suitcase-lugging to do once she got to the airport, and then at the other end in Malaga. She'd have to find somewhere to stay the night there…maybe a few days…until she could sort out accommodation and get her head around the new life she was going to make for herself.

One that was going to be so very, *very* different from what she had thought it was going to be.

But her mind was made up. There was no changing it now.

My baby—my decision. The only way it can be.

The heavy stone was still in her stomach, weighing her down, pushing the ever-present sense of nausea into her gullet. But it wasn't the physical impact of her pregnancy that was making her feel like this—feel as if she was being crushed to the ground...

She turned to start walking along the pavement towards the bus stop at the end of the road. Her feet dragged as if she was wearing shoes of lead.

The car braking sharply as it slewed towards the kerb made her head whip round. Recognition drew a gasp of disbelief from her. And then dismay.

Raw, shattering dismay.

Nikos was leaping from the car, charging up to her.

Dismay exploded in a million fragments—shot to pieces by the tidal wave of an utterly different emotion that surged across every synapse in her brain, flooding it with its totality.

Nikos! Nikos—here—in the flesh—in front of her—alive and well and *real*!

Not the hopeless memory in her head that was all he'd been these last endless weeks since she had walked away from him in Bermuda.

But real—oh, so real. How he'd suddenly appeared on the street like this she didn't know—didn't care. She knew only that a searing flash of joy was going through her.

Then that searing flash of joy was gone—shot to pieces in its turn.

Her arms were clamped in steel. His voice speared into her in fury.

'You're *not* doing it. Do you understand me? You're not doing it. I'll never let you do it. I don't care what the law says—I will *never* let you do that!'

Rage was boiling from him, burning in his eyes, and his face was twisted with anger as his words struck into her. She could only stare at him, not understanding...

Nikos saw the incomprehension in her face, layered over her shock at seeing him, and it maddened him yet more.

'How could you even *think* of it? How *could* you?'

The paper in her hand fluttered from her fingers to the ground. Automatically she tried to bend her knees to pick it up, but Nikos was still pinioning her and she couldn't move. He saw her movement and his eyes went to the letter on the ground. With a snarl he seized it himself, staring at it. His face whitened.

'Thee mou...' His voice was hollow. 'You're going there now—aren't you? *Aren't you?*'

From somewhere—she didn't know where—she found her voice. It was strained, as if it was being pulled unbearably tight.

'I didn't want you to know,' she said.

But it was too late now—the written proof of her medical appointment had revealed everything to him.

Another snarl broke from him. 'No! You were going ahead with it without even telling me, weren't you?'

Greek words burst from him—ugly and accusing. She didn't know what he was saying—only that it contained fury. Sickness rose in her. Dear God, she had been right in her decision not to tell him.

She made herself speak again as he stood there, the betraying letter in his hand, his face contorted with fury.

'It...it seemed the best thing to do, Nikos. I...I didn't want to involve you in any of this...'

'Involve me?'

He stared at her as if she'd spoken in an alien tongue.

Then a sudden, sickening realisation hit him. His hand, which had been still clamped around her arm, dropped away. He took a step back.

'Is it mine?'

Three little words—but in them a wealth of accusation. She paled, and he heard his voice going on, cutting at her with slashing words.

'It's a reasonable question to ask. After all, I picked you up easily enough, didn't I? Maybe you got a similar offer when you went off to New York without me? Maybe *he's* the guy who got you pregnant?'

She gasped as if he had struck her. *'No!'* she cried, the word tearing from her in rejection.

Emotion leapt in his eyes. 'So you admit it's mine? You admit it—and yet here you are, with the evidence of your damnable intentions in your hand, and you were going to say nothing to me—*nothing*!'

She shut her eyes, misery overwhelming her. 'I told you—I thought it would be for the best. It wasn't an easy decision, Nikos—truly it wasn't.'

More Greek broke from him, dark and furious. 'You never wanted to be pregnant, did you? Don't tell me otherwise, because I won't believe it.'

Her features convulsed. 'No—I didn't want to be pregnant,' she said, the words torn from her. 'When I realised it seemed…it seemed…'

Nikos supplied the words. 'An end to your freedom?' His voice was heavy, crushing.

'Yes. Pregnancy seemed…seemed the last thing I wanted…' She spoke faintly, as if the words could barely be spoken.

He turned her appointment letter over in his hand, his eyes never leaving her. 'And so you decided to re-gain your freedom,' he said, and now his words were not just heavy and crushing—they were swords, stabbing into her, strike after strike, pitiless and condemning. 'You decided to end the pregnancy.'

He saw her whiten like a sheet. The blood drained from her face. Inside him, unbearable fury lashed. Fury and something so much more.

All she wants is to get rid of the baby we created between us. It means nothing to her but a burden, a curb on her freedom!

And that was why she had bolted. Because surely she must have known that the moment he knew she was carrying his child there could be only one outcome?

For a second—just a fraction of a second—he felt his heart leap within him.

Mel—back with him. Back with him and bringing with her a gift even more precious than herself.

He felt his lungs squeezed, the air crushed from them.

But she didn't want that—didn't want him. And she had never wanted his baby.

Instead she wanted what she was set on doing now. What that starkly condemning report had told him. The report that had informed him she had been spotted entering a high street charity for a walk-in consultation.

The comment in parentheses had been unemotional.

We would advise our client that this particular charity is supportive of pro-choice options for women with unplanned pregnancies.

In a single sentence he had read heaven—and hell.

She was staring at him now, still as white as a sheet. She felt the words he'd thrown at her sear into her brain like a burning brand of accusation. Her mouth opened.

Words were desperate to take shape, to fly across the gaping space between them, to counter the dreadful accusation he had hurled at her.—

'Nikos! It isn't like that. It—'

But he was cutting right across her, stopping her speaking.

'Don't try and defend it. You can call it what you like, but we both know the truth of what you are planning to do.'

The terrible words were like knives, slashing at her. She could not bear to hear them. She gave a cry, backing away as if he had struck her physically. Features convulsing, she thrust past him, out into the roadway.

She had to get away—oh, dear God, she had to get away.

There was a screech of brakes, a hideous sound of squealing rubber. And then, as if in some horror movie slow-motion, Nikos saw the car hit her…saw her frail, fragile body crumple like paper and fall to the tarmac.

CHAPTER ELEVEN

HE WAS THERE in an instant—a heartbeat. The space of time between living and dying. He was yelling—he could hear himself yelling—but it was as if it were someone else. Someone else yelling as he saw that fragile figure crumple to the ground. Someone else yelling like a madman for an ambulance.

Because he was on his knees beside her, horror in his face, his eyes, in his whole being.

Let her be alive! Dear God in heaven, let her be alive. It's all I ask—all I beg! Anything else—anything else at all—I can bear. But not that—oh, not that!

It was all that consumed him in the eternity it took for the ambulance to arrive.

She had a pulse—it was his only desperate source of hope—but she was unconscious, inert, scarcely breathing, still as white as a sheet.

I did this to her. I did it. The punishing accusation went on and on in his head.

The paramedics tended her, phoning ahead to the hospital that they were bringing her in, checking the car's driver for shock and whiplash.

Nikos piled into the ambulance with her. 'Is she going to be all right? Please God, tell me.'

But the ambulance crew were adept at tragedy, and

only gave platitudes to him. There could be no answer to that question until she was in A&E…

Time stopped…time raced. Time blurred.

When the ambulance arrived at the hospital the emergency team fell to work. Nikos hung on to the doorjamb of the resuscitation bay and prayed—prayed with all his strength.

'Just *tell* me!' He was beyond coherence.

One of the doctors looked up. 'Looks like only bruising, lacerations—no sign of internal damage…no lung damage,' he reeled off. 'One cracked rib so far. No skull trauma. Spine and limbs seem OK, though she'll need a scan to check thoroughly.

'And she's coming round…'

Nikos swayed, Greek words breaking from him in a paean of gratitude. Mel's eyes were flickering, and a low groan sounded in her throat as consciousness returned. Then, as her eyes opened fully, Nikos could see her expression change to one of anguish when she saw all the medics clustered around her.

'My baby,' she cried. '*My baby!* Oh, please—please don't let my baby be gone. Please, no—*please, no!*'

Immediately the doctor responded, laying a calming hand on her arm.

'There's no sign of a bleed,' he said. 'But we'll get you up to Obs and Gynae the moment you've had your scan and they'll check you out thoroughly. OK?'

He smiled down reassuringly and Mel's stricken gaze clung to him. Then, before Nikos's eyes, she burst into crying. 'Thank God. Oh, thank God,' he heard her say.

Over and over again…

And inside him it felt as if the world had just changed for ever.

'Thank God,' he echoed. 'Thank God.'

But it was more than the life of his unborn child he was thanking God for—so, *so* much more…

Then the emergency team were dispersing, and a nurse was left to instruct that Mel be wheeled off for a scan and then up to Obs and Gynae. Once again Nikos was prevented from accompanying her, and frustration raged within him. He needed to be with her—needed her to be with *him*.

After an age—an eternity—he was finally told that she was in Obs and Gynae and that her scans, thankfully, had all been clear. Again, Nikos gave thanks—gave thanks with all his being.

He rushed up to the obstetrics and gynaecology department, heart pounding…

There were more delays there—more being kept waiting, pacing up and down. He focussed on one thing, and one thing only—getting to Mel. And then finally—finally—he was allowed to see her.

She was in a side ward, blessedly on her own. She was conscious still, but her face was pale—apart from the grazing on her cheek from where she'd collapsed on the tarmac after the impact. Her face whitened yet more as the nurse showed him in.

He rushed up to her—then stopped dead.

The expression on her face had stopped him in his tracks. She was looking…*stricken.*

He felt a hollowing out inside him. Horror washed through him again as he saw in his head that nightmare moment when the car had struck her and she'd crumpled like paper.

Then another emotion seared through his head.

His eyes fastened on her, desperate to read in her gaze what he absolutely, totally *had* to know. He heard in his head her terrified cries down in A&E.

'My baby,' she'd cried—and he could hear her cry still. *'My baby! Oh, please—please don't let my baby be gone. Please, no—please, no!'*

Relief, profound and infinitely grateful, had ripped through him that at that moment—at that moment of extreme danger to her baby—she had realised she wanted it. Realised how precious it was. How precious *she* was.

'I nearly lost you—I nearly killed you...'

He took a jerking step towards her. Saw her expression change.

'Oh, God, Mel—I'm sorry. I'm so sorry.' The words burst from him.

Words shaped themselves on her lips. Were uttered with difficulty and strain and a terrible emptiness. 'You thought I wanted to kill my baby.'

It wasn't an accusation, only a statement. But it came from a place he didn't want to exist.

He swallowed. 'I know—I know you don't. I heard you, Mel. I heard your terror when you came round—you were terrified for your baby.'

He saw her hand move slightly, unconsciously, to lie across her abdomen. Sheltering. Protective.

Emotion stabbed within him. 'Mel, I—'

His voice was jerky, but hers cut right across it.

'How could you think that, Nikos? How *could* you?' Her eyes were piercing—accusing. Horrified.

A rasp sounded in his throat. 'You said yourself that you didn't want to be pregnant. That it would be an end to your freedom.' He took a ragged breath, memory searing through him. 'And I kept remembering how you told Fiona Pellingham that you didn't want a baby now—'

Her face worked. She acknowledged the truth of what

he'd just said—knew she had to face it. 'That was my first reaction, yes—but it wasn't the only one, Nikos. Truly it wasn't. But it was so...so complicated.'

Complicated... Such a weak, pathetic word to describe the searing clash of emotions that had consumed her as she'd stared at that thin blue line on the pregnancy testing kit.

They were there still, consuming her. Anguish churned inside her that Nikos should think...should think...

He was staring at her. 'You were on your way to an abortion clinic—I saw the appointment letter.'

Her face contorted. 'It was an antenatal appointment. That's all it was! To have a check-up before I fly to Spain tonight. How could you think it was for anything else? How *could* you?'

She took a shuddering breath.

'My old GP is miles away, and I'd have had to wait days for an appointment. So the woman at the charity made an appointment for me at a mother and baby clinic.'

He was staring at her still. Still not making sense of things. 'It's a pro-choice charity,' he said, his voice hollow. 'They arrange abortions for women who have pregnancies they don't want.'

Her features were screwed up. 'Yes, they do, Nikos. But they also help with all the other alternatives, as well. Like single-parenting—raising a baby alone.' Her expression changed again. 'How do you know I went to that charity?'

He took a deep breath. This wasn't the way he'd thought it was going to be—this moment of finding her again. Shock still reverberated through him—shock upon shock. He remembered the terror as he'd read the report that had totally changed everything—for ever. It had given him the most wonderful gift he could imagine—and threatened to tear it from him in the same moment.

Mel—carrying his child.

Mel—wanting to destroy their child…

Mel—crumpling to the ground as the car hit her, nearly destroyed by his accusation.

Cold snaked down his spine like iced water as he realised how hideously close he'd come to losing everything—everything he was most desperate to keep.

'I…I've been trying to find you. I sent investigators to search for you. They found you, finally, where you were staying—and they saw you there. I only just got their findings now—when I landed at Heathrow. I've been in Hong Kong. There was a typhoon.'

His jerky, staccato words ground to a halt.

'I've been trying to find you,' he said again.

It was, he knew, the only thing he had to say to her. Nothing else mattered—nothing at all.

Except that I've found her. That she's alive, that she carries my child!

Emotion flooded through him.

Our child—she bears our child.

Wonder and gratitude soared in him. He felt weak with it.

She was staring at him.

'You were trying to find me?' Her voice was faint.

'*Yes!* Mel—Mel, I—'

But she cut across him. 'Oh, dear God, I wish with all my heart you hadn't. I wish you'd never found me.' Her face buckled. 'Never found me and never found out about the baby.'

Her voice was anguished. Inside her that same impossible conflict of emotions was still warring, tearing her apart.

Oh, dear God, what a mess this is—what an unholy, impossible mess!

She felt again that stabbing wound, the lashing blow that she'd felt when she'd heard the full import of his words—the cruel accusation he'd hurled at her that had made her want to run, to flee straight into the path of the car that had nearly killed her—nearly killed her baby.

Nikos's baby—that I didn't want him to know about—Because if he did...

'I never meant to involve you in this, Nikos,' she said, her voice twisted, her eyes pleading.

He was staring at her again. 'What do you mean, *"involve"* me? Mel, this is *our* child. Our baby!'

How could she talk like this? Say she hadn't wanted him to know?

Words she had said earlier now registered with him—something about going to Spain, taking a flight that day...

The cold snaked down his spine again.

Had he not sent his investigators to find her she would have disappeared again.

And I'd never have known—never have known she was carrying my baby—our baby!

Fear at what had so very nearly happened gouged at him.

She was answering him—her voice low, strained.

'It doesn't have to be, Nikos. It can just be *my* baby. That's why I went to that pregnancy charity—I needed someone to talk to about not telling you about the baby. She...she helped me make my mind up. And then she went through the practicalities of raising a child single-handed, without paternal involvement, taking all the responsibility on myself.'

'*Thee mou*—why? *Why?* Why even *think* like that?' The words broke from him.

She didn't answer—couldn't. Could only press her hand against her abdomen again, feeling…needing the reassurance that her baby was safe—*safe*. The baby she would raise on her own, as she had come to realise she must. Because anything else was…impossible. Just impossible…

She felt her throat tighten. To see Nikos again—here…so real—but for him to be as far away from her as he could be…

He saw the emotion on her face. Realised what it must mean. She hadn't wanted him to know she was pregnant because she didn't want him *involved*.

Didn't want him in her life.

After all his hopes…all the hopes that had soared within him as he'd stood in his office in Athens…when he'd realised that he and Mel were nothing, *nothing* like his parents. That what they had between them could never descend into the bitter farce that was his parents' marriage.

But now his hopes were ashes in his mouth. Heaviness filled him.

She wants her freedom—the freedom she's craved for so long—the freedom she left me for and still wants.

The freedom he could not take from her—*must* not take from her.

Not even for the sake of the child she carried—*their* child. The child she wanted to raise on her own—free of him.

He sought for what he must say now. Letting go of

his hopes…letting them fall to the ground, dashed to pieces…

'You must have known…' he said, and his voice was hollow, but so, *so* careful. 'You must have known that I would…stand by you, Mel.'

He was picking his words with infinite care. All that she had said to him while they'd been together, about how precious her newly gained life of freedom was to her, came back to him like blows.

It was why she left me—to safeguard her freedom. Why she walked out on me when I wanted more of her than she wanted to give.

He would let her keep that freedom—he must. He would not try to chain her to his side in a life she did not want. If she wanted to raise their child herself he must let her—he *must*.

Whatever it cost him.

He came towards her now, took the hard chair that was near the bed and sat himself down on it. Took a deep, steadying breath in order to say what he must say now that she'd made it crystal clear that she'd never wanted to tell him about her pregnancy. Never wanted him *'involved.'* The word twisted inside him like snakes.

'You know I'll stand by you, Mel. There'll be no money worries. I'll see to everything. Look after you, whatever you choose. So you can live wherever you want—well, anywhere child-safe, obviously.'

She heard him speak, and each word was like an arrow in her. But with each word she knew irrefutably that after all her anguish and turmoil, her longings and her fears from the very moment she had seen that thin blue line on the pregnancy test, that she had done what had proved the right thing to have done. She knew she had made the right decision in determining to head for Spain, not to tell Nikos about being pregnant, not to burden him with it…

But it was too late now—he knew she carried their child. And now she would have to take the consequences of his knowledge. Protect herself from them as much as she could.

A pang went through her…

He made as if to reach for her hand, then stopped, drew back. Then he spoke again.

'I know how vital your freedom is to you, Mel. I'll protect that for you as much as I can—make as few demands on you as I can. So long as from time to time you let me…let me—'

He stopped, unable to continue.

Let me see my baby—my child. Let me see you, Mel—let me be a part of your life, however small…

He swallowed, forced himself to keep going, to keep his voice studiedly, doggedly neutral—impossible though it was to do so, when inside he was holding down with brute force what was burning inside him.

'But please, Mel, don't disappear without my knowing—that's all I ask. I have…responsibilities…for you… for the baby…'

The word tolled in her brain. *'Responsibilities…'* Yes, that was all it could be to him. He'd been angry—furious—and understandably so, when he'd thought she wanted a termination. But now that he'd realised she wanted this baby—how terrified she'd been when she'd thought she might lose it—now it was just a question of…*responsibilities.*

Responsibilities she would—*must*—keep as light as possible for him. She must assure him of that.

'I won't…impose on you, Nikos. Financially I'll be

all right. I have the rental income from my grandfather's house, and until the baby is born I can work. I'm going to base myself in Spain, probably, because I can live cheaply there. There are various child benefits I'm entitled to claim as well—that woman at the charity explained it all to me.'

'Impose?' he echoed. 'Mel, this is *my* baby you're talking about. It goes without question that I'll take care of everything.'

She shook her head violently. It hurt, but she didn't care.

'Oh, Nikos, that's why I wish to God you'd never found out. I know how scarred you are by your parents chaining themselves to each other. That you never want to run such a risk yourself. That's why you only wanted a brief romance with me. The last thing you want is to be trapped—trapped as you are now—trapped by unplanned, unwanted fatherhood. And that's why I was never going to tell you about the baby. So *you* could be free.'

Her voice was anguished, no more than a whisper now.

'If you'd never known about the baby we could both have been free of each other...'

For a moment...for an eternity...there was silence.

Then... 'Free of each other?' Nikos's echo of her words dropped like lead into the silence.

Abruptly, he let go of her hands. Pushed the chair back roughly. Got to his feet. Paced about the narrow room. Turned back to look at her. Tension radiated from him.

'Your freedom to roam the world after all those years looking after your grandfather—mine to avoid any kind of repetition of the snake pit that is my parents' marriage—is that it?'

There was something strange in his voice—something that made her stare at him. Not understanding. Not comprehending.

He didn't wait for an answer—just ploughed on. That same strange note was in his voice, the same strangeness in his face...his eyes.

'All my life I've run scared,' he said. 'Scared and, yes, *scarred*. Scarred by what I've had to witness between my warring, snarling parents. Tearing each other apart...tearing their marriage apart. And I dreaded, *dreaded* that I might end up doing the same.'

He took a breath—a shuddering breath.

'I vowed I would never run that risk. And I vowed I would never get involved with any woman who could endanger that vow. I only ever wanted temporary relationships. Nothing...deeper. Nothing...longer. Nothing longer than a holiday romance.'

There was a twist in his voice now, and it was heavy with irony. Bitter self-mockery.

'Just the way you did.' He took another breath, felt it razoring his lungs. 'We were so well suited, weren't we, Mel? In our own different ways we wanted the same thing—our freedom.'

He gazed at her—at the way she lay there, at her golden hair, her beautiful face—and a thousand memories came rushing to his head of those glorious days they'd had together—so good...so *good*.

So *right*.

And in the golden wash of those memories came knowledge, pouring like a fountain through him. Confirming—in a tidal wave of emotion—what had swept over him when he'd set out to find Mel again—to beg her to stay in his life.

He stilled. Thrust his hands deep into his trouser pockets. Stood there immobile, unreadable. Then something changed in his expression. He seemed to stand straighter—taller.

He looked at her lying there, her body ripening with their baby…their child-to-be.

'I want a new freedom,' he said. His voice was different now—resolute, adamant. 'The freedom not to be scarred by my parents' marriage—not to be fearful of repeating their mistakes. The freedom, Mel, to say finally what I have crushed down up to now, because I don't want to put on you what you do not want. You want your freedom—honoured and preserved—and I won't try and hamper you, or constrain you, or curtail you in any way. I know how hard-earned it is, how well deserved it is. You have your scars, too, Mel, but for all that I still want a new freedom.'

He paused, took a razor-edged breath. Then spoke again.

'I want the freedom to say this, Mel.' He took another breath, just as sharp, and absolutely vital to his existence. 'You said if I hadn't known about the baby we could have been free of each other.'

Between them, the silence stretched. Mel could not speak, could say nothing at all, for suddenly there was no breath in her lungs—no breath at all—and still the silence stretched between them.

Then… 'I don't want to be free of you.' Nikos's voice seared into the silence. 'When I saw that car hit you— oh, God, I thought you were dead. I thought you were *dead*! That I'd lost you for ever. And it was the worst moment of my life.'

It felt as if his heart was being impaled, speared again by the terror he'd felt as he'd watched her crumple to the ground. He relived that moment of absolute nightmare, knowing with grovelling gratitude to all the powers-that-be that he'd been spared. Knowing with a blaze in his head, in his heart, that he could not go on without speaking.

He surged on. It was too late to stop now—far, far too late.

'I want you to come back to me so much. I can't help hoping…hoping against hope…that despite everything—despite all that you've ever said to me—you might just—just…' He took a final ragged breath. 'Just want to come back to me. That you might just,' he said, and his eyes could not leave hers…not for a second, not for an instant, 'want to make your life with me.'

He had said it. Finally he had said it.

His heart was bared now, and it was beating for her and her alone. And if she spurned it—if she looked at him with pity, with rejection, after hearing words that had only made her want to flee from him the more—then he would bear it. But if he didn't put his words out there, then she might never know…never guess…just what he felt for her.

'I don't want to be free of you, Mel. I *can't* be free of you. You're in my head, and in my thoughts, and in my blood. You're in my *heart*, Mel…'

His eyes were blazing…the blood was roaring in his veins.

'There's only one freedom I want, Mel. I want to be free to love you.'

There was silence—absolute silence.

Nikos's gaze lasered down at her, willing her to speak. To say something—anything. But she simply lay there, her face as white as ice. Then he saw slow, thick tears start to ooze from beneath her eyelids.

He was at her side in an instant—a fraction of a second. Seizing her hands, clutching them to him.

'Mel! Don't cry—oh, my darling one, don't cry. I'm sorry—I'm sorry that I said all that to you. I should never have burdened you with it.'

But she only wept more, and he had to scoop his arm around her shoulders and cradle her against him. She wept into him—tears and tears and more tears. He soothed her hair and held her close, and closer still. And then, somewhere at his shoulder, he heard her speak. Muffled and tearful.

Carefully, mindful of how fragile her body was, he lowered her back upon the pillows. But she clung to his hand still. Her eyes swam with tears.

'I want that freedom, too. Oh, Nikos, I want it more than anything in the world!' Her face crumpled again. 'I want to be free to love you, free to *tell* you that I love you. And to love you the way I do.'

She wept again, and he held her again, and she was as light as a feather. For all the world weighed nothing now—nothing at all.

'I missed you so much,' she sobbed. 'I tried so hard not to miss you, but I did. All the time in America I missed you. I missed you wherever I went. Everywhere without you was...*awful*. I wanted you with me. On the Staten Island Ferry, at the top of the Empire State Building... I wanted to laugh with you in Las Vegas, revel in all its gaudy garishness. And I wanted you to stand beside me at the rim of the Grand Canyon and look down a mile deep into the earth. I wanted you everywhere I went. And you weren't there, Nikos, because

I'd walked out on you—and I'd walked out on you because…because…'

The sobbing came again, and once again he was soothing her, stroking her hair, clasping her hand tight, so tight.

'Because I knew that if I didn't go then, I'd never go. And I *had* to go—it was a holiday romance we had—only that. That was all you wanted—and all I wanted—all I thought it would ever be. But it wasn't, Nikos—it wasn't, it *wasn't*… But it had never been *supposed* to be anything more than a holiday romance because I wanted to be free—free like I've wanted to be for so, *so* long.'

She pulled away from him, her face working, full of anguish.

'When I first found out I was pregnant I…I was distraught. I was terrified that I'd be plunged back into having to take care of another human being just when I'd got my own life back. But at the same time I felt my heart leap with joy. I had a *baby* growing inside me—a wondrous new life—and it was *your* baby, Nikos. Yours. And I realised…I realised…' her eyes were clinging to his and her hands were clinging to him '…I realised, Nikos, that all I wanted on this earth was to be free to love my baby—free to want my baby more than anything else in all the world. And because of that…because of that—'

She broke off, tears welling again, her voice choked with emotion, with discovery.

'Because all I wanted was to love my baby I knew…I knew—oh, Nikos—I knew it meant I was free to love. Free to love *you*. Love you the way I wanted to. The way I'd feared to because it was loving my poor grandfather that kept me by his side so long. I feared love would be a tie. And I thought all I wanted was to be free of all ties. Free of all bonds.'

Tears flowed down her cheeks and she felt her heart must surely overflow with the emotion now pouring through her.

'But to love *you*, Nikos, is to be free.'

He moved to sweep her to him, but she held him back, fear leaping in her eyes.

'But *am* I free to love you, Nikos? Am I? You talked of standing by me and "responsibilities". And—'

'Mel, my darling one, I said that only because I didn't want to burden you with my wanting you the way I do. With my wanting, more than anything in this life, to be your husband—your devoted, loving husband—the father to our beloved child—with you, my beloved wife.'

She gave a little choke of laughter and of tears. Of happiness and bliss.

'What fools we've been. Denying what we both craved.'

'Each other!' Nikos finished, and then he swept her to him, wanting no more pointless words, no more unnecessary doubts, no more fleeting fears.

He was free, finally, to hold her, to embrace her, to kiss her—to love her. As she was free to love him in return. And they were both free to love the child she carried.

Free to be happy with each other—all their lives.

A cough sounded from the doorway. They sprang apart. The nurse took in Mel's tear-stained face and frowned slightly.

'Happy tears or sad tears?' she asked enquiringly, with a lift of her eyebrow.

'Happy,' said Mel and Nikos in unison.

The nurse's gaze went to their fast-clasped hands,

and she nodded. 'Not too much emotion,' she advised, with another nod and a smile. 'Not good for baby.'

She picked up the notes from the foot of the bed, glancing at them. 'Overnight stay for observation,' she confirmed. Then she glanced at Nikos. 'I'm sorry to tell you this, but it's not actually visiting hours at the moment. It's only because your—'

'Wife-to-be,' Nikos inserted, throwing a glance at Mel.

'Your wife-to-be,' echoed the nurse dutifully, 'has come up here from A&E.' She looked again at the pair of them. 'It's visiting hours at six, so come back then. In the meantime…' her mouth twitched, and her expression was sympathetic now '…you've got five more minutes.' She whisked out.

Nikos turned to Mel. His heart was soaring. Soaring like a bird in flight.

'Will five minutes do it?' he asked her, his brow lifting questioningly.

Mel shook her head. She was floating somewhere above the surface of the hospital bed—she didn't know where. Didn't care.

Had it been so simple? Had a holiday romance been the real thing all along?

I wanted freedom, but my freedom is here—here with Nikos. Here with our child, waiting to be born.

She felt her heart constrict. Whatever names Nikos might want, one she knew. If their baby was a boy it would be named for her grandfather. The grandfather she had loved so much. Not the stricken husk he had become, but the loving, protective grandfather she remembered so clearly.

Oh, Gramps—you wanted me to find a good man— and now I have. I have!

'OK,' said Nikos. 'Well, if five minutes won't do it…' his eyes softened as he gazed down at her, the woman he had claimed the freedom to love '…how about fifty years?'

Her face lit. 'Sounds good to me,' she said. 'Sounds *very* good!'

He bent to kiss her. 'To our Golden Wedding Anniversary, then, and all the golden years between.'

'To our golden years together,' echoed Mel, and kissed him back.

EPILOGUE

THE CHRISTENING PARTY at Nikos and Mel's newly acquired family-sized villa on the coast outside Athens was crowded with guests. Mel sat in almost regal splendour on the sofa, and young Nikos Stephanos Albert—already known as Nicky—lay on her lap, resplendent in his christening gown, fast asleep, oblivious to all the admiring comments that came his way.

The vast majority of those came from his doting parents, and Nikos, standing beside the sofa, was gazing down at his newborn son with an expression little short of besotted, accepting all the homage as nothing more than perfectly right and reasonable. Their son *was* the most amazing baby ever, and no other could *possibly* be even a fraction as wonderful.

They were not alone in this view, for Nikos's parents shared it with them.

'Hah!' exclaimed Stephanos Parakis proudly, gazing benignly down at his grandson.

'He looks like you,' said his wife fondly. His *new* wife.

Nikos's eyes tore themselves away from his infant son and settled with approval on Adela Parakis. Even if she hadn't turned out to be a very calm and level-headed divorcee of forty-plus, rather than the sultry mistress he'd assumed, Nikos would have approved of her. For she had been the catalyst that had finally triggered his parents' decision to call time on their tormented marriage.

One of the catalysts, Nikos acknowledged.

The other was the elegant silver-haired man at the side of Nikos's mother—the new Principessa Falesi. The widowed Principe had met her at a party in Milan, and such had been his admiration for her that his mother had received with equanimity the news that her husband wished to remarry.

Now, as Principessa, she was enjoying a new lease of life—and of beauty. For as her son's eyes perused her they could see that his mother had clearly undergone a facelift, chosen a dramatically more flattering hairstyle and, if he were not mistaken, had a few additional discreet nips and tucks, as well.

He was glad for her—glad for both his parents. Glad for their late happiness with other partners, and glad that their respective remarriages had enabled them—finally—to be civil to each other…especially when they now had a common fascination with their grandson.

'He has my eyes,' observed the Principessa with complacent satisfaction, approaching with her new husband.

'He does,' Mel smiled. Nikos's mother was being very gracious towards her, and Mel wanted to keep her that way. So she didn't point out that *all* newborns had blue eyes.

Nikos refrained from telling his mother that, actually, his son had his wife's eyes—which just happened to be the most beautiful eyes in the world…

Memory struck through him—how Mel had flashed her sapphire eyes at him in that very first encounter, and how they had pierced him like Cupid's proverbial arrow.

Happiness drenched through him. And disbelief.

A holiday romance? How could he *ever* have been idiotic enough to think Mel—wonderful, fabulous, adorable, beloved Mel—could be nothing more than a holiday romance? She was the most precious person in the world to him.

Along with Nicky, of course.

Instinctively he lifted Mel's free hand in his and wound his fingers warmly into hers. She shifted her gaze to look at him, love shining in her eyes.

'A daughter next, I would recommend,' the Principessa said to Mel.

'Oh, yes,' agreed Mel. 'That would be ideal.'

'But you must watch your figure, my dear,' her mother-in-law reminded her.

'I fully intend to aspire to be as elegant as *you* in that respect,' Mel assured her, and nodded admiringly.

The Principessa gave a little laugh, and bestowed a careful smile of approval on her daughter-in-law. 'You must visit us in Milan, my dear, when my grandson is old enough to travel,' she said, catching her new husband's arm.

'Oh, that would be *lovely*!' enthused Mel. She glanced up at Nikos. 'Wouldn't it?'

'Yes, indeed,' he said hurriedly. 'Are you leaving already?' he asked.

'Alas, we must. We are flying home this evening.'

The guests were starting to disperse, and shortly after his mother's departure Nikos's father left as well, informing his son as he did so that Mel, Nicky and he were also invited to visit himself and Adela whenever they liked.

Nikos thanked him heartily, and saw them both to their car. As he came back into the villa Mel was in the hallway, cradling Nicky, who was now wide awake.

'He needs a change,' she said cheerfully. 'Want to help?'

'I wouldn't miss it for the world.' Nikos grinned. 'Do you mean a nappy-change? Or a change out of that metre-long silk embroidered concoction he's wearing?'

'Both,' said Mel. 'And then, if you won't think me a bad mother, I'll hand him over to Nanny, and you and I can sneak off to dinner before he needs his next feed.'

She gave a wry little smile of gratitude. It was amazing, she acknowledged, just how easy motherhood was when there was a nanny on hand. And when the baby's father was as devoted and willing as Nikos was.

'Great idea,' Nikos said with enthusiasm. 'It's more than time I had you to myself again.'

As they headed upstairs to the lavishly decorated suite that was Nicky's nursery Nikos said, 'By the way, we've been invited to a wedding—'

'Oh? Whose?' asked Mel interestedly.

Nikos gave a glinting smile. 'Would you believe Fiona Pellingham—and Sven?'

Mel gave her gurgle of laughter. 'His name's Magnus,' she said. 'But it's lovely news. I'm so glad for her.'

'Well, you were the matchmaker there,' Nikos reminded her.

Mel smiled fondly at her husband. 'And she was ours in a way, too, if you think about it. If she hadn't been pursuing you, you'd never have asked me out.'

Nikos put his arm around her shoulder. 'I'd have found another reason,' he answered. 'There was no way I could ever get you out of my head.'

She paused at the top of the stairs to kiss his cheek.

Her eyes were soft with love. 'Nor me you,' she assured him.

The dark eyes glinted with wicked humour. 'Love at first sight, was it?'

She spluttered, remembering their intemperate sparring at that first prickly encounter in the sandwich shop. 'We got all the aggro out of the way,' she told him firmly. 'Oh, and on the subject of sandwich shops—I heard that the Sarrie's Sarnies franchise is going great guns. Thanks to your business loan.'

'Well, didn't I promise that if his turnover increased I'd consider funding his expansion?' Nikos reminded her as they gained Nicky's bathroom and got to work on the delicate task of parting him from his ornate christening robe.

'He's very grateful,' Mel assured him. 'And so,' she added, 'is Joe. For sponsoring that new homeless shelter he's in, and the medics for addiction and alcoholism treatment.'

'Well, I'm grateful to Joe in return,' Nikos riposted. 'When I showered him with all those damn pound coins you'd dumped on me in your splenetic rage...' he ducked as Mel swung him a playful thump of objection, then lifted Nicky free of his gown '...I realised you were right about more than just how the booze was killing him—that you were *entitled* to be put out about the way I behaved to you. And that I owed you flowers to make amends.'

Mel gently laid their infant son down on his changing mat. 'Well,' she said, throwing another wicked glance at her husband, 'you can go on making amends.' She stepped aside. 'Go on—your turn for the nappy-change.'

'I couldn't just hand you the clean nappy, could I?' Nikos asked hopefully.

'Nope,' said his wife sternly.

Her husband dropped a resigned kiss on her forehead. 'It's a price I'll pay willingly for a happy marriage,' he told her.

Mel reached up to him with her mouth. 'Correction,' she told him. 'For the happiest marriage in the world.'

She took a wad of cotton wool, holding it at the ready for Nikos, talcum powder in her other hand.

Nikos grinned. 'Right, as always,' he agreed.

Then, with a squaring of his shoulders, he got to work to prove to the woman he loved just how much he loved her…

And beneath their joint ministrations the child who had brought them back together gazed cherubically up at the two people who loved only him more than they loved each other.

* * * * *

THE RETURN
OF ANTONIDES

ANNE McALLISTER

For Anne

CHAPTER ONE

"GETTING MARRIED IS EXHAUSTING." Althea Halloran Rivera Smith Moore collapsed into the back of the cab and closed her eyes, unmoving.

"Which is why you're only supposed to do it once," Holly said drily as she clambered in after her sister-in-law. She pulled the door shut and gave the driver her address in Brooklyn.

As the taxi edged back out into the late Saturday afternoon Midtown Manhattan traffic, Holly slumped back in against the seat. "Those dresses were horrible." She shuddered just thinking about the pastel creations she'd tried on all day. It wasn't as if she hadn't worn identically repulsive bridesmaids' dresses for Althea's other weddings.

"This is the last time." Althea put her hand over her heart. "I swear. I'm just too impulsive."

In the eight years since Holly's wedding to Althea's brother Matt, Althea had marched up the aisle three times. And into divorce court each time shortly thereafter.

"But not anymore. This time is different," Althea assured her. "Stig is different."

Swedish professional hockey player Stig Mikkelsen had nothing at all in common with the aloof doctor, the extroverted stock broker and the pompous professor Althea had married previously. Stig had swept into Althea's life six months ago, charmed her, teased her and refused to take no for an answer. He'd overturned her resolve never to walk down another aisle, and best of all, had somehow given Althea the greatest gift—helping her return to the sparkling, cheerful woman she had been before her three marital disasters.

For that alone, Holly blessed him. So when Althea began making wedding plans and asked Holly to be her "one and only bridesmaid, please, please, please!" Holly had gritted her teeth and agreed.

She'd even silently vowed—if necessary—to force herself into another stiff, ruffled, pastel cupcake of a dress. But even with just the two of them to please and all of Manhattan's gauziest wonders to choose from, they hadn't been able to find "the perfect bridesmaid's dress."

"Stig will know what we need. I'll take him next time," Althea said.

"He's a nice guy," Holly allowed. But if he went dress shopping with Althea, he should be nominated for sainthood.

"And he's got teammates…" Althea shot her a speculative look. "Single ones."

"No," Holly said automatically. "Not interested." She crossed her arms over her tote bag, holding it against her like a shield.

"You don't even know what I was going to say!"

Holly arched a brow. "Don't I?"

Althea had the grace to look a tiny bit abashed, then gave a little flounce and lifted her chin. "Some of them are very nice guys."

"No doubt. I'm not interested."

"You're not even thirty years old! You have a whole life ahead of you!"

"I know." There was nothing Holly was more aware of than how much of her life there still might be—and how flat and empty it was. She pressed her lips together and made herself stare at the cars they were passing.

Suddenly Althea's hand was on her knee, giving it a

sympathetic squeeze. "I know you miss him," she said, her voice soft but thick with emotion. "We all miss him."

Matt, she meant. Her brother. Holly's husband. The center of Holly's life.

Just thirty years old, Matthew David Halloran had had everything to live for. He was bright, witty, handsome, charming. A psychologist who worked mostly with children and teens, Matt had loved his work. He'd loved life.

He had loved hiking, skiing and camping. He'd loved astronomy and telescopes, basketball and hockey. He'd loved living in New York City, loved the fifth floor walk-up he and Holly had shared when they'd first moved to the city, loved the view across the river to Manhattan from the condo they'd recently bought in a trendy Brooklyn highrise.

Most of all, Matt had loved his wife.

He'd told her so that Saturday morning two years and four months ago. He had bent down and kissed her sleepy smile as he'd gone out the door to play basketball with his buddies. "Love you, Hol'," he'd murmured.

Holly had reached up from the bed she was still snuggled in and snagged his hand and kissed it. "You could show me," she'd suggested with a sleepy smile.

Matt had given her a rueful grin. "Temptress." Then he'd winked. "I'll be home at noon. Hold that thought."

It was the last thing he'd ever said to her. Two hours later Matt Halloran was dead. An aneurysm, they told her later. Unknown and undetected. A silent killer waiting for the moment to strike.

Going in for a lay-up at the end of the game, Matt had shot—and dropped to the floor.

Simultaneously the bottom had dropped out of Holly's world.

At first she had been numb. Disbelieving. Not Matt. He couldn't be dead. He hadn't been sick. He was healthy as a horse. He was strong. Capable. He had his whole life ahead of him!

But it turned out that Holly was the one who had her life ahead of her—a life without Matt. A life she hadn't planned on.

It hadn't been easy. All she had wanted to do those first months was cry. She couldn't because she had a class full of worried fifth graders to teach. They looked to her for guidance. They knew Matt because he and Holly took them to the marina on Saturdays to teach them canoeing and kayaking. They shared her grief and needed a role model for how to handle it.

Psychologist Matt would have been the first to tell her so.

So for them, Holly had stopped wallowing in misery. She'd wiped away her tears, pasted on her best smile and resolutely put one foot in front of the other again.

Eventually, life began to resemble something akin to normal, though for her it never would be again—not without Matt to share it.

But even though she had learned to cope, she wasn't prepared when friends and family began trying to set her up with another man. Holly didn't *want* another man! She wanted the man she'd had.

But ever since last summer Althea had been dropping hints. Holly's brother, Greg, a lawyer in Boston, said he had a colleague she might like to meet. Even her mother, a longtime divorcee with not much good to say about men, had suggested she take a singles cruise. At Christmas Matt's parents had begun telling her she needed to get on with her life, that Matt would want her to.

She'd always done everything Matt wanted her to. That was the problem!

"At least you're dating Paul."

"Yes." A few months back, Holly had determined that the best way to deter meddling family and friends was to appear to have taken their advice and gone out. Charming, handsome, smart, a psychologist like Matt, Paul McDonald was *like* Matt. But he *wasn't* Matt. So no danger to her at all. It just kept well-meaning relatives and friends off her back. And she knew she wasn't leading Paul on. Long divorced, Paul was a complete cynic about marriage.

"If you married Paul," Althea said, oblivious to Paul's lack of interest, "you wouldn't have to hare off across the world to sit on a coral atoll somewhere." She gave Holly an indignant glare. "I can't believe you're even considering that!"

Joining the Peace Corps, she meant. Last fall, fed up with the emptiness of her life and admitting to herself at least that she needed to find a new purpose, a new focus, Holly had sent in her application. They had offered her a two-year teaching position on a small South Pacific island. She was to start preliminary training in Hawaii the second week in August.

"I'm not considering. I'm doing it," she said now.

"Paul can't talk you out of it?"

"No."

"Someone should," Althea grumbled. "You need a man who will make you sit up and take notice. Paul's too nice. You need a challenge." Abruptly, she sat up straight, a smile dawning on her lips. "Like Lukas Antonides."

"What? *Who?*" Holly felt as if all the air had been sucked out of the universe. She was gasping as she stared at her sister-in-law. Where had *that* come from?

"You remember Lukas." Althea was practically bouncing on the seat now, her cheeks definitely rosy.

Holly felt hers burning. Her whole body was several degrees warmer. "I remember Lukas."

"You used to follow him around," Althea said.

"I did not! I followed Matt!" It was Matt, damn him, who had followed Lukas around.

Lukas Antonides had become the neighborhood equivalent of the Pied Piper from the minute he'd moved in the year he and Matt were eleven and Holly was nine.

"Ah, Lukas." Althea used her dreamy voice. "He was such a stud. He still is."

"How do you know?" Holly said dampeningly. "He's on the other side of the world."

Lukas had spent the past half dozen years or so in Australia. Before that he'd been in Europe—Greece, Sweden, France. Not that she'd kept track of him. Matt had done that.

Since Matt's death she hadn't really known where Lukas was. She'd received a sympathy card simply signed "Lukas." No personal remarks. Nothing—except the spiky black scrawl of his name—which was absolutely fine with her.

She hadn't expected him at the funeral. It was too far to come. And thank God for that. She hadn't had to deal with him along with everything else. For a dozen years now she hadn't had to deal with him at all. So why was Althea bringing him up now, when he was off mining opals or wrangling kangaroos or doing whatever enthusiasm was grabbing him at the moment?

"He's back," Althea said. "Didn't you see the article in *What's New!*?"

Holly felt her stomach clench. "No." It was the end of the school year. She didn't have time to read anything except student papers. "What article?" *What's New!* was a hot, upscale lifestyle magazine. Out of her league. She wouldn't normally read it anyway.

Since getting engaged to Stig, Althea always read it. Sometimes she was even in it. Now she nodded eagerly. "Gorgeous article. Just like him." She grinned. "He got the centerfold."

"They don't have centerfolds in *What's New!*" But the image it conjured up made Holly's cheeks flame.

Althea laughed. "The centerfold of the magazine. There's a double-page spread of Lukas in his office. Big story about him and his foundation and the gallery he's opening."

"Foundation? Gallery? What gallery?"

"He's opening a gallery for Australian, New Zealand and Pacific art here in New York. Big stuff in the local art community. And he's heading up some charitable foundation."

"Lukas?" If the gallery and the centerfold boggled her mind, the notion of Lukas heading up a charitable foundation sounded like a sign of the apocalypse.

"It's in this week's issue," Althea went on. "He's on the cover, too. Surprised it didn't catch your eye. The gallery is in SoHo. They showed some of the art and sculpture in the article. Very trendy. It's going to draw lots of interest." Her grin widened. "So is Lukas."

Holly folded her hands in her lap, staring straight ahead. "How nice."

Althea made a tutting sound. "What do you have against Lukas? You were friends."

"He was Matt's friend," Holly insisted.

Lukas's move into the neighborhood had turned Holly's life upside down. Until then she and Matt had been best friends. But once Lukas arrived, she'd been relegated to tag-along, particularly by Lukas.

Matt hadn't ditched her completely. Solid, dependable, responsible Matt had always insisted that Holly was his friend. But when Lukas's father took them out in his sailboat, she hadn't been invited.

"Go play with Martha," Lukas had said. It had been his answer to everything.

His twin sister, Martha, had spent hours drawing and sketching everything in sight. Holly couldn't draw a stick figure without a ruler. She'd liked swimming and playing ball and catching frogs and riding bikes. She'd liked all the same things Matt did.

Except Lukas.

If Matt had always been as comfortable as her oldest shoes, Lukas was like walking on nails. Dangerous. Unpredictable. Fascinating in the way that, say, Bengal tigers were fascinating. And perversely, she'd never been able to ignore him.

If Lukas was back, she had yet another reason to be glad she was leaving.

"He's made a fortune opal mining, apparently," Althea told her. "And he's parlayed it into successful businesses across the world. He's got fingers in lots of pies, your Lukas."

"He's not *my* Lukas," Holly said, unable to stop herself.

"Well, you should consider him," Althea said, apparently seriously. "He's handsomer than ever. Animal magnetism and all that." Althea flapped a hand like a fan in front of her face. "Seriously hot."

"Hotter than Stig?"

"No one's hotter than Stig," Althea said with a grin. "But Lukas is definitely loaded with sex appeal."

"And knows it, too, I'm sure," Holly said. He always had. Once he'd noticed the opposite sex, Lukas had gone through women like a shark went through minnows.

"Well, you should look him up—for old times' sake," Althea said firmly.

"I don't think so." Holly cast about for a change in subject, then realized happily that she didn't need to. The taxi had just turned onto her street.

Althea shrugged. "Suit yourself. But I'd pick him over Paul any day of the week."

"Be my guest." Holly gathered up her sweater and tote bag.

"Nope. I've got my man." Althea gave a smug, satisfied smile.

Once I had mine, too, Holly thought. She didn't say it.

There was no reason to make Althea feel guilty because she had found the love of her life and Holly had lost hers. "Hang on to him," she advised, getting out her share of the taxi fare.

"Put that away. The taxi is on me. I'm sorry we didn't find a dress. Maybe next Saturday…"

"Can't. I'm going to be kayaking with the kids from school next Saturday." She'd only missed going today because Althea had begged her.

"Then maybe I'll take Stig. Do you trust me to do it on my own?"

Trust her? After Althea had dressed her like a cupcake with too much frosting three times before?

Wincing inwardly, Holly pasted on her best resilient-bridesmaid smile. "Of course I trust you. It's your wedding. I'll wear whatever you choose."

Althea gave Holly a fierce hug. "You're such a trouper, Hol', hanging in with me through all my weddings." She pulled back and looked at Holly with eyes the same flecked hazel as Matt's. "I know it's been tough. I know it's been an awful two years. I know life will never be the same. It won't be for any of us. But Matt would want you to be happy again. You know he would."

Holly's throat tightened and her eyes blurred, because yes, she knew Matt would want that, damn him. Matt had never focused on the downside. Whenever life had dealt him lemons or a broken leg—though it had actually been Lukas who'd dealt him that, she recalled—Matt had coped. He would expect her to do the same.

"The right guy will come along," Althea assured Holly as she opened the cab door. "I know he will. Just like Stig did for me when I'd given up all hope."

"Sure," Holly humored her as she stepped out onto the curb and turned back to smile.

Althea grinned. "You never know. It might even be Lukas."

* * *

Lukas Antonides used to feel at home in New York City. He used to be in tune with its speed, its noise, its color, its pace of life. Once upon a time he'd got energized by it. Now all he got was a headache.

Or maybe it wasn't the city giving him a headache. Maybe it was the rest of his life.

Lukas thrived on hard work and taking charge. But he had always known that if he wanted to, he could simply pick up and walk away. He couldn't walk away from the gallery—didn't want to. But being everything to every artist and craftsperson who was counting on him—and the gallery—when for years he had resisted being responsible for anyone other than himself made his head pound.

Ordinarily, he loved hard physical labor. Throwing himself body and soul into whatever he was doing gave him energy. That was why he'd taken over the renovation of not only the gallery, but the rest of the offices and apartments in the cast-iron SoHo building he'd bought three months ago. But the gallery cut into the time he had for that, and getting behind where he thought he should be was causing a throb behind his eyes.

And then there was his mother who, since he'd got back from Australia, had been saying not so sotto voce, "Is she the one?" whenever he mentioned a woman's name. He knew she was angling for another daughter-in-law. It was what Greek mothers did. He'd been spared before as there were other siblings to pressure. But they were all married now, busily providing the next generation.

Only he was still single.

"I'll marry when I'm ready," he'd told her flatly. He didn't tell her that he didn't see it happening. He'd long ago missed that boat.

But more than anything, he was sure the headache—the pounding behind his eyes, the throbbing that wouldn't go away—was caused by the damned stalagmites of applications for grants by the MacClintock Foundation, which, for his sins, he was in charge of.

"Just a few more," his secretary, Serafina, announced with dry irony, dropping another six-inch stack onto his desk.

Lukas groaned and pinched the bridge of his nose. The headache spiked. He wasn't cut out for this sort of thing. He was an action man, not a paper-pusher. And Skeet MacClintock had known that!

But it hadn't stopped the late Alexander "Skeet" MacClintock, Lukas's cranky friend and opal-mining mentor, from guilting him into taking on the job of running the foundation and vetting the applicants. He'd known that Lukas wouldn't be able to turn his back on Skeet's plan for a foundation intended to "Give a guy—or gal—a hand. Or a push."

Because once Skeet had given Lukas a hand. And this, damn it, was his way of pushing.

Lukas sighed and gave Sera a thin smile. "Thanks."

"There are more," Sera began.

"Spare me."

Sera smiled. "You'll get there."

Lukas grunted. For all that he'd rather be anywhere else, he owed this to Skeet.

The old man, an ex-pat New Yorker like himself, had provided the grumbling, cantankerous steadiness that a young, hotheaded, quicksilver Lukas had needed six years ago. Not that Lukas had known it at the time.

He would have said they were just sharing digs in a dusty, blisteringly hot or perversely cold mining area in the outback. Skeet could have tossed him out. Lukas could have left at any time.

Often he had, taking jobs crewing on schooners or yachts. He'd leave for months, never promising to come back, never intending to. But for all his wanderlust and his tendency to jump from one thing to next, there was something about opal mining—about the possibilities and the sheer hard work—that energized him and simultaneously took the edge off his restlessness. For the first time in years, he had slept well at night.

He felt good. He and Skeet got along. Skeet never made any demands. Not even when he got sick. He just soldiered on. And at the end, he had only one request.

"Makin' you my executor," he'd rasped at Lukas during the last few days. "You take care of things...after."

Lukas had wanted to deny furiously that there would be an "after," that Skeet MacClintock would die and the world would go on. But Skeet was a realist. "Whaddya say?" Skeet's faded blue eyes had bored into Lukas's own.

By that time the old man had seemed more like a father to him than his own. Of course Lukas had said yes. How hard would it be? He'd only have to distribute the old man's assets.

Skeet had plenty, though no one would ever have guessed from the Spartan underground digs he called home. Lukas only knew of Skeet's business acumen because Skeet had helped him parlay his own mining assets into a considerable fortune.

Even so, he had never imagined the old man had a whole foundation up his sleeve—one offering monetary grants to New Yorkers who needed "someone to believe in them so they could dare to believe in themselves."

Who'd have thought Skeet would have such a sentimental streak? Not Lukas. Though he should have expected there would be a stampede of New Yorkers eager to take advantage of it when the news spread.

He'd had a trickle of applications before the *What's New!* article. But once it hit the stands, the postman began staggering in with bags and bags of mail.

That was when Serafina had proved her worth. A fifty-something, no-nonsense mother of seven, Serafina Delgado could organize a battalion, deal with flaky artists and cantankerous sculptors and prioritize grant applications, all while answering the phone and keeping a smile on her face. Lukas, who didn't multitask worth a damn, was impressed.

"Sort 'em out," he'd instructed her. "Only give me the ones you think I really ought to consider."

He would make the final decisions himself. Skeet's instructions had been clear about that.

"How the hell will I know who needs support?" Lukas had demanded.

"You'll know." Skeet had grinned faintly from his hospital bed. "They'll be the ones that remind you of me."

That was why the old man had created the foundation in the first place, and Lukas knew it. Back when it mattered, when he was in his twenties, Skeet hadn't believed in himself. Deeply in love with a wealthy young New York socialite, poor boy Skeet hadn't felt he had anything to offer her besides his love. So he'd never dared propose.

"Didn't believe enough in myself," he had told Lukas one cold day last winter, fossicking through rubble for opals.

They didn't have heart-to-hearts, never talked about much personal stuff at all. Only mining. Football. Beer. Skeet's sudden veer in a personal direction should have warned Lukas things were changing.

"Don't pay to doubt yourself," Skeet had gone on. And Lukas learned that by the time Skeet had made something of himself and had gone back to pop the question, Millicent had married someone else.

"So, what? You want me to play matchmaker to New York City?" Lukas hadn't been able to decide whether he was amused or appalled.

Skeet chuckled. "Not necessarily. But most folks got somethin' they want to reach for and don't quite got the guts to do." He'd met Lukas's gaze levelly. "Reckon you know that."

Then it had been Lukas's turn to look away. He'd never said, but he knew Skeet had seen through his indifferent dismissal to a past that Lukas had never really confronted once he'd walked away.

Now, determinedly, he shoved all the memories away again and forced himself to go back to reading the applications. It was the first week of June. The deadline for application submissions was two weeks away. Now he had thousands of them. Even with Sera sorting through them, he needed to read faster.

He stared at the paper in front of him until his eyes crossed…then shut…

"Grace called."

Lukas's head jerked up. "What?"

Sera stood in the doorway frowning at him. "She says to pick her up at her grandmother's at a quarter to eight. Were you sleeping?"

"No. Of course not." Though from the hands on the clock above the file cabinet he'd been closing his eyes for over half an hour. Now he tried not to let his jaw crack with a yawn. He'd winced, realizing he had forgotten all about Grace. She was Millicent's granddaughter, and Lukas sometimes wondered if she were Skeet's own attempt at matchmaking from beyond the grave. The old man had found out a bit about Millicent's life over the years. Chances were he'd known about Grace. He raked a hand through his hair. "Why didn't you put her through?"

"She said not to bother, to just give you the message." Sera studied him narrowly. "Are you all right?"

"I'm fine." Lukas stifled another yawn. "Just bored."

"Go meet Grace then," Sera suggested with a grin. "You won't be bored."

"Can't. Got to finish this." He glanced at his watch. "Time for you to go home, though."

"Soon. I have a few more applications to go through. You can do this," she said briskly in her den-mother voice. Then she shut the door behind her.

Lukas stood and stretched, then paced the room, trying to muster some enthusiasm for dinner with Grace. He shouldn't have to muster enthusiasm at all.

Grace was wonderful. His mother liked Grace. Sera liked Grace. Everyone liked Grace. Grace Marchand spoke five languages, had degrees in art history and museum conservation. She coordinated special exhibits for one of the city's major art museums. She was blonde and blue-eyed and beautiful, looking a lot like her grandmother must have half a century ago. Skeet would have loved her.

Because of that, Lukas had taken her out several times since—to dinner, to a concert, some charity functions, a couple of command-performance family dinners. Grace was good company. She knew which fork to use, which was more than he often did. In his new more social role, he was grateful for that. But regardless of what Skeet might have been plotting or Lukas's mother might be hoping, he wasn't marrying her.

And now he really had come full circle because his head was throbbing again.

The door from the outer office opened once more, and Sera came in.

"I thought you were leaving?" Lukas said sharply.

Sera nodded. "On my way. Just finished the applications. There's one that you should see." She waved the envelope in her hand.

"I don't want to see another application tonight." He held out a hand to ward her off. "I've had it up to my eyeballs. Every person in New York City wants me to give them half a million dollars."

"Not this lady." Sera waved the envelope again. "She only wants half a boat!"

Lukas felt the words like a punch in the gut. "Half a—? *What?*"

Sera shrugged, grinning as she set the papers on his desk. "Half a boat. Can you believe it?"

Lukas crossed the room in three long strides and snatched up the papers from the desk. There was only one woman in the world who would ask him for half a boat— Holly.

Holly. After all these years. Lukas wasn't bored anymore. His heart was pounding even as he stared at her signature at the bottom of a typed business letter on ivory paper.

Holly Montgomery Halloran. Firm, spiky, no-nonsense letters—just like the woman who had written them. He exhaled sharply just looking at her name. The letter had a letterhead from St. Brendan's School, Brooklyn, New York. Where she taught. Matt had told him that a few years back. The letter was brief, but he didn't have a chance to read it because with it, fluttering out of the envelope, came a photograph of a sailboat.

Lukas snatched it out of the air before it hit the floor and, staring at it, felt a mixture of pain and longing and loss as big as a rock-size gouge that there had been in the hull when he had last seen the boat in person. Someone—Matt—had repaired the hull. But the mast was still broken. Snapped right off, the way he remembered it. And there was still plenty of rotten wood. The boat needed work. A lot of work.

Lukas felt a tingle at the back of his neck and faint buzzing inside his head. He dropped into his chair and realized he wasn't breathing.

"Yours?" Sera queried.

"Half." Lukas dragged the word up from the depth of his being. It sounded rusty, as if he hadn't said it in years.

Sera smiled. "Which half?"

There was no answer to that. He shook his head.

"I thought you must know her," Sera said gently. "Holly?" Because, of course, Sera had read the letter.

"Yes."

Sera waited, but when he didn't say more, she nodded. "Right. Well, then," she said more briskly. "Well, you deal with Holly and the boat. I'm off."

Lukas didn't look up. He waited until he heard the door shut. Then he picked up the letter, not seeing anything but the signature. Then he shut his eyes.

He didn't need them to see Holly as clear as day.

He had a kaleidoscope of memories to choose from: Holly at nine, all elbows and skinned knees and attitude; Holly at thirteen, still coltish but suddenly curvy, running down the beach; Holly at fifteen, her swingy dark hair with auburn highlights, loose and luxuriant, her breasts a handful; Holly at seventeen, blue eyes soft with love as she'd looked adoringly at Matt; Holly at eighteen, blue eyes hard, accusing Lukas when Matt had broken his leg; and then, two weeks later, Holly on the night of her senior prom—beautiful and nervy, edgy and defiant. Then gentler, softer, laughing, smiling—at him for once.

And then Holly in the night, on his father's boat, her eyes doubtful, then apprehensive, then wondering, and finally—

Lukas made a strangled sound deep in his throat.

He dropped the photo on the desk and, with unsteady fingers, picked up the letter—to read the first words he'd had from Holly Halloran in a dozen years.

CHAPTER TWO

WHERE THE HELL was she?

Lukas stood on the marina dock, hands on hips, squinting as he scanned the water, trying to pick Holly out of the Saturday-morning crowd of canoes and kayaks and pedal boats that were maneuvering in a sheltered basin on the banks of the Brooklyn side of the East River.

He should have been hanging drywall in one of the lofts above the gallery or helping set up the display cases in one of the artisans' workshops. He should have, God save him, been reading more of the apparently endless supply of MacClintock grant applications.

Instead, he was here.

Because Holly was here.

Or so the principal of St. Brendan's School had promised him.

Three days ago, as he'd read her stilted, determinedly impersonal letter requesting that he join her in making a gift to St. Brendan's School of the sailboat he and Matt had intended to restore while they were in college, because she was "tying up loose ends before she left," a tidal wave of long-suppressed memories and emotions had washed over him.

He could, of course, keep right on suppressing them. He'd had plenty of practice. So for all of thirty-six hours he'd tried to push Holly back in the box he'd deliberately shut a dozen years ago.

It was over, he'd told himself, which wasn't quite the

truth. The truth was, it had never really begun. And he should damned well leave it that way.

But he couldn't. He couldn't just sign the deed of gift she'd attached to the letter. He couldn't just walk away. Truth to tell, the mere thought of Holly was the first thing to really energize him since he'd come home.

So on impulse, he had called St. Brendan's and asked to speak to her.

Of course it had been the middle of the school day. Holly was teaching. The secretary offered to take a message.

Lukas said no. He could leave a message, but she wouldn't call him back. He knew Holly. If she had wanted to talk to him, she would have given him her number in the letter. She'd have written to him on her own notepaper, not printed out an impersonal little message on a St. Brendan's official letterhead.

He got the message: Holly still didn't want anything to do with him.

But it didn't mean she was going to get her way. He called back and spoke to the principal.

Father Morrison was pleasant and polite and had known instantly who Lukas was. "Matt spoke very highly of you."

"Matt?" That was a surprise.

"He volunteered here. He and Holly taught extracurricular kayaking and canoeing. Matt wanted to teach the kids to sail. Right before he died, he told me he had a boat they could use. After... Well, I didn't want to mention it to Holly. But she brought it up a few days ago, said she had written to you hoping you'd agree to make it a gift to the school." The statement had been as much question as explanation.

"I want to talk to Holly," Lukas said, deliberately not answering it. "I've just moved back from Australia. I don't have her phone number."

"And I can't give it to you. Privacy, you know," Father Morrison said apologetically. Then he added, "But you might run into her at the marina. She still goes there most Saturday mornings to teach the kids."

"I might do that," Lukas said. "Thanks, Father."

So here he was pacing the dock, still unable to spot her. He hadn't seen Holly since her wedding ten years ago. Every time he'd been back since—less than half a dozen times in the whole decade—he'd seen Matt, but never Holly.

She had been visiting her mother or at a bridal shower or taking books back to the library. Maybe it had been true. Certainly Matt seemed to think nothing of Holly's excuses. But Matt didn't know Holly was avoiding him.

Now Lukas jammed his hands into the pockets of his cargo shorts, annoyed that she was so hard to spot, more annoyed that he cared. His brain said there was no sense dusting things up after all this time. He probably wouldn't even recognize her.

He'd recognize her.

He knew it as sure as he knew his own name.

A day hadn't gone by that Holly hadn't wiggled her way into his consciousness. She had been a burr in his skin for years, an itch he had wanted to scratch since he'd barely known that such itches existed.

A couple of days after his family had moved from the city out to the far reaches of Long Island, he had met Matt. They had been standing under a tree near his house, and Lukas had said his dad would take him and Matt sailing, that it would be cool to have a new best friend.

And suddenly a skinny, freckle-faced urchin dropped out of the tree between them and stuck her face in his. "You can't be Matt's best friend. I already am!" She'd kicked him in the shin. He'd pulled her braid. It had pretty much gone downhill from there.

Lukas had two sisters already. He didn't need another girl in his life, especially one who insisted on dogging his and Matt's footsteps day after day after day.

"I was here first!" she had insisted.

"Go away! Grow up!" Lukas had told her over and over when he wasn't teasing her because he knew her face would get red and she would fight back.

But it was worse when she did grow up. She got curves—and breasts. She traded in her pigtails for a short shaggy haircut that accentuated her cheekbones rather than her freckles. She made her already huge blue eyes look even bigger with some well-placed eye shadow. She got her braces off, wore lipstick and sometimes actually smiled.

But never at him.

Except…sometimes, obliquely, Lukas thought she watched him the way he watched her.

But her focus was always on Matt. "I'm marrying Matt." Holly had said that for years.

Hearing her, Lukas had scoffed. And at first Matt had rolled his eyes, too. But he had never been mortified by her declaration as Lukas would have been.

"That's Holly," he'd said and shrugged. Then, when he was fourteen, he told Lukas that he'd kissed her.

"Holly?" Lukas felt as if he'd been punched. "You kissed Holly?" Then, hopefully, he'd asked, "Was it gross?"

Matt's face had turned bright red. "Nope."

It couldn't be different than kissing any other girl, Lukas had thought. So he'd done that. And then he'd kissed another. And another. He couldn't believe Matt kept on kissing only Holly.

Then, Christmas of Holly's senior year in high school, they'd got engaged.

"Engaged?" Lukas hadn't believed his ears. It was ludicrous, he'd told Matt fervently. He'd told Holly the same thing. "You're crazy," he'd said. "How can you think about spending the rest of your life with one person? You're not in love!"

But they hadn't paid any attention to him. And when

he'd tried to make it clear to Holly, well, let's just say she hadn't got the message. In fact, she'd hated him even more.

Then, when Matt was twenty-two and Holly just twenty, they had tied the knot.

Lukas had been on the other side of the world when he got Matt's call to come home and be his best man.

"I'm in Thailand!" Lukas had objected. He'd been crewing on a schooner that summer, basking in sunny days, balmy nights and the charm of a bevy of intriguing, exotic women. He hadn't been home for three years, had no intention of going to the wedding.

"There are planes," Matt had said. "Get on one."

Lukas had argued, but Matt was implacable. "You're my best friend," he'd insisted. "You've always been there, always had my back."

The words had stabbed his conscience. "Fine," he'd muttered. "I'll come."

He'd done it. Had even managed a toast to the happy couple at the reception. Then he'd got the hell out of there, lying about the departure time of the plane he had to catch. He'd been back in Thailand twenty-four hours later—back to his real life, back to being footloose and fancy-free. Matt could have marriage with its boredom and sameness.

Lukas had been telling himself that for a decade now. Today was no different, he thought as he shaded his eyes with his hand and squinted out across the water. It was just a matter of putting the past to rest.

And then he saw her.

One minute he was scanning the water where everyone pretty much looked alike paddling their canoes and kayaks and pedal boats in the confines of the marina. The next moment his gaze locked onto a woman in the back of a canoe out near the breakwater. There were two kids in front. And in the back there was Holly.

His heart kicked over in his chest. He didn't know how

he'd missed her before. There was, as always, a purpose-fulness about her. Everyone else was splashing and floun-dering. Holly was cutting through the water with ease and determination, as if she knew what she wanted and aimed to get it.

She hadn't changed a bit.

He remembered when she hadn't known how to paddle a canoe, and, taking advantage of that, Lukas had refused to let her come with him and Matt.

Her chin had jutted. Her eyes had flashed. "I'll learn."

He'd scoffed. "From who?"

It turned out his oldest brother, Elias, was no proof against big blue eyes. Elias had taught her, and the next time they went canoeing, Holly had come, too.

Suddenly there came a whistle from the car park. A man wearing a green St. Brendan's T-shirt waved broadly. "Bring 'em in!"

With greater or lesser skill, the paddlers turned their canoes and kayaks and headed for shore. Lukas kept his eyes on Holly. He could see her talking to the students, giving instructions to back off a bit and let the earlier ar-rivals dock first.

She still hadn't seen him, but she was close enough now that Lukas could study her more easily. Gone were the lux-uriant dark waves she'd worn at her wedding. Now she had the same pixie-ish look she'd had as a child. Most of her face was hidden behind a pair of sunglasses and she wore a sun visor for shade, as well. The boy in the front of her canoe said something that made her laugh. And Lukas's breath caught in his throat at the husky yet feminine sound.

"Gimme a hand, mister?"

Lukas looked down to see a kayak alongside the dock and two boys looking up at him. One held out a line to wrap around the cleat. Lukas crouched down to steady the kayak while the boys scrambled out. Then he helped them haul it out so they could carry it up to the waiting van. Out of the corner of his eye, he kept an eye on Holly's canoe where she was talking to her students. She was still several feet away from the dock.

One by one, as the canoes and kayaks came up against the dock, Lukas helped them all until finally when he turned back there was just one canoe left.

Holly sat in the stern, unmoving, her sunglass-hidden gaze locked on him. No question that she'd seen him now.

Lukas straightened nonchalantly. "Holly," he said casually. "Imagine meeting you here."

The boy and girl in the canoe looked at him, surprised. Holly's sunglasses hid her reaction. She still didn't move as the two students brought the canoe against the tires lining the dock, and Lukas grabbed the bow to hold it for them.

The boy scrambled out, followed by the girl. Holly stayed where she was.

"Thanks, mister," the boy said.

"You're welcome." Lukas had seen all the St. Brendan's canoes now, and this one, with its deep, narrow hull, was far nicer and swifter than the wide-bottomed trio he'd helped pull out earlier. He let his gaze slide slowly over it, then brought it to rest on the woman who hadn't moved. "Nice canoe. Yours, Holly?"

"How come you know Ms. Halloran?" the girl demanded.

"We grew up together—I've known Ms. Halloran since she was about your age."

The boy's brow furrowed, as if he couldn't imagine either of them being that young. "You kiddin'?"

"Not kidding." Lukas held up three fingers. "Scout's honor."

"You were never a Boy Scout!" Holly blurted.

"Ah, she speaks," Lukas drawled.

Her freckled cheeks were suddenly a deep red.

"I was a Cub Scout," Lukas said, "when I was eight. You didn't know me when I was eight."

Holly gave a muffled grunt. She still didn't move to get out.

And knowing her, she probably wouldn't, unless Lukas forced the issue. "Nice to see you again, too, Hol'. It's been a long time." He held out a hand to help her out of the canoe, daring her to refuse it.

She muttered something under her breath that sounded like "Not long enough."

And of course, she ignored his hand. Instead, she set the paddle on the dock and shoved herself up, trying to step sideways at the same time so as to avoid his outstretched hand.

In a flatter-bottomed canoe, it might have worked. In this one, she'd barely edged sideways when the canoe tipped.

"Oh!" she yelped. "Oh, hel—"

"Ms. Halloran!" The kids shrieked as Holly pitched, arms flailing into the water.

Lukas couldn't hide the unholy grin that stretched across his face.

More kids came running. So did the men loading the canoes onto the trailer with St. Brendan's van. Lukas didn't move.

Holly sputtered to the surface, hair streaming, sunglasses gone, those all-too-memorable blue eyes shooting sparks in his direction. He still couldn't stop grinning.

All around him kids clamored. "Ms. Halloran! Are you okay?"

"Ms. Halloran! You fell in!"

"You're s'posed to stay in the center of the canoe, Ms. Halloran!"

One of the men who'd come from the van pushed past Lukas, a hand outstretched to help her. "Are you all right?"

"She's fine," Lukas said abruptly, stepping around the

man and reaching to grasp her arm. He hauled her unceremoniously up onto the dock, steadying her with a hand against her back, aware of the warmth and suppleness of her body through her wet T-shirt even as she shivered. "Aren't you fine?" She sure as hell looked fine, her nipples pebbling beneath the cotton of the shirt and her bra. He swallowed.

"Of course I'm fine," she said brusquely, clearly unaware of the spectacle she presented as she turned to the students. "I slipped. We've all done it, haven't we?"

At the fervent bobbing of heads, Holly grinned, shaking her hair out of her eyes. "So, I'm just today's reminder. Do what I say, not what I just did. Now, let's get the canoe out." And with a deft move, she twisted out of Lukas's grasp to haul the canoe up onto the dock.

If the T-shirt was a temptation, it was nothing compared to the way her shorts plastered to her rear end. Lukas's mouth went dry. The other men and boys seemed to be appreciating the view, as well.

Stepping between Holly and her interested audience, Lukas wrested the canoe away from her, simultaneously snapping at one of the teachers. "Get her a towel. The rest of you, give me a hand."

Everyone jumped to obey, and by the time Lukas and the boys wrestled the canoe onto the dock, Holly was wrapped in a towel.

The man who had provided it held out a hand to Lukas. "I'm Tom. Thanks for helping her out."

Lukas grinned. "It has always been my pleasure to pull Holly out of the water."

"Usually after you pushed me in," Holly retorted.

Tom blinked. "You two know each other?"

"We're old friends," Lukas said.

"He's an old friend of my husband's," Holly amended. "Lukas Antonides."

Tom Williams beamed. "Great. He can take you home then."

"I ride the bus!" Holly protested.

Tom raised doubtful brows at her sodden clothes and streaming hair. "They aren't going to let you on like that."

"I'll take a taxi."

Tom shook his head. "Not likely, Hol'."

"It's all right," Lukas said. "I'll take her."

Tom beamed and grabbed Lukas's hand, pumping it up and down again. "I wouldn't want to leave her to get home on her own, and I've got to get these kids back to school. See you Monday, Hol'. Come on, gang." He clapped two of the boys on the shoulder, then herded all the kids up to the van.

Holly didn't speak until they were all out of earshot. Then she said, "I'm not going with you."

"Right," Lukas said. "You're just going to stand here until you dry."

He could hear her grinding her teeth. She didn't look at him, just hugged her towel tighter and stared at the departing van. Lukas didn't care. He stood there and drank in his fill of Holly Halloran.

It felt oddly like reaching an oasis after a lifetime of wandering in the desert. He had spent so many years determinedly not thinking about Holly that it was hard to believe she was actually here in front of him.

She was definitely no less eye-catching than she had ever been. Her bones were sharper now, her eyes set deeper. Tiny lines fanned out at the corners of them. From laughter? From sorrow? God knew she'd suffered that. Lukas wanted to reach out a finger and touch them.

No doubt he'd get a slap for his trouble. That wouldn't have changed, either. Except once. Once she'd let him touch her.

"What are you doing here, Lukas?" Her voice cut across

his memories, jerking him back to the present. She was looking at the Manhattan skyline, not at him. There was nothing inviting in her tone.

"You wrote me a letter," Lukas reminded her.

Her fingers tightened on the towel wrapped across her breasts. "I sent you a deed of gift and asked you to sign it. Or to tell me if you wanted to keep the boat yourself."

"I read that."

"So, I repeat, what are you doing here?" The afternoon sun made her hair look more auburn than brown, like spun copper.

"I figured we could talk about it." He paused. "I wanted to see you."

Wanted to see if whatever he'd once felt was still there. It was perverse, he supposed, how Holly's contrariness had always sharpened his senses. Going head-to-head with Holly always exhilarated him, made him feel alive. As a boy he hadn't understood the subtext to their encounters, hadn't yet connected the dots. It was all about attraction. His brain had finally recognized it at fifteen. His body had known it sooner—probably from the very moment he'd met her when he'd been shaken and stirred, both at once. He'd put it down to the suddenness of her tumbling out of the tree and confronting him. His heart had pounded and his pulse had raced the same way they were doing now.

The way they had the night he had incurred Holly's everlasting wrath, the night he'd crossed the line.

And heaven help him, Lukas wanted to cross it again. He'd been gone for a dozen years, had dated more women than he could even remember, and they'd all paled in comparison to Holly. His best friend's girl, and he'd never stopped comparing other women to her! He wanted to touch her again now, wanted to feel the softness of her skin and to trace her curves, to kiss her lips and still the chatter of her teeth. Good lord, her lips were blue!

"Come on," he said abruptly. "Let's get you home."

"I don't need you to—"

"Don't be an idiot, Holly. I'm offering you a ride. Nothing else!"

For the moment.

For a dozen years he'd told himself that the past was past, that they'd all moved on, that what he'd felt was kid stuff, that he was well over her. After all, when he'd come back to New York, he hadn't sought her out. He hadn't even considered opening that door again. Not until Wednesday when he got Holly's letter.

And when the door had opened anyway, he knew he had to see her again. But even this morning he had been convinced that everything he'd ever felt for Holly wouldn't stand the test of time. She had been the dream girl of his past, the one girl against whom he'd measured all the others he'd met since.

But he really hadn't expected to do more than make his peace with the past—with her. He expected to feel maybe a little nostalgia—and a twist of guilt.

But seeing her now, he knew it wasn't going to be as simple as that. He felt the guilt, all right. But he didn't feel nostalgia.

He felt as fierce an attraction as he'd ever felt. Some elemental connection that he'd never felt to another woman. He had a lot more experience now than he'd had back then.

Yes, she was obviously still holding a grudge. But he had to believe she'd changed, too, that she couldn't hate him forever. Could she?

Lukas slanted a glance at the girl who had stirred his blood, at the woman apparently capable of stirring it still, and knew he was going to stick around and find out.

For all that he suspected he should, he couldn't walk away.

CHAPTER THREE

THE MINUTE SHE saw Lukas, Holly had felt her heart kick over in her chest. All the years of pretending he didn't exist blew right out the window. It was like being eighteen again—young and intense and, above all, foolish.

And there was nowhere to run. Nowhere at all.

For years every time Holly remembered the night of her senior prom, she had done so with a bucket load of guilt—and a heart load of resentment.

It never should have happened, she told herself. And it was all her fault.

She should have been stronger. Firmer. She should have said no, right from the start, when Matt had broken his leg.

At least it hadn't been her fault he'd broken his leg. That had, of course, been Lukas's—just as every hair-raising, death-defyingly stupid thing Matt and Lukas had ever done could be laid squarely at Lukas's door. In this case, two weeks before her prom, Lukas had persuaded Matt to climb Mount Katahdin in Maine.

Holly had not been invited.

She couldn't have gone anyway because, while Matt and Lukas were sophomores in college and their schedules that Friday were free, Holly was a senior in high school with classes every day. Besides, it was the weekend she was getting her dress fitted for the prom, not to mention that her mother would have freaked out if Holly ever dreamed of going camping with two guys, even if one was her fiancé.

Lukas thought their engagement was idiotic. He had

looked confused, then appalled when she had held out her hand to show off her ring. "What's that?" he'd asked warily.

And when she'd said, "I'm engaged," he'd stared at her in disbelief.

"To get *married*?"

"No, to wash windows." Holly had rolled her eyes. "Of course to get married. What do you think?"

He had thought they were out of their minds, and he hadn't hesitated to say so. He'd told Matt he was foreclosing on his options too early, that he had no idea what other women were on the planet, that he would never know what he was missing. He didn't tell Holly anything. Obviously he considered Matt to be the one making the bad choice. She'd wanted to smack him.

But Matt—her dear, dependable Matt—had just laughed and said, "I'm not missing anyone important. I've got the only one who matters." And he'd wrapped an arm around Holly's shoulders, hauling her hard against him, the two of them presenting a solid wall of defiance in the face of Lukas's scorn.

Only then had Lukas turned to Holly. "You can't be serious." His tone had said he wasn't joking. Their gazes met and something flickered between them that Holly immediately suppressed. Attraction? Connection? She had never let herself examine it too closely. Lukas Antonides was far too powerful, too unpredictable—too intensely *male*—for Holly to handle.

"I love Matt," she had said flatly. It was true. Matt was comfortable, predictable—every bit as male as Lukas, but without the intensity she found so unnerving.

Lukas hadn't disputed it. But he hadn't shut up, either. Over the following weeks he had told her she was too young. He'd questioned whether she knew her own mind.

Deliberately Holly had turned a deaf ear. "What do you care?" she'd asked.

If he'd said, "I love you," what would she have done? Holly laughed at herself for just thinking it. Lukas love her? Ha! Lukas had been going through girls for years!

He'd scowled then. "I don't want you making a mistake."

"I'm not making a mistake."

But Lukas didn't seem to agree. As winter turned to spring, he'd found ways to keep them apart. In February he and Matt had bought the battered old sailboat in New Haven. It wasn't seaworthy. It would have sunk in a bathtub, but Lukas had convinced Matt they could repair it.

"It will take months," Holly had pointed out. And that would be if they worked on it every weekend, which would mean Matt would have less time for her.

"We can sail around the world after we graduate," Lukas had gone on, undaunted.

"I'm getting married when I graduate," Matt had reminded him.

Lukas had shrugged dismissively. "Who knows what will happen in a couple of years. You can at least help me work on it," he'd said to Matt.

So, good friend that he was, every weekend that spring, Matt had worked with Lukas on the boat. Holly had barely seen him. The one weekend he had said he would come home turned out to be the weekend she was doing the final fittings on her prom dress.

"No problem," Matt had said. "Lukas wants to go to Katahdin."

Feeling hard done by, Holly had said shortly, "Let him."

"He wants me to go, too. It'll be a change from working on the boat. And you're going to be busy anyway."

So Matt had gone—and had broken his leg. Which was how Holly had ended up with Lukas as her date to her senior prom.

"I won't go," she'd told Matt. "No way."

Matt had looked at her from his hospital bed, foggy-eyed

with anesthetic. "Of course you have to go. You already have your dress," he reminded her the day after he'd had half a dozen screws and a plate put in his left leg. "You've been counting on it."

"I don't mind staying home. Truly. Lukas doesn't want to go with me. He doesn't even like me."

"Of course he likes you. He's just…"

"Bossy? Opinionated? Wrong?"

And though she could still see the strain and pain on Matt's face, he had laughed. "All of the above. It's just the way he is. Ignore it. It's your prom. And Lukas should take you," he added grimly. "It was his idea to go climbing. He owes me."

No doubt about that. But Holly was sure Lukas would refuse. She was stunned when he didn't.

"Why?" she'd demanded suspiciously.

"Because he understands responsibility," Matt said, looking completely serious.

She should have said no then. She hadn't, telling herself that arguing with Matt would make him unhappy. It might also make him wonder why she was protesting so much. Holly wouldn't even let herself think about why she was protesting so much.

She didn't want to think about Lukas, about how when he wasn't irritating her, the very sight of his muscular chest, lopsided grin and sun-tipped shaggy hair made her blood run hot in her veins.

It meant nothing. She was engaged to Matt.

Still, she wasn't prepared two weeks later when she opened the door to Lukas, drop-dead gorgeous in a dark suit, pristine white shirt and deep red tie, for the impact of six feet of walking testosterone. The sheer animal magnetism of the man made all Holly's female hormones flutter in appreciation while her brain screamed, *No! No, no, no!*

But she could hardly send him home. What would she tell Matt?

So she pasted her best proper smile on her face and tried to pretend she was completely indifferent. Yes, he was gorgeous. Yes, he smiled and chatted and charmed her mother. Yes, he brought her a corsage, which he fastened just above her left breast, standing far too close for comfort, so close that she could smell a hint of pine in his aftershave and see the tiny cut on his jaw where he'd nicked himself shaving.

She leaned toward it instinctively, then jerked back, practically getting herself stabbed by a florist's pin in the process. "Sorry," she muttered, mortified. "Sorry."

He just smiled his engaging Lukas smile, the I'm-so-sexy one she had seen him turn on other girls but which until that moment he had, thank God, never turned on her.

"It looks good on you," he said. It was a spray of tiny deep red roses. Delicate and aromatic. She drew a breath, trying to draw in the scent of roses to blot out the pine of his aftershave, to blot out Lukas.

But Lukas wouldn't be blotted.

Worse, he unnerved her by being a perfect gentleman the whole time. He didn't tease, he didn't mock. He didn't mention Matt or their engagement at all. He took her to dinner before the dance. It was expected. And Holly had thought they would go to one of the trendy upscale local places where most of her classmates went to see and be seen. But Lukas took her to a quiet romantic Italian place where he seemed to know everyone.

Holly couldn't help looking surprised.

"We don't have to go here," Lukas said. "But I like it. It's a little lower-key."

Since when was Lukas lower-key? But Holly had nodded, glad they weren't in the midst of a crowd. There might have been safety in numbers, but there would also have been lots of questions about what she was doing with Lukas, why she wasn't with Matt.

They'd get asked at the dance, of course, but they wouldn't become a conversation piece there. Holly didn't want to be a conversation piece. "It's fine," she said. "I like it." She managed her first real smile of the evening then, one that didn't feel as if it had been welded to her lips.

Lukas smiled, too. Electricity arced between them—sharp and frighteningly genuine. "I'm glad," Lukas said.

Holly wasn't sure if she was glad or not. Tonight Lukas was everything Matt had assured her he would be: polite, charming, an easy conversationalist. When the waitress brought their menus, he didn't tell her what she ought to order. He asked what she'd like to eat.

It was a sort of dream date—an intoxicating, heady experience. Unreal, almost. Holly kept waiting for him to revert to the Lukas she was accustomed to, but he never did.

At the dance, when she expected he would do his duty, dance once or twice with her, then disappear with the more interesting, flashier girls, he stayed by her side all evening. She wondered aloud whether he wouldn't rather dance with other girls, but Lukas simply shook his head.

"I'm happy," he said as the music started again. Without another word, he swept her into a dance while Holly's mind spun and her body responded instinctively to Lukas's powerful lead. One of her hands was gripped in his hard, warm fingers, more callused than Matt's, rougher to the touch, giving her another tiny stab of awareness. Her other hand, resting on his shoulder beneath the smooth, dark wool of his suit coat, felt the shift and flex of strong muscles.

When she danced with Lukas, her eyes were on a level with his lips. Instinctively she licked hers and stumbled, red-faced, at where her thoughts were going.

"What's wrong?" Lukas pulled her up and held her closer.

"N-nothing." She tried to put space between them,

averted her gaze from his lips. "What're you doing?" she demanded as Lukas only drew her closer.

"It's called leading." The soft, almost teasing murmur in her ear sent a shiver to the base of her spine.

He led. She followed. Their bodies touched. The experience was nothing like the warm, slightly zingy buzz she experienced when she and Matt danced. No, each touch with Lukas felt electric, a shock to the system, a different sort of awareness altogether.

"Relax." He breathed the word in her ear on a warm breath that did anything but relax her. She felt alert, aware, awake as she'd never been awake before. Expectant— though what she was expecting, she would not have dared to think.

Lukas didn't say anything else, just moved with the music, drawing her with him, easing her closer. His hand slid to her hip, but went no farther. And gradually, unable to remain alert and wary every moment, Holly realized that she was relaxing. She found joy in the movement, in the rhythm, in the warm nearness of Lukas's body. He made her feel oddly protected.

They danced almost every dance, far more than she ever would have with Matt, who much preferred to stand on the sidelines and watch while he talked sports with the guys. But Lukas danced. And eventually he began to talk, too, recounting what they had been accomplishing on the boat, then telling her what they had seen mountain climbing in Maine.

"So you don't think breaking his leg is all we did." His smile was wry.

Holly gave him a doubtful look, but she couldn't help smiling and sharing a moment of rapport with Lukas. He asked her about her classes, and he surprised her by talking about his own courses.

"I don't know what I want," he said. "I just try things.

See what I like. I've got geology this semester that is kind of cool. And—don't laugh—but I like Latin. But what the hell do you do with Latin?" He shrugged. "What about you? What are you going to do?"

Holly, disarmed by Lukas liking Latin, found herself telling him about her own plans and dreams. "Nothing grandiose. I want to get married, have a family. I've always wanted kids."

"Me, too," Lukas said. Another surprise. "Not anytime soon, though," he added quickly. "Not ready to settle down yet."

She wasn't at all surprised by that. "Before I have kids, though," she went on, "I think I'll teach."

"You'll be good at it," Lukas said. And when she raised a questioning brow, he shrugged. "You should be able to handle a classroom. You always kept me in my place." His wicked grin flashed, inviting her smile in return, and Holly did.

The whole evening was like that—Lukas attentive and fun to be with—a Lukas that once upon a time she had dared to imagine might lurk beneath his teasing, baiting, infuriating exterior. But if that Lukas ever even existed, he'd seemed far out of reach.

She shouldn't even be thinking about him that way. She was engaged! She was going to marry Matt!

So she deliberately closed her eyes and tried to pretend that he was Matt. But the aftershave was wrong, the way he moved on the dance floor was smoother, easier. His height was wrong, too. She opened her eyes again at the feel of something feathery touching her forehead and saw Lukas's lips so close they could kiss her brow. Holly sucked in a careful breath and shoved the thought away.

Why were there so many slow dances tonight?

Holly longed for something fast and furious to burn off her awareness, to give her some space. But when the next one was fast, it was no better. Seeing Lukas's body shimmy and thrust to the music while she did the same, created something elemental, primeval, between them.

Holly tried to deny it. It was only dancing, she told herself. But their bodies were in sync, moving, shifting apart, coming together. And at the end Lukas grabbed her hand, then spun her out and reeled her back into his chest so that his body spooned against hers as he wrapped her in his arms.

"Oh!" Holly's body was trembling, her heart hammering. His hands cradled her breasts. One of his legs had slid between her own. Holly tried to get her balance, to pull away. But her overheated body wanted nothing to do with that. She turned to stare breathlessly up at him.

Lukas was breathing hard, too. His cheeks were flushed, his forehead damp, his hair tousled across his forehead. Her fingers itched to brush it back, to feel its silkiness between her fingers. Deliberately, she knotted those fingers into fists.

"Hot work," he muttered. "Let's get something to drink."

"Yes." Before she went up in flames.

He got them each a soft drink, and they stood watching as the next dance began. It was a slow one again. Romantic. If they danced now, Lukas would pull her into his arms. Holly felt her body trembling.

"Let's sit this one out." Lukas's voice was gruff.

"Yes." Holly nodded and took a desperate gulp of soda, praying that it would cool her down. But nothing cooled her down that night. Amid the kaleidoscope of lights and sounds, of fast dances and slow, she was seduced by the moment, by the night. She told herself it wasn't Lukas making her feel this way. But she had to admit he had made it a night to remember. He'd been the Lukas she'd dared to dream he could be.

When the prom ended, several friends were heading

off together for a late meal. Had she been with Matt, no doubt they would have joined them. Holly expected Lukas to breathe a sigh of relief, bundle her into his car and take her straight home.

But when her friend Lucy called over, "Do you guys want to come to Woody's?" Lukas had looked at her.

"Do you?"

She hadn't expected that, and was ready to say no, sure he'd had enough of the evening, of her. But before she could answer at all, he went on. "That's what you do on prom, isn't it? Stay out till dawn?"

Stay out till dawn? With Lukas Antonides? An inappropriate flutter of anticipation tickled her. "Well, I—"

He raised a brow. "Would you go with Matt?"

"Sure, but—"

"We'll come," he said to Lucy. He slanted Holly a grin. "After all, I'm standing in for Matt."

So they went to Woody's, an upscale version of a fifties diner, full of her classmates, all laughing and talking, still on a high from the dance. Lukas, to her surprise, fit right in. He talked sports and surfing and sailboats with the guys. He was easy and charming to their dates.

They squashed into a booth with three other couples. Holly would have been comfortable with Matt shoved in next to her, would have relaxed when he slipped an arm around her. But when Lukas did it, she could feel every inch of the hard muscles of his arm. She was more aware of the heat of his body pressed hard against her than of anything anyone was saying.

She was sure Lukas wasn't aware of her with the same intensity. His knee bumped hers, then finally settled against it, and he didn't seem to notice. He kept right on talking to Sam, Lucy's date, even as his fingers played with a strand of her hair. If she turned her head even slightly, her lips would brush his fingers. Holly shivered and looked straight ahead. It didn't mean a thing. It was just Lukas. He didn't mean anything by it.

But her whole body was thrumming with awareness by the time they left Woody's. The noise subsided when the door shut behind them. The night breeze on her heated skin made Holly shiver.

"You're cold," Lukas said. "Here, have my jacket." He made to shrug out of his coat.

Wear Lukas's suit coat still warm from his body? Holly shook her head quickly. "N-no, thanks. I'm fine. It's lovely out here, isn't it?" She did a pirouette in the parking lot, looking up at the night sky, trying desperately to get her bearings, to get her feet on the ground.

Lukas glanced up briefly, then looked straight back at her. "Not as lovely as you."

Holly stared at him in shock. Was she losing her hearing? Imagining things? "Was that a compliment?" she ventured.

"I can give them," he said gruffly.

"Not to me."

His mouth twisted. "Don't let it go to your head." Now he sounded more like the Lukas she'd always known, but perhaps just a little bit kinder. Then, like the gentleman he had never been until that night, Lukas opened the car door for her, then shut it once she got in.

"You know, one of the things I hated most about you—" she said when Lukas got in and shut the car door.

He had been about to put the key in the ignition. Instead, he stopped and looked at her, startled. Then a corner of his mouth quirked up. "Just one? I'm sure you have a whole long list."

She did, but this was one she felt compelled to share. "Yes, but listening to you guys talking back there reminded me of this one."

Lukas raised a brow, waiting for her to speak.

"I hated that you wouldn't let me go sailing with you. You used to take Matt out with your dad and your brothers, but you wouldn't take me." She probably shouldn't even be admitting that it had mattered.

Lukas looked thoughtful, then he nodded, put the key in the ignition and turned it. The car hummed to life, but he didn't put it in gear immediately. Instead, he stared straight ahead in the dimly lit parking lot as if making up his mind about something. Deciding if he should apologize? That would definitely be un-Lukas-like.

Finally, he turned to her. "You want to go sailing? I could take you sailing."

"When you and Matt get your boat finished?" Holly said with a tiny smile. "The twelfth of never?"

"No. Now." There was a rough edge to his voice. And though it was dark in the car, Holly could feel his gaze on her as if he were touching her.

"Now?" she said doubtfully. "Tonight?"

"Don't want to take the boat out in the dark. But when it starts to get light… How about that? We'll end the night with a sail." And he gave her one of those amazing Lukas Antonides grins that would have caused a saint to cave in to temptation.

Holly was no saint. Besides, it was just sailing, she told her sensible self, the one that was telling her to say no. He was, for once, being kind. It was Lukas's way of making up for years of thwarting her. Was she supposed to throw it back in his face?

Besides, she did want to go sailing.

And with Lukas? Well, this had been Matt's idea. Not hers.

He was playing with fire. Lukas knew it.

But he'd never been one to play it safe. And he hadn't

started this. It had been Matt insisting that he take Holly to the prom. What should he have done? Said no?

So he'd done it. He'd done everything Matt would have done—taken her to dinner, danced every dance with her, put his arm around her in a crowded restaurant to make more room for her friends. And if he had heightened his own desire with every touch, well, he could see desire in Holly, too.

He had seen the way she'd looked at him tonight. Her cheeks had been flushed, her nipples had become hard pebbles beneath the midnight silk she wore. Lukas was twenty years old, not a virgin. He knew something about the response of women's bodies when they were aroused. Holly had been aroused. By him. And God knew he was aroused by her.

He should take her home. She was Matt's girl. Not his. He had no right. But what if she was making a mistake marrying Matt? What if she wasn't as in love with Matt— as committed—as she believed she was?

Don't go there, Lukas told himself.

But he couldn't bring himself to take her home. He'd offered her a sail. It wasn't betraying Matt to take her for a sail. Lukas put the car in gear and headed toward the marina.

Halfway down the dark, narrow highway, Holly said, "I can't."

Lukas, shoulders tense, turned his head sharply. "Can't what?"

"Go sailing! How can I in this dress?"

He breathed a sigh of relief. "No problem. There's stuff on board. Shorts, T-shirts. Jackets. You can wear something of Martha's. It'll be fine."

She swallowed. "Oh. Well, good." She didn't sound wholly convinced.

Lukas expected she would find another reason to call a

halt to things. But as he kept driving, Holly was silent. She sat very still the rest of the way.

The marina parking lot was virtually deserted, allowing him to park next to the ramp leading to the dock. Some cars were still there because people had taken their boats out for the weekend. But no one was around. Lukas started to lead the way down the ramp, then realized that Holly had to pick her way carefully because she was wearing high heels.

He went back and swept her up into his arms.

"Lukas!" She wriggled against him.

His half arousal went to full-on just like that. His jaw tightened. "You want me to drop you? Stop squirming!"

"I can walk," Holly protested.

No. He wasn't relinquishing her now. He strode down the ramp, getting a faceful of hair and a breath of citrus shampoo for his effort. "Hold still!"

"I am!"

She was. He was the one who was moving, causing her body to rub against his. Lukas swallowed a groan. By the time they got to the boat and he let her slide down his body to put her feet on the deck, he was in a state of temptation and torture both. It was worse to let her go.

"Martha's stuff is below," he said gruffly, leading the way down to the galley where he pointed to one of the tiny bunk rooms. "Put on a bathing suit. We can go for a swim."

Holly looked at him, startled. "Swim?"

"There's a beach just on the other side of the shop." Lukas jerked his head in that direction. "We've got a couple of hours to kill before it starts to get light." He could think of other more pleasurable ways of killing that time, but he knew better. He needed cold water. Lots of it. Now.

He thought she would object, but after a second's hesitation, Holly nodded. "Good idea."

When she disappeared into one room, he went into the other and stripped off his clothes, grateful for the cool night air on overheated skin. Then he dragged on a pair of board shorts and went back up on deck where he stood staring up at the sky, his body rock hard from a combination of desire and tension, as he wondered again what the hell he was doing with his best friend's girl.

"Just doing what he asked me to do," Lukas muttered aloud. Matt would have kept her out all night, he reminded himself. It was what you did after prom. It was a tradition. Matt wouldn't have taken her for a sail, though. Matt had nothing to take her for a sail in.

No, Matt and Holly would have been doing something else entirely. Lukas cracked his knuckles fiercely, trying to avoid thinking about Matt and Holly making love when he so badly wanted to do it himself.

It was almost a relief when Holly climbed back up the steps. Except the sight of her—even in Martha's sensible one-piece maillot—was enough to cause his self-control to slip another notch. Even the fact that she had a towel draped over her shoulders with the ends hanging down in front shielding her breasts from view didn't help. Her long legs were bare and tempting in the moonlight.

Lukas sucked in a breath and jumped back onto the dock without waiting for her. "Come on," he said over his shoulder and headed back toward the parking lot and the beach on the other side of the closed shop as fast as he could.

The whole place was deserted. But the moon and the lights in the parking lot illuminated the steps so that finding their way down to the beach was easy enough. He walked ahead, needing the space, only stopping to wait for her at the edge of the water.

She didn't come. Instead, when he looked back, Holly had spread her towel and was sitting down.

"Sunbathing?" Lukas, self-control fraying badly, couldn't keep the edge from his voice.

"Guess so." Holly pulled her knees up toward her breasts

and wrapped her arms around her shins. "Don't let me stop you. Go on in."

Lukas stared at her. What the hell was she playing at? Maybe she knew he was coming undone and was giving him a wide berth. "Suit yourself," he growled. Then he turned and ran, flinging himself under the incoming wave.

The shock of the cold Atlantic in the middle of an early May night had the desired effect. By the time he broke the surface, he breathed a little easier. A glance back told him that Holly had stood up and was walking to the water's edge. He caught a glimpse of a long, lissome shape in the moonlight. Then she began to run into the water. He heard a shriek, then she dove under—and surfaced bare inches from him.

So much for dampened ardor. Lukas swallowed a groan.

"It's freezing!" Her teeth were chattering.

He resisted wrapping his arms around her. "You'll warm up. Come on. Let's swim." He took off, swimming away from her as he'd always done, never letting her catch him. And Holly swam after him.

Minutes passed. Half an hour. They did laps. They swam in lazy circles. Lukas finally slowed a bit to allow her to come alongside where she did the sidestroke, all the while keeping her eyes on him.

Lukas couldn't take his eyes off her. He should say something about Matt. Something to deflect his awareness, but nothing deflected his awareness of the girl swimming mere feet away. It reminded his fevered brain of one of those nature films they had showed in school, the ones that euphemistically described the mating rituals of exotic maritime animals. Not a useful train of thought. But apparently the only train of thought he had. It was all he could do not to reach for her.

"You're making me crazy," he muttered at last and abruptly turned to swim back toward the beach.

"What?" Holly sputtered. "What's wrong?" He could hear her splashing after him, but he didn't wait. Lukas needed space. He needed distance. He needed to stop wanting what he couldn't have. He didn't stop moving until he was back on the boat.

Then he turned to see Holly hurrying up the beach and across the parking lot after him, her towel wrapped around her shoulders. Her teeth were chattering like castanets when she finally reached the boat.

"Why didn't you say you were cold?" Lukas demanded. "You can take a shower." He slipped down the steps below deck and jerked open the door to the head. "There's plenty of hot water. Lots of towels. Get warm, I'll be on deck."

He changed swiftly into another pair of shorts and a sweatshirt, resolutely ignoring the sound of the shower and his imagination's notion of Holly's naked body beneath the spray. Instead, he made himself focus on getting the boat ready to go. He was checking the mainsail when he heard Holly's footsteps.

"What did you mean?" she said. Her voice was quiet.

He turned around then. She was wearing shorts and a baggy sweatshirt of Martha's that hit her midhip. They had never struck him as remotely sexy when Martha wore them. Put Holly in them and it was a different story. Lukas crouched down, showing sudden interest in the mast again, in case his interest in Holly was more obvious.

"You said I made you crazy." She had climbed up on one of the benches and was almost on eye level with him.

Lukas shrugged awkwardly. Was he supposed to tell her he wanted her? That he was crazy with longing for her—and she was engaged to his best friend? He put a hand back and rubbed between his shoulder blades and said the only thing he could think of. "You always argue."

"I didn't argue tonight!"

He grunted. "Most times you argue."

"So do you."

Lukas scowled, unable to dispute that. He turned his attention back to the mast. "We can go soon. Should begin to get light in half an hour or so."

He thought she might go away, look out to the east for signs of dawn. She didn't. She watched him. Then she asked, "Why did you agree to take me to the prom?"

"You know why. Matt asked me to." He flicked a quick glance up at her, then picked at a bit of loose brightwork with his thumb.

"Is that the only reason?"

His brows drew down, and he scowled at her. "Why else would I do it?"

Holly shrugged awkwardly. "I don't know. I just…wondered. Sometimes…" She stopped and looked away, staring out across the dark water. "Never mind."

Wondered what? Don't stop there! But damn it, she did. She didn't say anything else. And he couldn't make himself ask. He and Holly never had heart-to-hearts. They never talked about things that mattered. And he wasn't going to admit to anything when she wasn't saying how she felt.

"That's the only reason," he said gruffly. "I'm just doing what Matt would do. What Matt wanted me to do."

If he said it out loud firmly and flatly enough, would that make it true?

"Of course." Holly's voice was toneless. Was she convinced? Was she doubtful?

Did she want…him? Lukas rubbed his hand against the back of his neck, then he straightened, walked back to the cockpit and dropped lightly into it. Only one way to find out. He reached up and caught her hand, pulling her down off the bench to stand facing him.

"What?" Holly looked up at him, confused.

"What would you and Matt be doing now?"

Her eyes widened. "What do you mean?" She looked at him, confused and wary.

"You asked me a question. My turn to ask you one. I'm standing in for Matt, aren't I? What would you and Matt be doing?"

He felt her fingers twist in his as she looked away. "How should I know?"

"Kissing?"

She didn't answer, just pressed her lips together and refused to look at him.

"Kissing," Lukas affirmed softly, leaning in, so close now that he caught another hint of that citrus scent.

Her fingers pulled out of his hands. He let go, but only to catch hold of her wrists, then slid both his hands up until they rested lightly just above her elbows, drawing her closer.

"So I haven't been doing my job," he said, keeping his voice even, although he felt the tension rising within.

He would burn in hell for this. He knew it, but he couldn't help it. If she responded… If she wanted him, he would save her from making the biggest mistake of her life.

Holly flicked a quick glance up at him, then immediately looked away again, but it was too late. Lukas had seen a flicker of interest in that glance. He let go of her arms to touch her face, to turn it to look at him as he ran his thumbs along her jaw and slowly and deliberately lowered his mouth to hers.

Lukas's brain fogged over. His body took over. He had no plan. Hell, he never had a plan. He went with his gut—and other even more interested portions of his anatomy—doing what came naturally, tracing her lips lightly with his tongue. Teasing, testing, tasting…

And Holly didn't pull away.

The taste of Holly on his lips intoxicated him, made him tremble with the need that had been building all evening.

Evening, hell, it had been building for years. From a time when he was too young to understand, some gut-level instinct deep inside him that he couldn't begin to put a name to had zeroed in on her. He had wanted Holly before he'd barely known what such desire meant.

And it hadn't gone away—ever. No matter how hard he'd tried to make it, no matter that she belonged to Matt, no matter how many other girls he'd dated, kissed, touched in an effort to blot Holly out of his mind, she was still there. He couldn't explain it. Couldn't begin to try. He only knew it felt right to have Holly's mouth open under his, to have her body pressed against his, driving his need higher.

He would stop. Of course he would stop. But not now. Not yet. He had been denied so long. But just now, just for the moment, he needed this. Needed her. If she wanted to stop it, she would.

But Holly didn't pull away.

Instead, as his thumbs caressed her temples and his fingers tangled in her hair, Lukas felt her lips part more, allowing him to deepen the kiss, to slide his tongue between her lips, to touch hers.

If she'd pressed her lips together, he would have stopped. If she hadn't opened to him, if he hadn't caught the sound of a sigh escaping her and felt her tremble at his touch, he would have stepped back, let her go. But instead, she lifted her hands and laid them against his chest.

And she didn't push him away. On the contrary, her fingers curled into the fabric of his sweatshirt, clutching him close, hanging on.

Lukas moved closer, trapping her hands between them as his lips traveled along the line of her jaw, nipping, tasting. His fingers stroked down over her back, then slid up beneath the baggy borrowed sweatshirt to settle against silky-smooth skin.

There was the slightest hitch in her breath, but when he

began an easy, gentle stroking, she arched into him, her spine elongating, as if she welcomed his touch.

Lukas welcomed being able to touch her. No doubt about that. He'd wanted to touch her forever. But the closest he'd come had been when he'd pulled her pigtails or pushed her underwater. Except once. When she was fourteen they had been biking and she'd hit a rock, falling, hurting her wrist and gashing her leg. It was obvious that she couldn't ride home. So, leaving Matt to bring her bike, Lukas had carried her.

Holly hadn't argued about it. She'd let him take charge, hadn't resisted when he'd pulled off his T-shirt and wrapped it around her leg, then lifted her into his arms.

It was the only time he'd held her until tonight.

This was far better. Now he could run his hands over her back, relishing the lack of a bra that would have impeded his fingers' journey. He could slide his palms around to cup her breasts and nuzzle them beneath the soft cotton of the sweatshirt. Now he could trace the line of her spine and the waistband of her shorts. So he did.

And Holly didn't push him away. Instead, she drew her hands out from between them, but only to set them on his hips. She leaned closer and tentatively brushed her lips along his jawline. Everywhere her lips touched Lukas felt little sparks of electricity.

He groaned as hot blood pounded in his veins and he felt the thrum of wanting build within. But more than he wanted to take Holly, he wanted to know her, wanted to feel her tremble beneath his hands, and know that she was responding to him.

He sank onto the bench where she'd stood earlier, then drew her down onto his lap, into his arms, and kissed her again, even more deeply this time, tasting her, savoring her as she squirmed against him, curving her body into his.

Her bottom shifted against his erection, making him

even harder than he already was. His hands were unsteady as they stroked their way up her legs. She moved again, settling in, and Lukas had to edge his legs apart to ease the pressure just enough to keep from disgracing himself completely. Then he slid a hand around and up across her rib cage to find the soft swell of her breast again.

He cupped it in his palm and felt the nipple pebble as he rubbed his thumb over it. Holly whimpered and shifted under his touch, rubbing against him through the thin cotton of his shorts. Lukas's eyes squeezed shut.

But his hands kept moving, kept exploring. He drew lines up her thighs to the hem of her shorts, across the tops, down the sides. He drew circles on the insides of her knees, then his fingers ventured slowly up her inner thighs. He felt her breath quicken. His fingers slid back down and circled around her knees. His heart pounded in his ears.

He could hear hers, too, as his explorations grew bolder. His fingers skated under the hem of her shorts. Then they slid back down. He heard her swallow. She shifted, but she didn't protest. She seemed to be alert, attentive, waiting. Wanting?

Wanting what he wanted? Lukas eased her around so that she curved toward him, one of her feet on the bench, her knee bent, the foot dangling off where she sat on his lap. Now when his fingers slid up her legs, he had room to explore, to learn the warmth and softness of her inner thighs, to venture farther to the lacy edge of her underwear.

Holly didn't stir. Only her breathing quickened as Lukas explored the lacy boundary, stroked along it, then dipped beneath.

Holly sucked in a breath. He felt her tremble. Or was that him?

Lukas had had sex before, but not like this. He'd been in too much of a hurry before, too eager for his own pleasure, unaware—for his sins—of the girl he was sharing it with.

He wasn't unaware of Holly. Yes, his body was clamoring for completion, but Lukas ignored it, more interested in Holly than in himself. What would make her tremble? What would make her moan?

He desperately wanted to know Holly's mysteries, wanted to bring her pleasure even as he made her his own. So his fingers trembled as he parted her and touched the warm wetness of her. He knew what that wetness meant. It made him harder than ever. His fingers slipped between her folds, stroked her, and reveled in the way she arched against his touch, making a sound deep in her throat.

He wanted to tear her clothes off, and his. He wanted to plunge into her and take her with an urgency he'd never before been able to control. But tonight he forced himself to go slow, to give, not just to take. To draw a response from Holly even as his whole body trembled with the need of her. Then he heard it again—another whimper, and she was no longer holding perfectly still. Her hips had begun to rock in counterpoint to the rhythm of his stroking. Her thighs parted, giving him greater access.

Eagerly, Lukas took it, reveled in it. It didn't matter now what his body wanted. He wanted this—for her.

It was only moments until Lukas felt Holly begin to tremble against the stroke of his fingers. She shuddered, her hips rocking, her breaths coming in quick gasps. Then her whole body seemed to ripple as tremors coursed through her, rapidly first, then gradually abating as she buried her face against his shoulder.

Lukas cupped her, didn't let go as he felt tiny aftershocks against his fingers. In his lap Holly barely seemed to be breathing now. He could feel her heart hammering, but she didn't move. On the knife's edge of desire, Lukas didn't move, either. Didn't even breathe. Just waited.

Dared to hope.

Then, as if she were just discovering that she could move

her limbs, Holly began to move. Her movements were stiff, almost if she were coming back to life. Then her fingers uncurled from his sweatshirt and abruptly she shoved herself away from him, wobbling as she stood.

Lukas reached out to help her get her balance, but she jerked away, wrapping her arms across her breasts. "Take me home." There was a hoarse, almost desperate edge to her voice. She didn't look at him.

"What?" Lukas stared at her, stunned. "Take you—? But—"

He reached for her again, but Holly twisted away.

"I want to go home." Holly's voice was low and shaking. She tried to move past him toward the stern. "Now."

Lukas blocked her way and caught her by the arms. This wasn't the way it was supposed to happen! "Why? What's the matter with you?"

Holly lifted her face and gaped at him. "What's the matter with me? You don't know? You have no idea? You just— We just—" Her voice was shrill. He'd never heard it like that before.

She didn't finish the sentence, just yanked her arm out of his grasp and pushed past him, scrambling over the side of the boat and onto the dock. She set off toward the car, barefoot, never glancing back.

Lukas stared after her, dazed, confused, and still aroused enough that it almost hurt. He couldn't even move, and she was practically running. She stopped at the car, opened the door, jumped in and banged it shut after her. If she'd had the keys, no doubt she'd have driven off and left him there!

What the hell was wrong with her? He hadn't done anything she hadn't wanted! She'd had every opportunity to say no. It wasn't as if he'd actually *done* anything—as his body was only too willing to complain about!

Lukas winced and swore under his breath as he began to move about the boat, gathering up her dress and shoes, and his own clothes. His arousal began to abate a bit, but his fury and bafflement were growing exponentially as he stuffed his feet into a pair of deck shoes, then began to close up the boat. He took his time, grinding his teeth the whole while.

Only when he was sure his dad wouldn't even know he'd been here did he head back to the car. Holly was sitting in the front seat, looking mutinous, staring straight ahead. It was hard to equate her rigid, icy posture with the girl who had minutes before melted in his arms.

It wasn't hard. It was impossible.

Lukas tossed her dress and shoes on her lap. "You forgot something." His voice was bitter, ragged, raw. He couldn't help it.

Holly wadded them into a ball and wrapped her arms around them, still refusing to look at him.

Lukas flung himself into the driver's seat and stuck the key into the ignition, but he didn't turn it on. He just sat and stared at her for a long moment, willing her to face him, to talk to him, to admit that she'd wanted him just as much as he wanted her.

But Holly clearly wasn't admitting anything. Jaw tight, arms hugging her dress and shoes, she just said again, "Take me home."

He didn't move. "You're going to pretend it didn't happen?" he demanded. "It happened."

"I didn't *want* it to happen!" In the harsh glare from the lights of the parking lot, her eyes spat fire. "I love Matt!"

Lukas felt her words like a blow to the gut.

"You did, though." Holly's eyes glistened. Were those tears that were accusing him? "You got what you wanted, though," she said bitterly. "Didn't you?"

And wasn't that the joke of the century?

What *he* wanted? He wanted Holly understanding—and

welcoming—his feelings. He wanted Holly recognizing her own feelings for him.

Had he got that? Not even close, Lukas thought, his throat tightening. Yes, those were tears brimming. As he watched, one slid down her cheek.

Perilously close to crying himself, Lukas didn't bother to answer. He started the car.

In silence, he drove her home.

CHAPTER FOUR

LUKAS LEFT THE next morning.

Thank God his father, intending to go to Greece on family business, had jumped at the chance to send Lukas instead.

So Lukas had never had to face Matt, had never been forced to lie to his best friend's face about what had happened that night. He'd lain awake for hours after he'd dropped Holly off. He'd spent them tossing and turning, reliving every moment, aching with unfulfilled desire as well as the growing guilt and shame that came with finally admitting to himself that he'd misjudged everything, that he'd betrayed his best friend.

It was a blessed relief to get to the airport, to put miles between himself and the scene of the previous night's debacle and the people he didn't want to face.

He didn't call Matt. Instead, he sent a text from the airport, explaining the trip to Greece was a business emergency, that there was no choice, he had to go.

It was the truth.

But the bigger truth was that he didn't want to face Matt. And he couldn't face Holly.

He was raw and aching, and he could barely think about what had happened the night before without flinching away from the memory. He'd been so gratified at her response, had barely believed it was happening, yet at the same time thought he was proving a point. If she was responding, she had to realize that she couldn't blithely marry one man when she had feelings for someone else. For him.

But evidently she hadn't. She'd been furious.

So why had she let him touch her if she felt that way?

Lukas never did figure that out. And he sure as hell had no one to ask. Finally, he told himself it was just one of the mysteries of women. But it hadn't helped.

God knew what Holly thought of him after that night. Lukas didn't want to know. He knew what he thought of himself—that he had betrayed them all that night by taking what he wanted, by being selfish and immature and greedy. He couldn't have Holly. He had no right to her.

She didn't love him. She loved Matt.

Lukas felt sick.

The family business on Santorini had taken all of five days, but afterward Lukas hadn't gone back to New York. He'd stayed the whole summer in Greece building boats with his grandfather and crewing for a company that rented high-end sailboats for vacationers on the Mediterranean.

And while he stayed away, a tiny part of him dared hope that Holly would realize in retrospect what she hadn't realized that night—that she loved him.

But by autumn he knew it wasn't going to happen. He never heard a word from Holly. And all he had from Matt was a handful of emails. The first had thanked him for being a good sport and taking Holly to the prom, the second said that Holly reported that they'd had a good time, the third wondered when Lukas was coming home so they could work on the sailboat.

So Holly had never told Matt what had happened.

Lukas supposed he should be grateful that Matt didn't want to punch his lights out. Instead, he just felt guiltier. His other feelings—the ones towards Holly—hadn't changed. He tried to think about other women, deliberately—and desperately—losing himself in the lure of every passably attractive woman who smiled at him.

At the end of summer, he didn't go home at all.

Sometimes Lukas told himself he was being noble, refusing to go back and make Holly uncomfortable. In truth, he knew he was making himself as comfortable as possible by staying away. He couldn't face them. He had ostracized himself.

He hadn't gone back at all until Matt demanded he be best man at their wedding.

It was his punishment, Lukas realized—to attend their wedding, to stand there and watch Matt and Holly stare into each other's eyes as if they were the only two people in the world, then to have to reach into his pocket and hand over the wedding ring that Matt slipped onto Holly's finger. He'd even had to prepare a speech that he'd rehearsed so often he could say it in his sleep.

Matt had been amazed. "You? Prepared?" He'd laughed at the thought.

But sheer preparation was the only thing that had got Lukas through it. Then he'd toasted their happiness. He didn't dance with the bride.

"Sorry," he said right after the toast as he headed toward the door. "I've got a plane to catch."

He caught that plane and then another. He drank more whiskey than he should have, hoping it would take the edge off his pain. It hadn't. But he'd survived. He put all thoughts of Holly behind him. That chapter of his life was over.

He hadn't let himself look back.

When he heard of Matt's death, he had felt guilty and gutted—and he'd stayed away. He'd never let himself think about Holly unattached.

Until now.

And now, Lukas thought grimly, it was déjà vu all over again. The old turmoil was back. The awareness. The desire.

He had spent the past half dozen or so years growing up, becoming the adult he probably should have been then. He had focus these days. Purpose. He worked hard. He made better than a good living. He gave back to the community. He dated sophisticated, sensible women. Beautiful women like Grace Marchand.

And he was still hung up on Holly.

And Holly still hated his guts.

He looked at her now as she stood on the dock, arms folded, holding the towel across her chest, shivering with cold, determinedly ignoring him.

He didn't blame her.

"Come on, Holly," he said to her now. "Your lips are turning blue. Let me give you a ride home." He paused. "And an apology, as well."

An apology?

From Lukas? That would be a first. And for what?

As far as Holly was concerned Lukas Antonides had about a million things to be sorry for. She hesitated, wanted to hear more. But, typically, Lukas wasn't waiting around to explain. He was already striding ahead of her toward the parking lot, obviously expecting her to follow.

Holly darted her tongue out at him, feeling childish. Then, as he knew she would, she followed.

Walking behind Lukas was never a hardship. A woman would have to be dead not to appreciate the physical Lukas Antonides. In casual khaki cargo shorts and a faded red T-shirt, he should have looked no more imposing than the teachers she'd kayaked with from St. Brendan's. They worked out at the gym, but they seemed like milquetoast compared to the man moving ahead of her.

Lukas was lean with broad shoulders, narrow hips and hard muscular arms and legs that spoke of hard physical labor, not a gym membership. He moved up the hill with the grace and power of a panther at home in—and in charge of—his world.

But then, Lukas had always been in charge.

And he had always been gorgeous, with defined cheekbones, a strong jaw and deep-set gray-green eyes. But the angles and planes of his face were harder and sharper now.

The only thing soft about Lukas was his hair. It was still a memorable mixture of dark brown tipped with light, sun-streaked blond, though the blond wasn't as evident these days since his hair was trimmed neatly, shorter than the shaggy mop she remembered. He was still tanned, though she suspected that owed less to days on the beach or on boats and more to the natural olive tones of his complexion.

He had reached the parking lot now and turned for the first time to glance back and make sure she was there. The sun caught the dark stubble on his jaw, giving it a hint of the same burnished gold highlights in his hair.

Trust Lukas to turn stubble into an art form.

Matt would have laughed if she'd told him that. Then he'd have admitted wryly that Lukas probably could.

"He's the best-looking guy I know. Hands down," Matt had always said. "All the girls want him."

"Not all," Holly had been quick to reply.

"Not you," Matt had said wonderingly. He had always shaken his head at that, as if her choice amazed him.

But she had, deep down inside. She'd been as susceptible as all the other girls, even knowing Lukas as well as she did. The difference was she knew herself, as well. She knew, as a girl, that she could never handle a boy like Lukas. And so, while she had the occasional dream of domesticating the panther, she knew better than to try.

That was why his teasing got under her skin. It was like he knew she hankered after him and wanted to bait her at every turn. It was easier—not to mention smarter—to focus on the boy she trusted: Matt.

She should have remembered that the night Matt had deputized Lukas to take her to the prom in his place. If she had, she wouldn't have succumbed to Lukas's charm. She wouldn't have relaxed in his presence. She wouldn't have let him do what he had done.

Even now, a dozen years later, what Lukas had done that night—what she had *allowed* him to do—still mortified her. Her face still burned at the memory.

With a cooler head, she understood why he'd done it. He had railed at them about the stupidity of their engagement since Christmas. They were too young, they didn't know their own minds, they might marry the wrong person, they might not be the right person for the other...

And that night he'd set about proving it—to prove to Matt that he never should have asked her to marry him, that she must not really love Matt because, if she did, how could she have been tempted by another man?

She had let Lukas touch her. In the heat of the moment, she had foolishly allowed him to run his hands over body, to evoke sensations that she'd never felt before. Color her stupid, all right, Holly thought, but those sensations had caught her unaware.

It wasn't as if she hadn't made love with Matt. Before Christmas when they had talked about marriage, about commitment, about being together forever, they had made love.

The first time had been intense, but hurried, and—for Holly at least—unfulfilling.

Matt, while he had known more about lovemaking than she had, hadn't really understood the intricacies of how a woman's body responded to arousal. His own had responded fast and furiously, while Holly had been left feeling vaguely dissatisfied, as if there were something missing, something she hadn't experienced yet.

Something more.

Holly had never quite found that something more—until the night she'd gone to the sailboat with Lukas.

That night things had been different.

Lukas was different.

And when he'd kissed her, she hadn't said no. She hadn't pulled back. She'd been curious. Would it be different from kissing Matt? She had so little experience with other men, she wanted to know.

If Lukas had come on strong, she'd have had the good sense to pull away. But he had moved slowly, taken his time, actually made her eager with anticipation.

Get on with it, she'd thought. That was what a fool she'd been!

Until that night she hadn't understood that slower was better, that every deliberate touch just heightened her awareness, her expectation.

With Lukas expectation became all. The feel of his lips on hers had made her heart beat faster, the stroke of his tongue on hers sent shivers of longing through her.

And his hands—dear God—his hands on her body had made her quiver in response, the slow journey of his fingers over her breasts, then up and down her legs setting off waves of responsive desire that she had only barely begun to experience with Matt.

And that had been her undoing.

With Matt, there had been no opportunity for leisurely exploration, no chance to really learn what pleasures their bodies could give them on the way to climax.

Until the night Lukas had taught her.

Lukas! *Not* the man she loved. *Not* the man she was engaged to.

No, it had been his best friend—and, after that night, *her* worst enemy!—who had brought her to orgasm and had held her in his arms while she trembled and shuddered— then came to her senses and realized what they had done.

Humiliated and furious, feeling she'd been taken advantage of at the same time she knew she had allowed it to happen, Holly had been terrified that Lukas would go straight to Matt the next morning and tell him what she'd done.

She'd been shocked to learn later that day that he had actually left the country only hours later. He hadn't gone to see Matt at all.

Why hadn't he? Had he expected her to 'fess up and break off the engagement herself, knowing that she'd betrayed Matt? If she didn't, would Lukas tell him what had happened?

For days, weeks, months after that awful night, Holly had expected the other shoe to drop. Feelings of panic fluttered in her stomach every time Lukas's name came up. But he never came back.

And as far as she knew he had never said a word.

She was aware that she was holding her breath as she watched him walk down the row of cars. Consciously, carefully, she let it out. She had to stop overreacting to him. She wasn't a kid anymore. And whatever he did now, he couldn't hurt her anymore. He couldn't tell Matt what had happened between them.

She hadn't wanted to see him again. But now that he was here, maybe it was a good thing. One more bit of the past she could put to bed before she moved out to her coral atoll and discovered the path for the rest of her life.

She took a deep breath, then let her gaze follow him, looking for the Porsche mentioned in the *What's New!* article. His "dream car," he'd called it. A vintage model, green and low-slung and more powerful than a pride of jungle cats. The sort of car alpha men drove.

But even as she scanned the row, Lukas stopped next to an old stake-body truck, its back end half loaded with drywall and lumber.

"Come on," he called to her as he opened the passenger door to the truck.

Holly stopped, then blinked. "That?"

"I didn't bring the Maserati," he drawled. "You'd get the seats wet."

She gaped as she walked toward him. "You have a Maserati, too?"

"No. I have a Porsche. But I drive the truck, too. Easier to haul stuff when I'm working."

Holly's brows lifted.

"I'm restoring a building."

"Yes. I heard. Althea told me about it. And…I read the article," she admitted. "It's how I knew where to write to you." Holly felt self-conscious saying it, but refused to allow it to show. "You've done very well," she added, and then her cheeks did burn because she sounded so…judgmental. And prim.

Lukas's mouth quirked in a sort of wry self-deprecation. "Who'd a thunk it?"

"I didn't mean that!"

"No. I don't suppose you did. Surprised my mother, though. She always thought I'd come to a bad end."

"She did not!" Lukas's mother doted on all her children. Still, when Holly reflected on Lukas's childhood, she realized that between the broken windows and the broken bones, Mrs. Antonides probably had had moments of despair.

"Let's just say she's happy that her worst fears weren't realized." Lukas was clearing off the passenger seat as he spoke, removing a couple of paint cans and some tools. He stowed them in the back, then pulled out a towel, handing it to her. "In case you want to dry your hair."

Holly took it doubtfully. "You carry towels?"

"For a lot of years I never knew when I was going to see running water and indoor plumbing again, so I learned to take advantage of every opportunity."

"Of course you did," Holly replied drily, then realized he could read something else into that comment.

And had, for he cleared his throat. "Like I said, I owe you an apology for that."

Holly lowered the towel so she could peer at him over the top of it.

Lukas looked as uncomfortable as she'd ever seen him. There was a hint of red across his cheekbones. "I shouldn't have...taken advantage." There was serious color in his face, which amazed her. Was he embarrassed?

He hadn't seemed embarrassed then. He'd acted like he was mad because she'd been upset.

"It was my fault, too."

He shoved his hands into the pockets of his shorts. "It didn't feel like it was somebody's *fault* at the time."

"I shouldn't have let it go there." She pressed her lips together firmly. "You never told Matt," she ventured after a moment.

"Of course not." He looked indignant now.

"I did," she said after a moment.

Lukas's face went even redder. "You told him?" He looked aghast.

"Not...not everything," Holly muttered, her own face hot now. "I thought you still might, and I didn't want him to learn it from you."

Lukas was still sputtering. "You told him we..." But he didn't finish.

"I said...you'd kissed me." That was enough. She raised her chin defiantly and glared at him.

Lukas dragged in a breath, then pulled his hands out of his pockets and dragged one down his face. He swallowed.

"That's all you told him?" He sounded somewhere between wary and relieved.

"I didn't give him a play-by-play," Holly said, annoyed. "I didn't think he'd want to hear it."

"No," Lukas replied with feeling.

"But I didn't want it hanging over me, either, in case you decided to come back and rat on me."

"I would never have—"

"You were friends," she said quietly. "He didn't deserve that."

Lukas was wearing sunglasses so she couldn't read his gaze, but she saw his Adam's apple move, and he dipped his head, acknowledging her words. His jaw tightened. "No, he didn't. I had no right."

"No, you didn't." Holly was glad he realized that. "But it happened. So—" Holly shrugged as indifferently as she could "—I thought, 'I'll just tell him about the kiss. We'll laugh about it.' So I did."

Lukas's hand wrapped around the top of the truck's door frame, his knuckles white. "And did you?" he asked roughly. "Laugh?"

"We did." She didn't tell him how hard it had been to make a joke of it. But Matt would never have believed his best friend would have crossed the line. And he had given her way too much benefit of the doubt, as well. One of the things she loved most about Matt—and one of his biggest failings—was his tendency to believe the best of people always.

Lukas didn't speak for a long moment. His expression was unfathomable. Finally, he drew a breath. "Well," he said lightly. "No harm done then."

"No."

Not unless you counted Holly's mortification at knowing she had shared with Lukas something she hadn't yet shared with Matt. Later, thank God, she and Matt had learned to please each other.

But Holly could never forget that Lukas had been her first.

CHAPTER FIVE

SHE WAS LIVING in the same high-rise condo in Brooklyn that she and Matt had been in last time Lukas had been back in the country. He had been there briefly when he'd picked Matt up to go out for a beer.

Holly hadn't been there, of course. But Matt had shown him around the flat. It was small but modern, stylish and with spectacular views across the East River toward Manhattan. Lukas had wondered at their choice because he'd always imagined them returning to Long Island and raising a family. Maybe they would have if Matt had lived. It hadn't been the sort of thing you asked.

Now he wondered what Holly's plans were. In her letter she had said she was "tying up loose ends." Nothing else. And she wasn't saying anything now.

She'd offered directions to her condo, but other than that she hadn't spoken. And once he had tendered his awkward apology—for something he still didn't quite regret—Lukas had gone silent, as well. He didn't know what to say to her. He never had. It was why he'd always taken refuge in teasing, in baiting, because she had always touched something inside him he didn't completely understand.

Worse, she had always seemed to see right through his bravado. He winced inwardly at the thought of her having told Matt even an expurgated version of what had happened that night. And he squirmed more than a little at them laughing about it. But it hadn't destroyed their relationship at least, and with the hindsight of some hard-won maturity, he had to be glad of that. Matt and Holly had been right for each other, as much as he hadn't wanted to see it. They had known better.

He actually found that he was glad he'd been able to apologize, even a dozen years too late.

Lukas could have just dropped her off at the front door. It was clearly what she would have preferred. But he couldn't bring himself to do it. Whatever it was that had attracted him to Holly years ago still persisted. And things were different now. She didn't belong to Matt. So as they approached the condo building, before she could say, *I'll just get out here*, Lukas said, "We need to discuss the deed of gift."

"Why?" Holly looked at him, startled.

"I want to know more about the school, what they're going to do with the boat."

"I'll have Father Morrison send you a brochure on the school, and—"

"I want to talk to you about it."

"When?"

"How about now?"

He thought she'd refuse, would come up with some reason that it wouldn't work. She could have pleaded that she needed to shower and clean up, which she certainly did. But he waited, and finally she said, "I guess you'd better come up then."

She didn't speak the rest of the way up to her flat. Only when they were inside and he was drinking in an atmosphere of cozy simplicity with a world-class view did she say, "I need a shower before we talk. There are books and magazines on the table if you want. I have coffee and tea."

"I'll be all right."

"Well, if you want some, help yourself. The fixings are right there." She nodded toward the countertop in the kitchen on the other side of the bar that separated it from the living room.

But his attention had been caught by a stack of professionally done flyers on the bar. They advertised a condo for sale. Holly's condo.

Lukas picked up one of the flyers. "You're moving?"

On her way toward the bath, Holly glanced back at him. "Yep. In August."

"Find another place?" This one had never seemed like Holly to him. He wasn't surprised.

"No. I'm leaving."

"Leaving?" He frowned. "The city?"

"The country." And Holly gave him the first really bright smile he'd seen from her today. "I'm joining the Peace Corps."

Lukas stared, feeling oddly as if he'd been punched. "You're joking?"

Holly looked indignant. "You don't think I can do it, maybe I'm not tough enough? Not resilient enough?"

"Of course you can do it." Holly was one of the toughest, most resilient people he'd ever known. As a kid she'd taken anything he and Matt had dished out. And as an adult, well, she'd survived losing her husband, hadn't she?

"It's just—" Lukas swallowed—that he'd just got back, that he'd just seen her again. They'd finally made peace. "You live here," he protested. "You've always lived here."

Holly's smile faded. "I don't think 'always' is in my vocabulary anymore."

Oh, hell. Lukas opened his mouth and closed it again. He rubbed a hand over his hair. "So, you're leaving because of Matt? You don't think that's maybe a little drastic?"

"Dying was a little drastic," Holly said wryly.

"Well, yeah, but…" Lukas straightened his shoulders. "He didn't do it on purpose."

"I know that!"

"I know you know. It's just… I'm surprised, that's all. I thought you loved your job."

She gave him a wary look. "How do you know that?"

"Matt always said so. He said you were fantastic at it, that the kids loved you." Every time he'd seen Matt, his old friend had spent much of the time talking about Holly.

Lukas had told himself he didn't want to hear, but he had never changed the subject. In fact, he'd hung on every word.

"I like teaching," Holly allowed. "I like the kids." There was a renewed warmth in her tone, and he remembered seeing that warmth when she'd been with them that afternoon. "They were what kept me sane," she reflected with a wan smile. "After." After Matt's death, she meant. "They needed me. They made me focus on something besides coming home to an empty house. An empty life." She paused again, then her face brightened a bit. "But there will be kids where I'm going. I'm teaching there, too."

Lukas still wasn't convinced. "Where's there?"

"You won't have heard of it."

But when she told him, he had. It was a tiny South Pacific island he hadn't visited, but he knew where it was. Thanks to what happened on Holly's prom night, Lukas had done a lot of crewing in the South Pacific. He knew hundreds of little islands no one in their right mind would go to. He'd been to most of them. "And that's better than St. Brendan's?"

"Not better." She shook her head no.

"Well, then—" Lukas was ready to argue.

But Holly just shrugged. "I can't stay here. I can't do this anymore. It's…what my life would have been with Matt." Lukas could hear the aching loneliness in her voice. He had to make himself stay right where he was, not cross the room to touch her. "I need to find out who I am without him."

The same person you've always been, Lukas wanted to

say, but deep down, he understood. Her dreams had died with Matt. She needed to find new ones.

We can find those dreams together. He wanted to say that, too. But he couldn't. He knew better than to push. He had pushed her twelve years ago, trying to make her see what she didn't see at all.

"There's beer in the fridge," Holly told him, "if you'd rather. Excuse me. I need that shower." And she disappeared down the hall, leaving Lukas staring after her.

Holly took her time in the shower, needing to get her mind and her emotions on an even keel. So much for handling the boat issue with her letter to Lukas. Now she had him in her condo instead.

Worse, it wasn't a "boat issue" at all. It was a "Lukas issue"—and it always had been. She couldn't lie to herself any longer.

She had always, deep down, had a thing for Lukas. Not that she'd ever admitted it—not to anyone. Not even to herself. But for the past dozen years she'd been able to pretend it didn't exist because…well, because it hadn't.

She'd loved Matt. She'd married Matt. It had been the right thing for both of them. And if once upon a time she'd entertained brief foolish dreams of a relationship with Lukas, fortunately she'd known better than to believe it could ever happen.

As long as she had known him Lukas had been the most unsettled, least reliable person she'd ever met. If she'd ever been stupid enough to throw herself at him, she knew he might well have taken her up on it. But after he'd had a taste of her, he would have got bored. He never stuck with anything. The article in *What's New!* had made his varied enthusiasms and scattered career sound like positive things—and for an entrepreneur, maybe they were.

But you never built a lasting relationship on that. And

Holly knew herself well enough to know that, however much she changed direction now, if she ever started another relationship it would have to be with someone who felt the same deep, intense commitment she did.

"So remember that," she said, gurgling into the spray from the showerhead, "no matter how appealing you still find Lukas Antonides."

Because one glance of him face-to-face told her she was still susceptible.

Fortunately, Lukas wouldn't be around long. They would sign the deed of gift, chat about what he was doing, what she was doing, maybe talk a bit about Matt and the "good old days," and, in a matter of an hour or two, he'd be out of her life.

Tonight she would go out to dinner and a film with Paul and it would all be behind her. It was no big deal.

It was nice—and unexpected—that Lukas had apologized. Apparently, he had done some growing up, too. Good. They could act like adults.

Thinking about it like that—rationally, sensibly—eased the tension in her shoulders, allowed her to take deeper breaths, and by the time she got out, toweled off and dressed again, she was feeling much more in control.

Lukas had made coffee by the time she returned to the living room. She could smell it, and it made her stomach growl. He held a mug in his hands. He nodded at a second full mug on the counter. "Hope you wanted one."

Holly picked it up, glad to have something to hold. She took a sip. "So what is it you want to know?"

He shook his head. "A dozen years' worth of your life? Too much?" He smiled wryly. "Okay, so tell me what this program is all about and why Matt thought it was a great idea to saddle a bunch of kids with a nautical disaster."

"Because a lot of them are disasters themselves," Holly said. She moved to sit in the armchair that Matt used to sit in, wanting his presence to help her articulate what she was going to say. She gestured to the other chair or to the sofa, hoping that Lukas would take the hint. She didn't need him looming over her. Fortunately, he sat down on the sofa and put his mug on the coffee table. But instead of settling back, he leaned forward, forearms on his thighs, fingers loosely clasped, his full attention on her.

"There are a lot of at-risk kids there. Kids who haven't had a lot of chances. They see their little patch of turf and not much else. They don't know what else there is in the world—unless they see it on TV. So five years ago, after we came back from a canoeing trip to the Southwest where we'd seen groups of kids doing what we were doing and having a blast, Matt said, 'The St. Bren's kids would love that.' And it started from there."

"You took kids to Utah?"

"No. We started trying to find places that we could teach them canoeing and kayaking around here." They'd scavenged up used canoes and kayaks as cheaply as they could. "We took a few hand-picked souls to the marina on Saturdays." She shook her head, remembering. "It was a disaster."

Lukas's brows lifted. "Sounds like a good idea."

"Yes, well, they were afraid of the water. Not one of them could swim. And they didn't want to learn. Too far out of their comfort zone. We were pretty naive."

"You grew up around water. So did I."

"Yes. And we never gave a thought to how far they'd have to go to make that leap. We needed to start on the ground, let them dip a toe in a pool. So we started there. It was a slow process, but eventually we had some kids who could swim. And when they could, others wanted to. And then we started again with the kayaks and canoes. By this time we figured that they benefitted if they were involved with everything, if they were invested in patching canoes and making kayaks water worthy." She smiled. "Matt showed them how to do that. And they got good at it. They like canoeing. They like kayaking. And now they have confidence to try other new things. The boat— well, the boat was just sitting there. He'd given up on you coming back." She slanted a brief glance at him when she said the words. She didn't mean them judgmentally any-more, though she had for years. She had come to accept that Lukas didn't have much follow-through. And, person-ally, given what had happened on prom night, she was glad he'd stayed gone.

"I couldn't, could I?" Lukas said now. His gaze bored into hers.

Holly met it this time, but she waited for him to explain.

"I'd betrayed Matt. I'd hurt you. I—" he began, but then just closed his mouth and shook his head. "I didn't have much to stay for."

Holly wasn't sure about that, but the way he said it didn't brook any argument. And this was Lukas, she reminded herself. He wasn't known for staying power.

"Well, anyway," she went on, "Matt thought there were some kids who could work together, who could learn some planning and teamwork that way, if they worked on the boat. And he'd work with them. And then he would teach them to sail." She could still remember the light of enthu-siasm in his eyes when he'd talked about it.

Lukas still seemed to be listening intently. He didn't interrupt, he didn't jump up to pace around or crack his knuckles or say, *That's a dumb idea.*

All things that the Lukas she remembered would have done.

This Lukas just sat still and waited for her to continue. Holly swallowed and went on. "He had just talked to Father Morrison about it…the week before he died. But he said he had to make sure it was okay with you."

"Of course it would have been okay with me!"

"You know Matt," Holly said. "He did things by the book. You owned half the boat, ergo, he needed to ask you."

But writing to Lukas was something Holly had never felt up to. So she'd dropped the ball.

Now she said, "If it was so obvious that 'of course it would have been okay with you' why are we even having this discussion?"

Lukas shrugged. "I wanted to see you again. I told you that. And yes, you can have the boat. It sounds like a great plan." He settled back against the sofa now and took a long swallow of coffee. "But I'd like to see it first."

Holly stared at him. "See what? The boat?"

He nodded. "It's been a long time."

"Of course." She didn't ask why. Maybe he was feeling a little sentimental about what might have been. "It's at your brother Elias's boatyard. Just ask him."

"With you," Lukas said.

She almost spilled her coffee. "With me? You don't need me there."

"I want you there."

"Why?"

He shrugged. "It feels right."

"And if it feels right, do it?" Holly said acerbically. "Experience has proved that isn't always the best choice."

Was that a hint of color in his face? Green eyes met hers. "Come with me, Holly."

She couldn't tell if it was a command or a request or an invitation. She hesitated.

"Or are you chicken?" And there it was—the calculated, devastating Lukas Antonides grin, the one that had baited her a thousand times. How could she have thought he'd changed?

"You're such a bully!"

There was unholy glee in his eyes. "I'm not forcing you."

"No?" She glowered at him.

Lukas looked absolutely delighted. "Ah, there's the Holly I remember."

The Holly he remembered wanted to kick him. But maybe it was good to keep being reminded that he hadn't changed. He was Lukas, teasing, taunting, playing some game.

Fine. She'd go along with it. She'd get his signature on the line to deed the boat. And life would be back to normal. "Right. Okay. We'll go see the boat." She stood up and carried her mug into the kitchen.

"Now?" Lukas looked momentarily disconcerted.

"No time like the present." If she didn't go now, she'd have to agree to see him again. Lukas had been enough of a disruption for one day. She didn't need another one. She glanced at her watch. It was just past three. And as long as she got back in time for her date with Paul this evening, no problem. She turned and narrowed her gaze at him. "And after you see it, you'll sign the deed of gift?"

"I said I would, didn't I?" He looked offended.

"And of course you always do everything you say you'll do. Like spend a summer repairing a boat?" Holly raised a brow.

Lukas had the grace to grimace. "I'll sign it."

While she put on a pair of sandals, he called his brother to ask about getting into the boatyard, then hung up and said, "We have to run by his place for a key."

Elias lived in Park Slope, not that far from where Holly lived. She said, "I'll wait in the truck," when they drove up in front of his brownstone twenty minutes later.

"Not a chance. I said I wanted the key and Elias said, 'Great. You can stay for dinner.'"

"I can't—"

"Don't worry. We're not staying for dinner." Lukas hopped out of the truck, then came around to open her door. "But this is family. I can't just grab the key and run. It doesn't work like that. I have to go in, smile, ruffle the kids' hair, say how much they've grown." He sounded bored at the thought, but he stood there expecting her to get out of the truck.

Holly hadn't seen Elias in years and she had never met his wife or kids. "How many kids does he have?"

"Four. It's a madhouse." Lukas rolled his eyes. "Prepare yourself."

But there were no little kids at the door, only Elias, who did a double-take when he saw Holly, then grinned broadly. "Hey, Hol'! Long time no see." Ignoring his brother, Elias pulled her into his arms and gave her a warm hug, which she returned. Then he held her out at arm's length and studied her.

"You're coping," he decided, and she remembered that she had in fact seen him at Matt's funeral, but not since.

"I'm coping," Holly agreed.

Elias nodded his approval. "So what're you doing with him?" He jerked his head at Lukas who, apparently used to brotherly disparagement, brushed past them both and went into the living room.

"We came for the key. She's fine. We're in a hurry, Elias."

Elias ignored him. "Everyone's in the kitchen." He looped an arm over Holly's shoulder. "Come on back."

Lukas sighed audibly. "What'd I tell you?" he said over his shoulder as he headed toward the back of the house. "Tallie is not feeding us," he added firmly.

"Whatever you say." Elias just smiled and drew Holly through a comfortable, cluttered living room, past two dogs, a Lego fortress and a bunch of dump trucks, haulers and steam rollers.

Holly gazed around almost hungrily. It was the living room of her dreams—one filled with the joy and photos and chaos of a growing family, like she'd hoped to have with Matt. But before she could do more than swallow the lump in her throat, a trio of boys came swarming down the hall.

"Hey, Uncle Luke! I got a new dump truck. Wanna dig with me?"

"Uncle Luke. We're makin' a robot!"

"Uncle Lukas, wanna see him walk?"

"Unca 'Ukas! 'Ick me up!" This last voice came when they'd reached the kitchen and a little dark-haired girl toddled into the mix and wrapped her arms around Lukas's knees.

Holly imagined he'd be looking for the nearest exit. But his impatience vanished. He scooped up the littlest boy, flipped him up onto his shoulders, then hoisted the little girl up in his arms and gave her a smacking kiss.

"How's my pretty girl?" He nuzzled her cheek and made her laugh. "Let's see that robot," he said to the older boys, and she could see that his eyes were alight with boyish enthusiasm.

Holly found herself oddly charmed as, still carrying the kids, he crossed the room to where a slender, dark-haired woman with a pixie-ish haircut was taking a sheet of cookies out of the oven. "Hey, Tallie."

Elias's wife was an adult version of the little girl in Lukas's arms. She set down the cookie sheet and threw her arms around him and her daughter. "Lukas! Where've you been? You'll stay for dinner, won't you?"

Lukas gave Holly a "what did I tell you?" look over Tallie's shoulder. "Thanks, no," he said. "We just came to get a key for the boatyard. This is Holly," he introduced her casually. "My sister-in-law, Tallie."

And as Elias's wife looked her over, Holly had the odd feeling that she was being sized up. Her narrow-eyed assessment was nothing like Elias's welcome. It felt almost suspicious, certainly measuring.

Instinctively, Holly straightened and stared straight back at her.

Her action made Tallie laugh suddenly and, still beaming, she swept across the room to envelop Holly in a warm hug. "Glad to meet you at last."

At last?

But before she could ask what that meant, Tallie stepped back and looked her up and down again. "Yes, you look like you can handle him." Then Tallie had turned her gaze on Lukas. "It's about time you brought her around." Her eyes swung back to Holly. "He's never brought anyone around before."

"Not—?" Holly began, confused.

But Tallie smiled at Lukas. "Helena says you're serious at last. About time. And she is beautiful, that's for sure. But why did I think her name was Grace?"

"I am not serious about Grace! It's my damn family," Lukas said as soon as he had hustled her out of Elias and Tallie's house. "They meddle. They don't know when to shut up." He flicked on the ignition, put the truck in gear and shot away from the curb as if he couldn't leave fast enough.

Holly, who had watched Lukas's face turn bright red when Tallie had mentioned Grace, only said, "Oh." She wasn't surprised that Lukas wasn't serious about Grace, whoever she was. Lukas had never been serious about anyone.

"You hit thirty and they think you ought to be married," Lukas muttered, the color still high along his cheekbones. He flexed his fingers on the steering wheel. Holly saw his jaw bunch and his brows draw down. "My mother likes Grace," he went on. "Thinks she'd make a perfect daughter-in-law."

"Maybe she would."

"Probably she will," Lukas agreed. "But she's not marrying me. I'm not marrying her!"

"No surprise there." Holly's tone was dry.

At her words, Lukas slanted her a glance. "What's that mean?"

"Just what I said." Holly shrugged. "I mean, how many girls did I watch you date? How many more must you have gone through since?"

Lukas grunted. "That was then." He seemed to be grinding his teeth.

Holly didn't see what difference it made. As far as she was concerned, whoever Grace was, she'd caught a lucky break. "Doesn't matter, does it?" she said. "Not to me, anyway."

She expected him to drop it, but he went on. "My mother is starry-eyed. And she likes a good story. The guy I worked with in Australia, the one whose foundation I'm working on here—Grace is his long-lost love's granddaughter. We've gone out a few times and now Ma thinks it would be 'poetic' if I married her. It's not going to happen."

"I believe you."

But he wasn't listening. "Ma wants more grandchildren." His eyes were on the heavy traffic heading out toward Long Island. He sounded aggrieved.

"Of course she does," Holly said equably. "Why shouldn't she?" Her own mother doted on Holly's brother Greg's two kids. She had been sad when Holly and Matt hadn't had kids. Holly had been sad, too. "You seem to like children," she added.

"It's no reason to get married!" Lukas strangled the steering wheel. "And I'm not marrying to please my mother."

Holly thought it unlikely that Lukas would do anything to please anyone but himself. "I'm sure you won't," she said mildly.

Lukas's jaw bunched. He stared straight ahead. "You like kids?"

Where had that come from? Holly nodded. "Yes."

"You don't have any." He sent a quick glance her way. His words were more question than statement. Holly wanted to say it was none of his business. But before she could, Lukas grimaced. "Sorry. None of my affair."

"We wanted kids. Lots of kids. Not at first. After Matt finished his PhD. But we didn't have any. Two years went by and I didn't get pregnant, so we went for tests. Everything seemed okay. The doc said we were 'trying too hard.' He said, 'Relax. You can't plan everything. Some things happen when you least expect them.'"

She glanced at Lukas. He didn't say anything, didn't even glance her way. But she was sure he was listening even though she wondered why she was telling him any of this. It was something she hadn't told anyone at all, not even her mother.

"He was right. Matt died—definitely unexpected." Holly's fingers knotted in her lap. She could hear the blood rushing through her veins, could hear the quickened beat of her heart. "And I miscarried the next week."

His gaze was on her then, searching her expression.

She looked away. "I was a month along. I…I didn't even know I was pregnant until…until I lost the baby."

There was a moment's silence. He didn't say a word. Then he reached over and wrapped his hand around hers.

It was the last thing she expected—warm physical comfort from Lukas Antonides. For once, Holly didn't pull her hand out from his grasp.

"I didn't have any idea," Lukas said at last, his fingers still wrapping hers. "I'm sorry." He hesitated. "No one said. After Matt died, I talked to my mom now and then. She said you were coping. She never said anything about…" His words dried up. His thumb rubbed the back of her hand.

Holly wetted her lips. "She didn't know. No one did."

"No one? Why not?"

"It was…too much." She sighed and tried to explain. "Everyone was already devastated by Matt's death. If I'd said…about the baby… They all knew how much we wanted a family. If they found that I'd lost the baby, too…" She just shook her head. "I couldn't tell them. I couldn't bear any more sympathy."

She knew it sounded strange. Ungrateful.

But Lukas just nodded. "I get it."

She raised her gaze to look at him, surprised. But Lukas's tone was quiet and calm and his fingers continued to squeeze hers in silent commiseration.

Oddly, it felt as if he really did understand. She supposed he might. Lukas had known her—and Matt—for a very long time. And while he might not know them the way their parents had, in some respects he knew them better.

Maybe, too, she had had enough space and time between herself and both excruciating events to actually speak of them and not have the emotions destroy her.

After Matt's death, friends and acquaintances had sympathized fervently, and often awkwardly, unsure what to say to "make things better."

Nothing could. But Holly didn't say that because that would have been rude. Instead, she was the one who ended up comforting them. She couldn't do more of the same after her miscarriage. She didn't have the strength.

Now she didn't need to have strength. Lukas gave it to her. He kept her hand wrapped in his, holding on firmly.

She was holding hands with Lukas Antonides. *Who'd a thunk it?* Holly thought with a wry inward smile. He had rough hands, workman's hands, calloused and competent, quite different from her husband's hands. But even though Holly knew from the article that Lukas's work now was largely behind a desk, he still clearly spent a lot of his time doing physical labor.

"Are you doing all the work on the building yourself?"

He slanted her a quick glance, and seemed to sense that she didn't want to talk any more about Matt or their unborn child. He nodded. Then his gaze grew self-conscious as it dropped to their linked fingers. "You'd think so, wouldn't you?" he said wryly. "But I'm only doing the grunt work. Painting, hauling, whatever the professionals don't do. My cousin Alex is an architect. He did the design for the renovation. And I've got a contractor now. He hires the workers we need. I do the rest."

She imagined Lukas did considerably more than he said. He'd never been a hands-off sort of guy. "What's it like?" she asked.

So Lukas described the gallery space on the first floor, the studios where some of the artists would be "in residence," working while people watched. He told her about the office space and the seven apartments.

"Some are even done," he added with a faint grin. "Mine is. And the one for my gallery manager, Jenn, who's coming on Monday. And two on the third floor. None of them would be finished if I were doing it myself. You should come see it," he suggested.

"Maybe." But Holly knew she wouldn't. Today was a one-off. Get the deed signed. Move on. "I'm getting ready to leave. I have to pack and still make the condo look presentable for potential buyers. I should have started a few weeks ago," she admitted. "But I couldn't get my mind on it until now that school's almost over."

"Haven't they tried to talk you into staying at St. Brendan's?" Lukas asked. "I figured they'd fight like hell to keep a good teacher."

"They asked. But it's time to move on. You should understand."

Lukas raised a brow. "Me?"

"It's what you did," she reminded him. "When you left."

Lukas let go of her fingers and put his hand on the steel-ing wheel, all the while keeping his eyes on the road. "That was different."

"Different how?"

He didn't answer, just rolled his shoulders in silence. She thought he wasn't going to answer. But finally he said, "It just was."

"So you're not going to talk about it?"

A muscle ticked in his jaw. "I'm not."

"But—"

"You've only got to think about it, Holly," he said gruffly.

She frowned. So, okay, he'd betrayed Matt. He'd said that already. And there wasn't anything to stay around for. He'd said that, too. But he'd left his degree half-done. He hadn't come back. She turned her head so she could look at him, try to see what had been turning the wheels in his head. But as always, what went on inside Lukas Antonides's thick skull was beyond her.

So she turned away and stared out the window. They were nearing the turnoff for the boatyard. The late-afternoon sun had dropped in the sky behind them. It beat on the back of her neck through the truck's window, but it was no longer as hot as it had been earlier. The boatyard was deserted when they arrived.

"I'll open the gate," she said. "The boat is around back of the boathouse. You can park there." She nodded toward a place near the office where she and Matt had parked when they had come here. "I'll show you where it is."

She didn't wait for him, though. It was the memories of Matt, she told herself, that were making her weepy. They had come out here only a couple of weeks before his death. Matt had been so eager to see the boat again, yet had walked slowly, holding back, almost as if he were afraid that it would be beyond repair. She knew he hadn't wanted to get his hopes up. Of course he had talked about Lukas that day, too. *Lukas and I were going to do this*, and *Luke thought we should do that*.

Of course Lukas had never been around to do any of it. But as always, any mention of Lukas had brought back Holly's feelings of guilt.

And now…coming here with Lukas felt like a very bad idea indeed. Behind her she heard Lukas shut the truck's door. Then his footsteps came across the gravel after her.

"Wait up!" he called. "Going to a fire?" he began with a grin when he reached her. But when he saw her face, his grin faded. "What's wrong?"

"Everything's fine. Come on." She started walking again. But Lukas caught her wrist and hauled her to a stop.

"You're crying." He sounded appalled, looking at her worriedly, out of his depth.

"It's okay. I was just…remembering…the day Matt and I came here." She swallowed. "He was so happy. He had so many plans. I…don't usually get weepy anymore. Sorry." She wiped a hand down her face.

"You don't have to apologize." Lukas's voice was gruff. "I didn't mean to bring it all back. Do you want to wait in the truck?"

"No. I said I'm fine."

He didn't look convinced. "It won't take me long. I just… wanted to see it again." He took a breath. His gaze was dark and serious, as if he were intending to lay some ghosts to rest, too. "Come on, then. Let's get it done."

She would have gone along without being held on to. But Lukas didn't let go of her hand, and Holly was exquisitely conscious of the hard strength of his fingers, though he grasped her lightly enough.

Only when they reached the boat itself did he loose her fingers, letting his own drop to his side as he just stared at it. Holly, watching him, couldn't begin to read the shuttered expression on his face.

As she watched, Lukas walked around the sailboat in silence, his expression hooded and unreadable. The boat's name, *Promise*, was still faintly legible on the bow. Matt had traced it with his finger and grinned. "That's perfect for the kids," he'd said. "A promise they can keep."

Unlike the one Lukas had made to you, Holly had thought at the time. She would have bet he didn't even remember it. But now, watching Lukas circling the boat slowly before pausing and hunkering down to examine the work Matt had done on the hull, she thought she'd been wrong. She saw sadness in his gaze. She saw a flicker of pain. Lukas ran his hand over Matt's patching effort.

Holly waited for him to acknowledge it, but he didn't speak. So she did. "Matt did a lot."

Lukas nodded. "Yes. He never said."

"Maybe he didn't want to make you feel like a slacker." It wasn't a kind thing to say. "I'm sorry," Holly said quickly.

"No." Lukas lifted his shoulders. "You're probably right. Will they work on it here at the boatyard?"

"I think so. Elias said they could. Tom, the guy you met, will be in charge."

"When will they start?"

"As soon as we give them the deed. Ready to go?"

"Not quite." Lukas nodded and hoisted himself up into the boat, then disappeared from view.

Holly glanced at her watch and shifted from one foot to the other. It was already after five.

Finally, Lukas reappeared. "Lotta work." He put one hand on the not-very-bright brightwork and jumped lightly back down onto the ground.

Holly nodded. "But it will keep them off street corners and out of trouble." She gave him a bright smile. "So, it's okay? Now you'll sign?" She was pulling the envelope with a copy of the deed of gift out of her tote bag even as she spoke.

A corner of Lukas's mouth lifted. "You're in a big hurry to get rid of me."

"Is there anything else you want to see? If not, I'd like to get back." She held the paper out, then pulled a pen from her bag.

"It's almost time for dinner. I'll sign it at dinner. Where should we go?"

Holly shook her head. "Sorry. I can't."

"Can't?" Lukas's brows drew down. "Or won't?"

"Can't."

Lukas looked skeptical. "You don't eat meals?"

"I'm going out."

"Out?" he said, as if he didn't understand the word. "You're going *out*?"

"I have a date."

A date. Holly had a date.

All day long he'd been treating her with kid gloves, tiptoeing around her very understandable grief for Matt—and all the while she'd been waiting to go out on a date!

Furiously, Lukas slapped paint on one of the gallery walls. Damn her! He tried telling himself that it didn't matter, that he'd lived without Holly Montgomery Halloran for his whole life, that it didn't matter what she did.

But his gut reaction to discovering that she was going out tonight—with a guy who wasn't him—put the lie to that.

"Who is he? What's his name? What does he do?" he'd demanded.

Holly had blinked at his intensity before she'd responded. "His name is Paul. He's a psychologist. A friend of Matt's," she had told him as he'd driven her back to her condo. "He's a good guy. You'd like him."

Lukas doubted that. Now he strangled the brush in his

hand, aware he was wishing it was Paul the psychologist's scrawny neck. Rationally, he told himself that Holly was entitled to date anyone she chose.

But it didn't stop the way he felt. Every bit of his possessiveness toward Holly that he had relinquished to Matt's greater claim years ago had come winging right back the moment Holly had said she was going out.

It didn't even matter that she'd told him it wasn't serious.

"We're just friends," she had said almost apologetically as she'd got out of his truck, refusing to let him to do more than pull up at the curb outside her place.

With benefits? Lukas had wanted to demand. But he'd managed to hold his tongue. "Friends?" he'd snarled.

"Yes. We go out together. Do things. Concerts. Ball games. I'm trying to get a life." She gave a vague wave of her hand. Then, at his scowl, she went on, "I'm in a hurry, Lukas. He's going to be here any minute. But—" and here, damned if she hadn't given him a bright cheery smile "—it was great to see you and catch up. Thanks again for signing the boat over to St. Bren's."

Then she'd waggled her fingers and disappeared inside her building as if she fully intended to never see him again!

We'll see about that, he thought as he thwacked the paintbrush hard against the wall.

CHAPTER SIX

"I WON'T HAVE IT!" Holly burst through the door to his office, red-faced and furious.

Lukas swallowed his astonishment—and the leap of his heart—at the sight of her. "You won't have what?" he asked mildly.

It had been a week since he'd seen her. A week in which he'd managed to knock out three walls, paint an apartment, read the best twenty-five grant applications, interview half a dozen gallery assistant applicants, show up at the first session of work on the *Promise* out at the boatyard and dream about Holly every night—sometimes twice.

He had picked up the phone fifty times at least, to call her "just to talk." And every time he'd put it down again because, God knew, he and Holly had never "just talked." But it would have been a place to start.

Now, apparently, he didn't have to. He looked past her toward the open door wondering how she'd got past Sera. Not that he was objecting.

As he did so, Sera appeared in the doorway. "I'm sorry! I was on the phone and she…she just…zipped past."

Lukas shrugged, still enjoying the heightened color in her cheeks. "She does things like that." He gave Sera a commiserating smile. "It's all right. I'll handle her."

"You won't 'handle' me!" Holly slapped her hands on his desk and glared at him. "You *can't* handle me, Lukas Antonides! I'm not Matt. You're not going to ignore me!"

Sera paused in the doorway. "Are you sure, Lukas?"

Lukas, never taking his eyes off Holly, nodded. "It's fine," he told Sera. "I've never ignored you, Holly." *Couldn't. Not even when I wanted to.*

Holly snorted. But at least Sera believed him. With one last worried glance, she backed out of the room. Lukas waited until the door had closed with an audible click, then nodded toward one of two leather armchairs not far from his desk. "Would you like to sit down? Can I get you a cup of coffee?"

"No, I wouldn't like to sit down! And I don't want coffee. I'm not staying. This is not a social call!"

"I gathered that," he said drily. "So what's the problem?"

She hugged her arms across her breasts. "I won't let you do to the kids what you did to Matt!"

Lukas sobered instantly. "What are you talking about?"

"You went to the boatyard yesterday."

"So?" That was a bad thing? He'd rung up Father Morrison on Monday and asked when they were meeting. He'd been intrigued by the idea of working with them—and tempted by the thought that Holly might be there. She hadn't been. But he'd still found the kids' eagerness compelling, and they'd been thrilled to learn about his connection to the boat.

"Why?" she demanded.

"Why not?"

"Because you're raising expectations!" Holly's voice began to rise again, too. "They'll expect you to come every week!"

Lukas tilted his head. "So?"

"So it won't work. You'll go a few times. Make them count on you—and then you'll drop them."

"No. I—"

"It's what you do, Lukas," she insisted, cutting him off. "It's what you always did. You always started something, then didn't finish it."

"The hell I—"

"You did," she insisted. "Remember the go-kart you and Matt were going to build?"

She'd had to go back a long way for that one, Lukas thought. He'd been eleven.

"And what about when you were going to learn to scuba dive?"

"I did learn," Lukas protested. "Just not then." The three of them had signed up for scuba lessons one summer in high school. But then his dad had asked him to go to Santorini to help out his grandfather for the summer. How could he turn down his grandfather?

"And then there was the sailboat. One minute you were full of plans, fixing it up, sailing around the world, and the next you're off to Greece for something better to do!"

"We both know why I had something better to do, Holly."

She stepped back as if he'd slapped her. She took a breath and let it out slowly before saying in a voice that wasn't quite steady, "So this is…*my* fault?"

Lukas shoved himself up out of the chair. "Of course it's not your fault! It's *my* fault! I told you that! But you know *why* I went." One of the reasons, at least.

She hesitated, then gave him a tight little nod. "So, am I supposed to thank you for leaving?"

"You could," Lukas said drily, "but I don't expect it."

Holly grunted and paced around his office. If she were a cat, Lukas thought, she'd be twitching her tail in fury. It reminded him of all the times she'd railed at him when they were kids. He'd been fascinated by her. She was so intense. So loyal. No one had more spirit than Holly. No one championed the underdog the way she did.

She had reached the end of the room and turned back to face him again. He could see her working to get herself under control. "Look," she said at last, "it's simple. I told you lots of these kids have had a rough time. They've been let down more than once. They need to be able to count on people."

"Got that," Lukas said.

"Which means if you act like you're going to be there, you have to be there."

"I'll be there."

"You might intend to be there—you might have intended to stick around and work on the boat, I don't know—but things happen!" Her face suddenly grew bright red again. No doubt they were both remembering exactly what "thing" had happened that night. "You run a damn empire now, Lukas! How do you know you won't have to dash across the world to do something important?"

"Because I run a damn empire, and I decide what's important." He met her gaze implacably with one as fierce as her own. "And if I say I'm going to be there, I will."

Their eyes dueled. Holly didn't give an inch, but Lukas wasn't backing down. It was obviously more important than he realized that he follow through with the kids. And admittedly, he hadn't given it a lot of thought when he went in the first place. Now he could see her point. He wasn't totally self-absorbed. He had grown up.

Still she stared into his eyes. He stared right back. Finally, Holly broke eye contact. She pressed her lips together and looked away across the rooftops of SoHo.

Outside, Lukas heard a siren. In Sera's office the phone rang. She'd better deal with it herself. He wasn't picking it up if she put it through.

"I'm not going anywhere," Lukas repeated. "I get it, Holly. I understand. And I *can* make time. I *will* make time." He raked fingers through his hair, then dropped his hands to his sides. He paused, once more letting his gaze lock with hers. "Cross my heart and hope to die, Hol'. I swear I will be there."

He did exactly that—crossed his heart—like a twelve-year-old. But he didn't know how else to get it through to her other than to use the words they had always used as children in moments of deepest commitment.

"You didn't cross your heart about the boat," Holly said faintly.

Lukas shook his head. "No."

He saw a flickering of something—a softening perhaps—in her gaze as she took a shaky breath. "Well, then, as long as you understand how important it is…" She hesitated, then shrugged. "I guess we're good." A bare hint of a smile tipped one corner of her mouth.

Lukas would have preferred a blinding smile, would have liked her to throw herself into his arms. Fat chance. But it felt like a watershed moment, and now he was the one who needed more convincing. He caught her hand, holding her where she was. "Are we good, Hol'?" His voice was rough.

She blinked. "What?" She shook her head. "I… Yes, of course."

He should have let go of her then. It was all the reassurance he was going to get. But he wanted more. What he wanted from Holly was only partly tangled up with what had happened with Matt. Just as much it was about what Lukas had always—though unadmittedly—felt for her.

And it wasn't just reassurance he was hanging on for now. It was for the connection, for simply the feeling of Holly's soft skin beneath the roughened calluses on his hand, for the quickened beat of her pulse against his thumb. He could feel the heat rising in him as he looked into her eyes. Any minute she would break contact, move away as she always had. Always—but once…

But she didn't. She stared straight into his gaze. And whatever they had been talking about blew right out the window in the face of the desire he felt for her.

"I want to kiss you." He couldn't stop the words, only

knew them for the truth they were. "You know that, don't you?"

Her cheeks went red, and she shook her head rapidly. "No!" She took a quick breath. "Not a good idea."

"Why not?"

"Because…because I said no." She wouldn't look at him.

"Afraid I won't follow through?" Lukas pressed. "Or that I will?"

She jerked away from him. "Stop it!" She crossed the room, put the desk between them.

"There's something between us," he told her. "Don't tell me you don't feel it."

She looked away, shook her head vehemently. "Can't you ever take no for an answer?"

"I can," Lukas said. "But I want to know you mean it."

She flicked a glance back his way. "I mean it." She thrust out her jaw defiantly.

He drew in a slow, careful breath. "Okay." He let the word out just as slowly. He had pushed her before and look where that had got him. Never let it be said that Lukas Antonides didn't learn from his mistakes. "We'll take it slow."

"We won't take it at all," Holly said fiercely.

He raised a brow. That was what she thought. She was back in his life now. He wasn't letting her walk out again without a fight. But he could afford to take his time—for a little while at least. But it went against all of his instincts. He felt like a panther trapped in a birdcage, trying to play by the canary's rules.

Holly apparently took his lack of a verbal reply as acquiescence. She rubbed her hands together as if she were trying to erase the feel of his fingers wrapping hers, then gave him a bright determined smile. "Well, I'm glad we understand each other. About…about everything," she added lamely.

Lukas dipped his head. Let her take it however she wanted.

"Thank you for…understanding about the kids. If you change your mind and decide not to go every week—"

"I won't."

The firmness of his tone must have got through to her. "Well, then, good. I guess," she added awkwardly. "I should go." She was already edging toward the door.

"Why?"

Holly looked confused. "Why what?"

He shoved his hands into his pockets. "Why go?" He glanced at his watch. "It's almost five. We could grab an early dinner."

"I'm going to Althea's for dinner. And Stig's. Have you met Stig?"

Lukas shook his head. "Which one is he?"

"The fourth. And final," Holly said. "I believe in Stig."

"I'll believe it when I see it." Lukas had heard occasional stories about Matt's sister's marital adventures from Matt. Since Matt's death he'd only caught the occasional rumor passed on by his mother. It didn't sound promising.

"You'll believe if you ever meet Stig," Holly assured him. She started toward the door again.

"What time's your dinner?"

"Seven. But I should get there early."

"At five?" Lukas gave her his best skeptical look.

"I need to call my Realtor. She's showing the condo now at this very moment to some lunatic film director." She shook her head. "A location scout saw it last week and thought it might be a good movie set. As if." She gave a small laugh.

"It's got a view."

"I've had a dozen prospective buyers come through since I've put the place on the market, and I haven't had a single offer yet." She looked a bit despondent. "I don't mind if the condo doesn't sell right away, but I'd like an offer I can close on before I leave. The view won't sell it," she said, going back to the current issue. "Lots of places have great views."

"Not this one." Lukas gestured toward the vista outside the tall, narrow windows that gave them a bird's-eye view of other buildings like his own. He was willing her to stick around, to let him get a toe in the door before she vanished again.

Now she came over to look out, too. "You didn't buy it for the view, did you?"

"No. It has great space. You haven't seen it, have you?" Lukas grasped at the straw he should have grabbed in the first place. "Let me show you."

Holly shook her head, moving back toward the door. "I'm going to Althea's."

"Right." Lukas shrugged easily. "And where does she live?"

"The West Seventies."

He nodded. "Yeah, well, it might take you two hours if you walk."

Holly made a face at him. But there was a light in her eyes that had always had the power to stir his blood.

Lukas grinned. "Come on, Hol'. You know you want to see it."

"You want to show it off, you mean."

"Yeah," he said, his grin widening. He breathed easier. "That, too."

"I've never seen anything like it. There's the most amazing art! Stunning textiles, murals, these astonishing fanciful birdcages. Birdcages, if you can believe it!"

Holly knew she was babbling, but her mind still boggled at everything she had seen in Lukas's gallery that afternoon. "And the jewelry…" She gave a shake of her head in near disbelief. "It's absolutely gorgeous. The workmanship is superb. And the opals are the most beautiful I've ever seen."

"You were impressed," Stig said drily, but he grinned at her.

"You could say that." Astonished more like. Partly because she had rarely seen so much appealing art all in one place. But also because it was evident that Lukas had had a very big hand in making it possible.

Of course the *What's New!* article had sung his praises. But articles like that were showpieces intended to paint things in the best light. But Holly's own tour of the gallery, coupled with the enthusiasm of the artists and sculptors she met, told an even more complimentary story.

He'd been eager to show it off, and having seen it now, she could understand why. He was fretting over details even as he showed her around, but she was sure it was going to be a success and she'd told him so.

"You think?" He'd sounded almost doubtful, but genuinely pleased.

"Of course," Holly had said. "The artists are all brilliant. They cover a wide variety of media, and every one of them has some particular gift, some talent that just grabs me."

It was true. She loved the airy textiles and the ornate and elegant birdcages. The wood sculpture was exquisite. The paintings covered the spectrum from primitive to sort of pseudo-impressionist to realistic to dreamy ethereal watercolors. She hadn't been able to decide which she liked best. And the jewelry—the opal rings and necklaces, the brooches and pendants—was simply out of this world.

It wasn't only seeing such wonderful works of art that enchanted her, it was that several of the artists were there, working, right in front of her. Lukas had introduced her to several of them.

"You can talk to them," he'd said. "Comment. Ask questions. Whatever you want. We want to make the art—and the artists—accessible," he'd told her. "We want people to understand the process, the artist's mind."

It was fascinating—and a brilliant marketing move. She could have talked forever with Charlotte, a textile artist who did amazing wall hangings. And the guy who made the birdcages, Sam, was as charming and quirky as he was talented.

He told her all about how he designed the cages, the materials he used, how long it took him to do one, even as he soldered tiny wire flowers in place, making them look like they were growing up the side of a Victorian house. "I have my own ideas," he said. "But I've done a few to order. Want a birdcage? We could have dinner and talk about it," he offered.

"She's busy." And Lukas had hauled her away peremptorily. "Well, you are," he said when she protested. "Having dinner at Althea's, didn't you say?"

"Yes, but I could have continued to talk with him."

"Not now. Come on. There's more to show you."

He took her through all the galleries, including one featuring opal mining. "A little background before we get to the jewelry," he said. There were blown-up photos of the land, the mines, the work he and Skeet had done. She would have liked to look closer, but if she lingered, he took her arm. And Lukas's fingers on her arm were a distraction she didn't need. So when she sensed he was getting impatient, she moved on before he could touch her again.

He showed her the whole building, top to bottom. She had, of course, seen his office when she'd burst into it earlier. But after he took her through the galleries and the studios and workshops, he brought her back upstairs and showed her around his top-floor apartment with its skylights and its twelve-foot ceilings and highly polished oak floors. Her whole condo could have fit in the main living space of his apartment. On one wall, his sister, Martha, had been painting a mural.

"She's not finished," Lukas said. "It's a work in progress. She's adding things as I think of them." So far she had done a panorama of what Holly presumed were significant places and events and people in Lukas's life. There was a New York City skyline, a South Pacific island, the deep reds and ochers of the Australian outback and the blue-and-white houses of Santorini. A man who looked rather like Lukas's friend Skeet was whittling a piece of wood. His parents were dancing at a wedding. Martha herself was with a man Holly guessed was her husband. Three little kids clambered all over them. She spotted the house he'd lived in on the beach in the Hamptons, the facade of the building in which they were standing right now, and a dozen other things— rain forests, old manuscripts, a rough-coated retriever-ish sort of dog—all symbols of Lukas's many interests, of the wide and various enthusiasms of his life.

And, of course, there was a sailboat. Not the one he and Matt had never repaired. This one was whole and skimming through the water. At the helm, looking toward the future, no doubt with his eye out for whatever would catch his fancy next, was a man with sun-streaked, windblown brown hair.

For a moment, Holly couldn't look away.

"When she gets going, there's no stopping her." Lukas came to stand beside her, so close that the sleeve of his shirt brushed her bare arm. The awareness was like a magnetic pull.

Holly moved back so she could get a broader view. So she could step away.

"She's got amazing talent. You should feature her."

"She's already showing at another place in the city. Besides, Martha's not Pacific. Not in any sense of the word," he added with a grin. "You remember Martha?"

"Yes." Martha had, in her way, been as much of a force as her twin. She had always known what she wanted and gone after it. No one in Martha's family was remotely arty or painted murals. Martha did.

"She'd like to see you again," Lukas said. "When she and Theo are in town—they live in Montana—we should get together."

"Sounds like a good idea," Holly said, certain she'd be gone by then. She glanced at her watch. "It's past six thirty. Gotta run."

She had chatted with him all the way down in the elevator, told him again what a great place it was, and, just for good measure, had reiterated that he didn't need to continue showing up for the kids repairing the sailboat as long as he stopped going now.

Lukas nodded. "No worries. I'll be there." And when she'd opened her mouth to protest, he'd said, "I crossed my heart, remember?" Sea-green eyes bored into hers.

"I remember."

"I'll even tell you all about what happened," he said. "Unless you're going to be there yourself."

"No."

"Then I'll tell you at dinner on Saturday."

"I don't—"

"You don't have a date, do you?" he challenged.

Unfortunately no, she didn't. And she wasn't a good enough liar to pretend she did.

He caught sight of a cab and flagged it down, then opened the door for her and shut it again, bending down to lean in the window. "I'll pick you up Saturday at six."

Something she wasn't telling Stig and Althea. God knew what Althea would make of her going out with Lukas.

"We have to go," Althea said to Stig, who was carving the roast.

Stig looked skeptical. "Birdcages?" But then he shrugged. "Why not?"

Althea beamed. "See?" she said to Holly. "Isn't he a dear? And he came with me yesterday and picked out your dress."

"Did he?" Holly tried not to sound as worried as she felt.

Althea nodded happily. "I took him to a couple of boutiques we missed. And he picked a dress." She smiled. "He says it captures the real you."

Which could be ominous. Holly wasn't sure what "real her" Stig was capturing—and how he knew, anyway. They were hardly bosom buddies. She got no clue from the man himself. Stig finished carving and sat back, grinning guilelessly.

"Tell me about it," she suggested.

Stig shook his head. "Wait and see."

"You can see it next week," Althea said, passing her the potatoes. "I can pick it up on Wednesday unless you want to try it on there for alterations?"

"I'll pick it up." She could deal with the alterations herself if Stig had picked something totally outrageous.

"I don't see you as a cupcake," Stig told her.

Well, thank God for that. But Holly didn't have time to worry about it. Over dinner Althea wanted to talk about the wedding reception, and after, when Stig took the dog for a walk, Althea pressed her for more details about Lukas's gallery—and Lukas.

"I didn't think the gallery was open yet, or we'd have gone," she said. "I thought the article said something about the first week in July."

"Yes. Lukas said that, too," Holly agreed. "But it's sort of a gradual process, apparently. Several of the artists are already there, and a lot of their work is already on display. But the hours are still limited."

"But he gave you a tour!" Holly could see the wheels turning in Althea's head.

"He wanted to show it off," Holly said dampeningly. "And it gets him away from going over the finalists for the MacClintock grant, which drives him nuts." He'd told her that.

"I can't see Lukas sitting still for long," Althea agreed.

"He's doing a lot of the actual carpentry on the apartments." For all that he disparaged his contribution, Holly understood that he'd done a lot of the finish work as well as what he'd described as "grunt stuff."

"I'll bet he looks good in a tool belt."

Holly was quite sure he did, too, and felt her face warm at the thought. Determinedly ignoring it, she talked about the gallery opening instead.

"He's waiting on the gallery manager," she said. "She's coming from Sydney next week. I gather she's very good at this sort of thing. Can do it with one hand tied behind her back—or from the other side of the world. But he wants her here before they officially open. So that's why they're waiting for the grand opening."

"You're going, of course," Althea said as she loaded the dishwasher. It wasn't a question.

"I might be back out at my mother's by then."

Althea looked up, startled. "At your mother's? Why?"

"I'm hoping the condo sells. If it does…I have to go somewhere." She took a swallow of the wine Stig had poured for her before they cleared the table. "I'm just doing wishful thinking here."

"You won't have to move in three weeks," Althea protested. "You haven't even sold it yet, have you?"

"No." She swirled the wine in her glass, staring at it moodily. "I'm just hoping I will. I don't want to have to deal with it long distance—particularly not 'out of the country' long distance. I should have put it on the market before now." Her brother, Greg, had told her at Christmastime to put it on the market then. But Holly hadn't been ready then. She'd only just made the decision to go. "I am going to have to get a storage locker somewhere soon anyway."

Althea finished putting the last dishes in, then turned the dishwasher on. Drying her hands, she turned to Holly. "It still seems insane to me. Giving up everything. Going halfway round the world."

It wasn't the first time they'd had this chat. Holly said, "I'm sure."

And not just for all the reasons she'd had before.

Now she also needed to put a world between herself and Lukas Antonides.

She might not know what she wanted out of the rest of her life, but it was perfectly clear what Lukas wanted—a roll in the hay or the urban equivalent thereof.

His "I want to kiss you" in that sexy sandpaper voice had sent shivers right down from her neck to her toes. Still did.

He hadn't done it, but he hadn't been joking. And if he had kissed her, he wouldn't have stopped there. When Lukas wanted something, he was single-minded. If he decided he wanted Holly, he would do his damnedest to get her into bed.

But scariest of all was Holly's fear that she might not stop him.

He waited for the other shoe to drop.

Ever since he'd helped Holly into the cab, Lukas had expected a phone call saying that something had come up, that she wouldn't be able to have dinner with him on Saturday night after all.

He deliberately worked with power tools all evening so he wouldn't hear the phone when it rang. But when he checked his voice mail before he went to bed that night, there was no message from Holly.

There were seven others, including one from Jenn, the office manager who was supposed to be arriving Monday.

"Ah, Luke," she'd said, her normal Aussie drawl powered by excitement. "Really sorry, but I can't come! Bryan's popped the question! Who knew?"

Lukas ground his teeth. Who indeed? And where the hell was he going to find a gallery manager at this late date? He wanted to tear his hair out.

The other six messages were from various family members, all inviting him to come out to his parents' place in the Hamptons the weekend after next.

"I miss you," his grandmother had said. "Why did you come back to New York if you don't come out here?"

"Theo and the kids and I will be at the folks' this weekend," Martha had said. "You know you want to see us."

"Week from Saturday, Mom and Dad's. Be there," Cristina had commanded.

Only his mother had been unable to conceal the real agenda. "The Panathakoses will be here all week," she'd said. "You remember their beautiful daughter, Angelika? She's looking forward to seeing you again."

Lukas had groaned. But he'd taken heart, too. At least none of the messages was from Holly.

Still, that left Friday—and all day Saturday—for her to change her mind, to come up with some excuse that he would have to argue with before he got to see her again. She didn't call on Friday—and he was in the office all day, trying to round up a new gallery manager and finishing a preliminary run-through of the final group of potential grant recipients.

It felt like the longest day in history as he kept himself almost tied to his chair, sensing Skeet gazing down the back of his neck. But at the end of the day he had a stack of twenty finalists from which to make his three choices. He also had a list of half a dozen possible gallery manager candidates that Sera must have pulled out of a hat—and he knew for a fact that Holly hadn't tried to reach him. There was no message on his phone, and Sera hadn't heard from her, either.

He was whistling when he went to the boatyard Saturday morning. The kids were delighted to see him, and he had to admit Holly was right: they had been counting on him being there.

That time passed quickly, but the afternoon dragged. He needed to talk to both his cousin Alex and to the contractor before he did more on the apartment where he was working. He'd done enough grant proposals to fry his brain permanently. And he still had four hours until he could legitimately appear on Holly's doorstep.

So he went over to Elias and Tallie's place for distraction.

"I thought you were supposed to choose the winners yourself," Tallie chided when he appeared in her kitchen and dropped into a chair and tossed a pile of grant proposals on the table in front of him.

"Yes. And I will. But I don't entirely trust myself," he admitted. He poked a finger at the stack of applications. "These are, in my estimation, the most promising of the lot. But I still want to bang some heads against the wall and say, 'Get on with it. You don't need a grant to get off your butt and make a change.'"

Tallie laughed. "Probably not what your friend had in mind."

"He should have," Lukas muttered. "But—" he raked a hand through his hair "—you're right. He expected me to be supportive." And if his lips twisted on the last word, well, there was just so far he could make himself go. "Anyway, I thought maybe you could give me your opinion. I promise I'll make the final decision," he added quickly.

Sounds of boys shouting and scuffling their way down the stairs interrupted them. Tallie glanced toward the stairs and winced at Digger's sudden bellow. "Not sure when I'll have time. Elias took a prospective client out for a sail today. So it's just me and the heathens."

"I'll take 'em to the park," Lukas said.

"You must be desperate. Be my guest." Tallie made shooing movements toward the door with her hands.

"Thea, too?" Lukas looked warily at his niece, who was banging her spoon on the kitchen table. She was somewhere on the not-quite-civilized side of three, but a force in her own right—as only a girl with three older brothers could be.

"No. She still needs a nap. And she might even get one with the boys gone. Can you keep them away until four?" she asked hopefully.

"My pleasure," Lukas assured her.

"Thank you. I should be doing it for you anyway," Tallie added. "I owe you."

Lukas's raised his brows. "You do?" He didn't remember doing her any favors recently.

"For what I said when you brought your friend—Holly—over last weekend. Calling her Grace." Even now the color flushed Tallie's cheeks.

Lukas's mouth twisted. "It worked out. Gave me a reason to explain who Grace is—and isn't—in my life."

"Is it serious? You and Holly?"

Lukas grimaced. "Nothing to be serious about."

"Really? I thought you looked interested. You certainly turned red when I called her Grace!"

Lukas shrugged. He had denied it for so long that it had become part of who he was—the guy who wasn't interested in Holly. But now he said cautiously, "I could be. Maybe."

Tallie laughed. "Well, don't bowl her over with your enthusiasm."

The boys bounced into the kitchen just then so he didn't reply. He didn't know what he'd have said anyway. What was there to say?

"Uncle Lukas is going to take you to the park," she told the boys.

Instantly, the stampede was on. Tallie smiled at him. "Go to the park," she commanded. "Have a good time. The boys will keep you busy. You won't have time to answer your phone."

Lukas gathered up bats and balls, baseball gloves, a football and a soccer ball, then chivvied Garrett, Nick and Digger out the door.

"Don't let them drive you nuts." Tallie fixed him with a hard look.

Lukas just grinned. "They're fine." The noise and bounce of little boys was easy to handle. It was the rest of his life—well, what he felt about Holly and what she felt about him—that threatened his sanity. He dropped his mobile phone on the kitchen counter.

"What's this?" Tallie said.

"I don't want any interruptions."

Tallie looked doubtful, but she didn't offer any other explanation—especially not the real one: that he didn't want a phone call from Holly telling him she had changed her mind.

But he wasn't entirely surprised when he brought them back shortly after four that she had left a message on his voice mail.

Lukas waited until he was back in his SUV to listen to it. "Sorry to leave it so late." Holly sounded slightly breathless and just a bit frazzled. "But I can't go to dinner. I've sold the condo and I have to clear things out. Maybe we can do it another time…like in a couple of years when I get back." There was a light strained laugh. "Anyway, thanks for the invitation. See you someday. Maybe. Love your gallery." And then there was a click.

See you someday. Maybe.

Another end—before it really began.

No. Not someday. Not maybe. There was something between them—always had been. For years they hadn't allowed themselves to discover what it might become. Maybe nothing. He had to admit that. Maybe he'd just been focusing on her because, in a sense, she was the one who'd got away.

Girls had normally flocked to him. *It's disgusting*, Martha said, *The way you practically have to beat them off with a stick. Can't any girl say no to you?*

One had. One did.

Maybe if he got her to say yes—and want him, mind, body and soul—that would be enough. Maybe, though, he was as guilty as Skeet of not going after what he thought he wanted. Did he want a foundation to help him do it?

Hell, no.

And what kind of excuse was selling her condo? It didn't mean she had to stop eating.

At least she loved his gallery.

You had to start somewhere.

The unexpected chime of the doorbell reached Holly even deep within the bedroom closet. She ignored it, swiped a hand across her damp brow and plunged even deeper into the mess. She had to get through it, pack what she intended to keep, and donate the rest to the charity shop on Monday. Then she needed to start on the books. God, the books! They were going to be far worse than the closet.

The doorbell rang again. Longer this time. Louder.

Not really. But if a doorbell could sound determined, this one did.

Holly sighed and muttered under her breath. There was only one person who rang her doorbell with that singular determination—Deb from across the hall, wanting to borrow a cup of sugar, a teaspoon of horseradish, a bag of mixed greens.

Holly was Deb's go-to alternative to the grocery store when she couldn't be bothered. And she didn't give up.

The bell went again—even longer and more persistent than the last time. Clearly, Deb wasn't going away. Instead, she was leaning on the bell.

Holly sighed and extricated herself from the depths of the closet and, irritation building, pasted on a long-suffering smile as she stalked to the door and jerked it open.

"What now? I've packed—" Her voice died.

It wasn't Deb. It was Lukas.

Clad in faded jeans and a pale blue button-down shirt, his jaw freshly shaved and a lock of sun-tipped hair drifting over his forehead, Lukas Antonides looked crisp and casual, and as drop-dead gorgeous as a Greek god.

Holly looked—and felt—like a warmed-over stew of irritation and exhaustion. "I told you I couldn't go out. Don't tell me you didn't get the message."

"I got your message."

And didn't pay any attention, apparently, because he walked straight past her into the chaos that was her living room.

Holly didn't have the strength to deal with him and the rest of her life. "Lukas! I said no. I have work to do!"

"Yeah. You're moving. In August, you said."

"Tuesday."

"What?" He stared at her.

"I sold the condo. And I have to be out by Tuesday."

Now Lukas's brows really did shoot up. "Tuesday? As in three days—" she could see him doing a quick mental calculation "—three days from now?"

"Not even." Holly glanced at her watch. "Sixty-one hours and thirty-two minutes from now. That's when we close."

"That's crazy. Doesn't make sense. No one does that."

"Fraser Holcomb does."

"Fraser Holcomb? *The* Fraser Holcomb?" So Lukas had heard of the hotshot young film director. Holly hadn't. She wasn't a big film buff.

"The very one." She followed Lukas back into the living room where stacks of too much stuff and too few boxes covered every surface. "I told you some location scout came and looked at the place."

Lukas waved a hand in the direction of Manhattan. "He liked what he saw?"

"Seems he did." Which was something of an understatement. Amber the Realtor had called her Friday afternoon and squealed, "He loved it! He thinks it's perfect!"

Holly hadn't believed her. It was too preposterous. It still felt preposterous even though she now had it in writing. "He made a cash offer yesterday morning. I told Amber I didn't have anyplace to go. She told him, and he said, 'She can rent a place until August for a hundred thousand dollars, can't she?'" She swallowed. "He offered me an extra hundred grand above the asking price for immediate occupancy."

Lukas whistled silently.

Holly let out a ragged breath. "I said yes. Amber would have killed me if I hadn't. And it really was too good to pass up," she admitted. "But now I'm panicking. I need to get packed up. Find a storage facility." She shook her head. "So I really can't…"

Lukas looked around for just a moment, taking it all in, then looked back at her. "Where do you want me to start?"

Holly goggled at him. "What? No! You don't have to do anything! I was just trying to explain why I can't—"

"I understand, but it's obvious you can't do this all yourself. You were trying to do it all yourself, weren't you?" His gaze was mildly accusing.

"It's my condo. My life."

"And since Matt died you don't count on anyone."

She flinched at his perception. "That's right," she said stubbornly.

"How's that working for you?" He said it gently, making Holly sigh in recognition of how badly it was working.

"I should hire a mover."

"No. You've got me."

The mulish look on his face said arguing was going to get her nowhere, and that she would be wasting precious time trying to change his mind. She shrugged. "Fine. Start boxing." She pointed toward the piles of stuff she'd hauled out of the closet, then she realized the flaw in the plan. "I don't have enough boxes."

"I do."

She frowned. "You?"

But he was digging his cell phone out of his pocket as he spoke. "Who just moved in?" he reminded her. "And we've got all that art we've just uncrated."

"Oh!" She actually felt a stab of relief. "Yes, of course."

He started punching in a number, then stopped to look at her. "Do you have an apartment to go to?"

"I'll go out to my mom's. I just need to get hold of her and tell her. She's not in the country now. She's in Scotland on a tour. I've been trying to reach her." Unsuccessfully, as it happened. She hadn't really planned to move in on her mother so early. A week, she'd thought. Maybe two right before she left. She hadn't planned on six weeks. "If I can't get hold of my mom, I can find a suite at the Plaza." She put all the bravado she could muster into her grin.

"And your stuff?" Lukas tilted his head.

She sucked in a breath. "A storage unit. I've called a few places."

"Are you wedded to the storage unit idea?"

"Why?"

"You could store your stuff at my place."

She shook her head. "No, I couldn't. I don't want to take advantage! I—"

"I suppose you could say no," Lukas said mildly. "Pay through the nose for some little storage unit where your stuff will bake all summer and freeze all winter."

"And of course it wouldn't at your place." Holly knew when she was being led down the primrose path.

"It wouldn't. I heat my building in winter, I air-condition in summer." He smiled.

Feeling virtual rope tightening around her ankles, Holly waited for him to go in for the kill. But he didn't say another word. He just waited, letting her stew. Letting her realize she was being foolish by saying no to his suggestion.

"I'm paying you," she said at last, feeling ungracious and guilty at the same time she felt a prickle of relief knowing that she wouldn't have to just take the first place she found without doing her homework—homework she'd intended to do and now didn't have time for.

"If you want." Lukas shrugged, but he didn't argue with her. "I thought I might pay you," he added after a moment.

Holly glanced at him sharply. "What on earth for?"

"Being my gallery manager until I can hire a full-time permanent one."

She stared, astonished. "Your…gallery manager? Don't be ridiculous. I don't know anything about managing a gallery."

"You can manage a classroom of sixth graders," he said as if that was all it required. "And you always kept a handle on Matt and me. Kept us focused. Kept me focused," he amended with a twist of his lips. "Matt was always focused."

"Not always," Holly murmured. He was perpetually being led astray by Lukas's next scheme or great idea. But she didn't say that. "You don't want me to manage your gallery," she said firmly. "You're just being kind."

Lukas looked genuinely astonished. "When have you ever known me to be kind?"

There was a sudden silence. Holly's instinct was to say she hadn't. But that wasn't entirely true. That night on his dad's sailboat, to her way of thinking, he had not been kind at all, but the day after, she had expected him to tell Matt what had happened—and he hadn't.

Instead, he had walked out of their lives.

"You can be," she allowed.

"Well, I'm not now. I'm looking out for my own interests, believe me. I need a gallery manager. Jenn isn't coming. And the chances of me finding someone like her are not great. It's going to take a while. I don't want to grab someone off the street."

"Like me," Holly pointed out.

"I want to take my time and do it right," Lukas went on just as if she hadn't said a word. "So I'm asking you to do it until you leave. Six weeks max. Long enough to give me a chance to gather a reasonable pool of candidates and find the right one—and in the meantime you have a place to stay. I showed you the apartment I'd finished for the manager," he reminded her. "You're welcome to it. Part of the pay. You can store your stuff there all the time you're gone. I've got a lot of space. And I know you can do the bare essentials that need to be done."

"What bare essentials?"

"People skills mostly. You've got 'em. I've seen you with people. You charm them. You calm them. You make them do the right thing. You made *me* do the right thing."

"I've never made you do anything!"

"Yes, Hol', you did."

Then he just rocked on his heels and looked at her expectantly. As if he knew what she'd decide, and he didn't even have to argue his case.

Of course she could say no. It would be the wise thing to do.

Taking Lukas up on his offer was crazy. Reckless. Especially when deep down she'd wanted him for years. And past experience proved that she hadn't been able to resist him.

How was she going to move into his building for six weeks and keep her distance, be his business manager and, in August, walk away without ever a taste of forbidden fruit?

She wasn't. It was as simple as that.

Holly was tired of being wise, of being sensible and responsible. She had chosen wisdom and responsibility and a slow hearth fire of love when she'd married Matt.

And look where that had got her.

No, that wasn't fair. She'd loved Matt. She could never regret that love, those years. But all the memories in the world didn't make her less lonely every night. They didn't keep her warm. And it wasn't enough to date Paul anymore. Paul was a place marker. Nothing more.

And Holly wanted more.

Somewhere deep inside her—or maybe not so deep inside her—she had felt that desire quickening to life. Maybe it had started last fall when she'd realized how hollow and empty her life had become. Maybe her move toward the Peace Corps was part of it, an attempt to help her find herself again.

Or maybe it was Lukas's gallery. There was an energy there that had spoken to her. She had felt it in the paintings, in the sculptures and textiles. She had spotted it in the fire of the opals set in silver. She had caught glimpses of it in some large photos that weren't part of the gallery offerings at all. They were snapshots really—of the land, of the mines, of Lukas and an old man she was sure had to be his friend Skeet. She'd wanted to look more closely at them, but Lukas hadn't given her a chance. He had urged her on to the next room to other displays.

Or maybe it was Lukas himself.

For the first time she faced squarely the temptation that was Lukas Antonides. A temptation she'd resisted—wisely—for years.

He didn't want what she wanted.

He didn't want commitment, permanence, family—the things she and Matt had valued. Lukas was a man of drive and enthusiasms, not of constants. He spearheaded efforts. He wasn't there for the follow-through.

But sometimes there was no follow-through.

Sometimes the man you had vowed to love and share a lifetime with wasn't there anymore. Sometimes all your hopes and dreams were dashed.

What then?

She would never find again what she'd had with Matt. It hadn't been perfect—neither of them had been perfect—but it was theirs.

And now it was gone. Playing it safe and responsible hadn't guaranteed a lifetime of happiness.

So why not take a risk?

She wasn't a child any longer. She wasn't a skittish, nervy adolescent.

She'd felt the pull of Lukas Antonides for most of her life. He didn't want what she wanted in the long run. But life wasn't only about the long run, she'd learned.

Six weeks ought to be long enough for both of them. In six weeks she would go off to the South Pacific and put the past behind her.

In the meantime, she'd take it one step at a time. One word at a time.

She said, "Yes."

CHAPTER SEVEN

Yes?

Lukas had been staring out at the Manhattan skyline telling himself to shut up, not to give in to pressuring her, not—for once—to push. At least not until she said no, at which point he was prepared to argue with her again.

And then she said…yes?

His gaze whipped around, and he stared straight at her. He expected her to be looking in the other direction—out the window, at the floor, anywhere but at him. He expected her to say, *Er, I mean, no.*

But Holly was looking straight into his eyes, not averting her gaze at all. Staring resolutely at him.

Like a deer caught in headlights. Well, maybe. But she didn't look precisely stunned. She looked intense, committed. Alive.

Lukas didn't let himself wonder what had prompted her. He didn't even know what had prompted him to make the offer. As always, he had responded to the circumstances. And, let's face it, he had done what he'd wanted to do. How could he not want her close?

So he'd jumped right out of the frying pan and into the fire. It wasn't enough to tempt himself by accidental-on-purpose meetings and invitations to dinner. Now he had drawn her into his building, his work, his life.

He would see her every day. They'd work together. Talk together. No doubt argue together. And then what?

Lukas had never done relationships. Not real, long-term,

committed relationships—except with people to whom he was related by blood or family ties. He wasn't sure he knew how. Or if he wanted to.

Cold feet, anyone? he jeered at himself silently.

But his feet didn't feel cold at the moment. They felt eager, alive, ready to run a marathon. *Hold that thought*, he counseled himself.

He grinned at her. "Terrific. Welcome aboard." He punched in a number on his mobile phone.

Charlotte, the textile artist, the one whose work Holly had particularly admired, answered at once.

"Rustle up as many of the bunch as you can," he told her. "We need lots of hands. And bring all the boxes and crates you can find. We're going to move in our new gallery manager."

And just like that, Lukas sorted out her life.

One minute Holly was suffocating in dust and clutter and far too many decisions—about what to keep and what to toss and where to put anything she hung on to—and the next, Lukas had taken over.

It was like the first time she'd gone white-water kayaking. She had been moving down a stream nice and easy—everything under control. And then she'd spied rapids ahead and instinctively began sculling backward, apprehensive, trying to size things up, to get a bead on a through-line, to keep control the way Matt had told her to.

Then all her planning, all her care vanished as she felt the surge of the water beneath her, lifting and pulling the kayak past the point of no return. The current simply swept her up in its power and carried her into the rapids. Then all she could do was pray—and hang on to the paddle for dear life.

Exactly the way she was doing now. Minus the paddle.

Lukas Antonides in action was a class-four set of white-water rapids. Within an hour half a dozen of the artists, sculptors and jewelry makers she'd met turned up on her doorstep with boxes and crates galore.

"What goes? What stays? Tell us what to do," Sam, the birdcage maker, said.

"We're experts at packing," Charlotte told her. "I'm so glad you're going to work with us."

The other three, Geoff and Paul and Teresa, nodded in agreement.

"Where's the boss?" Geoff asked, looking around with a grin.

"I'm the boss," Holly said firmly and wished she actually sounded like it. She still felt dizzy. "Lukas went to get pizza and beer."

By the time he got back, Holly and her helpers had blitzed their way through the kitchen and the hall closet. It was easier, she found, to have the others there, not just for the help, but for the distance their involvement gave her.

It was less painful to step back and say yes to this and no to that when Charlotte or Geoff held up something than it was to handle each piece herself and be caught by indecision or carried away by memories.

By the time Lukas got back, they'd cleared the kitchen and bathroom entirely. After a brief pause for sustenance, he herded the guys into her bedroom to begin dismantling the bed and carrying the dressers down to the truck.

"Hey, wait! I have to sleep somewhere," Holly protested.

"In your new apartment." Lukas was collapsing the bed frame as he spoke. "You're moving. Remember?"

Holly swallowed. She'd just assumed she'd have until Tuesday to get used to the idea. Lukas, as usual, had other plans.

"What about this tablecloth?" Teresa appeared in the doorway. "Save or sell?"

So while Lukas and the other guys got on with dismantling her life, Holly went back to the living room and made another decision.

She made hundreds before they were done. But by ten o'clock all the furniture had been ferried to the gallery building, and stacks of boxes containing things she knew she wasn't keeping stood in the middle of the otherwise empty bedroom. And another stack of boxes with the things she was storing at Lukas's were in the living room. The cupboards were empty. The bookshelves were bare.

Now everyone had gone back to the gallery to unload the truck except Holly—and Lukas. He was labeling the boxes in the bedroom. She had finished with the last box in the living room and, at a loose end, moved restlessly around the room. The lights of Manhattan gleamed like bright patterns of stars across the river. They looked familiar, unlike the mostly empty room in which she stood. She stared at them, remembering the first night she and Matt had spent in the condo. They'd sat up all night, huddled together under a blanket on the sofa, just marveling at the view.

"Ours," Matt had said and turned his head to kiss her. "We're going to make wonderful memories here."

And they had, too, Holly thought, swallowing around the tightness in her throat. Just not enough of them.

And now she didn't belong here anymore. There was nothing left.

She looked around, wondering where Lukas had got to.

She cocked her head, listening closely, and realized she could hear water running in the back of the apartment. There were muffled sounds and occasional clattering noises punctuating the sound of the water. Curious, Holly followed the sounds down the hall and into the bathroom. The door was open. Lukas was on his knees, scrubbing the grout around the edge of the shower.

"You don't have to do that!"

He sat back on his heels and looked around at her, then shrugged. "Okay." But he made no move to get up.

"I can clean it myself," she protested.

"Yeah." He straightened slowly and stood, eyeing her speculatively, and Holly began to realize what he was doing. Lukas wasn't on his knees in the bathroom with an old toothbrush in his hand because he was desperate to clean grout or because he thought she couldn't do it herself. He had been giving her space and time of her own.

She took a breath and smiled—a little wanly perhaps, but it was still a smile. "Thank you."

Lukas's gaze flicked over her. "You okay?"

"Yes." Then, more firmly, "I'm fine. I will be fine."

"Of course you will be," he agreed. "Are you ready to go?"

She tilted her head, considering. "Unless you want to scrub the rest of the grout?"

He grinned, getting to his feet. "I believe Fraser Holcomb can do the rest."

He was an idiot.

His own worst enemy.

The guy least likely to get laid on the planet.

All of the above.

He now had temptation on his doorstep 24/7—and it was his own damn fault.

Lukas sprawled on his bed, staring up at the skylight, and wondered when the hell he was going to get a clue.

Not only had he pushed his way in when she had clearly left a message telling him no, he'd got the bright idea of hiring her to be his gallery manager, then moved her into the manager's apartment where she would be right there in his building for the next six weeks. Underfoot.

Then, heaven help him, he'd shared a glass of wine with her and had the unfortunate realization that she was shattered from leaving the last home she'd shared with Matt, whereupon he had somewhere—somehow!—discovered the scruples to tell her good-night, turn his back and walk out the door!

God.

Lukas thrust his fingers through his hair and flung himself over onto his stomach. It didn't help. In fact, it was worse. It brought his arousal into direct contact with the friction of the bedclothes and made him more desperate than ever.

He either needed the brains to recognize how far gone he was on Holly—and how far she wasn't gone on him—and so keep her at a distance instead of tormenting himself with the knowledge that she was sound asleep in her bed four floors below him, or he needed to be unscrupulous enough to pursue a woman who was still in love with another man.

But this—having her right under his nose every day and still keeping his hands off—was likely going to kill him.

He rolled over to the other side, then, irritably, flipped onto his back.

He'd bet Holly wasn't tossing and turning. She'd looked completely spent by the time they'd got her furniture where she wanted it and had made up her bed.

The others had helped bring things up, but then Holly had thanked them profusely and sent them away, saying they'd done enough. She'd tried to send him away, too. But he'd had to offer to help.

He could hardly insist she move in, then abandon her the minute she got there. He probably should have. Being there with her, in the intimacy of her bedroom—even one primarily filled with boxes—hell, it was like having her on his dad's sailboat all over again.

She'd dug out a pair of soft, pale blue sheets and they'd stood on either side of the bed, spreading them and straightening them. And it was all Lukas could do not to make some comment about spending the night in them. God knew he wanted to.

But he'd seen her hollow-eyed exhaustion, and he'd witnessed the emptiness in her expression as the condo had stopped being her home and had become just a holding space for pieces of what had once been her life with Matt.

He could get her out of the condo, but he couldn't intrude on her memories. She deserved to have them, to remember the man she'd loved and lost. She had been silent on the drive across the bridge into Manhattan. He'd seen her fingers twist in her lap, and he'd wondered what he was doing bringing her here.

Certainly not what he'd hoped in the mad moments he'd pushed for her to come. It had seemed like a perfect opportunity to get her where he could spend time with her, get to know her again—without being the odd man out this time. Charm her off her feet. Go to bed with her.

But she hadn't even been able to look at him while they were putting sheets on her bed. And he'd been ready to cut his losses and head out the door when she'd said quickly, "I have a bottle of wine. We should drink a toast to my new life."

Anyone less likely to be embracing a new life than the Holly who'd smiled tremulously at him would have been hard to imagine. Her face was pale, her eyes deep-sunken. She looked as if she was going to shatter any second.

But maybe a glass of wine would settle her, make her sleep. And apparently he was a glutton for punishment, because Lukas had found himself nodding. "Sounds good."

She'd found the wine without too much trouble, and even came up with a corkscrew to open it with. "Charlotte labeled the kitchen boxes very thoroughly," she'd said with a laugh.

But she'd fumbled with the corkscrew and muttered in

frustration. So Lukas had taken it from her and done it himself. "Got glasses?"

She'd rooted in another box and produced a pair. He'd poured, then set the bottle down and raised his glass to her. And Holly had looked at him with her eyes wide and terrified looking.

Lukas didn't speak. He didn't know what to say that wouldn't make things worse. Then at last Holly smiled, a small, twisted smile. "To the future."

It sounded as if she was expecting one unmitigated disaster after another. But as long as she didn't say so, Lukas could drink to that.

He clinked his glass to hers. "To the future."

She had taken a sip, then followed it with something close to a gulp, after which she had coughed herself silly. Lukas had taken her glass and set it on the counter, then didn't know what to do with his hands. Patting her on the back—touching her at all—was out of the question.

She'd laughed, a little desperately to his ears. "God," she'd muttered. "I'm hopeless."

Lukas had shaken his head. "No. You just need a good night's sleep," he added. "Everything will be all right in the morning."

Of course it wouldn't. It was just one of those platitudes his mother used to tell him. "Let's hope so," she'd said.

"Right. I'll go. Let you get some sleep." He gulped down the rest of his wine and turned for the door.

Holly followed him. "Thank you, Lukas."

Her voice sounded breathless and achingly sexy, and he needed to get out of there before he did something he'd regret. He gave her a wave of his hand without even turning around. "G'night."

Then he had shut the door behind him with a solid thunk.

So he hoped to God she was sleeping now. She'd been tired enough. As for him—well, no rest for the wicked.

Another of his mother's platitudes. And one better suited for the occasion.

From outside Lukas heard the wail of a siren, reminding him that there were people with greater problems than his. The clock on his dresser read 2:42 a.m. He wasn't going to sleep.

He wanted to get up and go knock down a wall, get rid of some of the tension. But there were no walls that needed knocking down. He groaned and rolled over again.

And that was when he heard the knock.

Knock? There was no one in the building but him.

And Holly.

Holly was knocking on his door? He half vaulted out of the bed before he dropped back again, breathing hard.

Suppose it was Holly. Suppose she needed him to fix the thermostat or maybe the refrigerator wasn't working. Suppose she was afraid of the dark in a new place and wanted him to sit with her until dawn.

Did she trust him enough to do any of those things in the middle of the night?

Did he trust himself? Lukas scrubbed his hands down his face. Trust himself? Ha. He slumped back against the pillows and assured himself that he was hearing things. Tormenting himself with imaginary knocks from a woman who, God help him, wasn't imaginary at all.

And then he heard it again. A little louder.

Definitely not imaginary.

Lukas shoved himself up and yanked on a pair of jeans, the better to disguise the lingering evidence of arousal. Then he put his game face on and padded barefoot to the door.

A glimpse through the security viewer confirmed his worst fears—Holly, hair mussed, in shorts and an oversize T-shirt, shifted from one foot to the other, raised her hand to knock again, then let it drop to her side, fingers twisting.

Once more she half raised it, then cradled it in her other hand, turned and started to walk away.

He didn't even hesitate. Lukas jerked open the door. "What's wrong?"

She spun back to face him, eyes wide, her mouth opening in a soundless O as she met his gaze. He saw her throat work once, then again.

"What's wrong, Holly?" he asked again, doing his best to keep his voice calm, steady, the exact opposite of his hammering heart. "What do you need?"

She dragged in a breath, then straightened her shoulders. Her gaze never left his. "You."

Lukas hadn't heard right. He gave a shake of his head. "What?"

"That's right, Lukas. Make me repeat it." Her mouth twisted. "You, damn it. You."

As she came back toward him, her breasts jiggling beneath the soft cotton of her shirt, Lukas caught his breath. She wasn't wearing a bra. He remembered what it was like to slide his hands under her shirt, to stroke her there. His fingers curled into fists. He dragged his gaze upward, which turned out to be just as bad. She had devilishly kissable lips.

"For what?" his voice rasped. Because if this had to do with fixing a light or some other damn household emergency, he was going to shoot himself.

"What do you think?" She stopped barely a foot from him, looking up into his eyes, hers challenging him the way she always had as a kid. He didn't think of her as a kid now. He hadn't thought of her as a kid for years. All he really thought was how much he wanted to take that extra step, haul her into his arms and feel those soft breasts against his bare chest, press the fierceness of his desire hard against her.

"Holly." He shut his eyes and ground his teeth in frustration.

"Mmm?" Why the hell did her voice sound almost like a purr? Was that her breath he felt against his collarbone?

"Holly!" he protested, strangling on her name.

Her hand came up, went flat against his chest and pushed. He took a step back into his apartment. Holly followed.

"Holly," he warned. "Don't start something you're not going to finish."

"I intend to finish." She sounded almost fierce and she was still close enough that he felt her breath on his bare chest. "Why did you ask me to move in?"

He shrugged. "Why not? I've got space. I need a gallery manager. I figured you could do that."

"I have no clue how to manage a gallery."

"Then why did you take the job?" he demanded. She wasn't the only one who could push. Two could play this game, damn it.

"Because it gave me an excuse." Holly edged even closer. "We want an excuse, don't we, to get what we really want?" Her voice was soft, enticing, and just a little edgy.

Lukas's breath caught in his chest. Her eyes were deep pools of midnight, so deep he felt he could fall straight into them. "What do you mean, what we really want?" he said roughly. Since when had they ever wanted the same thing?

"I told you what I want." He could hear his heart beat in his chest. "You."

There was no doubt what she was talking about now. Bed. That was what she was talking about. Sex. Lukas frowned.

"Don't you act like you don't want me, Lukas Antonides! Don't you dare try to pretend you were just doing me a favor, giving me a roof over my head!" She poked a fierce finger into his chest. "Because that isn't what this is about. Is it?"

Lukas's jaw tightened. "So, you just want to go to bed? Have sex? And then what?"

Holly shrugged "I don't know. If it's good, maybe we could do it again?" She looked almost hopeful.

And Lukas almost laughed. It would be good. He had no doubt about that. But he still didn't move. "Say we do," he said almost conversationally, which was a far cry from the way his body was clamoring to do just that, "go to bed. Have sex. More than once," he clarified. "What then? What's the point?"

Holly's eyes went wide. "What's the point? It's sex, for heaven's sake! That *is* the point! We go to bed—multiple times, if necessary—and we get it out of our systems. Once and for all!"

"Get it out of our systems? Sex?" He stared at her.

"Not sex," Holly said hotly. "Each other!"

Not likely, Lukas thought. If he could have got Holly out of his system, he'd have done it years ago.

"You won't even have to break up with me," she went on cheerfully. "It's perfect. We can have a six-week affair. Then we go our separate ways. I head off for the far side of the world, and you do whatever you're planning to do next. Simple. See?"

Lukas saw. He thought she was completely out of her flaming mind. It made him furious at the same time it made him desperate.

"You think that'll work?" Pardon his skepticism.

"Of course it will work."

If she were taller, she would have been nose to nose with him now. As it was her breasts were within a millimeter of touching his bare chest. He caught a whiff of citrus scent, enticing him further.

He lifted a hand and touched her cheek, ran his finger

down it to linger at the point of her chin. She held herself
absolutely still, didn't even seem to be breathing. He wanted
her breathing. Panting. Eager. Desperate for him.

He bent his head just as Holly lifted her hands and laid
both against his chest.

It was like being branded. Lukas's jaw tightened. Everything else did, too. His nipples beaded under the touch of
her palms. She rubbed them over him experimentally. He
swallowed a groan and lowered his mouth to hers.

CHAPTER EIGHT

THE KISS BEGAN SLOWLY, almost gently, echoing the kiss of long ago, as if Lukas were leashing his passion, keeping everything under tight control.

Then his tongue touched hers. And Holly could taste him on her lips. Instinctively, hers parted to give him entrance, wanting more. The kiss became harder, more urgent, almost desperate.

It felt exactly the way she felt—the way she had been trying *not* to feel for so long that it was a relief to not have to try to resist. She wanted what Lukas wanted—to touch, to taste. More than taste—to devour.

Of their own volition, her hands slid up the hair-roughened muscular expanse of his chest. She felt tiny nubs beneath her fingers, tweaked them and heard him groan. Holly swallowed his groan, darting her tongue between his lips to touch his teeth even as his tangled with hers. His hands, hard and warm and calloused, slid beneath her T-shirt, drawing her even closer, claiming her.

It wouldn't last, Holly knew that. It was desire. Lust. Passion. It was sex, just as Lukas had said. And it would run its course. It wasn't love. For it to be love, it had to be mutual. It had to knit together two people, create a relationship, make them better and stronger together than they were apart. They had to want that.

Lukas didn't. He'd made it clear more than once.

Love was what she'd had with Matt—a sense of completeness that they had shared. A bedrock of enduring love that worlds—galaxies—could be built on.

This was a shooting star.

But what was wrong with a shooting star? It was short and sweet and stunningly beautiful. And when it burned out, as Holly knew it would, it couldn't possibly hurt more than losing Matt had. And she would have the memory of Lukas. She would never have to wonder.

And wasn't that better than no star at all?

She assured herself it was. And she promised herself she wouldn't get burned. It was just pointless to keep denying the attraction. Everything she'd believed in when she'd married Matt hadn't prevented her from losing him.

She wasn't counting on keeping Lukas. She was going into this with her eyes open. It would be fine.

Still, when Lukas growled, "What are we waiting for?" into her ear, she felt a shiver of panic. But the feel of his lips on hers fed her desire, and she stopped fighting it and gave herself over to the need. She wrapped her arms around his neck and nuzzled his jaw.

Lukas lowered her to the bed, then settled next to her, a hand braced on either side of her. His eyes were dark, and yet she could see the hunger in them. And when he lowered his head and kissed her again, his mouth hot and hungry, Holly met his kiss with a hunger of her own.

Her hands slid over his back and the hard muscles of his arms and shoulders. While he was lean, his muscles were most definitely those of a man who worked hard physically. She loved running her fingers over him and feeling the tremor of those hard muscles beneath her hands.

Lukas's own hands were doing explorations of their own, sliding beneath the hem of her T-shirt, tracing the line of the waistband of her shorts. Holly remembered how it felt to have his hands on her. He made her quiver. He made her moan.

The sound seemed to please him. Abruptly, Lukas shoved himself to his knees and drew her up with him to grab her shirt and pull it straight over her head. Then he sat back against his heels, a smile curving the corner of his mouth as he cupped her breasts in his palms.

Self-conscious despite her best intentions, Holly shifted to cover herself. But Lukas stilled her hands. "Don't."

His gaze settled on her, then he bent his head and kissed each of her breasts, teasing her nipples to hard, tight buds, made her gasp and grab his shoulders as his tongue skimmed over her heated flesh, leaving exquisitely sensitive trails.

Stardust trails, Holly thought, giving herself over to the moment—to the man.

And then she ceased to think at all.

Holly. In his bed.

At last.

Holly's hands on his bare back, nails scratching lightly, sent exquisite little bolts of electricity straight through him, making him even harder than he'd been. But when her fingers slid around to the snap at the waistband of his jeans, he stilled them even though his own fingers shook as he pulled hers away. "Wait." His breath came in quick gasps. He shoved himself back and up on one elbow.

Holly stared at him, eyes wide and uncomprehending. "Wait?"

"Just. Slow. Down." He could only manage one word at a time, and there was a tremor in his voice as well as in his hands. He felt like a teenager, lacking control, desperate for release. A release he craved at the same time he wanted this to last.

"No...hurry." His mouth twisted. "We've got...all night."

Then he dipped his head and buried his face in her hair, drawing in more deeply the tantalizing citrus scent that had always said "Holly" to him. He nibbled her ear, pressed kisses along her jaw, slid his hands down her sides, then up over her breasts.

"How come you get to do things?" Holly's voice was plaintive. He could hear a tremor in it that made him smile.

"Because you want me to." He lifted his head and looked down at her. "Don't you?"

She swallowed. It was answer enough. Still watching her face, he drew one trembling finger down between her breasts, circled her nipples, then bent his head to lave them again with his tongue. He smiled when he heard her breath catch.

"Lukas!" His name hissed between her teeth. She reached out and caught his hand in hers. But she didn't stop him. His lips pressed kisses where his fingers had gone. His tongue traced the same path, pebbling her nipples, making her squirm.

She trembled as he rubbed a thumb over the exquisite softness of her breasts, then cupped them, nuzzled and nibbled them. Holly let go of his hand to grab a handful of his hair. It made him smile, and he bent his head and moved lower, down across her flat belly to the waistband of her shorts. Then, as her hands slipped down to clutch his shoulders, he drew a fingertip along the edge of her waistband and felt the muscles in her abdomen contract. She shifted under his touch.

Lukas flicked open the button, then eased down the zip and tugged the shorts down over her hips, then drew them down the length of her legs. Ah, those legs. God, he loved her legs.

Tossing the shorts aside, he made himself slow down, appreciate every moment as his fingers played back up from her ankles again. He followed them with his lips, kissing her knees, then sliding between them so he could do the same to the insides of her thighs.

"My turn," she said fiercely, pushing herself up to fumble with the zip of his jeans. He didn't stop her this time, even though he was on the edge and very nearly tipped right over when her fingers opened his zip and found him. Lukas's teeth clenched as her hand wrapped his hot flesh, tentatively at first, then more firmly. A harsh breath slipped between his teeth.

"Slow," he warned, teeth clenched.

It was close to the best thing he'd ever experienced—Holly touching him, learning his body—almost as wonderful as touching and learning hers. She could have shattered him right then if he'd let her. He wouldn't.

He stilled her fingers, then drew her hand away from him, felt the aching loss of her touch, but focused instead on her. He stroked lightly along the edge of the waistband of her panties, dipping beneath to trail a finger through the soft curls at the apex of her thighs. She trembled and shifted as he bent his head to plant a kiss there. And then another and another, before hooking his fingers around the scrap of lace and sliding them slowly down her thighs. Then he sat back and beheld Holly Montgomery Halloran naked before him.

"Dear God, you're beautiful."

He'd imagined this for years. Holly had figured so regularly in his nighttime fantasies, especially after the night of her prom, that he'd told himself that the real woman couldn't possibly live up to them.

But she did.

She was everything he had imagined—and more.

The curve of her hip, the length of her legs, the small pert mounds of her breasts, the triangle of curls that hid her mysteries all enticed him. He wanted to explore them all. First the soft smoothness of her skin drew his touch. He ran a hand over her from her shoulder over her hip, down her leg to her toes. He bent her leg, ignored the tantalizing hint of mystery that bending her knee uncovered, and instead kissed her toes.

"Lukas!"

"Mmm." He kissed them one by one, then let his fingers walk up her instep, trace her right ankle, then her left. Then he walked his fingers up her calves again to trace the backs of her knees, the exquisite softness of the insides of her thighs—torturing himself with anticipation. *Wait*, he told himself. *Wait.*

His thumbs brushed lightly against the curls where her thighs joined. Holly bit her lip, held perfectly still. She'd held still the night on his father's boat, too. She'd gripped his shoulders so hard she'd left tiny bruises that he'd cherished long after they had disappeared. And she'd let him touch her. He touched her now. More deeply. Slid a finger through folds that were wet. For him.

"Lukas!" Holly's voice was urgent.

"Mmm?" He breathed on her there.

"There is slow and then there is slow!" She sounded somewhere between lust and laughter.

Lukas laughed raggedly, then kissed her, touched his tongue to her. There.

She jerked. Her knees pressed against his ears. "You are driving me insane!"

"I know." He was driving himself insane, too.

"How would you like it if I did that to you?"

He groaned. "Do you think I'd tell you to stop?"

"Excellent." Abruptly Holly sat up and looped her fingers over the waistband of his jeans.

Lukas started to do it himself, but she batted his hands away. "My turn."

"Hol'—"

"We're going slow," she reminded him, all seriousness, then slanted him a wicked smile. "You'll love it."

She was going to kill him. He made a noise deep in his

throat. But he knelt back on his heels stoically, watching as Holly came up on her knees before him in all her naked glory and slowly—inch by inch—no, centimeter by centimeter, slid the jeans down his hips, then coaxed him up off his heels to pull them off, to run her hands over him, taking her own sweet time.

He groaned, then gritted his teeth as she found him again and clasped him in both her hands, stroked him. His hips bucked. "Holly!"

She smiled. "Exactly."

Then she put a hand against his chest and pushed him back against the mattress. He reached for her, to pull her down on top of him. But she twisted away, moved to the end of the bed, bent her head, kissed his toes.

Lukas's fingers knotted around the sheet. "For God's sake!"

"See what I mean?" Holly looked up brightly with another of those maddening smiles. She slid between his legs, and he reached for her to lift her and settle her against him where he needed her most. If he didn't get her there soon—like, in an instant—it would be too late. Her merest touch would send him right over the edge. If she reached out a finger and touched him now, it would be all over.

"Wait, I thought you said—" Holly began, grinning at him.

But Lukas wasn't waiting any longer. "Enough waiting." He pulled her close, then rolled her back onto the bed and pressed his body against hers. He couldn't hold back, couldn't pace himself. Not now.

Holly didn't resist. She wrapped her arms and legs around him and opened to his kiss, to his need. She met him kiss for kiss, move for move, fitting her body, tight and hot and slick, to his, welcoming him in.

It was heaven. The years, the days, the minutes of tortured anticipation were over and even though Lukas did his best to make it last, he couldn't fight his need any longer. He slid into her, a single hard thrust, and she met him, digging her fingernails into his back as she arched against him. They shattered together.

And, as Lukas had known it would be, it was good.

The morning after.

Holly woke thinking those very words, and trying to articulate what had happened so she could put it in a box she would call My Affair with Lukas and then, in slightly less than six weeks' time, could close firmly and stick on a shelf at the back of her mind.

But at the moment, she just lay there in the early-morning light and watched Lukas sleep.

Lukas.

She had gone to bed with Lukas Antonides. Had had sex with Lukas Antonides. She had spent so many years furious with him, or fighting with him or pretending he didn't exist that it fairly boggled her mind.

She lay there, studying him, trying to think things through, then deliberately stopped herself. There was nothing to think about. She had no expectations. For six weeks she was going to live in the moment. She wouldn't let herself want anything else—wouldn't even let herself consider anything else.

Just live, she told herself. *Be in the moment.* The moment, after all, was the only thing you ever really had.

And this was a moment she hadn't expected to ever have—a time to contemplate Lukas unmoving except for the soft draw and exhalation of his breath. That was novel in itself. But so was seeing him looking young and unguarded.

Young, well, she had seen that before. But she didn't think she had ever seen Lukas unguarded. The edgy watchfulness or quicksilver enthusiasm she normally associated with his expressions were entirely absent. There was a gentleness to his mouth now. His lips looked softer. And heaven help her, Holly knew now exactly how soft that was.

And how persuasive.

She wanted to curl up next to him and go back to sleep. But she felt oddly energized, as well. And if she were going to really be his gallery manager, she had unpacking to do and material to read from the artists that Charlotte had given her last night.

Besides, she didn't know what it would be like when Lukas woke up. It could be awkward. Holly had no experience of "mornings after"—except with Matt. She didn't know the protocol of brief affairs.

She slid out of bed and let herself take one last look at him. She had six weeks with this man—as long as he didn't tire of her sooner. But she wouldn't think about that, either. *Live for the moment*, she told herself again.

She would. For six weeks she would.

And then she would walk away unscathed.

When he awoke, Lukas was alone.

It was nearly nine. He hadn't slept till nine in years. But he'd slept like the dead after making love to Holly. He lay back and folded his arms under his head and grinned, energized, replete—and hungry all over again. He went downstairs and banged on the door to the gallery manager's apartment.

Holly opened it, color touching her cheeks as she looked up at him. "Hey." Her voice was soft, a little hesitant.

"Hey, yourself." And he hauled her into his arms and kissed her. She tasted like sunshine and apples and something singularly Holly. God, it was good. "Have you had breakfast?"

"Just this." She waved a half-eaten apple at him. "I'm still looking for my granola."

"We can find it later. I know a great brunch place." He grabbed her hand. "Come on."

"I should work." She gestured at the artists' info spread out on the bar.

But Lukas shook his head. "I'm your boss. I say we have brunch."

He took her to a little place not far from the gallery. It was unpretentious and undiscovered by any but the locals. But there were enough locals that they had to wait for a table.

Since he'd been back in the city, Lukas had found himself edgy, aware of too many people going too many places, always in a rush. Over all the years he'd been gone, he had grown used to space, to horizons, to the only noises being the ones he or those he was with made themselves. The cacophony that was New York had irritated him in a way he hadn't expected. And he hadn't been able to blot it out until now.

Being with Holly made the rest of the world recede. He wasn't busy thinking ahead, wondering where he needed to be next or what he needed to do.

He knew instinctively that he was right where he was supposed to be, sitting across a tiny table from the one woman who could make him laugh and think and want to argue, all within the space of a minute.

He might—oh, once or twice—have thought it would be nice to be back in bed with her. But it would happen, he promised himself.

"What are you smiling about?" Holly asked.

She had been telling him about Althea's upcoming wedding, and Lukas supposed he should be sympathetic. But it sounded like another of several weddings too many.

"Just thinking about taking you to bed," Lukas replied.

The color rose in her cheeks. She rolled her eyes. "Well, stop!"

"I like thinking about it. I like doing it. I thought you did, too." He raised a brow at her.

She focused on cutting her French toast. "Yes," she said.

Lukas grinned. "Good. Right, then. Althea's wedding. When is it?"

"End of July. Right before I leave." She told him the date.

"Same day as the reception," he said. "For the grant winners. It's going to be a big deal at the Plaza. The mayor and all that." He grimaced.

"Well, you probably won't have to wear pastel," Holly told him philosophically.

Lukas blanched. "Pastel?"

Holly smiled. "Never mind."

"Want a bite of my omelet?" He held out his fork to her. She nibbled off it, then licked her lips. "Very tasty."

Lukas groaned. "Now can we talk about going back to bed?"

"No. We need to go back to the gallery so you can get me up to speed on this new job I've agreed to do."

So after one last cup of coffee, they headed back to the gallery where Lukas spent the rest of the afternoon on the gallery floor and then in the manager's office showing Holly the ropes, and periodically suggesting they go back upstairs as he had plenty of things he could show her there.

Holly just smiled and shook her head. She took her new job seriously, it seemed, peppering him with questions, half of which he didn't know the answers to. But he gave her the basics, explained the books, and gave her information about the opening coming up, and realized he should not have been so confident as to leave it all in Jenn's hands.

"She put some of it in place from Sydney." He knew that much. He said so as they walked back to her condo late that afternoon. They'd spent hours that could have been more interestingly occupied getting up to speed on work. "You can call her. You should call her. And I'll help as much as I can." He felt guilty handing the mess off to her. It had been a spur-of-the-moment suggestion, and he'd been amazed she had agreed. "Sera can help, too."

"It'll be a challenge." Holly unlocked her door and opened it. "But I'll do my best."

"Of course you will. And it'll be fine." He started to follow her in, but she turned to face him instead.

"So let me get going on it."

"What?"

"Go away. I have work to do."

"It's Sunday!" he protested.

"Which means I have one day to get my head around everything. I repeat, go away."

"But—"

"And don't pull out the 'I'm your boss' card," Holly said unrepentantly. "It's what you wanted—a trade-off, remember? I work for you, I get the apartment until I leave. We agreed," she reminded him. "And I mean what I say. I do what I say."

Holly kept her promises. She always had. It was why she'd been so angry with him the night of her prom: because she was engaged, she had made a promise to Matt and felt she had broken it with him. He raked a hand through his hair. "Fine. Go for it. If you have questions, follow the noise. I'm going to go find a wall to knock down."

She spent the rest of Sunday afternoon going over the artists' material, getting a feel for what they did, and then went back downstairs to see how it was displayed. She carried a notebook and made copious notes. And all the while she did so, she was aware of the sounds of destruction coming from upstairs. Lukas at work.

The thought made her smile. She could imagine him shirtless, working with a crowbar, muscles flexing and bunching. She wondered if he was wearing a tool belt. She was almost tempted to go up and see. But she didn't.

She was living in the moment—and the moment was here in the gallery, getting a grip on what she needed to do.

There would be time for Lukas later, she was sure of it.

And she was right. He banged on her door at seven and said, "Enough work," in an authoritative tone. "Come and eat."

"I have to change. Where are we going?"

"To my place," he said. "And as far as I'm concerned, you don't have to wear anything at all."

She took a shower and put on clean clothes and went upstairs, reining in her skepticism about Lukas's ability to cook. But he really had made dinner—spaghetti and meat sauce, a fresh green salad and crusty hot garlic bread.

She was amazed. Matt couldn't boil water. She'd given up trying to teach him how to do anything in the kitchen. It was easier to do it herself. But it was wonderful to actually have a man cook for her—even one who had her out of her clothes and back in his bed before she could offer to wash the dishes.

"That's what dishwashers are for." Lukas was busy yanking his own clothes off, his gaze devouring her nakedness.

"Yes, but you have to load them," Holly protested.

"Not now. We have better things to do."

They did. They made love until the wee hours of the morning. Then they slept, wrapped in each other's arms.

Living in the moment, Holly thought, could be addictive.

She would have liked to spend all day there. But Lukas was already up and shaved. He was fixing breakfast when she emerged from the bedroom, still tender in places she had almost forgotten about.

"Morning." He kissed her with lingering thoroughness, then said, "Gotta stop that or I won't be meeting the mayor this morning." He set a bowl of oatmeal and raspberries in front of her.

"You're meeting the mayor?" Holly raised her brows.

"More likely one of his flunkies. We're going over logistics for the reception at the Plaza." He shot back his cuff and consulted his watch. "And I'm going to be late. Will you be okay here?"

"Of course," Holly said. "I've got my work cut out for me."

"You don't have to," Lukas said.

"Oh? You got me here under false pretenses, did you?" A corner of her mouth twitched.

"Any way I could get you," Lukas said. He snagged a suit coat off the back of a chair and shrugged it on. "I'll be back by lunchtime."

Holly finished her breakfast, then loaded the dishwasher with last night's dishes and this morning's, then turned it on. She went back into Lukas's bedroom and straightened the bed, letting herself remember how they'd spent the night. Her cheeks grew warm just thinking about it.

"Live in the moment," she reminded herself. Lukas was heading uptown. It was time for her to get cleaned up and go to work.

She turned up in Sera's office half an hour later to ask for whatever material she had that she'd been saving for Jenn. "Lukas said I should get it from you," she told his assistant.

"You're the new gallery manager?" Sera's eyes were like saucers. A knowing smile lit her face.

Holly felt her own cheeks reddening. "Just for six weeks," she said. "Less if Lukas finds someone else."

"What happens in six weeks?"

So while Sera pulled up files and printed out material, Holly told her about the Peace Corps.

Sera's surprise was evident. "You're going away? For

two years? And Lukas is okay with that?" she said doubtfully.

"It's not Lukas's decision," Holly told her.

"I wonder if he knows that," Sera murmured as she col-
lated the material and put it in a folder.

Holly was sure Lukas knew it. She was sure it was exactly what he wanted. But she didn't say any of that to Sera.
She just thanked her for the files and said she'd be back to
pick her brain later.

The job, she discovered, was just as Lukas had said, not
unlike teaching. The better you knew your students, the
better job you could do. The same thing applied to the gallery. The more she knew about the artists and their work,
the better job she could do promoting them with the public, and the more she could help them get the best out of
the gallery and vice versa.

It was no hardship to get to know them better. They had
stopped whatever they'd been doing on Saturday night to
help her. She wanted to return the favor.

So besides going over the material Sera gave her, she
went from studio to studio talking to the artists. She learned
a lot about them, which she had expected. She also learned
a good deal about Lukas, not just from what they told her,
but from those blowup photos she hadn't had time to really
look at the afternoon he'd first given her a tour.

They were photos of what she inferred were some of the
mining sites where Lukas worked. They were blowups, of
dirt and rubble and two dusty men, one much older, thin
and wiry with gray hair buzzed close to his skull and wire-
rimmed glasses perched on the end on his nose, the other
lean, yet muscular, the ends of his normally sun-tipped
locks even blonder in the harsh Australian sun.

They were candid shots, taken by friends, Holly presumed. But they captured well the relationship of Lukas

and the old man. They were working together, talking together, standing together, covered with dust, their arms slung around each other's shoulders as they beamed at the camera. In the last shot they toasted each other with broad grins and pints of beer. Lukas looked as happy—and as satisfied—as she had ever seen him. And the pride in the old man's eyes was evident.

She understood very well why Lukas felt an obligation to see Skeet's foundation was a success. The rapport between them was obvious. It was beautiful.

It gave her a greater appreciation for Lukas than she'd had before. She'd known him as a boy and as a self-absorbed young man. She didn't see that here. She saw something deeper, something valuable.

What she saw there, she soon discovered, extended to the attitude of the artists toward the man who owned the gallery.

"He understands us," Charlotte told her.

"He listens," Teresa said. And she went on to tell Holly about how it was when she'd whined to him about lack of opportunities, that he'd said, "What would make it better?"

"I just babbled," Teresa told her. "Told him how wonderful it would be to have access to a North American market, to be promoted on the other side of the world. I didn't see it ever happening. I was just talking. But he made it happen."

"He lets us alone," Charlotte said. "He doesn't try to get us to do particular things. He never makes suggestions. Not even about how we display our work in his gallery. He's determined that it's ours, not his."

Not one person said, *He's bossy. He's autocratic. He thinks he knows it all.*

He certainly wasn't micromanaging her. He found her when he came back at lunchtime and asked if she wanted peanut butter and jelly or pâté de foie gras.

"What?" Holly was behind the desk in the main gallery reading over a spreadsheet.

He repeated it. "I've got peanut butter upstairs. Or I can take you out."

"I need to keep going. Jenn left a list of appropriate region-specific foods, but I have to find a caterer who can actually make them." It was a good idea to serve Australian, New Zealand and Pacific finger foods and desserts. But it was going to take a bit of effort to come up with a provider.

"Fine, but you have to eat," Lukas said, drawing her to her feet.

"I need to make phone calls."

"Right. Peanut butter and jelly it is."

He made a mean peanut butter and jelly sandwich. Holly had to give him that. But after he did he let her go back to work. He didn't turn up every ten minutes to make suggestions or to boss her around. There was the normal amount of noise in the gallery until about four o'clock, when the pre-opening hours closed to the public.

Then the banging and hammering began. Holly found she actually liked hearing it. She liked the images it called to mind. But when it stopped just after six, she found that her imagination was lacking.

Moments after it ended, Holly looked up to catch her breath at the sight of a sweaty, grimy, shirtless Lukas Antonides standing in her office doorway, wearing jeans—and a tool belt. Holly swallowed at the sight.

"Time to quit," he said.

"No more walls to knock down?"

"Not if I want the building to keep standing. Let's take a shower."

"Lukas!"

He grinned unrepentantly. "Come on, Hol'. You know you want to wash my back."

She wanted to wash a great deal more than that. She

wanted to wash all of him. Holly swallowed a whimper. Then she drew an anticipatory breath and stood up. "All right. Let's."

Sometimes over the days that followed, Lukas felt as if he'd died and gone to heaven.

He had Holly in the office, bright-eyed and eager, yet still businesslike, every day. He had Holly in the kitchen—sometimes his and sometimes hers—for breakfasts and dinners. She was a good cook—and she ate his own attempts with relish.

"A man to cook for me?" she said. "Be still my beating heart."

His own heart beat a whole lot more rapidly when she was around. He had expected that the reality of Holly might well pale compared to his youthful dreams of her. How often, after all, did the real thing ever measure up?

But Holly more than measured up. The memories of her had always outshone any girl or woman Lukas had ever dated. But she outdid herself, as well.

For a man who had always had his eye on the horizon, who'd spent his life in pursuit of what was beyond it, this was a whole new experience.

He didn't want it to end. What the hell did Holly need to go halfway around the world to find herself for? She was doing fine right here with him.

There was no question that taking Holly to bed was amazing. But they got along well outside of bed, too. He remembered she used to like baseball so he'd invited her along to his softball games. She came and cheered him on.

He tried to get her to come with him to the boatyard where he worked on Wednesday afternoons and Saturday mornings with the St. Brendan's kids. "You want to come," he said because she quizzed him eagerly about everything when he came back.

But she wouldn't come. She told him, "I have work to do."

"Work can wait," he told her.

But she shook her head. "It's my job." And Holly was determined to do what she had promised to do.

He had no complaints. The minute she'd taken over as gallery manager, things started getting done. She didn't know everything that needed doing. She wasn't familiar with galleries and artists and who the people to know were. But she figured out very quickly who to ask. She even called Grace and asked her advice.

"Grace Marchand?" Lukas stared at her, surprised. She was making dinner in his kitchen, looking completely at home. He liked coming in at night to find her there. "You know Grace?"

"No, but you do." Holly tore up lettuce for a salad with brisk efficiency. "I said I was working for you, and I needed some advice. She was happy to help. We're having lunch together tomorrow. You're not invited," she informed him cheerfully.

And thank God for that, Lukas thought. But he couldn't help wondering how things were going the next afternoon. And he made it a point to turn up in her office to remind her about his softball game that afternoon.

"How was Grace?" he asked, just a little warily.

"She's brilliant. She'd make a great gallery manager," Holly told him. "All the right connections. She can get anything in the city done before dinner. Seriously, Lukas, you might think about it. I can see why your mother thinks you ought to marry her."

"No," Lukas said firmly. "Just no," he said again when her eyes widened at his vehemence. "Not interested."

Holly let out a sigh. "Well, you'd better find someone," she said. "It's not that long until I leave."

She still talked about leaving. There was a copy of her itinerary tacked to the bulletin board in her office—and some Peace Corps official mail reminding what inoculations she was expected to have before she left.

"Good thing I'm not needle-phobic," she said cheerfully the day she went to get her typhoid shot.

Lukas found he wished she were. And he didn't like being asked his opinion about what sort of clothing she should plan on taking to a South Pacific climate.

It was all he could do not to tell her to forget the South Pacific climate, that she was staying right here. But if he told her that, then what? He kept his mouth shut.

In bed they didn't have to talk about inoculations or proper attire or anything else. They made love. And there, too, Holly exceeded expectations. She was as willing, eager and inventive a lover as he could have hoped for. And she welcomed his lovemaking with passion and enthusiasm.

He daydreamed his way through the grant applications, doing his best to whittle them down. His heart caught in his throat when he watched her at work, nibbling on the end of her pen as she contemplated something she was reading, or licking her lips at the sight of a particularly tasty snack one of the artists brought in, and his mind flashed back to those lips on him, that tongue making him crazy with need.

He was going crazy right now. He'd just come back from a meeting at the Plaza and stopped by her office to discover her at her desk, sucking her pen as she read.

Holly looked up. "Oh. You're back." She smiled. "Did you say something?" She twirled the pen across her lips again, then ran her tongue over the top of it.

Lukas felt blood pumping where it had no business pumping at the office in the middle of the day. He started to straighten, then changed his mind and cleared his throat instead. "No. And stop teasing."

"Me?" Holly looked briefly surprised, then gave him a smug grin. "Hadn't realized I was." But the speculative look in her eyes made his temperature go up another notch.

"You realized." And if she hadn't at first, she certainly did now. "You want me to make love to you right here in the office?"

Holly tipped her head, a smile playing at her lips. "Is that a threat?" she asked. "Or a promise?"

Holly had never thought of herself as wanton. She never would have considered making love with Matt on a desk in the middle of the afternoon. But Lukas brought out the devil in her, the one who, when pushed, had learned how to push back, the one who was determined to grab these few weeks and live them to the fullest.

And why not? They were two consenting adults. They knew each other well—well enough to press each other's buttons, especially now that Matt was no longer there to be the steadying influence between them.

If Lukas could stand there, leaning against the door-jamb of her office looking sexy as sin in a light tan suit, a dark brown shirt and a green, jungle-patterned tie that brought out the gold in his hair and the jade in his eyes, why shouldn't she flirt a little in return?

"If you keep looking at me like that, it's a promise." Lukas shoved away from the doorjamb, pushed the door shut and locked it behind him.

Holly felt a kick of desire go straight through her as he advanced purposefully across the room. She stood and came around the desk, meeting him head-on. "How nice you had a meeting with the mayor," she said, purring as she reached for him—and his tie. She loosened it and slipped it off his neck. "I think I can find a use for this."

She found a use for it. Several. Both on the sofa in his office and later that night in his bed.

It was heady and exhilarating, making love with Lukas. He brought out a side of her she'd never known she had. With Matt things had been steady, calm and responsible—

even their lovemaking. With Lukas, it went from fiery to tender, from passionate to gentle. With Lukas, anything went.

An affair with Lukas was everything she'd ever imagined it would be. And more.

Sated from their loving, she curled against his side, feeling her heart rate begin to slow. But her desire didn't slow. She raised her head and looked at him, traced his features, memorized them.

She wanted... No, she didn't.

She wouldn't let herself want. But sometimes she caught herself wishing... And she knew she couldn't even let herself wish.

Because he was Lukas. He was the man with his gaze on the horizon. He made no long-term commitments. He traveled light.

And even if he stayed in New York, he would move on from her. So she needed to move first.

"Remember that," Holly murmured, and she settled once more into the curve of Lukas's shoulder and laid a hand against his chest.

Lukas lifted his head and turned it to look at her. "Remember what?" His voice sounded soft and smoky across her cheek.

Holly hesitated, then tamped down the desire for more and shifted to press a kiss to his whisker-roughened jaw. Then she let her hand slide slowly down his chest, across his taut belly, then lower. She would take her joy where she found it. Here. Now.

She wouldn't ask for more.

CHAPTER NINE

THE GALLERY OPENING was a resounding success. All because of Holly.

Lukas was delighted and justified. He'd hired her, after all.

Holly, of course, credited everyone else. Lukas knew better. She might have got the names of useful people and lists of things that needed to be done from other more knowledgeable people, but Holly had done them. She had made it happen.

And she was the one who moved effortlessly among the guests now, smiling and talking with them, extolling the virtues of this artist and the vision of that one.

She had taken the time to get to know each one of them, both as artists and as people. As he watched her introduce Charlotte to the mayor, Lukas grinned. Normally painfully shy, Charlotte had blossomed under Holly's nurturing support.

"She's fantastic," his sister-in-law, Tallie, murmured into Lukas's ear as she followed his gaze. "A good choice, Lukas," she added with a smile.

"Yep." Lukas leaned against the wall, knowing he should be out there, too, glad-handing the visitors, schmoozing with journalists and hobnobbing with the bigwigs. But for just a moment he took a step back, let himself watch, let himself dream.

It wasn't too far-fetched to imagine doing this with Holly again. Doing this with Holly forever.

Forever? As in…what? Ask her to marry him?

He waited for the notion to feel like a punch in the gut. The idea of getting married had always felt like that before.

When Tallie had mentioned marrying Grace, the very thought had him envisioning a life sentence, a noose around his neck. Grace was a great person. Terrific girl. Smart. Capable. Beautiful. Not one he could ever imagine spending a lifetime with. Nor was any girl he'd ever dated. Marriage in the abstract he believed in. Antonides men married.

Except sometime in the past couple of years he'd begun wondering if he wasn't the exception who proved the rule. He'd reached the age of thirty-two and he hadn't had the least inclination to propose to spend his life with anyone.

He watched as Holly, having got the mayor and Charlotte talking, turned away, already looking around to see what else needed doing. Her gaze traveled the room, lit on him, and when their gazes connected, she smiled.

No, in his entire life, Lukas hadn't ever wanted to propose to anyone.

Until now.

In December, when she'd agreed to a two-year stint in the Peace Corps, Holly had begun counting the days until her training began. And she'd marked them off with increasing enthusiasm as time passed.

Two weeks ago she had stopped counting.

She wasn't even aware she had done so until the Wednesday after the gallery opening. Lukas had left the bed before dawn, going to meet Elias and sail a boat with him out to Greenport for one of Elias's customers.

It was one of the rare mornings since she'd moved here that she'd awakened alone, without Lukas's arms around her or her burrowed into his side. Refusing to lie there and focus on the awareness of how much she missed him, Holly jumped out of bed and went to shower.

It was while she was making herself a bowl of cereal that she noticed her calendar and realized for the first time that several days weren't marked off. More than several. Two and a half weeks' worth of days. The last day she'd marked off was the day she had moved out of her condo.

The day she and Lukas had begun their affair.

Affair. It meant temporary. Shallow. Meaningless. Nothing more than an itch to be scratched. Obviously the attraction wasn't going away by ignoring it. She'd tried that. *So do something about it*, she'd told herself. *Have a fling. Discover that Lukas Antonides is everything you ever thought he was—gorgeous, sexy, talented, energetic— but also impetuous, inconstant, egotistical.*

She had been sure she would be ready to walk away when the time came. She'd imagined she'd be ready to run!

But she wasn't even crossing off the days on the calendar. She was living in the moment—and enjoying every minute of it. But the fear was growing inside her that she had made a mistake, that she'd tempted fate by going to bed with Lukas.

That she was falling in love with him.

No! No, she wasn't. She couldn't be. She wouldn't let herself!

It was just that she was alone, that Lukas wasn't there to distract her. "Might not be back until Thursday," he'd told her last night, grimacing as he relayed the news. "Depends on how much time Elias has to spend getting the buyer up to speed. And if he wants to stop and see the folks on the way home."

Lukas's parents still lived on the shore in the big house where he had grown up. Holly knew from things he had said over the past couple of weeks that, for all that he'd been away a dozen years, Lukas was close to his family.

"You should stop and see them," Holly said.

"I would," he said, "if you came along. You could stop and see your mother."

"And tell her I'm living with you?" Holly hadn't even told her mother she'd sold the condo yet. She hadn't wanted to explain why she'd moved to Lukas's. She knew what her mother would think—that she was foolish, she'd get hurt, she should never take such a risk—and she didn't want to hear it.

"You're not living with me," Lukas pointed out. "You have your place. I have mine."

"But we seem to be in the same place a great deal of the time," she reminded him, nuzzling his whiskered cheek. "But we don't need to be together every minute. I have work to do here. A job, remember?"

"I never got to take you sailing."

"Another time."

"Promise?"

"Yes. Of course. As long as we do it before the first of August. Enjoy the day with Elias. Go see your parents. Don't even think about me."

But she thought about him.

It was because the opening was over and she had time to breathe, she told herself. It was because he wasn't there in front of her, coming up with ideas, making demands, distracting her, teasing her, kissing her. But all day long her mind was filled with a kaleidoscope of images.

She helped Teresa hang a new painting and remembered Lukas on a ladder, hanging another one, scowling as he tried to make sure it was perfectly straight. She fixed a peanut butter sandwich for lunch and smiled at her visions of Lukas slapping jam on bread as he made her lunch. Back down in her office, her mind went immediately to Lukas in black tie the night of the gallery opening, looking far handsomer than any man had a right to. She had another memory of him that night as well—of him bending down to listen to his grandmother lecture him. Then she had straightened his tie and patted his cheek as if he were a small boy. And Lukas had kissed her. The memory made Holly's eyes well.

He was so good with all his family. His grandmother, his parents, his siblings, even Martha, who was at pains to give him grief. He doted on his nephews and nieces. She had visions of Lukas with his nephews swarming around him, grinning broadly as he hoisted his niece onto his shoulders so she could be princess of them all.

She sat at her desk and tried to focus on writing a press release. But the last time she'd tried, Lukas had carried her off to bed. And of course, then she couldn't help but close her eyes and see Lukas naked in her bed, eyes slumberous, yet hungry and intent, focusing just on her.

"Ah, there you are!"

Holly jumped a foot as Althea swooped into her office, all smiles, and with a dress carrier bag over her arm. "Look what I've got!"

Holly felt a sinking sensation. "Oh. How nice."

Althea rolled her eyes. "Oh, ye of little faith. You'll love it. Truly. Stig says it's you. I just hope you won't outshine the bride," Althea added wryly.

"No chance of that. You've always been a beautiful bride."

Althea laughed. "All that practice. But Stig picked my dress, too, so I'm feeling pretty confident." She thrust the dress bag at Holly. "I'm just the messenger, and I'm late for a hair appointment. Let me know how it fits. If you need alterations, we can get them done next week." And she was gone as quickly as she'd come.

The dress bag hung over the back of a chair in her office the rest of the afternoon. Holly ignored it, even though it began to take on the proportions of an elephant in the room. She carried it upstairs after work, but she didn't take it out of the bag. She didn't want to be depressed. Then Charlotte and Teresa and a sculptress called Gwen invited her to go out for pizza.

"Since Lukas is gone," Teresa said, "we thought you might come."

Holly went. And after the pizza, Charlotte headed back to work on a wall hanging, but the other two wanted to go clubbing.

"Come with us," Gwen urged her and Teresa nodded her head.

Holly couldn't remember the last time she'd gone clubbing. Maybe after she and Matt were first married. Another lifetime ago. It wasn't her scene. But if she went back to the apartment, she knew what would happen. She would be faced with the dress—and she would miss Lukas.

"I'll come," she said.

It was nearly midnight when they left the club, and just past when Holly let herself into the building and climbed the stairs to her apartment.

"Stay in mine," Lukas had suggested. "Then I could come home and find you in my bed."

Holly had shaken her head firmly. "I'm sleeping in my bed."

But faced with it—as big and white and empty as an Alaskan winter—she was tempted to go upstairs. There, of course, she would find an even bigger bed, but it would have Lukas's scent on the pillows. And she could sleep in the T-shirt he'd worn yesterday.

Which just went to show how far gone she was, Holly thought, disgusted with herself.

August had better hurry up and get there. She was getting too soppy for her own good. But at the same time, she didn't want it to come at all.

Her brain muddled, Holly took a shower. But there were reminders of Lukas there, too. Yesterday morning she'd washed his back, had trailed her fingers down its muscular planes, then had slid her hands around to soap the front of him. Her body heated again now remembering the feel of slick, firm flesh beneath her fingers, and remembering what had happened after.

Abruptly, she shut the water off and got out of the shower. It was when she was putting on sleep shorts and a T-shirt—her own—that she spied the carrier bag with the bridesmaid dress hanging on the closet door.

She wanted to ignore it. But if it needed alterations, she would have to get them done. Wearing a frilly cupcake dress was bad enough. Wearing one that didn't fit would be even worse.

She slid the zip down on the carrier bag and opened it, then stared. "Oh, my word."

Anything less like a cupcake would have been hard to imagine.

The dress was red, a deep, vivid red. A dark, sultry lipstick of a color. There wasn't a frill or a flounce or a furbelow in sight. There wasn't much material at all, to be honest. It was a minimalist sort of dress, Holly decided as she took it out of the bag and gave it a shake. She sucked in her breath.

Very minimal indeed. And elegant. And sexy. And Stig thought it was "her"?

She had never worn anything quite so clearly sexy in her life.

Heart beating faster now, Holly slipped it on, then twirled in front of the mirror, astonished at the picture she made. The dress fit perfectly, molding her curves smoothly without being tight. The nearly shoulder-to-shoulder neckline plunged in a vee to the tops of her breasts, accentuating the soft roundness hidden beneath the silk. Three-quarter-length sleeves hugged her arms, giving the dress a sophistication that bare arms would not. And the flare of the hem just above her knees swirled, making the silk rustle as Holly turned in front of the mirror.

"Can I rip that off you?"

Holly spun around to see Lukas standing in the doorway. She felt a kick somewhere in the region of her heart. "You came back? It's one o'clock in the morning!"

"Didn't want to miss curfew." He crossed the room. "Couldn't stay away from you," he said in a low, rough voice, reaching for her.

"Don't touch! Althea will kill me if anything happens to this dress."

"This is the cupcake?" Lukas looked astonished.

"It's not a cupcake," Holly admitted. "Be careful!" she cried as he spun her around and moved in to nuzzle her neck.

"Then don't wear enticing dresses." He kissed her nape, sending shivers down her spine. Holly squirmed. "Hold still," he muttered as he slid the zip down carefully, then skimmed the dress off her shoulders.

It dropped to the floor, leaving her naked to his gaze. Lukas's breath hissed between his teeth. "God almighty, Hol'!" His voice was strangled.

"I just got out of the shower," she said defensively. She scooped up the dress, holding it in front of her, as if he hadn't seen it all before. "Then I remembered I hadn't tried it on. Althea needed to know if it needed alterations."

"It doesn't need alterations." He still sounded stunned.

Holly felt wobbly at the sight of him. "I didn't think you were coming back tonight." She fumbled with the dress and the hanger.

"You're the one who's going to wreck it." Lukas took it out of her hands and hung it up again. "I came home because you're here. But you weren't in my bed."

"Because you weren't there."

Lukas took her in his arms. "No worries," he said and

scooped her up in his arms, carrying her into her bedroom. "We've got a bed right here."

Every day Holly lived in the moment.

She said yes to going out to his parents' place in the Hamptons for the Fourth of July. She played with his nieces and nephews and chatted with his brothers and sisters and even smiled in the face of his grandmother's obvious approval, even though she knew Lukas's *yiayia* believed there was more going on between them than was really there.

It wasn't her job to protect Lukas's family from their misinterpretations, she told herself. Let him explain after she was gone. But even though she told herself that, she couldn't help feeling guilty.

"I don't like lying to your family," she told him after they were back in the city.

"Well, stay then," he said.

Holly looked at him, startled. Then she shook her head. "No, I can't."

She refused to let herself be tempted by the idea. He didn't mean it. He didn't love her. He didn't want to marry her. And even if he did...

Holly wouldn't even let her mind go there.

Live in the moment. It was her mantra. She said it a dozen times a day as the weeks went on. And she was having a wonderful time, she had to admit that.

They went kayaking one weekend. It was fun to camp out with Lukas. Very different from similar trips she'd taken with Matt. Lukas was more spontaneous and, surprisingly, more willing to listen to her suggestions. Lukas had seemed a little apprehensive about taking her when she'd wished aloud that she could go kayaking one more time before she left. But once they got there, he was fine. They even talked a bit about Matt, and it seemed to take the edge off his apprehension.

"I thought it might make you sad," he told her on the way home.

"I thought it might, too," Holly said honestly. "But I just had a good time. Thank you."

The next weekend they kept his nephews from Saturday afternoon until Sunday night. It had been Digger's idea. He and Holly had hit it off when he discovered that she knew the names of all kinds of road-grading equipment and had half a dozen kids' books about it.

"I'll give them to you," she promised Digger. "A few less things to keep in my storage area," she told Lukas.

"Can I have them now?" Digger asked, eyes bright.

"How about next Saturday?"

"Can we have a sleepover?" Digger wanted to know.

"Of course," Holly said.

"I only have sleepovers with you," Lukas complained that night.

"Not next Saturday," Holly told him. "You know you're glad to have them. And it will give Elias and Tallie a bit of a break."

"Nobody's giving me a break," Lukas muttered.

But they'd all had a good time. Digger had even looked at Holly and said, "We should keep her," to his uncle when the boys were going home.

"Suits me," Lukas said.

Holly told herself to not even think about it. But it was getting harder and harder to live for the moment when the moments seemed to want to add up to something more. Of course that was only in her mind, and Holly knew it.

She couldn't tell what was in Lukas's mind. Most of the time he was all smiles, charm and good conversations. But sometimes he grew remote, distracted. At night when they made love, he could be tender and gentle or passionate, almost desperately intense. Maybe he was tiring of her and didn't know how to say so. Maybe he was trying to recapture the enthusiasm of their first days together.

Holly didn't know. She didn't dare ask.

She just told herself it would be good when August finally got here. Soon their affair would be over. They would go their separate ways.

Holly knew Lukas couldn't go to Althea's wedding with her. It was the same day that the MacClintock grant recipients were being feted along with recipients of several other grants at the Plaza. Lukas had to be there.

So she was surprised when he came out of the bedroom, still knotting his tie, that morning and said, "Save me a dance."

"A dance?"

"At the reception." He was looking remote and distracted, though, even as he said it, and she wondered why he had.

"You won't have time to come to the reception."

He shot her a moody look as he shrugged into his suit coat. "I'll be there."

He wouldn't be.

Holly knew Lukas. Lukas dealt with what was in front of him. He was a man who responded to the moment, and today would be full of moments requiring him to deal with the MacClintock Foundation winners, the mayor and lots of other movers and shakers of the Big Apple. He wouldn't have a moment to think about her.

Which was, Holly assured herself, actually just as well.

They only had a few days left. She needed to wean herself away from Lukas, stop thinking about him day and night.

Althea's wedding was a perfect chance to do that. Just as Lukas wouldn't have time to think of her today, she'd barely have a moment to give him a thought. It was a relief to get to the hotel where the wedding party was changing into their finery. She was hustled up in one of the elevators to the thirtieth floor where Althea, her mother, a hairstylist and a makeup artist swooped down upon her.

"Hairstylist? Makeup artist?" Holly gave Althea a wide-eyed disbelieving look. None of her other weddings had required such expertise.

Althea shrugged. "I've got a famous groom. What can you do? There's press here. I don't want them to think Stig is marrying beneath himself."

"He's not," Holly assured her.

"But there will be stories," Althea's harried mother, Laura, said. "Stig and Althea haven't made it a secret that Althea has had a bit of trouble, er, making up her mind. The least we can do is look elegant and put-together."

Elegant and put-together sounded like a plan. Holly did her best to get with the program, to focus on the wedding, all the while wondering where Althea found the courage to give her heart all over again. Sometimes Althea seemed shallow, vague and flighty. Today, though, Holly thought she was incredibly brave.

"Sit." The stylist pointed Holly to a chair. "We don't have much time."

This wedding was a bigger madhouse than any of Althea's other weddings had been, and yet Holly recognized that this time there was a sense of rightness that the others had lacked. Maybe it was the look Holly saw in Stig's eyes as he looked past her to watch Althea come toward him down the aisle. Maybe it was the tears that had brimmed in Althea's when she spoke her vows. Or the way they kissed the first time as man and wife.

Holly didn't know. But as the wedding turned into the reception, as Stig and Althea danced together, were toasted and celebrated, smashed wedding cake in each other's faces and never ever stopped smiling, she knew she was happy for them, happier than she'd been at any of Althea's other weddings.

She sat at the head table and watched them swirl around the floor once more, this time in the company of many of the other guests, and she smiled, too. Theirs was the way weddings should be. For once she didn't compare it to her own wedding. Barely even thought about it.

"Dance with me."

Startled, Holly turned and looked up.

Lukas stood behind her, a somber expression on his face.

"What's wrong?"

"Nothing's wrong." His tone was almost curt.

"But…the Plaza? The mayor—?"

"The mayor is charming the first MacClintock Foundation grant winners and their extended families. Probably enough people to win him the next election. He couldn't be happier. Dance with me," Lukas said again and held out his hand, waiting for her.

But even as he did the music ended. The next piece was moody, almost plaintive, with lots of soulful clarinets. It touched a chord deep in Holly's breast. Echoed the way she felt.

One last dance. One more memory. Savor it, she told herself, and she put her hand in his and stood.

Effortlessly, Lukas steered her onto the dance floor and took her in his arms. It felt warm and right. The place she ought to be. And Holly couldn't resist. She let herself be wrapped in his embrace.

More than let. Relished it, drew strength from it, sustenance. So much for weaning herself away. She laid her cheek against the smooth summer wool of his jacket, felt the easy glide of muscle beneath, and gave herself over to the music, to the moment.

To the man.

When it ended, Lukas said, "Let's get out of here."

"I'm the bridesmaid!"

"They're married," Lukas said impatiently. "Your job is done."

And once more he drew her with him, this time toward Althea and Stig, who were in conversation with Althea's parents. *Matt's* parents.

"Say goodbye," Lukas instructed her.

But before Holly could open her mouth, Matt's dad, Joe, stuck out his hand to greet Lukas. Then Laura wrapped him in a warm embrace. "We've missed you," she murmured. "So glad you're back. You must come out and see us."

"I will," Lukas promised, the huskiness in his voice telling Holly that his promise was more than perfunctory. "Soon. We have to leave now."

All four—Stig and Althea, Joe and Laura—turned their gazes from Lukas to Holly. Four sets of eyebrows lifted. Althea was, of course, the first to speak.

"Of course you do!" she said with every bit of warmth of which Althea was capable—which Holly knew from years of experience was a lot.

"I don't have to," Holly began. "If you need me to stay…"

"I think I am the one she'll be needing now." Stig gave her a grin and a wink. "Nice dress, don't you think?" he said to Lukas.

"Very nice." Lukas's voice was clipped, his arm possessive around her. *I can hardly wait to get her out of it.* Holly heard the words as if he'd spoken them aloud. She was sure Stig did, too.

"Go," Althea said, making shooing motions. "I'll call you when we get back from our honeymoon."

Holly nodded. She wouldn't be here, but Althea was a smart woman. She'd figure it out.

Lukas had brought his Porsche. He tucked her into it wordlessly, then went around and got in the driver's side. If Holly had thought the cab of his truck shrank when he got in, it was nothing compared to the suddenly minuscule confines of the Porsche. She looked over at him, willing him to smile.

But he'd gone into one of his distracted moods. He put the car in gear and they were off.

Another night he would be regaling her with stories of the event with the mayor and the grant recipients, charming her, making her laugh as she saw it through his eyes. Lukas could do that. He'd done it millions of times. Notably, she recalled, the night of her senior prom.

But tonight he drove straight through Saturday-evening midtown traffic, jaw tight, eyes straight ahead.

Fingers knotted in her lap, Holly didn't speak, either. But by the time they reached Union Square, her nerves were beyond frayed. "What's wrong?"

"Nothing's wrong." But there was an edge to his voice.

"Tell me."

"Not now" His fingers flexed on the steering wheel. He stared straight ahead, focusing on heavy midtown traffic.

Holly turned in the seat to see him better. "Lukas, what's going on?"

"Just wait."

"Since when can't you drive and talk at the same time?"

His jaw bunched. "I can't drive and propose marriage at the same time!"

Holly stared at him, stunned. "What?"

"Oh, hell." He shot her a hard look. "You heard me."

Had she? Holly swallowed. Marriage? Lukas was proposing…marriage? She couldn't find any words.

"Would it be such a bad thing?" Lukas demanded. "I thought we had a good month." He hit her with the glare again. "Didn't you think we had a good month?"

"Yes," she said faintly. "But…"

"But what?"

"It was an…affair." Just saying it made it sound weak

and insubstantial. Nothing like what she'd experienced. And yet…

"An affair?" Lukas fairly spat the words. "So, I was just an itch you wanted to scratch?"

"As I was for you," Holly retorted.

"You're more than an itch," Lukas told her. He slammed on the brakes at a red light and cursed under his breath. "You couldn't wait, could you? You had to push."

"Me, push?" Holly gave a sharp laugh.

"You could have waited till we got home."

"You could have acted less like you were going to the dentist!"

They glared at each other. Holly looked away first.

"It's green," she said. "The signal."

Lukas ground his teeth and stomped on the gas pedal. Neither of them said another word until they reached the door of her apartment.

There, Holly fumbled with the key in nerveless fingers until Lukas took it away and opened the door for her. "Thank you," she said primly. "Good night."

But of course, Lukas came in before she could shut the door on him. "I love you, damn it," he said raggedly. "I want to marry you."

"'I love you, damn it'?" Holly echoed.

He raked a hand through his hair. "You know what I mean! It's more than an itch, Holly. It's a future. You feel it. You know you do." He reached out and caught her by the arm, hauling her against him. "You love me, too."

Holly didn't deny it. She didn't fight him. Couldn't. She wanted him too much.

She knew the depth of her foolishness, then. She had lied to herself when she'd believed she could have these few weeks with Lukas and walk away from him satisfied and unscathed. She had thought that being aware was being in control. She was wrong. It would hurt.

But staying would hurt worse. She had to go.

But not yet. Not without this—this touch of his lips, the warmth of his arms around her, the silkiness of his hair threaded through her fingers, his hands skimming down the zip on her sexy dress, then easing it off her shoulders, letting it slither to a pool at her feet.

"You love me," Lukas whispered against her ear. "And I love you."

Then he lifted her and carried her into the bedroom and laid her gently on the bed. His eyes were hooded, the skin taut across his cheekbones, his lips barely parted, breathing softly and close—so close she could feel the heat of his breath on her cheek.

She took his face between her hands and ran her thumbs across his brows, then across those sharply sculpted cheekbones, memorizing each detail before pressing her lips to his.

Lukas groaned. He toed off his shoes, then sat up, fumbling to drag off his tie and undo the buttons of his shirt.

Holly's hands wrapped his, held them still. "Let me. Please." Her throat ached as she spoke.

Lukas let out a harsh breath. "Go ahead then."

She took her time, slipped the tie off his neck, then with fingers almost as unsteady as his, she undid the buttons one by one, tugged his shirttails out of his trousers and pulled it off, then skimmed his undershirt over his head. Pressing kisses to his chest, she brought her hands down to his belt buckle, worked it open, slid a hand in to caress him.

"Hol'," he warned, his hips surging against her. She would have taken longer, would have had him as strung out as she had been that night so many years ago. But Lukas was done with that. His patience gone, he peeled off his trousers and shorts, shed his socks and bore her back onto the bed.

Then he had his way with her, took his time, kissed his

way from her breastbone to the apex of her thighs. He settled between her legs and skimmed his fingers up them, then parted her, touched her, stroked her.

Holly tried to hold still, but couldn't. She twisted beneath the friction of his fingers as they heightened her pleasure. And then he moved over her, came down to her and entered her fully, and the two of them were one.

For an instant he held himself still, his gaze dark and intense bare inches above hers. "I love you, Holly. I've always loved you." The words were harsh and hoarse. They seemed dragged from the depths of his being. Holly's fists clutched the sheets, her toes curled as he began to move. Slowly. Deeply. As if he were touching the very core of her being.

If she let him, he could touch her there. She knew it. She nearly sobbed with the knowledge. She twisted, matching his thrusts, letting go of the sheet to rake her fingernails down his back, then clutching him close as he drove them both over the edge.

She cried out. She said his name.

He slumped against her, his body sweat-slick, his heart hammering so hard she could feel it against her own. He lifted his head and looked down at her, a hint of a smile on his lips. "So," he said raggedly, "you want to argue with that?"

Holly couldn't argue. She couldn't even speak. She just looked at him, drank him in. Then she shut her eyes and breathed deeply, held him close.

The sun was high in the sky when Lukas woke. He knew where he was, tangled in the sheets of Holly's bed. He remembered the passion, the intensity, the love they had shared. And he smiled, recalling how she'd simply shut her eyes and gone to sleep beneath him. He'd lain there, savoring the feel of her body, nearly boneless now, slumbering beneath him. Finally, he'd rolled off, but only to tuck her against his chest and spoon his legs behind hers.

He sighed with contentment, then stretched and rolled over to reach for her again.

He was alone.

CHAPTER TEN

SHE WAS IN the kitchen. Or in the bathroom. She'd gone to her office. Or maybe down to the gallery to work.

Lukas bolted out of bed, then told himself that the flare of panic he'd felt at finding her gone was nothing more than an overactive imagination.

She hadn't left him. She couldn't have.

But it turned out his imagination was better informed than all his rationalizations. He found a note on the kitchen counter. As he picked it up, his hand shook.

Lukas, thank you for everything. I won't see you again before I go. It's better this way. I'll have a mover pack my things and store them. I'm sure you won't want to store my stuff. I can't tell you how much I appreciate all you did for me. PS: don't forget those kids at St. Brendan's will still need you. Thanks, Holly

Lukas's fist crumpled the letter. He felt gutted. He felt hollow. He felt sick. His throat was tight. His eyes stung.

So he was wrong again. She didn't love him, after all.

It was the first day of the rest of her life. And then it was the second. And then the third.

But no matter how hard Holly tried, she couldn't seem to live in the moment. She had spent the whole last week of her life in New York out at her mother's on Long Island. She told herself it was the right thing to do. It was what she'd always intended. It didn't have anything to do with leaving Lukas's at the crack of dawn so she wouldn't have to face him in the clear light of day.

She was doing the right thing, she told herself over and over. She was doing what she'd planned—and she was making things easier for Lukas. He might think he wanted to marry her, but he didn't mean it.

He could marry anyone—the remarkable, sophisticated, elegant Grace Marchand, for example. If he didn't want to marry a paragon like Grace, he certainly wouldn't want to marry her! She told herself that every day, too. And by the end of the week at her mother's, she had done a reasonably good job of convincing herself that was the truth. Besides, she was eager to get to Hawaii. That was something else she repeated again and again.

Her mother wasn't convinced. She looked worried every time she glanced Holly's way. "Are you sure you're all right?" she asked Holly.

"I'm fine," Holly assured her.

"Because you don't look very happy."

"I'm happy," Holly lied.

She would be—in time. It would be a relief when she got to Hawaii and started her training. She just needed something new and different—a new challenge to find herself.

Hawaii was different. All balmy breezes and sunshine. And the training was thorough and demanding and thought-provoking. Or it would have been, Holly was sure, if she'd been thinking about it. She didn't.

She thought about Lukas.

She showed up dutifully to every talk and had a hard time paying attention to a word that was said. In her mind, she kept seeing Lukas. She went to language classes and practiced and found herself wondering which ancient languages Lukas knew. She remembered the night of her prom when he'd confessed he liked studying Latin. She knew he even translated old documents sometimes.

"To keep my hand in," he'd said, then added wryly, "And my brain."

It had prompted her once to look him up in some scholarly indexes and she'd discovered he was there, that while he'd been out digging in the dirt with Skeet, he'd spent his evenings on ancient Sanskrit and Greek texts.

Every evening they prepared and ate local foods from the island she would be going to. It was a new program, an attempt to get them acclimated, to help them land on their feet. And while it was interesting and she learned it, it didn't stir her blood the way watching Lukas in the kitchen had.

Her mouth watered when she thought about the spaghetti he'd made. He had half a dozen recipes he'd got from his mother and grandmother that he had fixed for her, too. "You don't have to do all the cooking," he'd told her. "Or we can do it together. Then we can do this while we're waiting for the water to boil," he'd said with one of his lopsided grins. And then he'd kissed her.

She ached remembering how Lukas had used almost any excuse to kiss her. She ached remembering the feel of his silky hair beneath her fingers, his rough, whiskered jaw rubbing against her cheek. She ached whenever she thought about the way he always knew where to touch her—and how he could let go and allow her to learn what pleased him.

"Don't think about it. Forget him," she said over and over. But she couldn't stop thinking about it. And she feared she would never forget this past month as long as she lived.

She went through the motions of the program day after day. She attended the lectures, practiced the language, learned new skills. She tried to fill the emptiness in her life with what she was learning now, what she was planning to do.

And at night when the other volunteers were drinking

beer, laughing and talking and making plans, Holly walked on the beach alone.

It had seemed a brilliant idea last autumn when she'd looked into the project in the first place. But then she had finally come to terms with what had happened and had been trying to redefine her life after losing Matt. The Peace Corps had seemed to offer exactly what she needed to challenge herself, to do some good while finding out who she was and what she wanted to do with the rest of her life. It had been a good idea at the time.

Now it was too late.

Because she was, heaven help her, in love with Lukas Antonides. And all the lectures and language lessons and attempts to cook mysterious foods could not fill the hole that leaving him had opened in her life.

This wasn't like the hole Matt had left. His death had brought an irrevocable end to life as she had known it. And she'd had to face that there was no way to change it, no possibility to bring him back. She'd had to face that—and learn to move on.

But Lukas hadn't died. He hadn't left her.

She had left him.

Lukas had said he loved her. Had always loved her. The words echoed in her mind as she stood and stared out at the setting sun. Lukas had asked her to marry him.

And she had been afraid to.

Holly wasn't sure the exact moment she faced the truth—which wasn't that Lukas didn't love her, but that she was afraid to love him. She was afraid to open her heart, to risk the pain of loving again.

But it was too late to protect herself.

She already did.

Charlotte spun slowly around the cavernous space on the gallery's fourth floor and said, "It's getting very airy in here."

Lukas, halfway through knocking down another brick wall, merely grunted and kept on working, first with a crowbar, then a hammer and chisel. He wasn't knocking down any more walls than he and Alex had agreed on. Well, maybe a couple more, but it was his building, damn it. And he needed the exertion if he was going to stay sane. He'd thought about going back to Australia and digging again. He'd stayed because he had made commitments. No one could say he wasn't reliable, he thought grimly.

Charlotte stopped spinning and came over to peer closely at him. "Are you sure you're okay, Lukas?"

"I'm fine," he said shortly. They were all fussing at him. He knew they were concerned. He'd never thought he was the sort of guy who wore his heart on his sleeve, but they all knew he was pining for Holly. It was embarrassing. But he endured it. What else could he do?

Someday, he figured, he'd even get over it. Though since he'd carried a torch for her for two thirds of his life already, he wasn't going to hold his breath.

"A bunch of us are going out for pizza in about an hour," Charlotte said when he stopped hammering. "Want to come with us?"

Lukas shook his head. "No." Then, realizing how abrupt that was, he grimaced and added, "Thanks. Not hungry." He kept moving the chisel, whacking it with the hammer, moving it again. Each blow sent pieces of brick scattering to the canvas tarps below. Lukas wiped a weary forearm across his brow.

"You have to eat," Charlotte reminded him. "You're getting skinny," she said, assessing his shirtless frame.

"I eat."

Tallie saw to that. She kept bringing him food and inviting him for dinner. Ever since she and Elias had discovered that Holly had left, they'd been hovering like worried parents.

"Tallie left me, too," Elias reminded him. "Took me months to find her."

"I know where Holly is," Lukas said stonily.

"So go and get her," his brother said bluntly.

Lukas just shook his head. He couldn't tell them that Holly wouldn't welcome him if he did, that she didn't want him, didn't love him, that it had only been an affair to her.

"If we can do anything…" Tallie said, putting a hand on his arm as they were leaving. "If you want to talk…"

He didn't want to talk. For once in his life Lukas had absolutely nothing to say.

He stonewalled his family. He stonewalled Sera, who fretted about him whenever she came into his office and found him staring into space. He stonewalled Charlotte and the rest of the artists who kept trying to find helpful ways for him to convince Holly to come back and be the business manager again. He didn't tell them he figured she'd probably be happy to remain as the business manager if only he would go away.

Thinking about it now, his throat got tight. It wasn't the thinking that did it. It was because he was knocking down walls and there was dust everywhere. Too much damn dust.

"If you change your mind, we're leaving sixish," Charlotte said, then headed toward the door. "Leave a wall or two standing," she added. "We don't want the world to come crashing down."

God no, Lukas thought grimly, *we certainly don't want that.*

Charlotte had barely disappeared when his cell phone vibrated in his pocket. It would be Tallie telling him to come for dinner. He dug into his pocket, already deciding that he wasn't going over there tonight. Enough was enough. But it was Sera's name on the caller ID.

"I thought you'd gone home," he said when he answered.

"I was just leaving when someone came in who wants to apply for a MacClintock grant."

Lukas groaned. "We're done with that."

"For next year," Sera qualified. He could hear the smile in her voice. She knew he was so relieved to have it over for the year that she could tease a bit.

But Lukas had had enough of grant applicants for a while. "Tell him to come back next year."

Sera didn't say anything. She had learned by now that if she wanted something, she could always wait him out.

Lukas sighed. "Oh, hell, fine. Send him up. I'll discourage him myself." Or maybe he could kick the guy in the butt, give him some gumption like Skeet wanted.

Because look where gumption got you, Lukas thought bitterly. He, for example, had accomplished so much by laying his heart on the line.

He slid down the ladder at the sound of footsteps on the stairs and turned to meet the prospective MacClintock applicant.

It wasn't a guy. A slender, dark-haired woman was silhouetted in the late-afternoon sunlight that spilled into the room. Lukas glanced, and felt his heart kick over in his chest because it looked like… But he was dreaming. Had to be. It was a mirage. Like one of those damned oases that tempted camel drivers who had spent too long in the desert.

And then she came toward him.

"Holly?" Lukas dropped the hammer on his foot.

"Lukas! Oh, God, are you all right?" Holly didn't have time to stop and drink in the sight of him, didn't, in the end, worry that he would take one look and tell her to get the hell out of his life.

Once she saw the hammer fall and saw Lukas wince

with pain, all her own misgivings fled. She dashed across the room to kneel at his feet.

"Sit down!" she demanded, tugging at the hem of his faded denim jeans. She shoved the offending hammer away and tugged again, and finally Lukas sat. She fumbled off his work boot and sock to find a goose egg forming on the top of his foot. "We need to get ice on it."

"No," Lukas said. "We don't." And his hands grabbed her upper arms and held her still. His Adam's apple worked in his throat. "We need to know what you're doing here, Holly. *I* need to know." His eyes bored into hers.

And Holly knew she couldn't deflect the question. She smiled a little wryly. "Sera told you," she said softly. "I want to apply for a grant."

Lukas cocked his head. A tiny line appeared between his brows. "What're you talking about?"

Holly licked her lips. "Courage," she said, meeting his gaze, feeling herself drowning in those green depths. "I need some."

Lukas's expression seemed to close up. His jaw tightened. He looked away. "For the Peace Corps?" he said tonelessly. He didn't look at her. He was staring away across the room, as if looking at her would hurt.

Holly knew the feeling. She lifted a hand, wanting to touch him, to draw strength from him, then knew she couldn't. She had to do this on her own. "No," she said. "To tell you I love you, too."

Lukas's gaze snapped back to lock onto hers. "You—?" There was green fire in his gaze now, and hope in his eyes. "Holly?" His voice seemed to break.

Holly wetted her lips and nodded, then said them again. "I love you, Lukas. I do. I…didn't want to. I was afraid to."

"Afraid?" He sounded aghast. "I would never hurt you!" Then he had the grace to look abashed. "Once I did," he admitted. "Probably more than once, but I swear I won't anymore. Not ever. Not if I can help it," he added wryly. "I'm not very good at this."

Holly shook her head. She took his hands in hers, felt his fingers tighten around them. "You're very good at it," she said, and meant it. Once she'd allowed herself to believe what Lukas had told her, she realized how much effort he had made on her behalf. "I'm the one who's not," she admitted. "I'm the one who didn't trust. I told myself it was because you couldn't be trusted—"

"Imagine that," Lukas said wryly, but he was smiling now.

"But it wasn't you. It was me. I didn't trust myself to believe. I didn't think I had enough to make you happy. To keep you."

"For God's sake, Hol'!" he protested. "You've had me from the day you fell out of that damn tree!"

She laughed. "You wanted to throttle me!"

"Because I was eleven. When you're eleven that's what you do."

"Really?"

He nodded. "I think deep down, I've loved you for years."

Holly lowered her eyes, looked at their clasped hands, then raised her gaze again to meet his. "I loved you, too." She swallowed, then tried to explain. "I loved both of you. You were so different. He was warm, steady, constant, responsible."

"And I was not," Lukas said frankly, giving a rough laugh.

"You were…scary." She loosed one of her hands, lifting it to touch his cheek. "I never knew where I stood with you."

"In my heart."

Holly blinked at the prompt certainty of his response. "You had a funny way of showing it. Pulling pigtails. Trying to run off. Teasing."

"Like I said, I was eleven. I didn't do hearts and flowers. And by the time I woke up to what I should be doing," he said ruefully, "Matt already was."

Holly nodded. Neither of them spoke for a long moment, both of them, she was sure, thinking about Matt. "He kept me safe," she told Lukas.

"I know. He was the better man."

"No," Holly said quickly. "He was no more perfect than you are, than I am. And," she admitted for the first time, "you might have been right that we were too young to get engaged—"

"I wanted you for myself," Lukas told her. "I didn't deliberately mean to hurt you that night. I wanted you to give him up, pick me instead." He shook his head. "Thank God you didn't. I wasn't mature enough to get married then. Matt was."

"He was the right man for me at that time."

Lukas nodded. "Yes." He took her hand. He ran his fingers over it, then clasped it in his, firm and strong. He didn't say a word, just looked at her. Holly knew what he was asking. She could see his heart in his eyes.

"I don't need a grant," she told him. "You've given me the courage. I'm still scared—not that you don't love me, but that I'll lose you, too."

"No! I promise—"

She touched his lips with her fingers. "You can only promise to love me, Lukas, as I promise to love you. That's all we can do." She gave him a tremulous smile. "So. If you're still offering, I'd love to marry you, Lukas Antonides."

He took her into his arms before the words were out of her mouth. His kiss was fierce and possessive, and Holly met him with a desperation all her own. He got brick dust all over her—on her clothes, on her face, in her hair. He might have got it in far more scandalous places, but as he was sliding his hands up under her shirt, she shifted to give him more access and accidentally kicked his injured foot.

Lukas winced.

Holly felt sanity returning, at least momentarily.

"Up," Holly insisted, standing, then hauling a limping Lukas to his feet. "You need ice, compression, rest, elevation."

"Bed," Lukas translated, grinning. He looped an arm over Holly's shoulders, then lifted a hopeful brow as she helped him hobble toward the stairs. "You are the best thing that ever happened to me, Hol'. I love you."

Holly went up on her toes and brushed her lips against Lukas's. "I love you, too." It still scared her. But not as much as being without him did. "And yes, my love," she said with an impish smile, "a bed sounds like a great idea. I think we can arrange that."

* * * * *

LET'S TALK

Romance

For exclusive extracts, competitions
and special offers, find us online:

f facebook.com/millsandboon

y @MillsandBoon

◎ @MillsandBoonUK

Get in touch on 01413 063232

For all the latest titles coming soon, visit

millsandboon.co.uk/nextmonth

JOIN THE
MILLS & BOON
BOOKCLUB

* **FREE** delivery direct to your door

* **EXCLUSIVE** offers every month

* **EXCITING** rewards programme

50% OFF
YOUR FIRST
PARCEL

Join today at
Millsandboon.co.uk/Bookclub